I0762018

About the author:

Jill Marley lives in Wellington Point in Queensland and has a lifelong interest in writing and literature. In 2013, she spent an English summer in a quaint cottage in Holt, Norfolk, UK. She was inspired to write this story when a fisherman told her about Shipden, now two kilometres from the end of the Cromer pier.

The Missing Village is her third novel. Jill absolutely loves writing historical fiction. The three novels are: *The Missing Village* (longlisted for The McKitterick Prize, Society of Authors, London), *The Reunion*, and *Riverina Bluebells* (soon be published).

All her life she has loved to write. She still hordes the immature scribblings of stories written in old exercise books and a biscuit tin full of teenage diaries. Jill has four adult children and two gorgeous grandsons. A tertiary teacher for nearly thirty years and now a full-time writer, experienced traveller and observer of life in an uncertain world.

She's on Facebook as an author and has a personal travel blog, which contains much loved views of the North Norfolk area, where this story has been set, over a period of several hundred years.

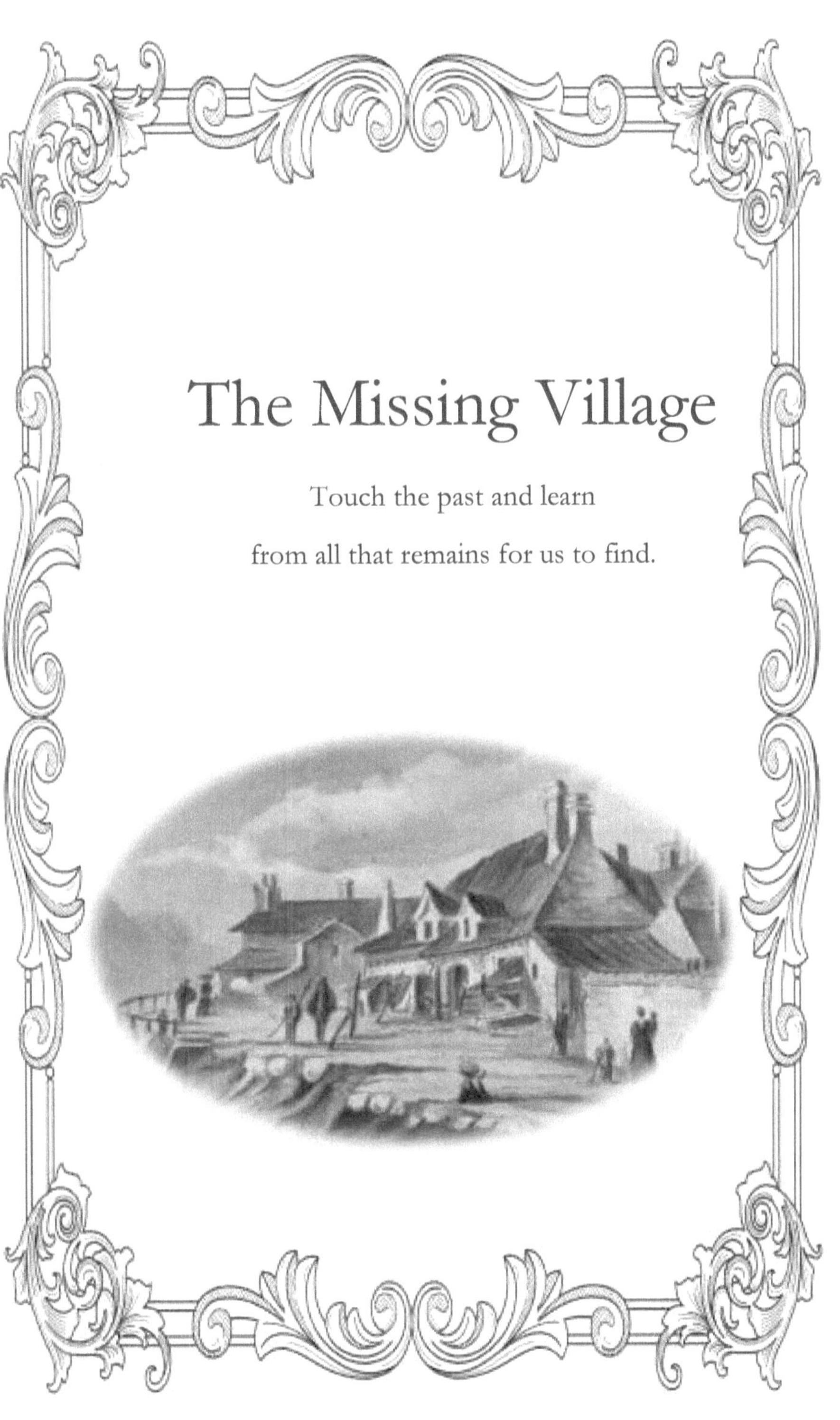

The Missing Village

Touch the past and learn

from all that remains for us to find.

Editor: Brigitte Prince

Painting on the cover: *Peasant Girl* Charles Pearce (1851-1914)

Paintings within the book are available at:

commons.wikimedia.org/wiki and *cromerdictionary.co.uk/*

- Intro page*: Old Shipden* (anon) online
- Chapter 2: *Woman in white dress and straw hat*, by Charles Sprague Pearce (1851-1914)
- Chapter 3: *Peasant Girl* Charles Pearce (1851-1914)
- Chapter 4: *Baby's Lullaby,* Mary Cassatt (1887)

Raggedy Men of Cromer Pier used with kind permission of the poet, Lynn Woollacott.

First published in December 2025.

Set in 12/24 pt Georgia, for hard copy and screen font. The Georgia typeface was designed by Matthew Carter for Microsoft in 1993 and developed with Thomas Rickner as a serif typeface.

Historical fiction. ISBN 978-1-7638598-1-4 (hardback)

ISBN 978-1-7638598-0-7 (paperback) ISBN 978-1-7638598-2-1 (ebook)

A catalogue record for this book is held at the Qld State Library 2026.

A catalogue record for this book is available from the National Library of Australia

Dedicated to:

Angie Timms, an inspiring and enduring friend who, despite living on the other side of the world, has helped to shape this story. Her kindness and generosity of spirit is only matched by her willingness to help others.

Cromer 1888

Prologue Medieval North Norfolk – 1348

The box was finished. He'd toiled on it for weeks, every evening since he'd moved into the cottage in Crowmere. It was plain to look at, heavy enough so it would sink to the deepest depths of the German ocean. A world of water washed away everything and everyone that mattered to him. But he'd eventually have his victory. The outer box would not corrode, would not be penetrable by sea nor man. Inside was a delicately carved box he'd made for her as a wedding gift. Each item inside would return her contagious smile to light up this dark world.

He moved into this flint cottage so nobody would suspect his desire to be with her. His sombre moods were dull to live with anyway. The village was flooded, the country riddled with plague, famine, hunger and destitution.

The whole village made it clear that they didn't want him around now that he had brought the wrath of God upon them all. He felt broken inside. He'd let his parents down, and everyone he ever knew in the village. His heart felt heavy.

He pondered on the unnatural storms eating away at Norfolk hillsides until they exposed chalky, pallid cliffs. The long, thin fingers of each surge seeped into every crevice, reaching under the far edges of the village until the land above collapsed into the waves below.

Was it all his fault? Truly, he'd done what was best for his young wife. He'd do it all again, no matter what the consequences were. The salty smell of the sea, the sharp, whipping rain, his boots caked in excrement and mud. Anything for her. How can that be wrong in the eyes of a loving God?

Chapter 1 – 2013

They walked together to Roma Street station the day she left to return to Sydney. Josh waited with her on the platform as others climbed aboard the Brisbane airport train. He kissed her and it seemed to him that she didn't want to let him go. Concern was written in new lines on her face, but he disliked her fussing. She pulled back, searched his eyes. The back of his head was throbbing. He composed his shoulders, told himself that he wouldn't have to wait on the platform much longer. She must've instinctively known the end was coming.

'See you soon,' she whispered, throwing her arms around his waist, and burying her face in his chest, holding on as if he were a rock in a raging sea. He didn't reply. Who knew what the future held? She had offered to stay a little longer, and he had wanted her to stay but knew she had to go. Family commitments he understood. It mollified and irritated him in equal measure. The constant throbbing seared into the back of his head, distracting him. He knew he needed to see his doctor as soon as possible.

A whistle pierced the air, and she was on a train again without him. The train pulled away from the platform. He paused and watched it disappear, taking her to the airport. He rubbed the back of his neck and turned his head left and right to slowly dissipate the pain. His eyes didn't leave the carriage she was in, waving through the open door just seconds before. He threw her one last kiss and each of them waved goodbye.

The house, when he returned home, was cool and still. Dull light crept through the study window as he watched dust motes dance above the shadows, just as it had been when they had left but now in silent witness. It was so quiet, his voice over the phone to his doctor's office echoed in the space.

A framed photo of the two of them stood on a shelf. He picked it up and looked at her laughing face, trying to convince himself that she was in the kitchen or outside by the roses and that she'd be back any minute, calling to him from the hall to come and join her. But her absence was everywhere, and he glimpsed, suddenly, how long the coming days, weeks, months were going to be. How .. unbearably .. long.

Her soft voice spoke to him as he looked at the cheerful photo. 'Josh, promise me you'll come down soon,' she'd said.

In the air, heavy now with her absence, all his senses were sharpened. A fly hit against the front wire screen door, a truck revved beyond the farm, changing gears in the distance. The lingering scent of her perfume. He imagined music playing on his stereo, of an awkward moment as she discovered his inept attempts at dancing the waltz. And how her hands had rested snugly inside his holey sweater, clinging to him on the back of his quadbike, listening for her laughter to bubble up as he sped through the paddocks, checking his cows and discovering more fun than he'd dared to hope for. Although he had never minded his own company on the farm and usually enjoyed an uncomplicated, simple existence, he couldn't help thinking that the happiness they had shared these past few days was special. He breathed a long, lingering sigh and reached for his phone to check for messages.

He realized he longed for company, even if it was just a text message. Grabbing at straws, memories of last night still fresh, he sat on the leather office chair, turned to his mobile and flicked through his photos. The local show, the wood-chop events, that dress, umm. He shivered at the thought of her fingers caressing him. He missed touching her so much. Somehow soothing, touching was a rousing indulgence, even when they sat to eat, their knees would meet under the table, like a magnetic force as though their bodies refused to be parted. But they did part, didn't they?

Photos forced us to see people before their future weighed them down; before they knew their endings. He smiled at the captured moment in Chinatown, her hand resting on his leg – was she being intentional in her actions? Was it the same affectionate signal he had sent to her, when his arm rested comfortably around her back, pulling her close to him? They were a happy couple, even though he'd been in pain when that memory was made. When she was with him, everything seemed to be in focus, now the fog will consume him until he's back into his normal routine again – the clarity and ease slipping to another time. Another visit. No-one should be alone, he thought. The whole house groaned, struggling to fill the space she had left behind. Tomorrow, he would go to visit his parents for a few days.

At Wellington Point, a long, crimson cloud stretched over the eastern coastline and the Coral Sea at dawn, bursting into a fresh, new morning. Pelicans floated near the pier, and two boys sat on their upturned buckets, their fishing lines visible through the clear waters below. Josh was leaning on the handrail watching a couple of tinnies pull out, packed with their Eskies and blokes looking forward to another day on the calm waters of Moreton Bay. Their laughter was the only sound in the crisp, cool air until they revved up their engine, disturbing the pelicans. He watched two of the birds in their awkward but perfectly balanced take-off, wide wingspan gently lifting them into the sunrise. Head and feet tucked into their bodies, he thought they were such aerodynamically efficient creatures, even with that beak. But only when they were flying. He sheltered his eyes from the glare of the rising sun. Another pelican swayed on his webbed walk towards the boys to eye-off their bait bucket. He looked almost comical in his gait. The bird flying was graceful in his zone while the other bird, out of his comfort-zone, waddled awkwardly. Josh knew what that was like.

That's how he felt when he was with her; out of his comfort-zone. Maybe she had felt the same unease. She not only lived one flight hour away, but it also didn't seem logical for him to move down there or for her to move up to Queensland. Long distance relationships were just too hard. He knew she would not understand his sudden reticence, for they were very close after this last visit. They had shared so much history which was what had attracted him in the first place – they went to the same high school, back in the day. Not that they spoke back then, but they did breathe the same air and remembered the same teachers and still knew the same students. He hadn't seen her for years, and then a school reunion caused her to message him through Facebook.

He kept walking around a circular path next to the calm waters of the bay, deep breathing the cool air. Six months had passed since he'd first visited her, when they'd decided to 'see what happens'. They had been emailing each other for quite a long time but he remembered wanting more, so he felt the time was right when he flew down to see her. From the start, that gentle and magnetic force of attraction was there. He was curious to see where it might lead them, even though it was going to be challenging with the distance. He recalled the road trip they did together five months later. It was exhilarating and scary and fun. They fitted together so neatly; it was daunting to think about not being together all the time. But how could they keep up that pace?

It was a Sunday when he collided with a hanging basket of petunias. Friends had arrived at his Maleny farm for lunch. She was already staying with him for a few days. Josh had organised a barbeque and marinated the meat, while she had made salads and sweets in his kitchen. He recalled a delicious lunch in the gazebo. After their visit, he had taken a short-cut onto the verandah, eyes down, and walked so fast into the hanging plant that he'd felt a crashing jolt. He'd tripped backwards and regained his balance before he fell into the roses. He smiled when he remembered she'd covered the swollen eye with a bag of frozen peas. As the hours passed, the pain in the back of his neck felt like whiplash.

At ten thirty, the doctor took one look at his MRI scan and ordered Josh into hospital for more tests. It was not whiplash, that much he understood. In time, he'd come to realize that absolute rest and blood pressure tablets would be necessary for him to survive. He had not thought of himself as overweight before, but he was a man with a large frame, six foot two or so. It probably crept on unnoticed. He had to lose weight. His doctor said no more flights, or anything energetic for quite a while. How he dreaded telling her that he could no longer be with her in any way. The urgency of his survival pushed him over the line, and he made that final decision to end their relationship. He loved her but it was all too hard.

On the plus side, his boss at the newspaper was understanding and didn't add pressure to the situation. Time and rest and pills got him back on an even keel. He had been able to do some work online and he was grateful for that. He didn't live far from his parents, so they all helped him along the road to recovery. He knew he had been lucky. He was alive.

Thirty-year-old Josh closed his book and rolled over on the picnic rug. The summer sun was beginning its descent over the calm waters of Moreton Bay. Where he walked, on paths sheltered by huge Poinciana trees in blood-red bloom, he saw Wynnum and Manly, where the Brisbane River met the bay. Electric lights twinkled, scattered on the outward tide beyond King Island. An industrial area for ships is not usually attractive, but, from a distance such as this, even the tall petroleum towers and ship loading docks looked glamorous against a western orange sky at sunset. The early evening brought grotesque shadows; the Moreton Bay Figs morphed into ghost-like configurations across the park.

He rolled up the blanket, collected the small basket holding a thermos of tea and bikkies, his book and his cap. His phone alerted him to a message. He took it out of his shirt pocket. He almost pressed the off button but thought that his boss might not appreciate it.

'Hey Tom, what's up?'

'Josh, I'm sorry to disturb you on your break but I'm in a bit of a bind. But, first, how are you feeling now, mate?'

'A bit jaded, but all good, thanks. The blood pressure pills and a bit of rest did the trick,' he said. He heard a few seconds of hesitation at the end of the line.

'Josh, say if you really don't feel up to this request. I could ask Cathy,' said Tom. 'I don't want to push you if you're not okay yet.'

He managed to convince Tom he was fine and was keen to find out what the assignment was. Truth was, Josh was bored and hated sitting around doing nothing.

'Well, I'll tell you what the offer is, and you let me know if you're up to it or not. Okay?' Tom continued. 'The bloke who's been covering the climate change assignment in England has just rung from a hospital. He's broken both legs in a car accident down one of those lanes they call roads over there. On the phone he sounded as mad as a cut snake! I'm flying him back home as soon as possible. In the meantime, I need someone to cover his patch for a while. Are you looking for an overseas assignment, mate?'

'Yes, always. That's really disappointing for him. So close to Christmas, too.'

'Well, that's true. What do you think, Josh? Do you want it, or do I call someone else?'

'It's an amazing offer. Thanks, mate. I'll check with my doctor in the morning if that's okay. I'm feeling great now, so it's just a formality. I'll need a script for the medication while I'm away,' said Josh. 'Then there's Christmas coming up. How much time are we looking at?'

'Dunno at this stage, Josh. You'll have it all sorted as quick as you can, I'm sure. I'll give you 'til tomorrow to think on it. Okay? As long as you're well enough to fly.'

'Sure, if that's alright. The doc assured me that the medication would sort things out and I already feel back to normal now. No problem. I'll give you a buzz as soon as I can. 'bye, Tom....and thanks.' He looked around. Gone were the kite boarders, gone were the fishermen, gone were the children who had been climbing the Fig trees.

Josh closed his mobile and put the picnic gear in his ute, all the while thinking about his editor's offer. He weighed up the facts. England at this time of the year was freezing but all the Christmas lights and decorations would be up. He might enjoy a white Christmas, but he'd be alone again during the festivities. He considered his parents and their excitement at having him come home for Christmas. The guilt weighed heavily. He hadn't been home for the past few years. He'd discuss it with them and, if they're too displeased with the idea, he'd knock it back. What a great opportunity for him, but ...

Since he graduated from their journalism program, he had longed to cover some international stories. Perhaps even work in a foreign country reporting back home on the bigger news stories. He got on well with his line manager and editor. Tom was always on the lookout for breaks, but Josh knew deep down that he still had a long way to go before he carved his name into headlines.

There were other considerations too. He spent most weekends on his farm near Maleny, tending to the jobs most cattle farmers needed to attend to. He'd need to ask someone to manage the farm if he went overseas. With the drought, the numbers of cattle he had were at an all-time low, so it wouldn't be a major task to keep an eye on the few remaining cows, although handfeeding could be a pain. He'd need to store plenty of hay bales before he left. His mate was a farm manager at a nearby property. He'd have a word with Col. See if he would like the extra work during his absence.

Josh climbed into his ute, turned the ignition on and circled the park before slipping it into low gear for the short climb up the park's exit road. His ute was pretty old; he'd bought it second-hand with his first pay back in 2008, so it took some patience to force it up the slope. He glanced to his left and saw Stradbroke Island with its white sandhills blotting out the side of a mountain and the lights of Dunwich lining the base. Nature had been generous apportioning beauty to this part of the world, and he loved visiting the village. To his right were the bayside suburbs of Brisbane. The sea this evening was crystal blue and sparkled as the sleepy crimson sun reached out to touch the tip of each tiny wave. He smiled. Makes a man want to turn his talents to poetry.

Main Road rolled out in front of him, lined with deep red canopies of Poinciana trees and he continued to turn things over in his mind. He might have to shelve his holiday back here for a while. He had to admit he felt a twinge of disappointment, despite the thrill of a temporary overseas posting.

Holt, Norfolk

A week later, Josh stood on Holt railway station, waiting for a restored steam train to take him to Sheringham, after a two-hour bus trip from Heathrow airport. He'd enjoyed a few days in London to recover from jetlag and had decided to do the most scenic route possible to get to his accommodation in Cromer. Someone back home had suggested The Poppyline. So, he wrapped his scarf tighter around his neck and swore he'd buy a coat as soon as he could, even if he never wore it again when he returned to Australia. A shiver ran cold down his spine. He rubbed his hands together and stamped his feet.

'Bloody freezing here,' he said to a young man nearby. 'I suppose there's better times of the year to visit.'

'Yeah. Cold. It's winter.' Josh thought the young man looked tense, but he persisted in conversation with him rather than look silly for not appearing to know which season it was.

'Last week I was lying on a picnic rug in the sun reading a book.'

The young man looked him up and down slowly.

'I'd have stayed there if I were you,' he said, turning a page of his paperback.

'Josh. My name's Josh.' The young man looked surprised at the introduction. Probably not the thing to do in England, so Josh gave a little wave from where he was standing, trying to be sociable. He immediately regretted opening his mouth. This guy was not the communicable type of chatty guy you might find waiting for a train in Queensland. His dark eyebrows furrowed in the centre of his wide forehead. He didn't look too pleased.

'Why do you want to know?' he mumbled, shuffling his red sneakers, his eyes darting up from under his long fringe every now and then, watching people as they passed by. Josh thought he seemed edgy. 'They call me Kyle mostly.'

'Are you going far, Kyle?'

'I live in Sheringham. Just thought I'd do it this way for a change.'

'That's where I'm going too. Sheringham station. I'll catch a taxi from there. I've booked a unit near the Cromer lighthouse for a while.'

'Not much of a tourist spot at this time of the year.'

He must've heard Josh's accent and assumed he was a tourist.

'Yeah. I'm here to work though. I'm a journalist for a newspaper back home.'

Kyle seemed more interested now. Josh met his gaze and felt somewhat uncomfortable when he noticed the four lip piercings. He stepped back a little when he moved his feet to keep the chill from settling into his boots.

'Are you writing about the Poppyline then?' Kyle asked.

'No, not a tourist story. One of the journalists I work with has landed himself in hospital, so I'll be taking over his job for a bit. Something to do with the environment along the North Norfolk coast, I've been told.'

'Ah. Well, there's a lot to write about there. Cliffs tumbling into the sea and such,' said Kyle. 'Sheringham has a rather unfortunate claim to fame, did you know? It was the first place in Britain to be bombed by a Zeppelin during the First World War.'

Josh heard a soft giggle behind him and noticed two girls leaning on the station post, one of them putting out her cigarette, the blond one in a red coat talking behind her raised hand.

The restored steam train was remarkable, made to look glossy new even though the old engine wheezed an exhausted sigh as it pulled into Holt station. Not many passengers opened the timber carriage doors when it arrived at the platform. The two girls stood too close to the train and vanished from his sight momentarily, engulfed by grey steam, the pressure hissing like a dragon and billowing around them. They screamed, laughed, and stepped back. Station platform volunteers moved to assist a few passengers off the carriages, carried bags a distance from the train and returned to help others.

'I've got to go now. Nice to meet you. Bye.'

'And you...' he was cut short by Kyle's agitated rush to get away. His hands were deep in his tattered duffle coat pockets, his head lowered. Josh watched him follow the two young women onto the first carriage while he jumped on board the second carriage with his backpack. Maybe this bloke was up to no good. No, he pulled himself into line. He should concentrate on getting to his digs in Cromer before letting his imagination take him to another story. It might be perfectly innocent, of course.

The girl in the blue coat had caught Josh's eye. She had dark hair and deep brown eyes. She had a laugh and demeanour like the woman he'd last seen on a different railway station, twelve thousand miles from here. He boarded the steam train, pushed his backpack ahead of him, pleased to deposit its weight in the luggage section. Soon, a shrill whistle broke through steam hissing outside his window.

As it gathered pace, he settled into the almost empty carriage and stared out of a window at the frozen white sky. The old timbers smelt of damp varnish, the leather seating was cold. The rhythm of the steam train lulled him into a sleepy daze, and he couldn't resist the warm memories jogged by the girl in the blue coat. His eyes felt heavy, so he relaxed and let it flow.

Carly and her friend climbed onto the steam train, unaware of the long-haired youth boarding after them. He sat behind blond-haired Rose, sunk back into the seat and pulled out a worn paperback to read. Half an hour later, both girls disembarked at Sheringham and walked towards the station exit, waving their pass at the ticket machine scanner as they discussed their weekend. Carly saw a couple, arm in arm, hurry through a puddle of lamplight. Neither of them noticed the dishevelled young man tucking a novel into his coat pocket and tracing their steps, until he sneezed. Carly turned, her eyes temporarily glancing directly at him. She smiled and continued to comment on her friend's story. At the gate, the girls separated, Rosie went in the direction of the town's high street. Carly turned towards the residential area and its sparsely lit street.

Lengthy shadows stretched across her path, ancient oaks with knobs and heavy boughs. She felt the evening air close in on her. She looked ahead and realized she was alone, pulled the collar of her blue coat up and quickened her pace.

Starlings flocked noisily in nearby gardens, a screeching sound in the misty evening. She turned her head to see if anyone was behind her, but she only saw a taxi disappearing down the street towards the train station car park. Then she heard a twig snap quite close to her. She startled and, again, she turned but still could not see anybody. Probably a cat, she decided. She sped up her walking pace. She felt aware of her breathing and her throbbing heartbeat. She turned her mind to something else before panic set in. She wondered how her cat was going back home. Silly cat was a bit wild when one of her sisters found her, so she used to like sneaking up on them and pouncing. She smiled at the memory. Jenny had looked as cosy as the soft kitten when she fell asleep, curled up with her cat on the blanket her mother had made. She won't panic. Probably just a cat.

Josh must've nodded off. It seemed no time had passed before the train had come to a noisy halt. He gathered his luggage and stepped through the gush of steam onto the platform in Sheringham. The girls, Kyle and another couple also got off the train, but he was the only passenger with luggage. No tourists this time of the year. From here, he would catch a taxi to his unit near the Cromer lighthouse.

He was immediately aware of the difference in temperature when he stepped from the train. He tasted the ocean air, salty and crisp with icy winds whistling past his ears. He could not help comparing it to the warm and salty air back home and there was a moment of loss. So, who wanted to be away from loved ones at Christmas? Nobody. He'd just have to ride it out and get on with the job so he could return before the intoxicating smells of summer faded, maybe even before Christmas. First thing tomorrow, he would contact the local college to see if he could hire someone interested in doing a bit of freelance photography work for him.

He stepped into the car park, where the taxi rank stood empty. He noted a sign with a phone number and pulled out his mobile.

'Hello. I'm at Sheringham train station. Could I please get a taxi to the Cromer Country Club in Overstrand Road? Five minutes? That's fine. Thanks. My name? Josh.'

He sat on his backpack and looked around. He heard the screech of starlings in a nearby tree, which caused him to look in that direction. They were probably startled by the young woman in the blue coat rushing by. She turned around a couple of times, maybe looking for someone but her friend must've gone the other way. He stood and took a couple of steps to get an unobstructed view. Just then, his taxi pulled into the car park. He climbed inside with his backpack, gave the driver the address, and closed the door. As the taxi drove down the street, away from the shopping precinct, he glanced in her direction, but she was gone.

Carly wanted to flee like a frightened rabbit, instead, she anchored herself to the spot, held tight to her handbag, turned and faced him. She felt that confronting him would empower her resolve to stand firm in a defensive stance. She'd read that in a magazine on self-defence for women but couldn't recall what else it had advised. The man in the shadows was short, stumpy, with a glow of him smoking a cigarette. She couldn't see him clearly, but she felt his gaze stripping her as she faced him, unmoved by the panic she was experiencing.

The young man mumbled something, but she didn't hear him. Drowned out by the sound of her own heartbeat thumping in her ears and the whisper of her own rapid breath suspended in the evening haze. A streetlight drew her attention to his reddish coloured shoes, but this was all she could see.

At first the words did not come, then she softly broke the silence. 'Why are you following me?'

She watched him as the cigarette glowed a little brighter, then her attention was drawn to it being tossed to the ground where his reddish-coloured shoe diffused its light into a puff of tiny stars. The wind rustled through branches of a nearby oak tree. She smelt smoke before she saw his shadow as he stepped out of interposed obscurity from behind the trunk of the oak.

'You shouldn't be so nervous, Miss.' She gaped at him, unable to speak for a moment. She tried assessing his intentions as he pushed his dark-rimmed glasses back on a wide, flat nose. He seemed vaguely familiar.

'Have we met? Do I know you? You've been following me since I left the station,' she accused. 'If you aren't following me, why are you behaving in such a secretive manner hiding behind trees and lamp posts?'

He was closer now and she smelt his stale breath, and tobacco lingered in the fabric of his coat. She estimated him to be about twenty, but it was hard to tell because of the long, greasy hair hanging lower than the top of his glasses and touching his shoulders unevenly. She sensed that he was probably, at that moment, harmless but she was alerted to a rush of anxiety which quickly tightened her chest and throat. She coughed, focused on him and stepped back a little as she continued speaking much louder than before.

'I felt quite frightened knowing someone was following me, and I couldn't see you in the dark. Are you nuts? Go away!'

He seemed to listen to her but didn't flinch. Suddenly, to her astonishment, he simply turned and walked away. She watched as he withdrew, a slight smile embedded on a youthful expression, and he receded into the frozen night. Carly allowed herself a long, slow breath before she turned and ran towards her guesthouse.

Now he was in England, Josh had to be careful not to knock his forehead after he entered a heritage building with very low ceilings and thresholds. His frame was not built for such an entrance, but the ancient pub in Cromer was where he'd arranged to meet with his new photographer, so he dodged a heavy timber beam and wandered over to the small bar. He glanced at his phone. He was way too early, surprised at how easy this place had been to find. He was hungry after walking along the clifftop path into Cromer. It had just started raining again. He had time for a bite of lunch.

Josh usually stood at the back of every gathering. He'd learnt to do this as a teenager when his height had gathered momentum. His height had seemed ungainly back then; awkward sometimes, but he liked to think his bulk made him more physically capable. His height gave him an instant power which he'd noticed early on. Someone once told him that being tall gave others an impression of strength, of dependability, and there was nothing fragile in his demeanour. The pub was quite busy. The sweet aroma of an English roast wafted from meals being handed over the counter to an elderly couple. The woman serving was middle-aged, friendly. She glanced over, acknowledged him with a smile.

'Be with you in a moment, sir,' she said.

He checked the menu board, decided on a toasted sandwich and a coffee. He wasn't sure how long he'd be staying, but it seemed cosy and welcoming. The people leaning on the bar turned to him. He smiled, felt a little uneasy at catching the waitress's attention before them.

Josh knew many people mistook his level of vulnerability, for he was quite shy. In the past, managers had made assumptions of leadership qualities, strong political or workplace opinions and he'd found it disconcerting. His almost gentle personality defied his build, and it came across as humility to those who didn't know him. He was a country boy, whipped off to the city to study and work in a whole new world. He grew up in south-western New South Wales, on a farm. Everyone told him how he'd inherited his handsome features from his father, and he'd often joked about his inherited receding hairline. As a teenager, he and his brother had jumped off the school bus feeling tired after a busy day at school, to be met by a solid routine of farm chores. He hadn't yearned for the social life other teens discussed during school lunch breaks. He was content with his freedom on the farm. He studied regularly, not easily distracted by socials or youth groups or sports like his contemporaries in town. He had enjoyed being part of a large country family who understood his need for peace and his curious hunger for knowledge. He finished school as dux of his year and won a scholarship to study in the city.

Maths always fascinated him. He didn't need a meeting to do his work. He preferred to work alone or with other similar-minded analysts. People who appreciated the awesomeness of a convoluted problem, who liked nothing better than estimating outcomes based on mathematical and complex pathways. He preferred to have a few loyal friends rather than many wishy-washy acquaintances. His strength was in his loyalty and focus. He was easily bored with large social gatherings where he struggled with their small talk. He was a man of facts and figures rather than one who could enjoy the frivolities of society.

At university, he met his future wife. His plans were simple. He'd thought that he would protect his family like little birds in the palm of his hand. When he was in his early twenties, full to the brim of love and testosterone, he would ward off evil intruders and sort out all their problems as they arose. He'd guard his beautiful wife with a passion into which he would quietly immerse himself. Nothing was going to get in their way. Until it did.

Cancer became an uninvited guest in their home and stole her away one Christmas Eve. He was a broken man for a long time. His confidence and concentration waned at work, so he took a break. He did some more study and enjoyed a change of career. After a while, he returned to the peace and quiet of the countryside; he bought a small holding of one hundred and fifty acres of lush cattle grazing country. He spent as much time as he could in Maleny, restoring his focus on life.

His lunch arrived soon after he ordered. He sat at the bar in the quieter end of the room adjacent to the other patrons. The toasted sandwich was steamy, the coffee hot. He glanced at the clock on the wall, eating the melted cheese and juicy tomato. He felt upbeat and looked forward to meeting his new photographer.

Carly had spoken on the mobile phone to a fellow called Josh. She could not believe her luck when she'd heard his Aussie accent and recognized the newspaper he said he worked for. He wanted to meet her in town somewhere to discuss doing some freelance photographic work for him. She looked up at the sign on the pub – The Albian. She thought this would be easy for a tourist to find as it's close to the church and the shops. Behind her, the howling wind from the sea filled the air with a salty taste. Although it was just after lunch, the sun was nowhere to be seen. Inky grey clouds started spitting more rain as she hurried to open the front door. Dark outside and cosy inside. She felt at home straight away when Zena and Steve looked up from the bar and smiled in her direction. She slipped off her blue coat and scarf and placed them on her arm. Winter in England meant wearing lots of layers of clothing and peeling it all off when inside houses or shops.

'Carly, hello,' said Zena. She and Steve owned the pub and always made patrons feel comfortable with their warm personalities.

'Hi Zena, g'day Steve.' She walked up to the dark-stained, wooden stool near the bar, smiled and shivered.

'What can we get for you today, Carly? You look frozen to the bone. You just never get used to our cold weather, do you?' Zena remembered her name, where she was from. They were impressive hosts.

'No, I won't get used to it. I'm waiting for some snow, but they keep telling me I'm in the wrong place for that.'

'Plenty of rain though,' said Steve. 'Taken any good photos lately, Carly?'

'I tried to take a few of the coastline this week but the weather ruined that plan. Although, I did get an awesome shot of the rolling fog from Sheringham pond park a while ago. Maybe I'll go back up there soon when the fog lifts.'

'Yeah. Good spot for photos of the pier and the Pavilion Theatre from there. What can I get you, then?'

She considered the list of brewed beers and settled for a hot coffee. 'I've got to meet a bloke here for a job in a while. Have you seen any strangers around?'

She searched the familiar dark timbered walls with a framed picture of the sailing ship and a bit further on, a darts board and a small telly, switched off. There was some soft music playing in the room, the ambiance quite relaxing.

'Strangers? Well, we like to think nobody's a stranger once they're in here,' he laughed. 'There's a chap who came in earlier and had a bit of lunch.' He glanced over to the wooden bench where this young man had been sitting but he'd gone. 'Maybe he's having a game of pool, or perhaps in the men's bathroom.'

'Or left already,' said Carly. 'He might be one of those people who need to be exactly on time for things. I'm afraid the bus was a tad late.'

She took the hot coffee mug from Zena and shrugged. 'I'll just sit here for a while and wait a bit, wrap my cold hands around this lovely, warm coffee and warm my nose.'

She walked over to a table near the central heater, thinking she'd be much warmer sitting right next to it. Already the warmth in the small pub was extraordinary compared with outdoors. She regretted the loss of the open fire as a focus of family life where everyone gathered, including the dog, to listen to the radio or read the newspaper. There was something missing with the central heating pipes lined up against the wall; an atmosphere only created by an open fire, crackling away on a hot grate. She recalled her mother describing the evenings spent in Norfolk when she and her siblings had gathered on a rug in front of their open fire. That was in the fifties when most people had an open fire, so she wondered if family life had changed for the better or worse since the advent of central heating. Her mother said they played board games on a rug near the fire and warmed their feet toward the flames. She remembered her being quite nostalgic in her reminiscing. It must've been so very different for her in the heat of the Australian northern summer.

'Carly.' It was Zena, breaking into her thoughts, who pointed in the direction of a tall man, who was standing at the end of the bar, looking at his watch. He had been in the other room. She put down the coffee mug, jumped up in a hurry and knocked over her chair. Her camera bag became stuck in the cross-rail of the chair. Coat, camera, scarf, everything but her coffee, scattered. The man looked toward the commotion and sprinted over to help clean up the mess.

Carly felt herself blushing. Her cheeks always went crimson whenever she was flustered. 'Thank you so much,' she said. 'Are you Josh?'

He handed her the camera bag and scarf and smiled.

'Yes, I'm Josh Campbell. If you're Carly Williams, it's nice to meet you.'

Josh stood outside the hospital, watching as the late afternoon sun began to set. It had been a week since he had arrived in Cromer. He realised it might take a while to get used to the sun setting in the east and adjusting to being on the other side of the world. Even cleaning his teeth and watching the water spiral backwards down the plughole was weird. He had his laptop in a shoulder bag ready to have a short meeting with his work colleague, who was a patient at the hospital until he was well enough to be transferred back to Brisbane.

At the nurse's station, he was directed down a long hallway to a private room. Well, it might not have been private, but John was alone in the two-bed room. His pinned legs were both resting on large pillows.

'G'day mate, how're you going? I'm Josh Campbell – your work replacement.'

'Hi Josh,' he tried to sit himself up and winced as pain froze him to the spot. 'I'm John.'

'I hope you don't mind me dropping in like this, John.'

'No, mate. Good of you to drop by. The boss said you'd be dropping by soon.'

Josh looked around and settled on the plastic chair behind the door. Near enough to hear but not too close. 'I don't suppose you have too many visitors from back home.'

'No. All poms. Love them to bits but I can't wait to fly home. Should be next week, I think.'

'Yeah. It's the only place to be when you're crook,' said Josh. 'So, what happened to you? I heard you'd been in a road accident.'

'Yes,' he smiled. 'A word of advice, Josh. Make sure you take a taxi when you need to go somewhere. Those tiny roads can be tricky and some of the houses were there before transport, so some villages have streets which wind around the edges of the houses. It's nuts.'

'Well, looks like you're on the mend now. Looking after you, are they?'

'Yeah, they are. The NHS seems to be doing the right thing by me.'

'Well, it's almost your tea-time, so I'll make my visit short this time,' said Josh. 'I just need to know what you're up to with work and what you'd suggest I start with. I hired myself a photographer on freelance. She's a tutor at the local college so she knows her stuff.'

'Oh, that's really awesome, Josh. She should work out fine. I know you want to get on with the job, so I'll have to ask you to take my flat keys and bring me my laptop. If you don't mind, that is...'

'No, I don't mind at all. Is there anything else you need while I'm at the flat?'

'No, thanks, mate. I have friends who are looking after me okay. It's just that they can't really dig in my work stuff. You know – privacy issues and so forth.'

Josh agreed to take his key and return the next day with the laptop and files he requested. He slipped the key into his back pocket, shook hands with John and left the room, as a trolley with his tea pulled up alongside his bed.

Next morning, Josh had driven to the hospital with John's laptop and was keen to download files onto his memory stick. They'd spent time discussing the potential outcomes and several ideas on presentation. He thought it was hard to pinpoint the defining moment when all this environmental consciousness began. Perhaps we've always known about it, but governments have been too slow to act. Is it the scientists and their warnings perhaps? Are we more educated now? Do we question things more?

We probably have a better idea when something doesn't seem right. Maybe the world has always been changing, moving, shaping the landscape over the centuries. It seemed to Josh that he would do his readers a disservice by only identifying the current issues when there's always been changes to adapt to. How could he show that to his readers? He didn't want to say it was only caused by recent policies, but there was no denying the industrial revolution certainly had things to answer for. But, according to John, he wasn't required to pinpoint an issue. His job would be to focus on what's been happening over time in this part of the world, not the reasons for them happening.

He decided to research some history of the local floods over the past few hundred years. He wanted his readers to compare and question what had changed, if anything at all. Over time, what happened if we took no notice of the warnings from history and science?

Maybe a series of articles in the weekend papers, he thought, jotting down some notes. He wanted to show the ordinary person what it might be like for people who lived in medieval times. He didn't want to preach to his readers but rather show them how it would've been for those families in the past who had lived with the results of inundation from the North Sea. Maybe he'd do a story from the nineteenth century too, and he already knew about that awful flood in North Norfolk back in 1953 so he could follow up on that with some facts. His fingers flew across the keyboard with these ideas and a plot began to form. He would go to the local museum with Carly soon and try to find the lady who owned the house he saw in the local paper. The article had said the cottage was tipping over a cliff like a seesaw. This should make an interesting and anecdotal story for his readers back home. Sad thing is – it's real and it's now - but he wanted the owner of the house to tell her own story.

His little unit seemed large and empty. There was an icy loneliness in travelling the world alone. The emptiness of hotel rooms is not the lack of furniture. He would wake up tomorrow, enthusiastic to meet the challenges ahead, submit his reports and return home. He could not forget why he was here in the first place. It was an exciting opportunity for him, and he couldn't wait to get started.

1880 *Woman in white dress and straw hat*, by Charles Sprague Pearce (1851-1914)

Chapter 2 - 1888

Sarah-Jane Fletcher would later recall hearing muffled screams and distant church bells, the eeriness of tiny bubbles tickling against her face, the horrific silence, the churning sea and her tight desperation for air. But the real struggle wasn't about any of that. It was the weight of her clothing; her leather-tied boots filling with sea water, her tightly worn under-clothing, her laced-up petticoat and heavy-woven cotton frock. She'd been sinking, tossed about by stormy undercurrents, when she stretched out to reach for a rope.

Grasping it, she pulled to test its strength. It was not solid. It didn't seem to be attached to anything at all, just floating about under icy salt-water. In her terror she did not consider releasing it, so she clung to it as the clothing she wore caused her to sink further into the dark abyss. Arms and legs flayed about as panic threatened, her throat tightened, her lungs were almost at bursting point. Her mind grew light. She looked up. The surface seemed smooth, light penetrated a rainbow until waves disturbed it. Her long hair floated above her and tangled in the rope her right hand was holding, triggering sharp pain when she glanced upwards. Then another wave pushed more sandy pressure down onto her face, into her eyes, lifting her body and dumping it in a circular motion through unrelenting waves. A whirlwind of underwater current tossed her upside-down. She lost consciousness with her hair entangled in the rope which she had to eventually release.

The boy knelt beside Thomas Blogg, who was his father and a local fisherman. He was also one of the lifeboatmen watching and waiting, unable to do anything else for this woman.

'Is she drowned, Father?' asked a wide-eyed, twelve-year old Henry.

Earlier, in the chaos around him, twenty-year-old Matthew had noticed a thick rope curled neatly on the Cromer pier when it suddenly stiffened. He'd held onto its slithering length and dived into the sea, pulling this rope up as far as he could. Four feet under, he noticed where the rope had tangled. The girl was swiftly sinking but, in the darkness, he could not separate her long hair from the twisted rope. He simply pushed her limp body with the end of the rope up towards the light, to the fresh wind biting the surface in soft sprays. She'd been heavily weighed down by her clothing, but he had no time to remove any of it. She simply required air, so, with all the strength he could gather, he thrust her body upwards, kicking and pushing with all his strength, until their bodies broke the surface and into the clarity and sounds of daylight.

The steam tug, *Victoria* of Great Yarmouth, was nowhere to be seen, though broken pieces of its hull were floating nearby, the gusty wind whipped its timber against barnacled pylons. Someone said there was a great chunk of the vessel stuck on a rock further out, not visible from here. He struggled and swum with all his might to pull her to the side of the pier, avoiding damaged timber and other people reaching out for help. At the pier, she was listless, saturated, and heavy.

People screamed, cried, called out. Thomas knelt over the edge, took her hands and pulled her up as gently as he could manage. Dripping and cold, Matthew followed her to the decking, and searched her pale face, her blue lips. He shook his head, emptied water from his ears. He felt ill and turned away, puffing, exhausted.

Thomas bent over her mouth and listened for her breath.

'No, lads. Wait .. I can feel a faint breath on my cheek,' said the lifeboatman, as he knelt beside her soaked remains on the wooden boards of the pier. People around them ran about, shivering under blankets, some dripping wet standing on the pier watching the horrific scene unfold, others still in the icy waters clinging to flotsam and still others sinking beneath the surface. Some begged for mercy, for help. He saw a young woman holding a child, the unrelenting waves picked them both up and threw them a further distance from the lifeboats. He saw fishermen join the rescue, their fishing trawlers near enough to throw out life jackets or ropes to those in the water. But he stayed with this woman.

'But she's so blue. All 'round her mouth. Icy blue, sir,' he cried, squatted, and held her head on his lap, the rope still entangled in her long hair. He tried to unravel the rope and hair, but the tangle persisted.

Sunshine broke through a low-slung black cloud strip. The girl turned over to her side, retched salty water from her stomach, her eyes now wide open. She struggled to sit up, confused at the mayhem around her. Her hands flew up to her tangled hair as she fell back on the pier, crying desperately, fear set in the depths of her welling eyes.

Thomas put his hand on her shoulder. 'Be all right now lass.' His son, Henry, breathed a sigh of relief beside him.

'The rope, sir. Should I cut her hair free?' asked Matthew. He nodded.

'Miss, hold still. We must release your hair from the rope. You've tangled yourself in it. Not all bad really. It saved your life, I'd say,' said Thomas. Matthew took out his knife and started cutting through the blond thickness, quite close to Sarah-Jane's scalp. The girl was shaking and stiffened when he finally cut through the last piece of hair. He held her wet locks in his hand.

He wondered at the power of being able to save someone's life after they had fallen into the sea. The idea felt like a red-hot poker. A jolt where he finally saw what his future might hold. He couldn't speak for some time but swore he'd work harder at being a lifeboatman, and spend his spare time teaching others to swim, for most could not swim to save themselves.

The young woman sat up, her hair scattered in clumps on her scalp, wild and wet. She crawled over to the edge of the pier, her eyes searching the water below.

'Nell? Molly? Catherine?' Sarah-Jane wiped her eyes with her hand again and again, trying to clear the tears. 'No, no, they must be there. Please help me find them.'

Her eyes dashed across silver sparkles dancing with wild abandon on top of the sea, flotsam and jetsam and people and wooden planks. She rolled into a small ball, bent sideways and was sick again over the edge, into the water. The young man who stayed with her placed a woollen blanket, crocheted in bright colours, over her shoulders. The weight of his hand lent her comfort at some primitive level. She gathered a deep breath and screamed out the names of her friends again, while the white cliffs on the shore seemed to light up from within, the sun now reflecting the colour of a dusky rose with flashes of gold. She knew today would be like no other in her life.

Then she saw him. In the distance a little, on the other side of the broken boat pieces. Richard. He'd know what to do. He always knew what to do in emergencies. She allowed a little hope to surface amid this horror they'd landed in. Her oldest brother was always dependable, and she set her eyes on his panicked features. His face, usually full and laughing, was like a deflated balloon, his head bent back and lying on the surface of the water as it washed over him. There was a wound above his eye, blood seeping to his chin and onto the wet plank. That's all she could see of his body, as he floated away from the wreck. Away from the pier. Why would he do that? Come this way, Richard, she wanted to say. She stood up so he might see her on the pier, she waved and the lad who'd saved her life picked up the blanket which had dropped to the boards.

'Richard, please...' she called. Her voice was lost in the cries and the wind. What would she do now? She felt that she was being buried alive under the weight of all this devastation. Her knees felt weak as she collapsed on the pier.

14th Century

Peasant Girl Charles Pearce (1851-1914)

Chapter 3 – 14th Century

Cartia Laman piled the kindling in her arms, cradled her precious cargo wrapped in a woollen shawl, tied it to her back and headed for home. A wintery night was creeping over the marshes; the sounds of feeding bats screeched through damp air. Henry, her older brother, who made the eerie woodland less frightening, stood at the edge of a path up ahead. They both knew the dangers which lurked behind the dark curtain of woodlands after sunset.

'Hurry, Cartia. We have enough wood for the firepit – let's go.'

'I'm sorry for my tardiness, Henry. I'm quite weary after such a long walk,' she tried to think of something hopeful to say to lighten his mood. 'These branches will be dry by morning if we warm them by the fire tonight.'

Rumour has it that thieves gathered in the woodlands at night to attack any passing pilgrim who might have a crust of bread or, better still, a bountiful purse.

'Cartia, you know the rules, home by sunset. No matter what. Pa will be furious.'

She glanced up at the slither of a moon risen above shadowy branches, felt the cold wind against her face as she hurried after him, with the dank kindling, her hair whipped out of its bun and flapping across her eyes. She pulled her scarf tighter, held onto it under her chin as she followed the sound of timber twigs when they crackled under his feet, just ahead of her. She tried to remember feeling warm under the summer sun, but gusts of ever-present icy wind from the German Ocean blew away her thoughts.

They walked into the sunset, all golden orbs in a dull, wintery sky. Cartia stole a moment, to hear the cracking sound of more heath-sticks snapped in two. The air was chilly - her breath dissipated into a fog. She glanced back at the stony road, a track which wound through velvet folds, mountains which changed shape as the light faded. She watched several rabbits bounce toward the coney-warrens there. She thought of her friend's family who farm rabbits on the northern side of Felbrigg, which overlapped the parish border near Shipden. Her friend's father was the resident warden, who had a lodge on the property. They bred rabbits for their smooth fur and delicious stewing meat. She rubbed her stomach, which rumbled at the thought of supper. If she wasn't quick, her mother would be cross, and she might miss supper tonight.

She would not dawdle a moment longer. Off came her scarf and she began to wrap more into her bundle of heath-sticks Henry had cut, tied it to her back again and raced after his inky silhouette as he made his way towards home with the larger firewood. She caught up to him near the windmill at the crossroads of Hall and Holt Roads. Several carts carrying corn were being unloaded, ready for tomorrow's work where they ground the precious local produce into flour. After the manor kitchens of the Abbot of Holme and the Bishop of Norwich retained their share, the remainder would be taken to Shipden markets the next day.

Henry knew the men well. They greeted each other as the two of them passed by. She adjusted her flaxen hair, plaited and tied up. Her fingers ran over her nosegay. It was looking withered, but she was alerted to the pungent smell of lavender sprigs. After a day outside labouring in muddy fields, she'd gathered a small bunch of wildflowers and a few herbs for a nosegay. She had tied it to her wrist with ribbon so she might smell fresh. Her eyes turned down, she scurried past the young men who had stopped work and smiled in her direction. Henry hadn't noticed, though she felt safer in his company.

The familiar stench signalled that they were almost at their village. A mix of mud, manure, drying fish, seaweed. Henry told her to keep walking while he relieved himself behind a tree before they exited the woodland.

Next morning, Cartia was pleased to walk down northern High Street, which continued into Jetty Street, past the cobbled marketplace and the dazzling German Ocean beyond. Two rocky streams flowed each side of the village and into the mouth of Shipden harbour, where fishermen tended to their fishing net repairs ready for tomorrow's catch. Behind her, the church of St Peter's perched at the top of a gradual rise and overlooked clusters of cottages to the south. Her family lived closer to the southern end of Shipden's small High Street. Several goats grazed along the hillside.

Henry stayed at the cottage farmyard to sort the wood they had gathered yesterday and piled it in the drying shed. He said he was going to walk along the beach to collect some timber from shipwrecks while the tide was out later. She hoped to see her sister, who lived in a cottage near farmland closer to Crowmere. Matilda would be at the beach most of the morning with her friends.

Women she had known all her life were gathered around on stools in a knitting circle near the shingled beach, for today the sun shone with only a slight breeze. Summer was on its way, if they were blessed. She became mesmerized by the constant rhythm of tiny waves which skittered along the beach. She loved to paddle in its shallows and let her toes sink into the saturated sand. Nobody went in too deep for fear they might drown. She heard that some of the fishermen could stay afloat and move about without sinking but she had no idea how they stayed on the top of the water, nor did she want to copy that behaviour. She was quite content with her two feet on the surface of the earth as God intended. Soon it would be warm enough to bathe again in their tub at the cottage. Even though she'd washed her hands and face every morning, taking particular care on Sundays, the family only had a full bath in their wooden tub several times a year. The last time she could remember a thorough scrub was at the end of last summer. She turned from the distant sound of waves breaking offshore, a potent smell of fish, salt and fishermen and walked over to her sister.

Cartia enjoyed her knitting lessons with her older sister, who had married two seasons ago and was now with child. Her gallant husband was riding to Blakeney town this day. Mati said he had inherited land valued at more than forty shillings this year so was permitted to vote in county elections. Matilda had met him in the field when they were planting the crop. She remembered him climbing from his steed and asking to be introduced. Henry was a year younger than Matilda, and an acquaintance of James Harmer, her future husband. Henry said he would discuss the matter with their father, and he would send a message to James in due course. He had turned from Henry, smiled at Matilda, bowed his head and left the field in a contented manner. She'd never forget that day.

'Good morning, Mati. Enjoying some sunshine?' she asked.

'Cartia, how are you? I wondered if you would come by today. I've brought some knitting needles for you to try a new pattern,' said Matilda, pulling at her small canvas bag. 'As I told you before, the pattern for our family is one which has been passed down from one generation to the next.'

'Thank you,' said Cartia, now seated on a stool and reaching for the wooden needles. 'I was beginning to become bored with plain square knitting. Although I have made a warm shawl for our mother with them.'

'And doesn't Ma love it? This pattern is special. It shows where a person comes from by the stitches you knit into it. It would also identify him if he drowned at sea and was washed up on a beach. Look at those fishermen nearby. Their mothers and sisters have knitted them the family pattern, and they look so warm.'

'The jumpers look a bit tight fitting.'

The other ladies laughed. Her sister replied,

'They are supposed to be tight to keep out the cold winds. Making a gansey is a labour of love; it can take a very long time to make each one. They're knitted in one piece with no seams making them less liable to tear along a weakness.'

'Ah. Just like me, she said, keeping it light-hearted. 'I have no seams.' The younger ones looked up from their work and laughed a while.

'I'll make a gansey for Henry. Is this the wool mother spun last summer?'

'Yes, and it's been beautiful to knit up. It's even and smooth. Henry will love a new gansey, Cartia. He doesn't have a wife yet, so I'm sure he'll appreciate you making it for him.'

'Cartia, you are growing into a lovely young woman,' said Mrs Bacon. 'Are you betrothed yet?'

She felt a wisp of panic. Why do they keep asking such a thing of her?

'When I was betrothed in my infancy, my prospective husband was only four years old, 'said Cartia. 'Sadly, the boy died at six from tuberculosis. Rest assured, my parents are always watching for a suitable husband for me, Mrs Bacon.'

The women who heard the conversation looked up from their knitting and smiled. They knew the pressure but also understood the need for her to feel secure in her future. After all, she was nearly fifteen and most of their children had left the family home around her age. Some had become apprentices in large houses, cooking and cleaning and in service until they married. She was the last daughter left at home, and she was able to learn these things from helping her mother, who was not young anymore at forty years of age.

'Our brother, Henry, is of the age to be courting now so he might be next to be wed. He has already started building a cottage near Jetty Street,' said Matilda.

'I saw him this week gathered with some of his friends on the land near the Lillyman's lease,' said Mrs Bond. 'He'll be a neighbour of mine when he and his wife move into the cottage.' She seemed quite pleased with that idea.

Her brother was strong and loyal, and a fisherman who hoped to inherit their father's fishing boat one day. Strange thing was – nobody asked who he was courting. It's family business, she guessed. Every woman there would've longed to know, but they would wait until announcements were made. It softened the blow on the young couple if negotiations did not work out for them. She knew that didn't mean they wouldn't watch and listen to gossip, so she kept quiet when nobody asked questions.

She had her own secrets.

1953

Mary Cassatt specialised in painting and making prints of children. When she was mastering dry point technique in about 1887, she made this fine print entitled *Baby's Lullaby*.

Chapter 4 - 1953

Right along the eastern coast of England, electricity had been cut hours ago. As the day wore on and darkness persisted, her husband lit the old oil lamp and placed it out of the reach of their five children. Cath knew someone might knock it off the shelf with their energetic ways in the small cottage, so that was enough to take extra care. The twins were still too young to get into mischief, four months old and so cute in their blue jumpers Gran had knitted them for Christmas. There would be no heating tonight apart from the range. It would be chilly if it hadn't been for knitted rugs and everyone squashing into the front room telling stories and singing tunes to drown out the constant sound of heavy rain. Cath was sure it hadn't stopped raining since the beginning of January.

The air smelt of soggy mud. She smelt it on everything. Even the twins smelt musty. She put Charlie back in his pram with Billy. No need for a proper cot for the babies. It was good enough for the other three. She'd heard that some parents used a bottom drawer of their dresser for tiny babies to sleep in, but her sister-in-law, Louise, had handed down her wicker pram after her Sally and Jane had outgrown it. A bit tattered, one of those low-slung fancy models in its day but just fine. They always made do. Since the war ended a few years back, everyone shared and pulled their weight. They helped each other out when babies arrived. Menfolk who returned from the war had just wanted to settle down and start a family. Fred said that they'd needed to get some normality back into their lives and so did their wives.

She wondered how her older brother, Bobby, managed to get to work in London. She couldn't imagine anything worse than sinking knee deep in muddy bog, or slipping and sliding through cobbled streets, to the railway station. She was glad her husband was off work. It's not possible for a thatcher to work in these conditions.

Fred had removed his sodden clothing and dumped it in the sink by the back door of the cottage. She could smell the caked mud scraped from his boots, now placed near the fire to dry. He had taken an umbrella to her brother's cottage, two doors up from theirs, to check on Louise, but he said the umbrella wrapped itself around his body in the fierce wind, whipped up from the North Sea. It penetrated bones and sent people to search desperately for shelter. She thought he looked relieved, though was his frown an indication of fear as he leaned against the cottage door, dripping onto the mat? She handed him a towel. No point in upsetting the children so she'd let it go.

Bob and his wife, Louise, had two daughters, who were playing quietly inside the cottage when Fred knocked on their door. He didn't go in; he was soaked through. He was just checking on their safety. Later, he told Cath he had smelt pea and ham soup cooking in Louise's kitchen, so their dry wood supply must be plentiful. He told her that the girls were occupied, sifting through their mother's jewellery box. The lacquered box with all Louise's crystal necklaces and fake jewels in it. The girls were trying on her pearls, keeping busy. He noticed Louise put the lock back on it and had them wash their hands, ready for their lunch.

Good old Fred. Always looking after others. Now, goodness knows when or if Bob can still get the train back home tonight. She supposed he'd stay in the city somewhere if the trains couldn't operate. He would trust us to keep an eye on things at home.

'That smells good, love,' he said, giving her a sodden hug. She wriggled free of him, Ginny and Tom laughed.

'I'm trying to get that musty smell out of my nostrils. It's a stew with dumplings,' she said, and stirred it a bit before popping it back into the Range oven to brown the top of the dumplings. Her daughter jumped up to steady the oven door.

'That's my girl. Thanks, Ginny.'

'Mum, I'm so hungry,' her daughter said, wide-eyed as she watched the stew pot slide onto the griller plate.

'And here I was thinking you were trying to be helpful, my girl,' she said. 'Well, it should only take another fifteen minutes or so and then you can fill your belly.'

'I'll get Tom and Lizzy washed up and ready, Ma,' said Ginny. She was christened Virginia, but nobody ever called her that. It had always been Ginny. She glanced over at the six-year-old, who skipped towards the utility room. The storm seemed to be gathering momentum. Cath could hear the water as Ginny poured it into a basin and called to the others to join her. Miss Bossy Boots. She'll make a good mother one day.

Fred lined up some more split wood next to the oven to dry out. She knew he was trying to keep a step ahead of their needs. When they married, Fred had taken on any maintenance as well as his thatching business while she was the home organiser. She considered she'd done a pretty good job organising all the home duties and the children.

It was not a grand house. It was a small cottage; the external walls dotted in flint cobble and ample room for the two of them. Now they're feeling the pinch a bit with five children to squeeze in. She inherited it from her grandmother, who had it left to her when

Great-Uncle Matthew, died. There was a beach hut at nearby Cromer too, but Bob's family needed the money, so it was sold. Kath wasn't easily distracted, stirring the cornflour mix into the stew, her mind wandering to that little beach hut. Bobby said there wasn't much left inside it, so he'd sold it as it was. The new owner would've sorted it all out by summer. She recalled a bench seat, a few old towels and blanket inside a box, a kettle and gas heater, an old and battered box used as a shelf for a lantern. Maybe the new owner cleaned it all out, but it did have a certain old-world charm about it as it was.

Here, in the front room, a radiogram stood silent in the corner, useless now with the electricity cut. The wooden table Fred had made them was sturdy and had two benches either side tucked neatly underneath. Her three older children were playing a board game on the mat which had belonged to her mother – they'd found it had survived the bombings in London even though the building had not. Over this side of the room, she prepared their food on the New World Rangette. Their cutlery and fine, bone crockery filled the buffet and hutch, and on the same side of the room was a sink with plastic bowl in it and next to the bench was a GEC fridge, also unable to work without electricity. Pots and pans hung from the rafters on large hooks near the stove.

Another room at the back of the cottage had a laundry basin and bucket with a lid for toileting during stormy weather. She will be glad when they could all use the toilet outhouse again but, until the rain stopped, the covered bucket attended to their needs. The outhouse, which was shared with Bob and Louise's family and Jo Hamilton next door, was too far to walk in the storm or at night. A hook hung discretely behind the door of the outhouse and near the bucket, with carefully torn squares of recycled newspapers. An old brick set-pot in the corner boiled their clothes. A tin bath hung on the edge of the windowsill, waiting for the Rangette to heat pot after pot so they could have a bath sometimes. Usually once a week, but the mud has meant a more regular cleansing routine. The cleanest person gets in first, the dirtiest last.

Upstairs, there was a double bedroom with a pink chenille bedspread, a box room and a loft with two dormer windows built into the thatched roof. The children shared the box room and the loft. The babies usually slept in their parent's bedroom but lately she has had them in the pram downstairs so as not to disturb everyone else during their four-hourly night feeds. The clinic said she should cut out their night feeds after seven weeks, but can you imagine the noise? It'd wake up the whole village.

She knew everyone in the street and was related to half of them in some way or other. They all shared a misshapen life of poverty since the war but together they all felt less deprived because everyone else was in the same position. They were all picking up the pieces and trying to re-build their communities when this terrible storm threatened to ruin everything. First the bombings, and now nature having its way with them. Their circumstances weren't unique from any of the other villages along the Norfolk coastline. They were across the board and Cath knew of many others who were not as well off as they were. There was always someone worse off.

'Tom, I want you to fetch me some vegetables from our plot out the back. Soon as this rain settles a bit. It's too violent now,' she said to her eight-year-old son. 'Can you manage that alright, do you think?'

'Yeah, Ma. I'll take my shoes off and see what I can find in the plot that's not under water.'

‘Good thought, Tom. You don’t want to ruin those shoes. Not too many boys have such a fine pair of leather shoes, so you would do well to keep them dry. Take the umbrella by the door.’

‘Yes, Ma.’

‘Fred, I hope your vegetables will survive these storms. A bit more than a few drops of rain, eh!’ she said to her husband.

Fred had changed into some dry clothes. He looked up from the mat where he’d settled playing with the children.

‘I don’t hold much hope for my little plot. Good thing if Tommy can find a few veg and bring them inside.’

‘We’ve survived so far these past years because you’re such a good gardener, my dear Fred.’

‘I’ll be able to re-build the plot after the storms, I’m sure, love. Plants don’t like too much water.’

Cath shook her head in disbelief, looked again outside the small cottage window and sighed. She felt that they had endured enough, but they don’t have any choice in the matter. Surely it couldn’t get any worse. Streaks of rain hit the windows with such ferocity she could hardly hear herself think. She placed a teapot on the stove to warm up, thankful for something to do.

Lizzy pulled herself up and clung to her mother’s apron, her thumb slipped into her mouth as thunder crashed around their cottage. Flashes of lightning lit up the gap in the door jamb and windowpanes and split the darkness from each upturned face. Cath bent down, picked her up and held her close. She didn’t have as much time as she would’ve liked with this child. She had been almost three when the twins were born and, since then, life had to be re-arranged around them. The twins and their demands were as relentless as that rain outside, so they all had to make sacrifices.

Two babies, double the work and double the love. The others took over the care of Lizzy. Fortunately, she was a generous and quiet child and only bothered Cath whenever the others were preoccupied with something worrisome like this storm. The twins lay in the pram, asleep with full bellies and not a care in the world, so she had time for Lizzy and sought comfort for herself, holding her near as more thunder echoed around the stone cottage.

'Tom, don't go outside now. We'll go without vegetables this meal. You'll be roasted on the pitchfork of a lightning strike if you go out now,' said Cath, carefully placing Lizzy down on one of the benches. 'You two can set the table and then we'll eat before the babies wake again.'

She figured it must've been their new teeth coming through early. Something certainly bothered them. Maybe one twin woke and disturbed the second twin. If only babies came with language built in.

The requirement to make-do was a constant constraint and this winter had meant that Fred had no opportunity to break the cycle and put them ahead a bit. As she ladled out the steaming stew, she considered his trade.

Word had it in the village that his thatching skills were exceptional, and she'd felt proud when she heard this. Many of the villages around North Norfolk carried his touch on their rooflines. Little straw rabbits or the shape of a dog or a horse tucked neatly into a corner of his straw plaiting. You'd have to look carefully to find some of them, but what sculptured beauty to behold and surprise. After tonight's storm – the last night of January – he should have work opportunities lined up for months. Repairing, replacing, mending, mentoring Tom and some of the other boys in the village, who wanted to watch and learn his trade. Until this storm stops, they'll just have to make-do. Fortune favours the brave, so they say.

The rain continued to pour down when the dismal day ended, an inky blackness filling each window. The oil lamp was still sending out flickers of light, like flames licking at the walls. The children had been tucked into beds in the box room and attic, and Fred was snoring in his chair with a book on his lap. Cath finished knitting her row of another matinee jacket, placed the needles into her workbox and gave him a gentle shake.

'Come on, Fred. Upstairs to bed with you. It's getting late.' He stirred, wiped his mouth with the back of his hand and blinked a few times.

'Yes, of course. Is it raining still? I haven't heard thunder for a while.'

'I'm afraid so, Fred.'

'I'll check the doors and windows. Maybe we should put a blanket along the door base to keep leaks out. It's possible that water might drain in here a bit. The land's pretty flat and the ground must be saturated by now.' Fred stood, stretched and placed the book on the arm of his chair. Cath watched as he rolled up a blanket and placed it at the base of the timber door.

'Are you coming upstairs tonight, love?'

'No, dear. Not yet anyway. I'll wait until the babies wake up for their night feeds. No point in disturbing everyone else.'

'That pram is a cumbersome thing,' said Fred. 'But I don't mind carrying it upstairs if that's what you think might be best.'

His soft words covered her and made her feel safe.

'No. I'll be right, reading here for a while. I won't be too much longer. You go up and get a decent night's sleep for the both of us.' She looked into his tired eyes, pushed a wayward hair back from his face and gently kissed his dry lips. Weary, he turned from her, patted his sons on their blond and fluffy curls, and headed for the stairwell.

'Alright, goodnight, my love. Don't be too long,' he said, yawning. It wasn't long before Billy woke up for his feed.

It was one o'clock when Cath put the second twin to her breast, and he nuzzled in. She always gave them individual feeding times every four hours. They all had their special idiosyncrasies, and she wanted to get to know each of them. Her mind drifted to the celebrations in August, when their twins were born.

Social structure in the village was pretty much set in stone, especially after the war when they longed for stability. While she had rested after the births, meals had been provided, the local nurse called daily to check the boys, and the other children were taken in by neighbours for a few days. She'd have done the same for them.

People knew their place and felt comfortable when they didn't overstep the clear marks set by their forebears. Even though it was 1953, Cath knew that social rank and acceptable codes of behaviour were instilled in each of them from a young age. She couldn't imagine what would happen if these expectations weren't met. Even though the war pulled women into the workforce and into men's roles, she was pleased to step aside for them when they returned from battle. Not all women felt the same, of course. There was her cousin, fighting to stay in her job as a truck driver. But not for her. She was like a broody hen on a nest and loved that she had a reliable and loving man who supported her family.

What if this solid sensible world was taken away from them again? What if their house was washed away or the village disappeared into the sea, or their rational existence suddenly became altered and confused again by another war? If we survived, we'd no longer exist in this house, in this village, in this well-defined world which generations before them had constructed. The old flint cottage in which they lived had been through many storms without too much damage; she shouldn't be concerned. Maybe she was just tired.

She can't say the same about those new homes the government erected recently. Many of the newer portables constructed after the war were temporary, not nearly as solid as their stone cottage. She wondered how they were coping tonight as the storm roared, and sounds became menacing. Their old world would be exposed as an assemblage of vacuities. Or maybe they'd clean it up and re-build in exactly the same structured way, just as they were doing to the old churches destroyed by bombs in places like Coventry, where her aunt lived.

It did not weigh heavily on her mind though. Normally, quiet moments like this, in the middle of the night feeding her babies, brought questioning depths to her thoughts. The rest of the day seemed mindless and repetitive by comparison. She knew that their identity as a thatcher's family was a given and there was security in that. Fred's father and grandfather had owned his business and the task of training up the next son was a responsibility Fred looked forward to. There were no choices to be made when they wed either. Her father knew of his father, and it had been arranged that the two should meet and consider a future together when she turned eighteen. She'd known Fred from school days. He'd seemed like the best possible husband in the village at that time. They were creatures of tradition, and it felt, somehow, safe and sound.

Someone could say that the past was already included in their future. Without this continuity and assured structure, Fred might be lost, unhappy, without a compass. As it was, Cath still loved this man, the father of her five children. She knew he was happy too just by the way he lived his life, smiling, content in their company. Their lives past and present had been in this village. The structure of their lives was not contaminated by contingency and a relativity of values they do not share together. They never argued on rights and wrongs. Cath knows how he ticks. He knows, most of the time, what her expectations are. It simply works.

The second twin stopped sucking, eased off her empty breast and flopped onto her arm. She lifted him onto her shoulder and rubbed his back with gentle strokes. She stole a deep, sweet breath from the baby's neck.

The oil lamp glimmered on and off, so she stood and turned it down. The baby belched. All was well, so Cath placed him in the wicker pram beside his brother, both sleeping soundly again. Billy's arms jerked upwards, his eyes opened and closed simultaneously as the gale raged from the east, the timber door pushing against the lock in a clicking noise with each gust of wind. She smelt the embers in the range, listened to the crackling of glowing coal in crisp air. There was a lull in the noise of the storm, though it continued to rain.

She was exhausted after her unpredictable day. A flicker of disquiet upset her stomach whenever she thought of her brother, probably struggling through the wrath of this storm to reach the safety of his home. He should've stayed in London overnight, but she knew him better than that. He would fight anything in his way to be with Louise and the girls. Maybe she could convince herself that he'd already arrived home and was sipping hot soup. The wind was wild outside; wilful and icy and howling around the cottages, beating against windows and rattling doors.

The air was thick with humidity; the smell was of rotting potatoes. She thought it wise to stay downstairs a little longer to make sure the twins settled in their pram, so she snuggled into Fred's cold, leather chair, her knees curled up to her chin and picked up his book.

Chapter 5 - 1888

The sea had been at low tide again that afternoon. Matthew O'Reilly thought the tide was much lower than usual for this time of the year. Local talk was that coastal erosion had been silting up the port too; that wouldn't have helped. At the end of the day, the question they all asked was, what on earth had the ship collided with? Sand banks, silt, rocks? What was hiding just under the surface of the water? He was aware that some of the locals were nodding. They knew more than he did on this matter.

He was new to the town. The locals at the pub whispered, bent as they were over their drinks, nodding. It'd been a strange day. He'd spent the afternoon wandering about, walking the pier, and along the cliff track among tall wildflowers. The wind gently blew him along to the south, to the lighthouse not far from Cromer town. While the locals had made him feel welcome, he'd felt the odd one out at social gatherings but that was to be expected. He also understood how close the locals were. He respected the fact that he'd never really fit in like they did, neatly, like a piece of a jigsaw. They'd been born and raised in Cromer and their parents and grandparents before them had been fishermen in the same town. They knew things he would never know. Instinctive things like the feel of the weather, when a storm might be brewing, why the gulls were making such a racket, watching for signs of danger in the sea he'd only noticed after they'd pointed them out to him. He was resigned to being an outsider, but he was also willing to learn from them, and, because of that, they'd made him feel welcome. But he hadn't really felt a part of their team, he was considered a stranger.

Still, he needed them. They knew more than he did about the local terrain. How was he going to prove to them all that he was a capable lifeboatman, a swimmer who was more comfortable in the water than out of it. His friends at Cambridge would've laughed at this thought. He didn't need to prove anything to them about his abilities in the water, not after winning a place on the inaugural university swimming team.

Of course, he would be hoping to get in some sea swimming practice while he was staying beside the sea. If he could find a casual job with a trawler for the summer break, he could swim after work. He had a few years yet to get himself into top shape. The first event would be held at the Kensington Pools in London against their rival, Oxford. In 1892, he would be in his final year of study, if it all worked to his plan.

He had met some fine student athletes at the trials last month. All muscles and brain combined. Many would've beaten him on another day, but his confidence flared as he dived into the pool and churned through the water that day. He knew, if he made the team, he would have friends for life as well as a notable achievement on his record. His future depended on it. The world awaited those who could perform well. Some of these young men had family they could rely on to support them, but he was on a scholarship awarded to poorer boys who performed well scholastically. He was hungry for success; they were in it to have a good time.

At this early stage, he had not really trained with his team-mates. They would have another event after the summer holidays to choose which one of the competitors would swim the individual freestyle events. Only two of them would be chosen so it would be competitive. He would like to go in the sprints, the one hundred yards, but would consider the medley, if the coach thought he was good enough.

But his mind was not made up. He would continue his studies and come here during his time off. Now, he was more interested in renewing acquaintance with that girl he rescued from the boat accident. She was most likely from Great Yarmouth, as that's where the pleasure steamer had come from. He had heard that most of the passengers returned by train the next day, so he was unlikely to meet up with her again in Cromer. Her name was Sarah-Jane Fletcher, according to the ship's manifest.

Shipden. It was all gone now. The lanes of flintstone cottages, the church and old manor houses, the sheep grazing on hillsides and the sloping pastures and woodland. He wondered what had happened to the fishermen and their families in the fourteenth century. They had most likely moved to nearby Cromer, or Crowmere, as it was once called, as there was a harbour with a wharf there. Matthew found the history of the village fascinating. A reaching out of past inhabitants. It was a reminder of the continuity of life, like a promise of a future still yet to come.

This summer was an unusually hot, dry season so far. Great for swimming in the waters of the German Ocean – now known mostly as the North Sea. This season, the sea levels dropped until the remaining stones of Shipden village emerged a couple of hundred yards beyond Cromer pier. It was proving to be a long walk from his bathing machine to the water for his morning swim, but he managed to achieve a decent hour or so training before the day began in earnest.

By the middle of summer, most the ruins of St Peter's Church were exposed. Nearby, cottage doorways, hearths and lower walls revealed themselves. The sea level continued to drop as warmer weather blanketed the beach. Matthew could walk out to the ruins now, stepping gingerly across pebbles. Among the rubble, a few hundred yards back from the village ruins, an imposing stone fireplace with its rounded columns was still largely intact, stone lined walls and the building's ornate gatepost rose out of the water behind it. Maybe it had been an old manor house. Wandering through the debris, he imagined the lives that would have gone on within those walls.

Closer to where the village would've been, he noticed a path beyond the church that led to a tall, shattered wall which was also exposed, along with what appeared to be a forty-five-foot church tower protruding from the sand and the remains of its lychgate posts on each side of a broken pathway. You could not miss it. The locals called the tower 'Church Rock'. It was here that the shipwreck had been stuck for quite a long time last year. Then explosives were brought in so other ships would not meet the same fate at very low tides.

There was an eeriness and melancholy in the piles of dirtied and shattered headstones from the churchyard. Graves, exposed to the ocean floor instead of a grassy churchyard. He wandered a few metres away to a separate stone circle, filled with sand, maybe a village well.

This sight was far removed from what he had imagined. He was awestruck by the pull of imagined sounds of children strolling along a leafy fishing village lane in tunics and cloaks; boys loitering by a stream near the cottages; villagers wandering the cobbled street to Shipden markets. Little girls, their hair long and unruly, skipping or playing hopscotch, throwing one of the many pebbles from the beach. These had been dark times in Shipden. The sea had destroyed all the fishermen's huts lined along the seafront, the hilly slopes eroded where St Peter's church had faced a hungry ocean. It had eaten away at the land beneath it and all their wooden sea defences. He imagined locals had tried their best, no doubt, and failed.

They were long gone. What remained of the fourteenth century village in the reign of Henry IV were a few stones of human debris, a cautionary reminder of human fallibility. How small and vulnerable he really was in the scheme of things. Gravestones too, some intact, some smashed as though tossed from a crumbling cliff. Only foundations of the solid flint and dawb variety were in evidence now. Crude cottages of this community left no evidence for nineteenth century witnesses, though local history tells of Shipden being a strong fishing port, a thriving market-town.

The pebbles were larger and sharper than on the beach front. He had tripped several times, as the larger stones were obscured with a mossy slime. He would need to tread carefully or risk falling. So, he moved with stealth, watching as he stepped forward, glancing along his pathway through the uneven surface. Ahead of him lay the tower ruins. On closer investigation, he was intrigued to find the walls largely intact but no church bell. He recalled his new friends teasing him in the hotel about this tower's bell chiming in the middle of storms. He smiled. Another folk story passed down from one generation to the next.

Others were also fascinated by this fleeting view of Shipden. An older couple nodded to him earlier, sheltered from the warming sun under their umbrella. Some children were playing closer to the hotel, not taking much notice of what the adults were doing or why anyone should be interested in a few old remnants of lives gone by. A fishman was picking around the ruins looking for bait, he assumed.

There was still a chill in the air from last night, but dappled sun mirrored off the town behind him, lending promise of another warm day ahead. For some time, he sat on one of the remaining lych gate stumps, looking around at the exposed bareness of it all. How he wished he had some company to discuss what was on his mind. Again, he thought of Sarah-Jane. If only he had one of those new camera setups to capture the rarity of this scene. Then, out of the corner of his eye, a reflection, a shot of blinding light from the sand, drew his attention back to the remains of the tower. It was a strange object that just didn't seem to fit amongst the flint and stone.

Chapter 6 –14 C, Shipden

In fields of swaying corn, Cartia loaded wooden carts with yellowed sheafs. A line of men slashed the stalks each gripping a sharp reaping hook and cutting succulent forage mainly for feeding livestock. Others would be baled and dried for winter months. The men held the plants in one hand, and, with a single, swift movement, they sliced through a grip of stalks as low as they could manage. She watched as they worked their way across the field. Behind them, straw lay scattered, and women were busy gathering it in. In front of them, tall golden sheaths moved in waves to the rhythm of a light breeze. And there he was, in the centre of that line of men, his strong, brown arm slowly lifting high above his curved, muscular back and coming down with one swift movement.

Cartia's secret.

It was her secret because he didn't know how she felt, let alone anyone else. Daniaen was taller than most of the men, with blond, wavey hair and bright sky-blue eyes. Most of the inhabitants of Shipden had brown eyes and dark hair, so he stood out. He had recently moved into the village for work and travelled by himself. That's all she knew about him but that was enough for her right now. She was content to admire him from afar, to watch and wait. There were so many questions to ask.

Mother told her that girls such as her must look to marry a man who was not above her station in life. In a way, she was relieved. She could marry for love, unlike the Lord of the Manor's daughters. She did not come with a dowry like the wealthy girls, who she had seen at the markets with their maids and their finery, every inch of them untouched for their prospective husbands. In some ways she felt jealous of the ease at which they sauntered about, while the rest of them pandered to their every need. She'd heard they had a room full of dresses, a maid choosing what they would wear for different occasions during the day. Why would a girl need more than two dresses? At the knitting circle, she heard these young ladies were often married off to men of great wealth and stature, who would insist on innocence and purity. More like a prized pig, she thought. That seemed in stark contrast to how her friends lived their lives.

They taught her what to do. Sometimes the men they worked with, and sometimes wealthy lads took advantage. The sooner she was married, the better protection she would have. Her own prosperity depended on marrying a reliable man, and she certainly hoped to do so soon. She had watched the other village girls marry local lads. Her older sister had the good fortune to marry a man who inherited land, but her friends were happy, snug in their village cottages, close to those they would know their whole lives.

Mother came to the common area with the pigs every afternoon in summer. The pigs grazed freely and deposited dung as fertilizer. She could take some time to settle near a tree and relax, knowing she wouldn't need to feed them so much when they returned to the cottage. Shipden had hay meadows and common land where they had the right to graze their animals. Each village family was given strips in all three fields. At home, stew gently cooked on the firepit, unattended.

Cartia could see her mother arrive and leave from where she worked in the adjacent field and often waved to her. Father left early to walk to the fishing boats even though the weather was unpredictable. If he were unable to fish, he would come home and help with the ploughing. The fields were ploughed three times: the first turned the stubble over, the second removed the thistles and weeds and the third prepared the ground for sowing. There was always a need for more hands to help so the whole family was called upon.

Farm work was a struggle but, by dinner bell, they had succeeded in saving the bulk of the wheat and cut it down. Each man was covered in sweat, working their way to the side of the field for refreshment at the call of their supervisor.

Some of the older women, who could no longer bend to gather the wheat or tie straw, spent the morning at the farm well, filled buckets with cold water and poured it into jugs placed on the cart. The older men attended to the horses which pulled these carts to the workers at different times of the day. In summer, cold water from deep inside the well was welcomed by the field workers.

Cartia worked for a smaller farmer. Marl and seaweed were used as fertilisers which left a pungent smell at first. They had already harvested one of the rye fields this week. The wheat would be completely harvested by next week before the weather turned the fields into slosh. The fallow strip was being prepared for tomorrow's ploughing teams to sow a late season of barley. Always something happening in summer as they reaped the rewards of a good harvest or cleaned up after a bad one. Villagers combined their oxen teams to get the job done in a timely manner.

'Our oxen teams manage quite well on this light soil,' said Daniaen to two men leaning on the water cart during a break. 'We just need a decent price at the mill.'

'Prices are lower than I've ever seen before in Shipden, my friend,' said Robert. 'We'll have to sell much of it at markets or crush our own corn for home baking.'

'Yes, this year will be difficult for everyone. As a community, we must pull together in many things,' said Tom. 'Daniaen, you're from the lowlands. Are you aware that we must give half our crop as rent and taxes? Our families need to grow corn enough to feed ourselves as well as provide for the landlord.'

'Yes, so I heard. In my opinion, the landlords have too much power here. I noticed all the cliff erosion to the village isn't harming trade and merchants seem to be wealthy too,' Daniaen said. 'If only the wealthy would try to stop the sea flooding the villages.'

'Yeah, that's true, 'said Tom. 'There's talk of building a pier. Not sure how that will help, but it's worth a try, I think. Thirty-six names appeared on the subsidy roll paying taxes. About forty-nine pounds and eleven pence all up. The Abbott will be pleased with that tally.'

'That's a considerable amount of tax from a small community which mostly fishes for a living,' he said. 'Did you count the number of oxen teams?'

'Yes. Quite a few arrived at sunrise to plough. The community is pulling together to get this harvest in before winter is upon us.'

'In Holland, I'm used to seeing horses do this work, but the land is different there and the soil very hard to turn,' he said.

'The markets are generating a profit for some people here. Let's hope the village has enough to store for winter.'

Cartia heard bits of his conversation as Mary and Tilly talked of other matters. She emptied her cup and turned towards the men.

'I love horses. They're so gentle, especially the large ones,' she said. All the squatting men looked up at her, but she only had eyes for Daniaen. For the first time, their eyes met in playful consideration of each other, and he smiled.

'The oxen are less expensive to feed, and they can be eaten when they die,' he said. After a while, he left the others and stood near her.

'I'm Daniaen de Rek,' he said. 'I know you are Cartia Leman because I already asked some of the other villagers when I first saw you.'

She tossed back her dark hair and laughed. 'Welcome to Shipden, Mr de Rek. Do you like living here or is it better in Holland?'

'Please call me Daniaen. My feet are not so wet here,' he said. 'My country is sinking fast, and I needed somewhere safe to live. The ocean constantly flooded our land and created lakes where our food grows. My whole family drowned in one of the many floods in the lowlands.'

'I'm so sorry to hear that,' she said. 'God has brought you safely to Shipden, Daniaen. I hope you'll be happy.'

'He has indeed,' he said. 'I hope this is not too forward of me. I am not yet sure of your customs. Cartia, would you like to go for a walk when the work is finished today? Perhaps we could walk along the cliff path.'

'That would be very nice. Why don't we walk to my family home for supper?' she asked. She could see her mother was sitting under the trees watching the pigs in the far field. She really should go and ask if they have plenty of supper to share but knew mother would divide whatever they had for a guest.

'I would like that very much,' he said, leaving her with a shy smile. 'What does your father do, Cartia? I look forward to talking with him. My father apprenticed me to learn how to build canals and dykes from the marshes.'

'That's a very useful apprenticeship. The marshes in Norfolk are causing problems further west. Is that why you've chosen to come here?' she asked.

'Yes, that was my intention and eventually, when I have saved a little more, I will look at perhaps building windmills or canals.'

'That's exciting. Your skills will be put to good use there,' said Cartia. 'My father is a fisherman. Always has been, like his father before him,' she said. 'There are seven boats in Shipden, and he owns one of them. We'll never go hungry as there are plenty of fish in the sea.'

'We have many fishermen in Holland too, along the coast,' he said, stepping in the direction of the other men, who were heading back to the crop. 'We can talk more later. See you after work, Cartia. I will come and find you. I promise.'

Chapter 7 - 1953

The train arrived from London and ground to a screeching halt. At 7.27 pm on Saturday January 31, 1953, Bob looked out of the carriage window into a pitch-black night. This was not a railway station, or was it? Hunstanton was the next stop, but he couldn't see any evidence of the station; doors remained closed, no announcements from the conductor, no visibility apart from gusts of hissing steam rising from the railway track and leaving his window fogged up. He could barely make out the shape of trees and, beyond that, a faint silhouette of a cluster of semi-detached houses. Rain was still teeming down in squalls, buffeting the carriage to each side. The village or wherever they had stopped was in a blackout, electricity poles criss-crossed over wires. The occasional candle flickered in a window of a house and was the only visible sign of life. Someone behind him coughed. He turned to see his fellow passengers, also trying to get home to North Norfolk.

He wrapped his coat closer and sank into its warmth. It was indeed a miserable trip home. Sudden sprays of rain, like volleys of sharp arrows, rattled against the windows of the carriage. His mind wandered to his family back home in this terrible storm. His lovely Louise, his two little girls. He was sure that his brother-in-law, Fred, would be checking on them, making sure they had enough fuel for their fire. His sister would be keeping her new twins fed and warm. It was a comfort knowing their cottage was very close to theirs. He was beginning to wish he hadn't gone into work today. London is still filthy from the coal fog last year, when people who had to travel there for work had coughed and spluttered on the walk from the train to their workplaces. They'd filled the hospital emergency ward. Some died. First the war made a mess of countless streets in London, then the fog and now this storm. What next?

Perched on the edge of their seats, half a dozen men in suits looked around for hints of what was to come. Sitting opposite one another, chatting, were a couple of ladies with their string bags of shopping, wrapped neatly with paper and tied with string. Nobody spoke for a while, expecting the train to push on again in a few minutes, maybe after another train would pass by in the opposite direction. A ticket collector appeared in their carriage, asking for tickets, thumping a small hole in the stub and returning it to each passenger.

'Your ticket, please, sir.' It was his turn, he reached into his top pocket and withdrew his return ticket.

'What's happened to the train?' he asked. 'Why are we stopped?'

'No concern, I'm sure, sir.'

'How long will we be sitting here for?'

'I don't know, sir. Here's your ticket, sir. Thank you.'

Not one for a bit of a tête-à-tête, the conductor lost his balance and stomped his foot down to anchor himself to the spot before he moved onto the next passenger. The carriage swayed too far to one side and steadied itself as he moved along the carriage. Wind gusts were becoming vicious, strong, worrying to everyone on board. Carriage lights flickered on and off. The conductor remained calm.

Outside his window, trees were ripped out of the soft earth after days of saturating rain. Maybe the line is flooded, he thought. Or a tree fallen across the line.

It was the not knowing that frightened him. He couldn't deal with a problem if he couldn't identify it. He heard other passengers moving about, shuffling, whispering in low tones. He wasn't the only one who was unsettled right now.

Bob felt a little claustrophobic cramped up with these strangers and all the doors jammed shut. He knew it was irrational to feel this way and he took a slow, deep breath several times. The light-headedness washed away, and he settled back into his seat. A baby he hadn't noticed before started whimpering at the far end of the carriage. It occurred to him how odd the situation was. It felt surreal, frightening, there was an eerie quietness in the air. Nobody knew what to do next. Should they yell and scream? Should they bang on the windows and doors to let them escape their confines? Should they be good British souls and behave in a quiet and orderly manner?

Every now and then, someone would stand for a while, and everyone else would stare at them. Christmas was right around the corner, so a bit of joviality and a few smiles broke the pattern and spirits remained convivial.

He longed to get moving again. He knew Louise would be worried when he didn't arrive on time, especially on such a stormy night. He imagined the boggy mud he would need to struggle through from the railway station to his home.

A sudden jolt. The steam train jumped forward and back and stopped again. Several moments passed, steam hissed in tufts and blocked the murky blackness outside. Lights flickered on. Two police officers, who were dressed in orange waterproof kits with plastic covers stretched over their uniform caps, entered through the sliding door between carriages. Dripping puddles, they asked for everyone's attention. He heard a loud crack of thunder, lightning shot across the sky, revealing endless silver rivulets of rain racing in every direction across the carriage windows.

Bob felt a rush of fear. He turned from the window to face the police officers standing nearby. Both men wore solemn expressions, which caused him to feel even more unsettled. Through the sliding door, he heard movement, shuffling, coughing. He really wanted to get off this train, but he knew he needed to listen carefully to instructions on how to do this. More deep breaths. At least, he consoled himself, we will finally hear what has happened and how they plan to resolve the situation.

'Ladies and Gentlemen, could I please have your attention?'

No problem. Passengers focused. They moved to the edge of their seats, bent forward.

'There's been an accident. The train cannot continue. Would you please gather your belongings and follow us to the emergency exit in the next carriage? There's no hurry at all, so do not panic. You will be safe.'

He breathed a sigh of relief after he'd heard that last sentence, looked around at his fellow passengers and smiled some reassurance. They had built a tie of camaraderie between themselves without consciously reaching for each other. Together they stood and collected their luggage. Sounds of people speaking after hours of silence felt soothing. There was no hysteria or upset voices at this news. A resolution had been found and those brave police officers were the heroes of the day.

As he walked past one of the police officers, he asked,

'Is the line flooded?'

'No, sir. The train collided with a bungalow,' he said, as though this was a perfectly normal expectation in these circumstances. 'It was washed onto the line at Hunstanton.'

Bob spent the night in a hotel room, which railway staff had arranged for all passengers who wished to continue their journey the next morning when the storm damage could be better assessed. He didn't sleep well. There was a young couple arguing in the room next to his and the continuous lashing of rain squalls hit against his window.

Twice, he had tried to phone his wife and his sister, Cath, during the night and again this morning, but all the lines were down. He was even more determined to get home as soon as possible. Of course, every one of the passengers felt the same urgency. Everyone looked forward to their own goose-down bed. Their safe place in a storm.

Passengers and staff shared scatterings of news they had gathered. A vision had worked its way into his head of the challenges ahead. War training a few years ago had sharpened his thoughts to be resilient, but he was reluctant to reach back.

The BBC news was not good. Hundreds of people had drowned, thousands were being evacuated, houses were washed out to sea. Someone told him of furniture floating in the streets. In Heacham, beach huts were swept half a mile inland near the station. He found it hard to take it all in. He still hadn't connected with anyone from his village or anyone who could tell him all was well at home and not knowing terrified him.

He sat with several other passengers during breakfast the following day and learnt of a bus leaving Hunstanton in the afternoon at two o'clock. He decided to book a ticket rather than wait any longer for authorities to clear the train line. No doubt the roads would also be clogged with debris but, unlike the train, a bus driver could take a detour.

Bob sat near the front of the bus as it heaved itself through slime, sometimes becoming stuck in mud, wheels spinning. Windscreen wipers seemed useless in this gale. He watched the bus driver, a rotund chap about fifty, negotiate the roads ahead, leaning over the steering wheel with his nose almost against the front window, wiping condensation vapour off with a cloth. Tom felt confident that the driver's experience would help them get through all this.

A break between storms enabled the bus to continue along the main route after a while. The road here was higher than the surrounding farmland, so most of it was not too bad. From that height, he observed whole families sitting on their rooftops waiting to be rescued by boats collecting people from their upstairs windows. The man next to him said that there had been nine feet of water through those houses.

As they moved more towards his village, it became impossible to advance any further as the roads had been destroyed, washed away or completely covered by sea water. Telegraph poles were jutting through swells, strewn across the horizon and scattered amongst the roofs of houses and treetops. His heart dropped.

As soon as he could, he would find a boat to take him to what might be left of his home, his family, his village.

Chapter 8 – 2013

Carly felt quietly confident after her interview with Josh yesterday. He seemed like an organised chap who knew what he was doing. He would contact her when he needed some photos to go with his articles. That suited her – she needed flexibility to balance her life between online tutoring and taking photos for his assignment. He seemed pleasant enough. Maybe a bit nervous but he hadn't been here long.

The sea mist rolled into shore, heavy and menacing, dissipating at the cliff-face; its path and promenade completely covered in a white haze. From the parkland north of the pier, Carly felt a tinge of disappointment at the vista below. Ever since she arrived in England two years ago, photography had become her passion. In fact, the local council hired her to tutor people, who needed a hand with new phones or iPads. She looked along the Sheringham precipice towards the beach at Cromer. There would be no digital activity for a while. Cromer pier stretched out into the North Sea, only visible in tufts of soupy air in eerie silence. She could not see any sun at all. It was a hazy, grey sky visible only when the fog cleared patches between tumbling rolls of sea-mist. She had never experienced this level of cold in Broome.

She wrapped her leather jacket tightly around her, turned and walked towards a large pond. She sat on a sheltered bench and watched a middle-aged man determined to sail his miniature sailing craft. She felt a bit lonely, so she went to talk with him.

'G'day. Do you mind if I watch your model boats for a while?'

The man glanced in her direction. He had a friendly ambiance about his stance, and he nodded. 'Sure. Not much of a day for sailing model ships, I'm afraid. Not enough wind to catch in the sails. Might as well pack it in.'

'Not much of a day for taking photos either. I've already packed it in.'

'Maybe later in the day when the wind comes up and blows the sea mist away. It's just sitting there and seems to be locked in.'

Carly noticed the fine workmanship of the miniature sailing boats he hauled out of the water. She saw the tiny sailors rigging the sails, climbing the mast. 'Did you make that ship yourself?' she asked. 'It's awesome.'

'As a matter of fact, I did. Thanks. The other one over there on the lawn is a very old model and I've been renovating it for a chap who had inherited it. I was hoping to sail it today to see if it's okay but unfortunately there's no wind. I'll have to come back another day, I think.'

'That's a shame. Nothing much either of us can do, I guess.' Carly watched as a smile seemed to change his concentration. 'No,' she continued. 'I think I'll walk over to the shops instead and have a hot coffee somewhere.'

'That'd be nice. There are some lovely coffee shops in Sheringham.'

'Do you want to come too?' She was astonished that she'd asked this stranger if he would like to join her, but he seemed like nice company and the grey day had closed in around her loneliness.

'Thanks for asking. No, I don't think so,' he paused, adjusting the tiller, but no matter what he did to change the leverage, his sailing ship was not going far today. 'Well, second thoughts; my wife is at the shops at the moment, so I'll pack up and walk down with you, if you like.'

'Maybe I could help you pack up. I don't have anything else to do.'

'Alright. Thanks. My name's Jack.'

'Hi Jack. I'm Carly Williams.'

She felt an instant warmth, a connection with Jack. The model ships were large enough for two people to carry them to the car comfortably and he placed them in the back seat with great care. She thought he might be sixty, not unlike her own father in his build. He had kind eyes and a genuine smile, though he obviously had a quiet and thoughtful disposition.

He locked his car and started walking towards the village high street, through an abundance of red rose bushes in a small parkland and past the old flint church on the corner. They talked about Sheringham as they manoeuvred themselves along the narrow pedestrian path. Like a lot of village streets, the footpath was single file for pedestrians and, sometimes, there was no path at all. She'd often find herself in a smaller village and up flat against a building waiting for traffic to pass.

It wasn't a long walk for them. The first shops appeared as they turned into the high street but in that time, she had grown accustomed to his presence. He stood for a moment with his hands in his pockets, looking down the crowded path ahead. She guessed he was searching for his wife.

'Well, I'll leave you now, Jack. Unless you want to join me for a coffee at Pungleberries? Do you know where that is?'

Before he could answer her, his phone rang, and he checked its screen. 'Excuse me a moment, Carly. It's the wife.' He moved a few steps back and spoke softly. When he came off his phone, he smiled and suggested the three of them meet at the cafe.

Anna was already at the coffee shop and soon they were getting on like long lost relatives. They seemed to have much in common with Carly's family in Australia; the same lifestyle, serving their local Methodist church – although her family was Catholic - and participating in their children's activities. The difference was not mentioned but she knew it might eventually come up in conversation. Not that she minded when people discovered that her mother had abandoned them many years ago, but it was not something one blurted out when first meeting people. She'd met other people who had resonated with her plight. Some had kept in touch, most didn't. Perhaps they prefer not to have it thrown up in their faces again. For her, she understood their point of view and pretty much kept it to herself most of the time.

'It's a pity you can't see the coastline in the sea fret. Perhaps it will lift later in the day for you to take some photos,' said Anna. 'Sheringham is a top vantage point for coastal photos,' said Anna, sipping her coffee.

'I'll walk back to the park later on then,' said Carly. 'My family back home likes to see where I'm staying and what I get up to.'

'How do you do that then?' asked Jack

'Well, my sister is on Facebook, so I post my photos onto her page, and she shows them around.'

Jack and Anna smiled and shook their heads. 'Modern technology in 2013. Isn't it marvellous, Jack?'

'Yes, it is. But I don't think I'd be bothered with Facebook though. Too many busy-bodies in this world as it is without encouraging more,' he said.

'Oh, but wouldn't it be lovely for Carly's family to follow her journey, Jack?'

'Yes, it would be nice. Especially as she's come to the other side of the world,' he said.

'A pretty little thing like you is always going to be a worry for your parents,' Anna said, smiling.

'Thank you very much. That's a kind thing to say,' said Carly. She was not used to compliments; not when she was at home with five brothers and two sisters. They were a large and happy family, but you were more likely to get into a scrape with one of them than receive a compliment. It hadn't been easy. Her father had done his best and she admired his endless love and support.

'Carly, it's been lovely to meet you and thank you for joining us. We're going to have to pack it in though,' said Anna. 'Our grandchildren are being dropped off at our place this afternoon for school holidays. They're twins, you know. They'll probably run circles around us, but we love them very much!'

Her father had always said that when Carly smiled, her whole face seemed to take a different shape. Her dimples appeared, her eyes lit up and her teeth seemed to sparkle. So, he often said. Who would want sparkling teeth? It reminded her of a comic book character. Her hair was dark, long and lustrous but today she had decided to tie it in a plait so the wind could not blow her hair across the lens.

'I love small children,' she said. 'Well, I'm assuming they are small. How old are they?'

'They're seven now, so this is only their first year in a proper first school.'

'I'm the oldest daughter in a household of children so I've had a lot to do with little kids of that age. If you need a babysitter or some help, give me a call. I'll write my mobile number down for you if you like.'

'Well, thank you, Carly,' said Anna. 'What a kind offer.'

'How long will they be visiting you?' she asked Anna.

'A couple of weeks, I think' she replied. 'It's the beginning of their holidays so they shouldn't be too bored. Our son, Carter, and his wife will be staying in a van down the coast. She has some sort of work to do on a coastal dig for a few days. We're hoping this weather improves for them, but the forecast predicts more rain.'

'It's so nice for the children to spend some time with you and Jack. I've never met my maternal grandparents,' she said. 'I bet the parents are pleased to get away for a while by themselves too.'

She wrote down her mobile phone number and her email address. 'Here you go then. Any time.' She handed Anna the card. 'You'd be doing me a favour. I never thought I'd miss the noise and hustle and bustle of home, but I do sometimes.'

Anna put her arm on her shoulder for a moment. 'Thank you, Carly. Let's hope it's a clear day tomorrow so you can take some photos of the coastline.'

Jack looked at his watch. 'Nearly time to go if we don't want to miss them. We'll have to walk back to the car, but it'll only take us fifteen minutes or so. I'll fix the bill. It's on us, Carly.'

'Well, thank you, Jack. Thank you, Anna. You've certainly made a dull day into an interesting one. This afternoon I'm going to take a bus to the old part of Sheringham and take a few photos at the church.'

'We live in Holt, Carly. That means we would drive right past that church. Could we offer you a lift?' said Anna. Carly was surprised at how quickly she accepted the offer. She never would have at home. One gets a bit brazen when you're a tourist, but her instincts had not failed her yet.

'If that isn't too far out of your way, that'd be awesome. Thanks heaps.' She stood up and followed Anna to where Jack was queued up at the till. 'I might as well take some shots inside a warm church. I love your churches over here and I believe this one at Upper Sheringham has an ancient trough I'd like to see. I've taken quite a few pics of church doors since coming to the UK.'

The early morning air hung still and menacing with dark clouds coming in from the west. It had been a dry night, but light rain was forecast for mid-morning. Carter Timms, flustered and irritable after driving from London with twins in the back seat, was looking forward to the pampering his mother would give him once they were inside their home. He imagined a warm cup of tea and some home-made cake near a crackling open fire. Christmas was around the corner, so he knew things could only get better as the excitement grew to fever pitch with their seven-year-old twins.

Tariq and Tasneem were full of bottled-up energy when they tumbled out of the family car. He and Aziza had already started unloading. Aziza wore a deep red shirt over her jeans and pulled her knitted cap down over her ears before trying to dress the children in their coats.

'I can't catch you in time, so you'll have to freeze until we get inside,' she said.

'At last. That journey doesn't get any shorter with a car full of noise. So good to see your smiling faces.' He held his parents tight for a while, then pulled back and returned to unpack his car.

'Oh, yes, we know what that feels like, son,' said Jack. 'We had our turn.'

'Do remember to bring the buckets and spades with you, dear. I know they'll enjoy going to the beach again, no matter what the weather is like.'

Carter had met his wife at the university in London ten years ago. He found her to be a fascinating and intelligent woman who was delightful company. At first, with English not being her first language, things had been a little strange for both, but they managed to plod through those challenges with only a few misunderstandings.

'We won't be going swimming, Aziza,' said Anna. 'I cannot swim, and Jack can only swim a bit. We don't like to take unnecessary risks with our beautiful grandchildren. If we change our minds, we have buckets and spades in our beach hut.'

'Do you still own that old beach hut, Mum? I'd forgotten about it. You and Dad haven't used it for years, have you?' said Carter. 'We will bring in some toys in case you change your mind, or the children want to dig in the garden. Cromer is not very far, and the children would enjoy getting out and about after being confined in London.' His wife nodded.

'I didn't even know the family owned one of those pretty little beach huts. What fun,' said Aziza.

'Mum had it left to her by Great-Grandma O'Reilly when we were kids. I don't think we've been anywhere near it since then. Not one of the swanky ones. In fact, I think she said it was once a bathing machine before they took off the wheels in the eighteen hundreds and painted it. Is that right, Mum?' said Carter. 'Not really beach people, my family.'

'That's right. In fact, I've had it painted recently. It's looking new again now. It's a nice blue and white theme. They built things to last back in those days,' said Anna.

'Did Dad paint it?' asked Carter.

'Not this time, dear. No. I had a leaflet in the mail about some work scheme for unemployed youth. A professional painter plus two other younger chaps called Gordon and Kyle, who were taught how to paint. I thought it would be a good idea to encourage them.'

'That was very kind, Anna,' said Aziza. 'You don't have to be beach people to enjoy a day relaxing at the beach in warmer weather. We know our twins are in the most capable hands, should you decide to go to the beach hut,' Aziza said.

The four adults made their way through the front door with suitcases wheeling along behind them. Jack held the door open for everyone and then closed the cold morning out.

'After you've had the delicious morning tea your Gran has baked for you, I have a surprise for the best-behaved people here.'

'What is it Grandpa?' asked Tasneem, a curious but cautious little girl with black hair and dark eyes. She was so much like her mother in many ways.

'Tell us, please, please, please.' Tariq said, pulling at his grandfather's hand.

'No, only the very best of manners at morning tea will get you a nice surprise, so let's have some cake. What do you say to that?' Jack enjoyed having the children around him. It reminded him of the hectic years when Carter and his brother, Stephen, were young and he'd wished he'd had more time for them. Now that he was retired, he had all the time in the world, and he intended to use it well.

Reluctantly, the children relaxed and joined the others around the dining table, more aware of their manners and behaviour. Anna looked relieved, it was relatively calm again and she sat down to sip her coffee. She wasn't really a tea-person but made a pot of tea served with a Victoria sponge she'd made early that day. She knew it was Carter's favourite.

'Aziza, tell me about the new project your archaeology studies have led you into? I understand it has to do with this area.'

'Not exactly in this area – more around the coast and Cromer.'

'Can you tell us about it yet?' asked Anna, who had an interest in local history. 'It's all fascinating to me.'

'Of course, I can. It's funny. I came to England to study archaeology at university to do this in my own country, in Egypt. So much had already been discovered but there is still so much more to find. It was exciting, and I was keen to pursue this for my career before I met your son.' She looked lovingly into the eyes of her husband. 'Now the officials in Norfolk, especially along the coast, are looking at how the many years of sea surges have damaged the cliffs and changed the whole shape of some areas.'

'That's one of the reasons we bought a house in Holt. It's a good fifteen minutes from the coast. We feel safer here,' Jack said.

'You have good reason to think like that with the history we have unearthed so far.'

'Aziza's team has its digs along the area we walk along whenever we're here for a summer holiday,' said Carter. 'Just down a bit from the ice cream shop.'

'Really? There's nothing there that I can recall,' Jack said.

Aziza's eyes glanced from Jack to Anna, and she bent forward, speaking in a mysterious tone.

Anna and Jack sat motionless, ready to absorb her secret. No wonder their son found this woman fascinating. The children were now bored, having had their fill of cake and milk. They were quietly colouring in a drawing of Santa which Anna had left beside their places at the table.

'Under the sea, there's the remains of an ancient shipping port and market village called Shipden, about two miles from the western side of the pier in Cromer. Did you know?' she asked her in-laws. 'That means the North Sea has come in about two miles and swallowed up everything in its path since the fourteenth century. Since then, it's been a missing village, along with others along the coastline.'

Carly opened her eyes and looked around her bedroom in Sheringham. The walls were covered in pastel florals up to the height of the picture rail which was capped with a piece of deeper blue trim about a metre from the ceiling. The light was a modern one, though the ceiling was still embossed. She guessed the boarding house updated to electricity with modern fittings at the end of the nineteenth century. She sat up, stretched and flopped back onto her pillow again to plan her day. She could smell bacon cooking downstairs. She heard the BBC radio announcer, who was giving the forecast for the morning. The pollen count is low. Good. Rain later. Again.

She put her legs over the edge of the double bed, slithered into a pair of warm Ugg boots and stood up. She turned and quickly made her bed look respectable and noted that she should ask for another blanket. There was a blanket box at the end of her bed, a large wooden chest with a padlock firmly in place. She couldn't simply open the box and retrieve an extra blanket for herself. She had to ask them to unlock it for her or borrow the key.

The bedroom next to her had been made into two ensuites. This house had so many rooms that this was repeated in several sections of the upstairs area of the house. A bay window, with a spectacular view of their garden from the window seat, was her favourite spot to curl up on lush pillows reading books, writing her travel blog or checking her emails.

The house was a bed and breakfast, mostly accommodating tourists for overnight stays or, particularly in the summer, families coming for an annual holiday. Carly had arrived in the summer of 2011 and planned on staying about a year but that had been extended to two years already.

On dark-weather days, when she was confined to her room, she would close her eyes and imagine she was at home. She would imagine the voices of her siblings in the hallway, their laughter drifting through the house as they ran on wooden boards, chasing one another. She imagined herself sitting on her favourite bench, reading a book under one of the frangipani trees, the aromas wafting from her memory for a few moments of bliss. She even felt a soft damp nose on her leg, looked down and imaged the dog, Molly, with a ball in her mouth. When she felt particularly homesick, she would start to plan her return journey, but then someone would suggest they go somewhere historical, and she'd grab her camera and go with them.

There were two reasons she felt the pull of staying longer. Firstly, she wanted to explore the world, and she was in striking distance of Europe's history. She hated London's crowded tourist attractions and old hotels, the only ones she could afford to use. Living where she did now, she had an affordable, pretty room and she was staying in an historical home. What more could she possibly want?

The second reason was the motivator which pushed her out of Broome and landed her here. She knew her mother's family came from Norfolk, and she wanted to meet them. They might be able to tell her where her mother is. So far she hadn't been able to locate them, but she'd not really put in the effort required either. What if they didn't know she existed? What if it was going to be a tremendous embarrassment to have her turn up on their doorstep?

She glanced at her phone. It was time for breakfast downstairs. Seven o'clock was her sitting. There were two early sittings, and this one was best for her. As she pulled on her hand-knitted jumper and jeans, her mobile shook. The caller was 'unknown' but she answered it anyway. 'Hello,' she said.

'Carly?'

'Yes.'

'Carly, it's me, Anna. We met at the coffee shop,' she said. 'Do you remember us?'

'Of course, Anna. How nice to hear from you. Is everything okay?'

'Yes, everything is fine. Jack and I are not used to having children running about, it's been a long time since our boys were at home,' said Anna. 'We were just chatting, and Jack suggested I give you a call.'

She wasn't really expecting to hear from Anna and Jack again after their morning tea at Sheringham two weeks ago. She had given them her contact details but didn't really expect to hear from them. She had thought they were just being polite.

'Anna,' she said. 'I'm so pleased you rang. I don't think I have anything on tomorrow that can't be moved around to another time. What do you have in mind?'

'Oh, that is wonderful.'

'How are you both surviving the onslaught?'

'That is why I'm ringing. I need your help. Do you mind?' Carly thought Anna sounded a bit tired. She knew how exhausting and demanding excited children can make you feel. After her mother disappeared, she had to pick up the pieces, put the family jigsaw back together and carry on. Her father had gone to the local pub most evenings, leaving her to sort out dinner and the little ones. She'd look forward to spending some time with Anna and Jack again and meeting the twins.

'No, I don't mind at all. What were you thinking – how can I help, Anna?'

'Jack and I would appreciate some 'us time' without little fingers being in everything and we wondered if it would suit you to babysit the twins while we vanish for a couple of hours tomorrow? We love them to bits, but we're exhausted. Of course, we'll pay you. What do you think?'

She paused for a moment to consider her plans. Josh hadn't contacted her yet, so he was probably still doing his research. He'd said he was into a story from the eighteen hundreds now so no need for a photographer. Her new class wouldn't be starting until next week. Her ironing could wait.

'I'd love that. But you won't need to pay me. What time would be better? There's a bus I can catch about ten and an earlier one – whatever suits you.'

After a long sigh at the other end of the phone, Anna replied, 'The ten o'clock bus will be fine, Anna. That way, Jack and I will be able to enjoy some lunch and do some Christmas shopping while we are out and about. But we insist on paying you some babysitting money, Carly.'

'Alright then. I'm not sure how long it takes a bus to get to Holt from here, but I shouldn't be too long after ten.'

'No rush and thank you so much. I'll ask Jack to meet you at the bus stop near the shops. I must go now and organise some play for a rainy day. Those heavy clouds look ominous.'

'Yes, I just heard on the radio that light rain is expected. I'll catch you tomorrow. I'm looking forward to meeting your twins. Bye for now.'

'Bye, dear. And thank you so much.'

Carly tapped her phone off and realized that she didn't feel at all homesick anymore. As she closed her bedroom door and headed downstairs for breakfast, she thought how fortunate she had been in meeting Jack and Anna. Sometimes, she thought, you find yourself in the middle of nowhere and, sometimes, in the middle of nowhere, you find yourself. It was one of those times.

Chapter 9 - 1888

Matthew O'Reilly had been living in Cromer for one year, so he had not seen the earlier destruction caused by coastal surges. Autumn had almost blended into winter. It had been several months since he had wandered through what remained of Shipden village and now the sea had draped the beach again and returned it to the same state as it had been for hundreds of years. A village, hidden. Standing on the precipice of the cliff walk, surrounded by tall wildflowers, he could just make out the shadow of Church Rock, tiny waves traversing its roofline at the tip, and, on his right, the new lighthouse stood. The old one had collapsed into the sea forty years ago. The remainder of the village had disappeared until the next extreme heat event dried the beach and left history exposed once again.

He smelt a salty breeze, which lifted his spirits, then turned and continued on his way along the worn path to Cromer. Purple tipped wildflowers swayed in gentle rhythm, dancing in the final days of autumn. Soon they would bunker down for the cold winter months. He glanced sideways and noticed some blue tractors on the sand below. One was pulling a dingy in, another was pushing a larger vessel to depths of waters not blocked with silt. Fishermen were on board, their warm caps pulled over cold ears and woollen sweaters visible from the top of the cliff.

At the base of the steps leading down to the beach, he turned to his right, towards several parked bathing machines. In the mid-distance, he relished the colourful contrast of the bathing machines against a pale, chalky cliff. Bright hues of deep blue separated sunny yellows and deep reds. On the shingle beach, simple sounds of children embedded memories for an uncertain future.

Matthew pulled out his key, ready to insert it in the lock. He had been undecided as to whether he should invest in one of the Cromer bathing machines, but he couldn't resist a bargain. It was half the expected price when he bought it last summer from one of the chaps at university, who only needed it for one summer. He told him that he needed the money to continue his studies. At the time, Matthew was in the process of building a cottage just outside the village and needed somewhere to live while it was being constructed. It was very small inside, but it was ample. There was a bench, some cushions, a small table and running water from a communal tap nearby. He washed in a handbasin, both himself and the dishes. Toilet amenities were provided on the promenade.

He was sheltered from the wind, and it provided a measure of privacy. Underneath the bench, he pulled out the old box he had rescued from the beach. For now, he used it as a side table on which he placed a lantern at night, and for a book to read to pass time in the evenings when he was too tired to socialize. The box was bolted and sealed, and he left it that way. His tools were back at his parent's home, so he was unable to open it. He was not in a hurry to open it anyway. It was probably just full of rusted junk. He was certain that it was not a pirate treasure chest as it was small and handmade. He guessed it was full of a worker's tools, perhaps of someone maintaining the church tower in ancient times. He would make good use of it as a nightstand now and open it another day.

Later this week, he had arranged to meet with a solicitor from Norwich, a firm his father recommended at Messrs Blake and Keith. He was to write his Last Will and Testament, for he was about to celebrate his twenty-first birthday. He would be officially of age with property and an inheritance from his grandmother which will pay for the construction of his cottage. His older sister would inherit his estate, at least until the day of his marriage. As he had yet to marry, Catherine was his nearest relative. He now held ownership of this old bathing machine and would soon be the proud owner of his small cottage. There would be title muniments and other legal documents, as well as his Will, to be held by the solicitor until his death.

He rolled out the padded mattress, spread it along the bench with a warm blanket and pillow. From the floral jug, he poured himself a refreshing drink and settled down to read his book. He looked forward to sorting his paperwork out later in the week, but tomorrow would be Saturday, his birthday, and he was expected to be at training with Mr Blogg and the lifeboatmen. He'd have an early night and hope to dream of Sarah-Jane, who seemed to have left the town altogether but remained in his dreams.

Sarah-Jane stood at the bay window in the parlour of the guest house, one knee on the blue velvet window seat and watched some birds on a branch, building a nest. The garden view was glorious even as autumn approached. Rows of deep crimson roses lined the path to the front gate where they met a neatly trimmed hedge. A gardener was raking leaves and filling his wheelbarrow. She was so glad to have found a vacant room available for her return visit to Cromer. Last summer evoked terrible unease. She couldn't remember what she felt in those panicked hours; she couldn't recreate the sensation of loss or the disorientation which she must have felt. Fear seemed to have blocked her mind from the tragedy.

She had stayed at Hotel de Paris after the incident, but they didn't have any vacancies this week. She'd been told that a trainload of tourists from London would be staying at the Hotel, so they recommended this guesthouse in nearby Sheringham. It proved to be a welcome retreat from the hustle and bustle of this holiday resort town. She had been shown to her room by a cheery woman, who had a young chap carry her luggage upstairs and place it on the bed for sorting into deep drawers. The walls were covered in tiny pastel flowers up to the painting rail. One chandelier was suspended from the ceiling and sconces were fixed to the wall above the picture rail. The woman explained they had gas lighting in the main rooms, but a candelabra was used to move about the house. She had been handed a modern paraffin wax candle, a wick trimmer and matches, and shown where the outhouse was situated. A chamber pot was under the comfortable bed for nights. Every modern comfort. She was given set times for meal sittings and shown where the dining areas were.

Although her memory was not at all clear of the events of the fateful collision, she was here to remember her brother, Richard, who had drowned. The Victoria was perilously perched on a pesky rock or something, which the authorities were planning to destroy. The vessel had been too difficult to move. She ordered a bunch of flowers to be delivered to her at ten. After breakfast, she would wait in the parlour until they arrived.

The carriage pulled up near some traditional Norfolk flint and pantile cottages in Holt Road. His body lay in the Cromer cemetery. Sarah-Jane paid the driver and carried the flowers to the graveyard across the road. The old Cromer town chapel stood the test of time. Beyond the church lay a stretch of newly laid railway tracks.

It was an overcast day, and she was grateful it was not raining. She noticed many gravestones bearing the symbol of drownings at sea. Fishermen who risked their lives on vessels not fit for rough seas or perhaps were tossed overboard in a storm. Richard was no fisherman. In fact, he couldn't swim at all. Even if he had been able to swim, he had no chance of survival. She remembered the cut on his head, watching him unconscious and floating away from the pier. They had been tossed into the sea. She was still astounded that she was able to be saved but could not recall how she was rescued. Maybe it will all come back to her now she's in Cromer.

The tiny chapel was surrounded by gravestones, but she had no trouble finding Richard's grave. The ground was freshly dug along a line near the wrought iron fence, tiny ivy creeping around the red brick corner post. A steam train chuffed past behind her, several children stopped in the field nearby and waved to passengers. Some of the old gravestones closer to the front gate dated to the sixteenth century. She found the cross with Richard's inscription on it, so newly engraved, it stung her soul. She placed her gloved hand on her heart and took a slow, deep breath. It was sad that Richard was lying there and not interred in the family plot in London, but this is where his soul was, and it was not going anywhere else. She placed the bunch of cream gladioli in a pot beside the marble cross and paused a moment to say goodbye.

Matthew sat in the waiting room of Messrs Blake and Keith several days after he was twenty-one. He didn't feel any different from last month but was proud to have reached his majority. Mr Blake's secretary sat nearby, typing on the Hansen Writing Ball typewriting machine. He was a tall, thin man, bespectacled with tiny round glasses. A manilla folder, tied with pink tape, was lying on his desk with notes pinned to the cover. A diary sat near a jar of pencils, nibbed pens and dipping ink.

Matthew watched him hit each key with gusto, staccato crisp and rhythmic. When he completed a page, he released the roller bar and lifted out the paper very carefully. Such an admirable skill. He imagined the man didn't want to re-type his work if the paper tore whilst being released from the grip of the machine. A buzz sounded on the side of his desk.

'Mr Blake will see you now, sir. Come this way.'

He collected his file and proceeded down the small corridor. Matthew followed him into Mr Blake's office.

'Good morning, Mr Blake,' Matthew said, as he shook his hand. He was an older man with a thick, grey moustache and bright eyes. He wore a business suit and tie of the older style, and his desk was almost empty. On the floor surrounding him were separate piles of individual files, with a safe in the corner near some filing cabinets. A single rope and pulley window, with glimpses of the street below, filled the whole wall behind him. The office was tiny, dusty and cluttered, but Mr Blake seemed to know where everything was situated.

'Come in, my boy. I should congratulate you on your recent birthday, Matthew. Your father has been a client of mine since we were at university together many years ago. Where has the time gone? It is indeed an important milestone for you, isn't it?'

'Yes, sir, it feels strange, but it is important in so many ways.'

'Now you make your own decisions. Where you go from here will be directed by the choices you make.'

'Yes, sir.'

'Your father tells me that you're a swimmer and you've started training with the lifeguards, as well as studying. Good for you, son.'

'Yes, that's right. Thank you, sir.'

Mr Blake opened his folder and began taking notes.

'So, we will be drafting your Will today, Matthew. Have you given this matter a great deal of thought? I hope so. I will ensure that the document would be accepted by a court of law on the event of your death, which we all hope will be many years from now.'

He nodded, laughed. Mr Blake mumbled into his moustache, but Matthew got the gist of what he'd said.

'Will I need to come back another day to sign the document?'

'Yes, you will need to make another appointment with my secretary, Mr Daly. It will take a day to type it, sew the document together and seal it for your signature. Can you come back then?'

He nodded again. 'Yes, Sir, tomorrow will be convenient.'

'Right, then. Let us begin. I have a list of questions to ask you, so I can produce your Will.'

Mr Blake eventually found the list and read out the questions. Matthew answered how he wished it to appear in the Will. It was a simple instruction really. Everything was to be left to his older sister, Catherine Jane. Mr Blake took notes and stuck these to Matthew's file.

'Well, that was painless, eh, Matthew? Can we also have you sign some conveyancing documents while you're here? In particular, for the sale of the property on which your cottage will be built.'

Chapter 10 – 14C

Cartia had never felt happier. Was this the man God had sent her to be with? She felt as though she was floating on air. Her eyes barely left him the rest of the day. Sometimes their eyes met across the field, and she felt excitement rush through her veins. Several times, Tilly had asked her if she was feeling alright and she had snapped her focus back to her job. She couldn't resist this man. He was like a gift. If her family approves, she will marry him. Of that, she was sure.

When the day was finally at its end, she told her friends that she was waiting in the field to take him for supper. They giggled and left her to calm herself. She could see in the far distant field that he was preparing to farewell his fellow workers and collect his warmer tunic.

Her body felt electric; she didn't know where to look. Never had she been with a man before. Tilly told her it might hurt but she couldn't imagine it. She stepped into the cornfield where the grains reached higher than her head. She spread her arms apart like a tree and fell gently backwards onto the soft earth, the dusty stalks snapping and breaking her fall. Nobody would find her there and tell her to leave. Perhaps. If he'd been sent by God, he would be able to find her, she told herself.

Within moments, he was towering over her.

'Are you waiting for me here, Cartia?' The sunset was ruby red behind him, as he undid his braies at the front. They fell open.

'Yes, I'm waiting for you. I can't wait a moment longer. Are we alone?'

'Yes, we are the last to leave.'

'Come lie with me before we walk home,' she said. 'But Tilly said I must warn you, you will be my first.'

'If you are sure, I will take great care.'

She lifted the side of her smock, as he slowly bent to push back her long hair. He lent in to kiss her lips and slipped himself between her legs as though it was something they did every day. Every fibre of her body felt alert and alive. She sank deeply into his eyes and time stopped still.

She smelt dusty plants and sweat, felt the gentle breeze on their intertwined bodies. At first, he was slow, gentle. They both breathed heavily and sweat ran, intermingled with daily grime. She wanted to scream but didn't want to alarm him. The heightened moment was soon reached. He fell to one side of her, breathing heavily. They laughed together, her hand resting in his.

'Are you alright, Cartia?'

'Yes. I think so.'

She sat up, holding her knees under her chin. She pulled her chemise and tunic over her knees and held his outreached hand as he lay puffing beside her. At fifteen, she was sure this would not be the last time for them to enjoy being with each other. But, for now, he was to be her secret.

'We should leave soon,' she said. 'Supper with my family doesn't begin until we're all home.'

'Cartia, will you come with me when I leave here?' he asked. 'Be my family?'

'When you have settled, you should return and we'll talk more then,' she said. She couldn't wipe the smile from her face. 'You will need to have a cottage near your new work.'

She stood, laughing nervously while he knotted his braies and adjusted his tunic. She felt brittle and relied on his cheerful confidence. They gathered their belongings and walked towards her home.

'Cartia, I will walk with you to your home but now is not the right time for me to come to supper or to meet your parents.'

'Why? Mother would find enough food for us all,' she said, one hand holding her stomach, which was gripped in fear that she'd misread his intentions.

'Cartia, I need to be clean and well-presented before meeting your family. Please do not be concerned. Although it is only a meal to you, it would be much more for me.'

She felt a warm confidence that he would support her, the best way he could. There was so much to learn.

It was Sunday and a day of rest for the field workers. Cartia had been woken as the sun rose to assist her mother in preparing bread and cheese early. She arranged clothes for the family to attend the village church service at St Peter's. She slipped into her day dress and apron and pulled on her shoes. She would change into her Sunday best dress after the chores were finished. A new energy, fresh and light, had settled on her since lying with Daniaen. She wondered if others could notice it too.

The cottage was no different from every other single storey building in the village. They all had sixteen feet from front to back, with a cauldron hanging over a pit fire in the centre of the room.

Kitchen tools and a brass cooking pot were hung on hooks from the rafter. Stools were scattered around a small wooden table and a bench lined the wall near one of the two windows. Nobody they knew owned chairs; they were too expensive. There was a wooden trunk in the corner where Mother stored her things, and it rested on the blanket box. It wouldn't take her long to sweep one room and toss some fresh straw about the hardened-dirt floor. She noticed the food scraps had been taken to the pigs and chickens already. Behind the woven wattle screen along one side of the room, Mother was busy fussing with the straw bedding and folding the sheet and blankets so she could air the straw. The disturbance caused a too-sweet smell of damp straw, dirt and mould. Several mice scattered when she tried to compact the straw. Mother was not alarmed.

After she collected the eggs, Cartia and her mother prepared for church. The water on the fire was warming, almost suitable for a wash. When she returned with the eggs, she placed them in the wooden bowl on the table and proceeded to undress. She placed rags next to the small wooden tub to wipe up. Mother was prepared, jug in hand. She stepped into the tub and bent over while warm water trickled down her body. She washed her hair for the first time in months. Lice had been a nuisance, but they don't seem to enjoy dirty hair and had left her at peace for some time. Nobody talked about it. There was nothing they could do. The herbalist suggested a few options, but the tiny eggs still appeared on clean hair. She found it best to keep her hair in plaits and under a hood.

She knew her breath was not fresh but no different from her friends. It could be a sign of illness, so it was important that she cleaned her teeth to eliminate the smell. Her last meal consisted of corn bread, and the tiny, crushed corn grains were stuck in between her teeth. To make sure her breath smelt fresh, she reached for the cardamom and liquorice. If these herbs were out of season, mother would make up a paste from aniseed, fennel and cumin. They all made her mouth feel fresh again. The tooth-drawer at the market would remove any decayed teeth but this was not something one looked forward to. The alternative, if she had a toothache, was to mix some mutton fat with the seed of sea holly. On these occasions, Mother would burn this mix and hold it close to her sore tooth, with a bowl of water under it to catch the tiny worms which the physician said had embedded themselves into her infected tooth. She had never detected any worms so far.

While Cartia dried quickly, dressed, and stepped into her shoes so the grit under her feet could be brushed off, mother undressed and stepped into the emptied tub. She refilled the jug with warm water and began to pour it over her mother. It took two jugs to fill the small tub.

She was glad water was plentiful now, after weeks of rain. After a day's work, it was tedious having to walk down to the village well near the church, queue for a turn at plunging the bucket down the wooden-edged shaft, pouring it into her own bucket and carrying it back to the cottage. She enjoyed talking to other local girls at the well, but the walk back home was heavy work.

She thought the whole room smelt damp and needed airing. Shutters were flung open, stretching the hide hinges and propping them apart with a stick. Ma washed her hair separately, using lavender water mixed in a copper basin hanging from a hook under the eaves.

Ma looked like a new woman in her Sunday-best, when she dabbed some lavender water on her wrists and brushed her long hair. It was only at times like this that her hair was let loose, and it made her appear years younger than she was. All married women in the village covered their hair. Young men admired the free-flowing locks of young single girls; she knew the reaction she could expect whenever she let her hair down.

Her mother brushed Cartia's long hair standing beside the window so she could observe any lice eggs. She then tied it up above her head so it would be well enclosed under her hood in church. She usually did Father's hair this way too, brushing it next to the light of the window. They talked of the dress she was sewing. Of the length of fabric.

'The clothier was right to be confused by the measurements,' her mother continued. 'He'd said that a foot in length may be the same twelve inches but a foot in cloth measurements was called an ell, normally forty-five inches. He told her twenty-seven inches if the cloth was Flemish. What a confusion!'

'Our red cloth is not Flemish, Mother, so you'll use an ell to measure. Will you show me how you do this soon? I need to learn more about sewing clothes,' she said.

Daylight washed across the cloudy sky at the angle of post-dawn when Cartia dragged the tub outside and leaned it against the woodshed. James was the only person she knew who owned a time piece, but she thought they didn't really need one. Life was routine. They were used to knowing when the angle of the sun touched different points and measured time by the length of shadows across their path. Although it was not often people had baths, they always washed their hands before and after a meal. They ate with their fingers, so cleaned their hands after eating too. The menfolk in the family would wash hands and face only today as time was running short. Families were walking past greeting her on their way to the church service. In the distance, she could hear the toll of the early church bell at St Peter's.

There would be no fishing boats leaving Shipden today until very late in the evening, so Father and Henry tended to two pigs in the far corner of the garden. It was really her mother's job to tend to the animals but, on Sundays, they all helped so they would not be late for church. She watched Henry fill the wooden bucket with water scooped from one of the barrels near the cess pit.

'Father, what do you think of the meeting with Martin Bartholomew later today?'

'Martin's a good man, son. We won't rush these things,' he said, pouring grain and vegetable scraps into the pig's trough. 'Let it go for now.'

'Sorry, Father. I can't help but be impatient.'

'Things will happen soon enough,' he said. 'Martin will come around here after church.'

'That's a good omen, Father, but do I have good enough prospects to marry his daughter?'

'Always a concern, of course, Henry. We are not wealthy, but we do a good trade with the fishing boat. Martin is a trustworthy man and will balance things up from a perspective of his daughter's best interests, I'm sure. I believe she has several prospects.'

Henry stopped in the middle of his chores and scratched his head. Lice again.

'The family fishing trade is steady work, and I'm strong and honest,' he said.

'Yes, son. It's not me you have to convince. Both of you were children together and she understands what it is to be in a working family.'

'I would like to court her and show her my intentions are honourable,' he said. 'I like her very much. Always have. She was the prettiest little girl in the village.'

'Pretty isn't important, Henry. Beauty fades. She needs to be able to support you in all your endeavours. That is important. She's been brought up with righteous values but what are her own dreams? Do they match your own?'

'Of that, I'm unsure. If I'm given permission to court her, we will talk of this. Before then, all I can do is hope I'm her most suitable match. I can't help but be attracted to her flaxen hair when the wind gathers it from her hood and when she laughs.'

'I understand better than you think, my boy. Men be attracted to women who are fairer than most and of child-bearing stature. That's just the way of things. How God intended us men to be for the procreation of children.'

Cartia watched Henry's face. His expression changed and his cheeks flared.

Cartia was sitting on the bench near their cottage door in the late afternoon when she noticed several people in the distance walking towards her. As they drew closer, she stood up and walked towards the front gate, waving. She hoped they would speak in English, but she could tolerate French if she had to, especially today. She found it more comfortable to speak the words of peasants and traders. The very idea that only French speaking people would be accepted in modern fourteenth century English society was, she felt, ridiculous.

Her friend, Gabby, came home for a brief visit last month and they had much to say to one another. She was sent to be a servant apprentice in the kitchens of the King. He spoke French and so did his lords, knights, and all his servants so Gabby had to revert to speaking French. She said noblemen who came to the palace had sons who were taking lessons in common English, and she'd been called upon to allow them to practise their new skills. Change was going to happen soon, she thought. The new King was young and enthusiastic with fresh ideas. He hired hundreds of men but few women. Gabby had been one of the first to be apprenticed on his castle staff.

Gabby told her friends that Edward of Windsor was only fifteen, one year older than she was, when he became King Edward III. She described the palace kitchens as enormous and her work never tedious, especially when guests came to the palace. She had told them how pleasant the new Queen was. He was sixteen when they were wed. The girls had wondered if French would continue to be spoken in the courts or if this young King would make changes. They hoped so, although it would not make any difference to the village, as they spoke in English, and, on more formal occasions, French, and the priests wrote in Latin. She wondered if today was to be a formal occasion or a simple gathering.

There were many things she'd like to learn but, for now, she was more concerned in learning skills in the home and working in the field to help support the family. Daniaen would leave the village soon, but he promised to return one day to ask for her hand in marriage. She needed to be prepared. Until then, he would remain her secret.

'God be with you, sir,' she said, welcoming their visitors. She opened the gate, and they entered the front garden. Henry and the rest of the family were sitting around the table inside the cottage, waiting for them to arrive after church.

'And with you, child.' Mr Bartholomew doffed his hat. His daughter stood behind his rather large body, still dressed in her Sunday best. She held open the wooden gate, and they strolled confident paces along the small stony pathway, Emma's petite hand resting on her father's arm.

Mother came to the door. Her cheery disposition filled the small cottage with love. These are people she'd known all her life, so Cartia wondered why mother was so overjoyed to greet them, but she welcomed the excitement. The men stood. After tea was shared and polite enquiries on health and the seasonal changes, both fathers left the cottage to check the pigs and goats and the more serious matters relating to Henry's proposal. It was mid-year so these animals would be taken to the empty fields where they had just recently harvested wheat and hay. All the village farmyard animals would soon clean up whatever was left of the crop while fertilizing the land.

Before long, a hand-fast ceremony was agreed and would take place in September. Emma's dowry included household utensils, tools, furniture, clothing and livestock. Henry's cottage would not have room for two pigs so the family would keep those. He did have space enough for a chicken coop.

The women tidied and washed the crockery in a wooden basin behind the cottage. Henry remained inside the cottage to sit with Emma alone for the first time.

Cartia picked some wildflowers from grassy slopes near the deer park at Felbrigg and carefully wound each stem into a chain. She was practising to create an unbroken ring of flowers to place on Emma's head for her wedding day. The two girls had become closer over the past few months since Henry was courting her and she was to be her maid on their wedding day. She even told Emma about Daniaen and introduced them one day in the marketplace. But he remained her secret to everyone else.

Her brother had vowed to wed in September at the celebrations of Michaelmas, but they did not want a church ceremony. Emma was very shy. She asked to keep the day special with just their families present. Henry was so relieved that she had chosen him above other suitors; the ceremony did not concern him at all. In years to come, they could be blessed by the local priest at St Peter's if they chose to. It wasn't important or illegal to marry outside a church.

As she threaded one stem into the tiny slit she'd made with her thumb in the stem of another flower, it occurred to her that families came together like this. One connected to the next person who was in turn connected to the next, from grandparents to babies. At both ends, they were vulnerable and had to be cared for by the stronger members. Her Grandpa drowned in the sea before she was born, but her dear old Gran lived until she was old at almost fifty years. In Shipden, there were quite a few widows of fishermen lost at sea.

The soft summer days were closing in earlier now. She smelt the fresh country air as it pulled at her hood, and she swore she would always live in the countryside.

'Cartia, bring me that cloth,' said Mother. 'You know; the red fabric Tom brought back from his pilgrimage to Walsingham last spring.'

'Yes, Ma,' said Cartia. 'That blood-red cloth? It's in the blanket box.' She went to the corner of the cottage near the straw bedding and lifted the heavy lid. There, under a pile of blankets, was some cloth for sewing garments. Younger brother, Tom, much to the surprise of his family, decided to join the priory as a priest. Although they don't see him often, her parents were very proud of him and looked forward to his visits with his tales of pilgrimages and exciting adventures. He spoke of towns along the journey which they hadn't known to exist, of the recent changes to an ancient monastery at Walsingham with twin Holy wells and healing baths. Tom said the abbey grounds were covered in snowdrops in spring. He was a bit of a dreamer, and they had been mesmerized by the way he'd explained all this to them around the fire one night. She carried the cloth carefully over to Ma.

'I thought I'd make a new dress for Emma to wear to her wedding,' said Mother. 'This wool is extremely fine. Lincoln Scarlett, it was called and was the most expensive in the Port of Boston shop.'

'That's such a beautiful cloth, Ma. Emma will love it, I'm sure.'

'I'll talk to her sister later today when I go up to the marketplace,' said her mother. She had already borrowed a dress belonging to Emma, so she would use that to determine where to cut the fine woollen fabric which she could wear for her wedding. They wrapped the cloth in a casing so it wouldn't spoil and placed some more dry herbs and lavender inside to protect the fine wool from vermin.

'She will look so lovely, Ma. Won't Henry be proud?'

'When I was wed to your father, my sister made me some lace to wear as a veil. I have always kept it for a special occasion such as this. Do you think Emma might like to use it?'

'Let's ask her later, Ma. Emma will have to come here for a dress fitting, won't she?'

'Of course,' said her mother, putting aside the intricate lace. 'I'll launder it, so it smells fresh for her. And I'll ask her to return it so you can wear it when your turn comes to be wed, Cartia.'

'What do you know of this, Ma? Are you teasing? Do you and Father have someone in mind?'

'No, not yet, Cartia. I need you here for as long as I can,' said Mother. 'You'll be fifteen soon, so it won't be long to wait.'

'Ma. I have a little secret to tell you,' she said. 'I've been with a boy I like very much. He introduced himself to me at work, but he is not from our village. He's the son of an engineering family from the lowlands. His prospects are good and he's very handsome.' She felt all giggly and silly. Mother stopped her work and sat down on a stool. For a while, she wasn't sure if she was angry or pleased with her secret. She just couldn't hold it in any longer and had to seek her thoughts on the strange feelings she'd experienced whenever he looked at her.

'What is his name, Cartia?'

'It's a strange name. He's called Daniaen de Rek. I waited for someone to call him, so I would hear his name when he first arrived.'

'We need to consider this carefully. If he's from a good family, and we must know his ability to provide for you. Or would you prefer your brother talked with him?'

The marketplace was particularly busy in Shipton village this morning, when Cartia accompanied her mother. Rain had held off for a brief reprieve, however the track to the cobbled area was muddy and the horse manure hadn't been scraped off the road outside some of the residences yet. But she wasn't going to let a bit of rain and mess spoil her day. The low harvest of recent times, the potential of drought and famine which people were talking about were not things she had any power over.

Her day dress was covered by an apron with a large pocket to store dried basil, chamomile, lavender and mint which they would buy to stuff into their straw bedding. With winter coming on soon, the rarely changed straw bedding was a paradise for vermin unless preventative measures were taken. Fleas and lice were only part of the problem. Rats and mice were unavoidable during the long months of winter when the warm central firepit attracted them to dry straw bedding, but she knew they did not like the smell of these herbs.

Walking in the shade of a row of merchant-houses, she stared through their square glazed windows at beautiful silks and other expensive fabrics from Asia. Behind her was a packhorse loaded with corn from local farms. A couple of priests passed by in their habits; crucifixes dangled from their belts. She looked at them, hoping one might be her brother, Tom, but it wasn't him. The noise was deafening as she walked closer to the centre of the marketplace. People selling their wares shouted over each other to attract buyers. Farmers were also driving their sheep and cattle into town, moving the animals to penned areas on the edge of the village. She noticed a servant shovelling horse manure from the entry to his master's residence.

'Going to market is my favourite past-time,' said Cartia to her mother. She nodded her hooded head and kept walking past the village well near the church of St Peter's. It hadn't rained since yesterday, and then only a few drops.

Carts, rattling on the cobbled street in front of them, were laden with produce, chickens in crates, fresh milk in large jugs and fresh cheeses. She recognised Daniaen's blond hair and lowered her gaze. She felt embarrassed, cheeks rushing rosy red. She concentrated on her mother speaking as they walked past but she nodded when he glanced at her. He stopped emptying the cart, smiled as he tipped his cap and watched her until she turned the corner.

'Life gets harder, young Cartia, so keep looking for the bright side of things.'

'Yes, Ma.'

'There's Emma's sister, dear. I'll see if she can take some time to talk about the dress and the lace.'

'As you wish, Ma. I will look around at the stalls until you're finished.'

She looked along the cobbled street. Signs hanging from walls. Not many of Shipden's residents could read or write, so they painted pictures on signs indicating what they were selling. The hotel had a bushel of barley on a pole. The fishmonger had a drawing of a fish. Blending in with all the noise from the market was the blacksmith's anvil, the clanging and hammering at their forge in the next street. It all felt so vibrant and alive. And home. How good it was to be alive. She turned around and skipped back the way she came, hoping to catch a glimpse of a certain blond-haired young man.

Cartia stood on the beach with Matilda and Emma, with echoes of rhythmic, lapping waves scuttling behind them.

'Over there, behind the tree,' said Emma, pointing. Her enthusiasm was contagious. The girls could barely see beyond the tree's shrubbery.

'Right. It's almost finished. Hasn't Henry been busy?' said Matilda, who was proud of her younger brother. 'He goes out in the fishing boat all morning and works on his cottage in the afternoon.'

'He has many friends who don't mind helping him build. They help each other,' said Emma.

How happy she was, thought Cartia. 'It's a good solid building, Em. You would be safe and secure in that home. Our brother has always been skilled in carpentry and in so many practical ways. He enjoyed doing this for you.'

'Yes, carpentry is something he could do if the fishing boats were called back in poor weather,' Matilda said. 'Carpenters can be paid up to five pence a day!'

Emma took a long breath, elation mirrored in her eyes as she ran up the gentle slope to the tree. The other girls followed at a slower pace to inspect their brother's half-built cottage. The structure was solid. Henry had constructed a framework of timber, then filled in the spaces with woven twigs. Finally, the twigs were daubed with mud which, when dried, made a hard wall.

'These internal walls will be covered in a plaster of animal hair and clay,' said Emma. 'We'll paint it with a lime mix once the thatching has been added to the roof.'

Emma stood in the middle of the timber structure which would be her home and glanced upwards at the sky. 'Soon those rafters will be blackened by our firepit, and years will roll past. Children may join us. Time doesn't stand still,' she said.

Cartia thought she looked dreamy and laughed. It was a dream they all hoped for and shared. 'Look! Henry has added an iron horseshoe to the rafters over the door jamb. Everyone who enters will be safe from the devil now.'

How superstitious they were. No harm in that, but she wondered if it would work. Everyone has foibles. Without even asking, she knew that Mother would have given Henry that iron horseshoe and also the iron nail on which it hung.

'Lovely, Emma. You must be very excited,' said Matilda. 'It's got two windows, but glazing would be too costly. Would you have external shutters to be closing it off?'

'Yes, I saw Henry working on the shutter lengths yesterday and he has already dried the rabbit hide for the top hinge,' said Emma. 'As you can see, there's two rooms which will be quite large. The cottage has a floor of stone foundations. I'm told that the ground is too sandy to have a dirt and straw floor like most older cottages set further back from the ocean.'

'The stone foundations will be much stronger. I heard father say they would work on restoring our old cottage in the summer. The top level of thatch needs replacing, and he's been collecting stone to build up the floor,' said Cartia. 'Now, Emma, about your wedding dress. I have a message from our mother. I know you're looking forward to trying it on. Even Mr John Hopkinson, the clothier, is keen to see it completed. He would like you to show it to him, if you please. You should call around to see Mother after dinner tomorrow.'

'You're so kind, Cartia. It's a fine red wool and will last a long time. So many good omens. Everything is falling into place,' said Emma. 'I'll be there after dinner. Is just before sunset alright?'

She crept up the hillside near the woodland where she wouldn't be disturbed. It was her secret place. There was the old oak tree she liked to lean on. She reached up between its branches. Her hand felt around inside the owl hole and found her work where she'd left it, wrapped in a cloth.

Satisfied, Cartia sighed and pulled out her new cottons to continue her tapestry. Green was the colour of young love. Blue for purity. She felt so excited for them. Her gift for Henry and Emma was almost finished.

There was a movement out of the corner of her eye as she sat on the warm grass. What was that? A rabbit maybe. No, too heavy footed for a rabbit's light bounce. Down the slope behind the poppies, dry leaves crunched and twigs snapped. A person approached in her direction. She sat very still with her work in her lap. Another noise. She chose to hide.

She tiptoed behind the trunk of the oak tree, taking shelter in case it was an undesirable character getting up to no good. The woods were beautiful, peaceful but they were also notorious for criminals, petty thieves. She did not normally come into the woods by herself, but everyone had been busy preparing for the wedding in the morning.

'Cartia, where are you?'

She was shocked to hear her name called. Footsteps crunched over the shingle path.

It was Daniaen de Rek. She showed herself as he approached her hiding place and smiled as his presence filled the space where she had sat only minutes before.

'Good to see you, Daniaen. Are you alone? Are you looking for me?'

'Yes, I'm alone and looking for you. Emma told me you were up here making her a wildflower headband for the wedding. I had to come and see for myself,' he said. 'It seemed like an opportunity to spend time with you before I must leave Shipden.'

'Oh, that's kind, Daniaen.'

'So, what have you been up to?'

'The headband is nearly finished. That's what I told Emma I was doing today. I've been sewing a gift for their wedding,' she said, showing her tapestry work to him. 'I've also got to finish off this headpiece.'

She demonstrated how she threaded the stalks together, he helped her collect some colourful flowers. He lay nearby and watched her every move, his eyes not leaving her for a moment. She laughed as he put some flowers in her hair, pulled her long locks to one side and kissed the back of her neck as she worked. He looked conflicted and she wondered why. They seemed so happy together. He lifted her chin so he could see her eyes and demanded her attention.

'I have something I need to tell you, Cartia. I came to tell you that I've arranged to work at a windmill construction north-west of here. I leave in the morning,' he said. 'I'm sad to leave you for a while, my love, but I will return for you as soon as I'm settled in my own cottage. Then I will speak with your father, and we will be able to say our own vows to one another.'

She stopped entwining the flowers and turned to face him. So that was the conflict. She must be strong and encourage him to find his best place in the world though she also felt a rush of heartache. Would he ever return? How long must she wait? These weren't questions he could find an answer for, so she didn't ask.

'That is good news. I'm pleased you were able to find a position which suits your skills, Daniaen,' she said. 'I'll wait for you, no matter how long it takes.'

'I'll miss you,' he said. 'We have found love together. We're fortunate to have found one another.'

Cartia knew that what he said was the truth, so she nodded, pushing back a tear. She ran her fingers through his hair and pulled him towards her, his touch so gentle that it felt like time was stilled for their hearts to gather strength to farewell one another. "

They embraced one last time before he walked her home. With a few belongings tied to his back in a blanket, he waved to her every few yards. She watched from their front gate as he disappeared over the horizon, in the direction of Crowmere. She knew the waiting had begun.

When her sister, Matilda, was betrothed to James, he was a tenant farmer with his own flint and brick cottage, so it was not unusual that they cohabited before their wedding ceremony. If any babies had been conceived and birthed during this period, they could've been legalised at the wedding ceremony, but their twins came several years later. Now it was different for Emma and Henry, who had announced their betrothal and banns were read out at St Peter's church recently. Her family insisted that they not live together until their wedding night as the cottage was not yet ready. It gave her time to get her glory box together and gave Henry a strong incentive to work faster. Cartia had to keep her secret until the time was right for her lover to return to the village. They didn't want a wedding service at a church. Both Cartia and Daniaen had already made plans for a simple ceremony, just as Emma and Henry would do.

Emma's own mother had died many years ago from tuberculosis, so Ma stepped up to help Emma. She had created a simple red dress for the wedding and Emma was going to be a beautiful bride. Mother was concerned that Emma's own mother had not given her any advice about marriage and her sister was living on the other side of Crowmere, with her young family so not readily available to have a talk about the many obligations a woman might have in marriage. She knew she should also speak to Cartia, so she called the two girls to have tea. They pulled up a stool each and she poured tea into pottery cups. While the girls enjoyed the treat, she started buttering some scones, hot from the coals.

'Girls, we need to talk about marriage and what is expected of you, especially when you and your husband make babies,' she began. The girls were both horrified and intrigued. This was not something people talked about over tea, was it?

'This is what I know and I'm passing this on to you so you will know as well. Now, for a wife, sex doesn't have to happen very often. There are restrictions placed on suitable times when married couples can engage in this activity.'

She made sure they were listening. They were.

'So, for example, the church has said that married sex is forbidden during these times: Sundays, sometimes Fridays and Wednesdays, the feast days of the saints, periods of fasting such as Lent or Advent, and during a woman's life when she is impure. Impurity is during your time of bleeding. It is also forbidden when a woman is pregnant, the first forty days after giving birth, and while nursing her baby.'

There were no rules, that she knew of, for when young women could enjoy the company of men. At least, not in the village. Depends on who they were, she thought. If they were of a high class, a Lady or a Princess, then there were strict obligations. For Cartia and others in the village, nobody really took any notice if a couple was discrete. Most of the girls she knew had met a special person in the village and quietly became a couple, sometimes at work in the field, or in private places like the wood. Some girls had told her they often had relations with boys they knew, just because everything was horrible in their lives and it made them feel wanted and cared for. She kept Daniaen a secret, but she longed to be held by him again. For now, she needed to listen to Ma. Marriage was a whole other matter. It felt solid, permanent, safer. There were church guidelines, and she needed to know what they were.

'Since the goal for a woman is mainly to give birth to as many children as she is blessed with and nurse them all into good health, she won't have much time to engage in sexual activity.'

'Life would get busy once babies arrive,' nodded Emma. 'And I hope to be blessed with many children. I love babies.'

'Emma, do you understand how these babies are made?' her mother asked. Cartia looked from her mother to her friend, focused on her answer.

'Henry said he would show me,' said Emma, softly. She was a shy girl who was probably feeling uncomfortable with the subject. 'I appreciate you telling me. I feel more prepared to be a married woman now. Did you know these things, Cartia?'

'No, I wasn't exactly sure. I'd heard there were religious rules, but I didn't know what they were until now. Thank you, Ma.'

'Remember, girls, I am here for you at any time. You can't possibly ask me a silly question.' She hugged both girls and they enjoyed the cooler scones with a dab of raspberry jam on freshly churned butter.

Before she left to go home, mother handed Emma a wreath of rosemary, as it was the night before her wedding. This was to symbolize loyalty, luck, and happiness. No fifteen-year-old in the world could possibly feel happier than she looked right now.

But Cartia did wonder about the rest of the story, untold and still a part of life's mystery. How she hoped her turn would come very soon.

The day of the wedding was overcast but not rainy. Almost everyone met at their cottage before strolling together down to the beach at low tide. Emma looked radiant in her soft, red dress, her clean, shiny hair was in a long plait with whirls of blond locks twisted on each side and gathered with ribbons at a chaplet of blue flowers. Mother's intricate lace piece was held on her head with a simple crown of wildflowers which Cartia had woven earlier. Henry was already there. He stood on rose petals scattered in a circle on the sand.

There was no wind, not even a breeze at low tide. Seagulls squawked constantly in the distance where several fishing boats were anchored, fishermen sorting and tossing fish entrails into the sea.

Cartia stood with them to one side as a witness, together with her family. And Emma's father and her sister's family stood on the other. Henry took his bride's small hands in his, and said the words,

'I take you as my wife, Emma.'

She looked into his eyes and said,

'I take you as my husband, Henry Leman.'

He slipped his grandmother's gold ring onto the third finger of her right hand.

The ceremony was over. He kissed both her hands. They were officially married.

Sunrise brought dappled light through the shutters and onto their new lives, wrapped tight together in each other's arms. Later in the morning, Cartia listened as Emma told her how it was for her to wake up and realize that she was a married woman. That her husband lay beside her in the bed. She showed her the gift he had given her the following morning. Cartia was aware that men often gave their new bride a gift on the first day after a marriage.

Emma pulled out her box from under the bed and opened it. Inside was Henry's gift. With care, she lifted it onto the table. Cartia's finger traced over the chiselled engraving of Emma's name on the lid of the wooden chest. She recognised it as a hard wood, which must've been difficult to work with, but he would've wanted it to last forever.

'What a beautiful gift, Em,' she whispered.

'That's not all. Look inside.'

She opened the box and saw the lace head-covering which Emma had worn at her wedding, with something wrapped within it. She unfurled it with care. She had no idea what the small object could be and was shaking in anticipation to find out.

'Oh, Emma. I've never seen anything so beautiful in all my life,' said Cartia. 'He must love you very much.' She was holding a marriage brooch. So pretty. It was circular and made from gold, set with alternating rubies and sapphires. She turned it over in her hand. There was an inscription written in French on the back. She had to ask what it said as Cartia could not read. She imagined the priest must have helped Henry to write this. The message on the back translated to - *I am here in place of the friend I love. August 1312.*

'Apparently, it's designed to be worn at the breast, near my heart. I shall wear it to church on Sundays.'

She promised Cartia she would treasure it always.

Chapter 11 - 1953

In the early morning silver light, Ginny pinned her tiny face to the upstairs bedroom window towards a crashing sound which had woken her. Lizzie had slept through the noise, so she didn't wake her. At the tiny attic window, she was straining on her toes to see outside. She closed her eyes to form tiny slits so she could see clearer through the wet squalls darting in all directions onto the glazed windowpane. She could make out a reflection of the streetlight in very wide puddles on the footpath near the front garden. She felt shivery cold in her nightie, so she pulled the knitted patchwork blanket from her bed and draped it around her shoulders.

'Ma,' she called from the attic, too scared to take another step in the dark hallway.

'Ma, I'm frightened.' It was her father who replied from his bedroom.

'What's up Ginny? Ma is downstairs with the twins,' he said.

'I think I had a bad dream 'cause I can't see what the big noise was,' she cried.

'It was probably a bit of thunder, love. Go back to bed.'

Then another crashing sound came from somewhere outside, in the distance, not from inside their cottage. She ran into her father's bed and hid her face in a pillow. He pulled her under the blanket and held her until she nodded off.

'No point in me trying to get back to sleep now, thank you, Miss Ginny. I'll go downstairs and make a cuppa instead.'

He slipped out from under the covers into his slippers and put on his dressing-gown. As he approached the top of the stairs, he wondered if the rain would ever stop. He could smell a heavy dampness in the air inside the house and he heard a gentle snoring sound below, which sounded familiar. Cath swore black and blue that she never snored; he smiled to himself. Halfway down the stairs on the small landing, he could not believe his eyes.

The blankets he'd used as draft blockers under the cottage door, were now floating. He looked about. Cath was curled up in his reading chair, still not wet, with a book on her chest so he touched her feet as he wadded past.

'Cath. Wake up. The boys .. are they okay?'

She sat bolt upright; took a few seconds to make out where she was. She tried to stand up and slipped onto the flooded sandstone floor.

'Pa, what's happening? Where are you?' He heard Ginny and replied so she'd know he meant business.

'Stay upstairs, Ginny.'

His heart was thumping too loud to hear her reply, but he heard her tiny feet scurry along the timber floorboards, and the squeak of her landing on the mattress. He reached out and held onto the woman he'd thought he had been through everything with, as she lifted each twin from the pram, now submerged up to the height of the carriage. Water had seeped through the wicker plaiting. She begged them to cry. Her voice, loving, gentle, was choking him up. He wiped away some tears and buried his face in her hair.

'No, no, no..' she whispered.

A crushing weight tightened in his chest. He held her and their babies while the melancholic greyness outside settled in his heart.

Chapter 12 – 2013

Aziza opened the kitchen curtain over the small window above the sink of the holiday van in Hemsby. Outside, it could only be described as a marshy, sandy, windy place in December. Hemsby was not too far from Great Yarmouth but far enough to avoid the winter-escape holiday crowds and Aziza was pleased to sit in the van and listen to the wind whistling around the small holiday park. In the dimming light of sunset, Carter had emptied the car, sorted their belongings into the various cupboards and stored their suitcases under the bed.

'Right, Aziza, where's that coffee you promised?'

'Coming right up,' she said. 'You were too quick for me!'

'Well, that's not such a bad complaint. At least I'm not held up tripping over the children's toys or books or indeed, the twins themselves,' he said, flopping down on the lounge. 'Looks like rain again and there's storm warnings out, according to the manager.'

'Oh, bother. I'd still like to do some reconnaissance of those sand dunes, if I can. Should take a couple of hours.'

'That's going to be difficult if heavy rain persists, love. Of course, you'll be careful, and, of course, I will come with you holding an umbrella, if necessary,' he said.

She expected that he would not leave her side as the sandy cliff was unpredictable now. The surge was all along the eastern coast and threatened everything in its path. Her team was interested in the geological makeup of the area.

'You can be my assistant, Carter,' she laughed. 'But I can't pay you very much.'

'I don't know about that,' he teased. They laughed easily. She enjoyed his company when he was not frustrated by the twins and other interruptions.

'We might be lucky enough to spot some seals in the sea tomorrow. Don't forget to take your camera. There've also been some breath-taking archaeological discoveries all around Norfolk which means the county can hold its own against the likes of Stonehenge and Sutton Hoo when it comes to heritage,' she said.

'Okay. Camera. Noted. Never know what we might dig up during your two-hour dig.'

'Wouldn't that be exciting? Some fellow dug up an object that was as old as two thousand years before Christ.'

'Man, that's ancient,' his eyes met hers. He was listening now, so she continued, handing him a steaming mug of coffee.

'Norfolk's team of air photo interpreters has now investigated many kilometres and mapped their findings. Part of that was around here where homes were washed out to sea during the past hundred years or so.'

She pulled out a file from her case and flipped through the pages. 'Here it is. Look at this map. It shows where the sites were seen from the plane when it flew along the water's edge. Of course, it was not in the middle of winter, so the sea was calm.'

He took a sip of coffee, put on his reading glasses and studied the map. 'Here we are, and running my finger up the coast a bit, I can see Cromer and Shipden's wreckage under the sea,' said Carter. 'I've always known it was there, but not many people take much notice. Not much left of it, I guess.'

'Shipden? Yeah. The village taken by the sea in the fourteenth century. There's a bit mentioned in the local museum about the village, but very little interest and it's not as complete as some of the other more recent villages taken by the sea,' he said. 'Not much left, I believe. A few walls, bits of a church, scattered stonework.'

'Probably because it's not the only village under the sea, Carter. The whole eastern coast has remnants of lost villages, and some are still threatened. Happisburgh's fourteenth century manor house, its Norman church and the lighthouse are all set to disappear over the next few years.'

'I'm more into how those people in Shipden lived their everyday lives back in the thirteen hundreds. A few bits of flint and a church tower are an interesting find, but unless we look at how the people lived and learn from them, what good is it?' said Carter.

'There aren't many records from back then. We know it was a fishing village which was granted a market by the King. We have a few church records written in Latin. Most people couldn't read or write. Yes, it would be great to push a button and stand on a street, watch the families, see what they ate, how they spoke, what was important to them.'

'You know, the cliff which fell into the sea in Shipden had been a hill with a church on top. The North Sea has been eroding these cliffs for a very long time,' she said. 'They try to hold it back, but it's all very temporary, in my opinion. The sea is just too strong, and the cliffs are too chalky or too sandy. We are getting better at it though. Cromer has some excellent retaining walls for sea defence, but it is something about which authorities must continue to be vigilant.'

'I read in the paper recently,' said Carter. 'that, if these storms become worse, Happisburgh residents will find themselves in the same position as a local farmer who ploughed a twelve-acre farm one night in 1845 only to wake the next morning after a storm to find the sea had covered his field.'

'That is why people like me do what we do, I suppose,' said Aziza. 'Research on paper is only as good as what we discover in the diggings. A pattern emerges when we do an archaeological analysis. We already know about the Black Death and have some insight into whether the plague killed a healthy population or kicked people while they were already down. Believe it or not, fifty million people died in that pandemic, or sixty per cent of Europe's entire population.'

'It's a fascinating assignment your team's been given, isn't it? We still have so much to learn from these people, and especially where they went wrong, so we don't repeat their mistakes. I mean, I get why Shipden fishermen wanted to live close to the sea when transport was by foot, but perhaps we should think about moving the villages inland now we have refrigerated transport for the fishing industry."

'I don't know anything about that, but, yes, perhaps we should change our ways to work with nature instead of trying to fight an endless battle,' she said. 'It's not just remnants of pots and flint which reveal how people once lived. I remember seeing some pollen analysis, which revealed how people gave up on Dunwich after 1338, when another great storm silted up their port.'

'Maybe that's the same year when Shipden village finally collapsed,' he said.

She placed the aerial map back in her file, while Carter moved to clear the table.

'I'm going to phone your parents now, Carter. See if the kids are behaving ... or not.'

'Yeah, okay. It's nice to have a break for a few days. We had a sensible discussion just now without being constantly interrupted. Be nice to phone and say good night.'

She was already missing Tasneem and Tariq, but she was looking forward to collecting samples of the cliff soil tomorrow. Rain, hail or shine.

The twins were full of life when they were together. Carly stood at the back door of Jack and Anna's cottage, watching her charges as they climbed an apple tree.

'Double trouble, eh?' sighed Jack, who was a patient grandfather but perhaps he felt like a little bit of an invasion was happening.

'Oh, yeah – it can be overwhelming when you're not used to it. You and Anna have certainly had your hands full with these two little visitors!'

Carly was familiar with the noise children made and their unique energy. What was troubling her then? It had been such a long time since she'd left Australia – nearly three years. Impressed upon her mind were the sounds and sobs of times past, as the oldest daughter of a large family without a mother. Well, not really without a mother. Her mother was most probably alive, but they didn't know where she was. All they'd been left with was a note her mother had placed on the well-scrubbed kitchen table when Carly was thirteen.

'The twins had a phone call from their parents last night before bedtime. Seems they're enjoying their freedom, even though the weather hasn't been the best,' he said.

'That's great. We all need to break away occasionally.'

'Yes, we do. Talking about having a break, Anna and I really appreciate you popping over to babysit for a while, Carly,' said Jack. 'Are you sure you will manage?' He sounded genuinely concerned about her, but he wasn't to know her background. Most teenagers were not left with a brood of children to care for; not to mention her poor father, who she loved dearly. She had watched his demise as he realized the lynchpin of his life would not be returning home.

'My pleasure. Anna gave me your mobile number in case anything goes wrong, so don't worry about us. We'll be just fine.'

The heavy burden of loss and grief doesn't only come with the death of a loved one. People went missing every day and their families never gave up looking for them. Grief had all but lifted now, but she still felt a deep sadness. Why on earth had her mother left them? People kept going, didn't they, no matter what? She had been so young at that time and struggled to keep up with schoolwork. Her father was said to have loved his wife to the point of obsession. Maybe his obsession was the reason she couldn't be traced when the police had her listed as a missing person.

Carly heard Anna and Jack in the hallway, Anna's laughter trickled through to the garden. They were so happy together, in their own little world. Jack called from the front entrance to say they were leaving.

'Have a great time. See you soon,' called Carly. The twins enjoyed their play too much to be concerned about what the adults were up to, but she did notice a few seconds of stillness before Tasneem reacted to her brother, who pulled her plaits.

Carly sat on the wall near the edge of the promenade. When she walked, she could think and sort things out in her head, but sitting was better for conversations with Josh. He walked at a pace that she found difficult to keep up over a distance and found herself puffed between words.

'What's wrong, Carly? You've stopped talking,' he said.

'Very funny, Josh. It's not easy to keep up. You have long legs.'

'Seriously, what's going on?'

'Okay. Sit here and I'll tell you.'

He was such a presence with his tall frame and when his blue eyes were focused on her, she just wanted to melt. He had hired her twice this week, and she thought she owed him some time to show him around Cromer. She didn't look at him directly and brushed her curls behind her ears while he settled on the stone wall beside her.

'You know I've been here for some years now, in Sheringham. It's a pretty place in summer and I'm happy here with my freelance photography and tutoring and so on. But that's not the reason I originally came to Norfolk,' she said. 'I came to find my mother.'

'Your mother? Does she live here?'

'I don't know really. I suspect she does. She was brought up here. When I was thirteen, my mother – for reasons I cannot fathom – left us. I thought we were very close. I never suspected she was unhappy. Dad was a mess for a long time afterward, the police got involved in searching for her as a Missing Person. I was the oldest child, so I was literally left holding the baby. Or babies...'

Josh nodded his head but didn't say anything. He listened intently as she related her story and her reason for staying on in England. Behind them, a North Sea breeze was blowing salty, white caps of foam at the pier.

'Are you still looking for her?'

'No. I've sort of given up. I have no idea where she'd be or even what her name is these days. She might've re-married and have an entirely new surname.'

'Yeah, but do you really want to find her again?' he asked. She wondered if he was being polite or if he really cared. It's always a risk telling someone your innermost secrets. He re-positioned himself to face her, as though he was keen for her to answer.

'Of course. That'd be awesome,' she said. 'It'd also be a bit awkward, but I'd love to solve the riddle of why she left us all without contacting us again. Maybe she doesn't want me to find her, so I have imagined this door closing in my face. What sort of mother has children and then leaves them to bring themselves up?'

'I don't know, Carly. Maybe she had reasons she couldn't tell you about at the time. Maybe she had mental health problems. Could be any number of reasons but I dare say you'd feel a whole lot better if you knew the truth. Is your father still alive?'

'Yes, he is. My Aunt Val and Uncle Peter keep an eye on him and the kids. Aunty Val couldn't have babies, so they sort of adopted us after Mum left. They're not really relatives of ours but have always been there for us.'

'That's nice. Good people. Your Dad must've been shattered,' he said.

She remembered how he had come home from the pub every night after having a skin full. He'd sooner write himself off than face making a meal or helping at home. The parish priest had called in after a while to have a long talk on the bench under the Golden wattle. It wasn't long after that when Uncle Pete would drive him home from work and Aunty Val brought the family casseroles or salads already made up. It saved us; she was sure of that.

'Yep, poor Dad. He loved her too much. Do you think that's possible? Can you love someone too much?' Carly looked across at him. He had paused to think, and she allowed time for this. He was such a deep thinker.

'Yes, an obsession is not really love, is it, Carly? I know, when people are first attracted to each other, there's a time when the world stops for them. It seems to crush everything else to the point where you can't breathe or think straight. Have you ever been bowled over with this kind of love?' he asked.

She watched his downturned face to look for signs of anguish or pain. She saw his diverted eyes, his head bowed, his hands clasped together on his lap. In getting to know someone, she always searched for how they projected their feelings without speaking a word. He looked up at her, wanting her to answer and she saw his eyes were filled with tears.

'Oh. Looks like I hit a raw nerve. Did I? So sorry to lay that on you, Josh. To answer your question, no, I haven't experienced anything like that yet. I hope I will one day. Sounds great,' she said, trying to smile and lighten the mood.

'There are so many mountains and valleys in life,' Josh said, his hand brushed a tear away. 'We'll all go through lots of those, I suppose. Ups and downs. It's how we handle them that matters. It tests our resilience and we hope we can grow from the experience.'

She decided to ask him more about his reaction at another, more appropriate time.

'Yep. You and I haven't been through wars or famines or pandemics, but our ancestors did, and humanity survived – we're here, aren't we? My teenage years were tough but always in the company of my family and friends. Just not my mother.'

'You travelling to the other side of the world was quite adventurous. I'd say you were a resilient person, Carly. I suppose it's been healing and peaceful for you to stay over here. Do you want to return to Australia one day?'

'Yes, of course I do. One day. The kids are not kids anymore. Dad's got himself a lady-friend now. Things have changed and improved for the better from my point of view. I'll return one day but not just yet. Maybe I need more crab salads before I leave. Cromer is quite famous for its crabs in summer.'

'I should try one, but I doubt if I'll be staying that long. Maybe next time. Get the story and go, my boss said. I'm working, remember?'

'Oh, right, yeah,' said Carly. 'You may be right about Mum struggling with a mental health problem. I hadn't really thought about that before now. We were pegging out the washing one day and she told me her twin baby brothers both drowned when she was young. There was a huge storm which engulfed the village for days. Homes were washed into the sea. It apparently drowned the boys somehow although their cottage was still upright. She wouldn't elaborate any further, so I left it.'

They both stood up and started walking towards the pier in silence. Carly walked past the lifeguards, who were practising their skills in a lifeboat. She overlooked them, walked further along the pier, and left Josh to watch the lifeguards. At the end of the pier, several people gathered, some fishing. She noticed an old man with a fisherman's cap drawn over on his tousled hair and stood near him. The old man doffed his cap as she approached.

'Mornin' Miss,' he said to her.

'Good morning. Bit chilly, brisk.'

'Yep. Won't be staying long.'

She turned, glanced back at Josh, who had stopped to observe lifeguards scattering when a whistle was blown by someone standing nearby with a stopwatch. The wind picked up, she wrapped her scarf tighter and turned towards the sea.

'Do you know about the village of Shipden, lass?' he asked, leaning on the railing.

'No. Is it nearby?'

'Yes, not too far,' he said, and pointed out towards the sea. 'Just a bit of a way out there somewhere.'

'Right.'

She wondered if he was the full quid, but she went along with it.

'Looks a bit damp to me,' she said, smiling.

'Aye, it is now,' he said. 'The sea flooded the whole village. Way back in the fourteenth century, they say. If you're interested, there's probably something about it at the museum in town.'

Josh came up behind them, stood next to her. Their arms touched briefly, and static electricity made her jump. Well, that hadn't ever happened to her before. Was this a message from above? She wasn't really superstitious, but you never know. He apologized and stepped back rubbing his arm. The distraction stopped her conversation with the stranger, but she did promise herself that she would visit the museum later and learn about this mystery village called Shipden. Josh might like to come too. This would knit into his assignment of collapsed cliffs, sea surges and history.

After her favourite Norfolk lunch of pungent cheeses, smoked fish and saltmarsh flavoured honey on fresh rolls, Carly felt ready for anything. She pulled out her pen and paper, shut the desk drawer slowly and opened her laptop. She needed some inspiration to write up a structure for the next week. A timetable, which she'd take with her today to show Anna and Jack. She could manage three days with Tariq and Tasneem if they would like her to help out. She had one more Zoom class to tutor but was free to help with the children most of the time.

Ah, the Christmas steam train. She'd be able to take her camera. The twins would enjoy taking a train to see Santa and there would even be Christmas food on board like fruit-mince pies and shortbread. She could organize tickets online after she had approval from their grandparents.

Of course, there's always the beach at Cromer, thought Carly. No ice-cream or swimmers but there's sand and fresh, salty air. We'd rug up. The sand would be wet but all the better to build sandcastles. We'd have to choose a day when it wasn't raining, which is almost impossible.

Most tourist attractions would not be operating until summer but there's the library or the movie theatre or a local Christmas pageant. They could wander along the high street and look at the Christmas decorations. There were a couple of good museums, especially the Henry Blog displays. She recalled her visit last year and knew the twins would enjoy the enormous lifeboat in the centre of the main room.

Anna and Jack had told her they had watched the lifeguard volunteers at their weekend training. She had told Carly of the Coastguard warnings on BBC lately. She would check closer to the day as there didn't seem to be any local, immediate problems. Besides, she would keep a watchful eye on the twins, wherever they went.

The plan was finished. Pity she couldn't print it off from her laptop – she must get that printer fixed one day soon. Carly emailed Anna and attached the plan, asking what they thought about it. Then she copied it all into her notebook. She uncrossed her legs, stuffed a hand-written plan into her day backpack and headed for the bus stop under a red-spotted umbrella.

Carly logged out of the virtual workshop on basic digital photography which she'd been Zoom tutoring on her laptop. That was the final session of four classes held over the past few Tuesdays online and she thought how pleased she was with the outcome. One more set of four classes would start next week. Students were all adults with Smartphones, and she showed them all the secrets of ISO, aperture, metering, focus and exposure adjustment and where some of the free photography apps were available to download. All her students had to do now was to submit some of their printed photos for assessment.

It was a regular source of income for her between photography sales and assignments. It not only paid the bills, but she also enjoyed teaching adults what they needed to know to take creative photos with their smartphones. Many of her students had only used their phones to make and receive phone calls. Some said they'd been keen photographers using their cameras but hadn't realized their smartphones were as adjustable as cameras were. A few of her students had just soaked it all up without saying a word.

She'd had a few shy students in the various groups. Probably not used to using a computer to attend classes before. They weren't all oldies either. She noticed that some were young people who had just wanted to listen without offering a comment. Perhaps they were used to one-way communication offered these days with a swipe or click.

She'd noticed one guy with long, dark hair hanging down his forehead, four small black piercings in his lips, wearing casual clothes – which may have been because he was at home. He had a Roman nose, pale skin, and a shadow beard. She didn't think he had uttered one word during the course. He stood out to her because of his impatience with others who wanted to comment or ask questions. His eyes darted back and forth, his hands couldn't keep still, and he constantly moved about in his chair. During one of these occasions, she'd suggested a break in case he'd needed to use the toilet or get a drink of water. Still, she wouldn't dwell on him. She never knew who her students would be, nor their level of knowledge or experience. Or even if they had mental illnesses or struggled with learning methods such as this.

She did know that there was a waiting list for her next four-week course, starting next Tuesday. Her phone rang.

'Hi Josh, good timing. I've just finished my class,' she said, picking up a pen ready to take down some notes. 'Yeah, that's all good. I'll see you the day after tomorrow then. Bye,' she said, pressing the off button.

She'd seen some of the teetering houses along the coast a few times over the past couple of winters. She felt terrible for the owners having to leave their homes. Josh wanted her to take a few photos of one house belonging to a lady who was now in a care home. He'd meet Carly on Thursday, after he'd taken this lady for a drive out to her old house, which was about to tip over the cliff.

Chapter 13 - 1888

The mid-afternoon sun was quite warm when Matthew left the solicitor's building. He adjusted his hat and stepped out onto the footpath. The street was abuzz with shoppers, scattered between carriages pulled by huge horses on the cobbled road. He glanced across the street at the inn where people were enjoying Devonshire teas with baskets full of groceries at their feet. He thought he might join them, so he stepped onto the road to cross. The air smelt of sea salt, and a mix of horses and, as he came closer to the inn, ladies adorned with lavender water. It was quite a contrast to the silence of the solicitor's office as he entered the long-established coaching inn.

'Table for one, please,' he told the owner, who waved at a young girl behind him. She came scurrying from cleaning a table.

'Claire, show this gentleman to table number eight,' he said.

He thanked the waitress, who would've been no older than his own little sister at twelve. She wore a black dress under a starched full apron. The table linen was also starched. A white cloth adorned by a vase of pansies in the centre, resting on a doily.

'The cream tea, please,' he said.

'As you wish, sir,' she said, giving a little curtsy as she turned to walk back to the gentleman at the desk. He wrote into an order book, tore off the carbon copy and handed it to the girl to take it to the kitchen. At the entrance, three young women, who were wearing modern straw bonnets made of velvet and straw, spoke to the owner and he called another maid to show them to their seats.

He watched as they fussed with their long dresses and petticoats and paraphernalia, the trappings of the wealthy.

He turned when he overheard a woman's distraught voice at the door. She appeared to be having some difficulty. It was clear, the owner did not want a single woman coming onto his premises. Maybe, it was presumptuous of her to attempt entry without an escort. His view was obscured by a large floral display, so he could only hear her voice. He thought how unfair it was that a single woman should be turned away on such a hot day. Without thinking too long, he walked to the desk and told the owner she was with him.

'I'm so sorry sir, I had no idea,' said the man. 'Ma'm, my apologies, please come this way. I will escort you to the table myself,' he said.

'That's very kind. Thank you, sir,' said the lady.

She didn't take her eyes off Matthew as they walked over to table eight. Hot scones had arrived at the table. Tea was brewing near the plate of light scones and fresh, clotted cream. He held out a cushioned chair for her and she sat down.

'What would you like to order for the lady, sir?'

'More of the same, please,' he said. 'And make it as quick as you can, so we can eat together.'

The owner, a white towel draped over his arm, turned and hurried away. The girl smiled sheepishly at him, and he looked away, a humility overcame his usual affable personality.

'I know you, sir. How have we met? Mr..?' she asked.

He looked closer at her features. Yes, he felt he knew her too. He would have to think more about this. Before long, they had become more open and relaxed with one another.

'Do you live in Cromer?' he asked.

'No, in London. I was here a year ago in a pleasure boat from Great Yarmouth,' she said. 'But the pleasure was not to be.'

'Were you involved in the accident at the beach?' he asked.

'Yes, I'm afraid I was. So were my brother and several of our friends, she said. 'It was to be a day trip to Cromer, but some of us ended up in the sea. Sadly, my brother, Richard, drowned that day.' She opened her lace purse and took out a handkerchief, wiped her eyes, and blew her nose.

'I was there, on the pier. I saw it all,' he said. It felt rude to stare into her eyes, but he couldn't help himself. He was drawn to her face, to examine her intently.

'Were you? Oh, my goodness.'

'An indelible memory, unfortunately, Miss,' he said. 'I'm so sorry for your loss. Please accept a stranger's condolences.'

'Of course, thank you,' she said. 'It was only this morning that I placed some flowers on my late brother's grave, so forgive me if I appear a bit raw in the moment.'

More tea and scones arrived, delivered by the young girl. She curtsied and offered to pour.

'That'll be all, thank you,' he said.

If he had been given a choice, the whole room would have been emptied to leave him alone with his guest. He couldn't believe his luck. He had searched faces in the streets of Cromer for so long to find this woman, and she had landed in his lap. He didn't want to mess this up now. He reached for the pot of tea.

'Do you have cream or sugar in your tea, Miss?'

'A little of both, thank you. I appreciate your kindness.'

'My pleasure. I think you can rest now, enjoy your tea. I cannot quite believe I'm seeing you again and in such an astonishing situation,' he said. 'May I introduce myself?'

'Yes, please do. I owe you more than you can imagine. I was feeling so alone and upset before you spoke up for me. I don't usually accept invitations from unfamiliar gentlemen, so you might do me the honour of an introduction now.'

'I'm Matthew O'Reilly, at your service, Miss,' he said, watching as her expression changed, and her face softened. 'And I'm in awe of meeting such a fine lady over a pot of tea. Please, indulge me. I wonder if I could ask you to remove your bonnet for a moment?'

She looked alarmed at such a request, amused by his impetuousness. 'Why would you want me to remove my bonnet, sir?'

'Because I think I know you already. Because you and I may not be strangers, although we've never been introduced formally.'

She was curious to understand him, so she looked around the room. Nobody noticed them, so she slowly untied the silk ribbon under her chin and removed her bonnet. Again, she checked the room. People were now starring at her, so it wasn't long before she replaced it.

'Now look what you've done,' she said. 'Was there a reason for you to embarrass me so?' she asked, adding strawberry jam and cream to her scone. It was a light-hearted remark, he decided, so he smiled. In fact, he found it hard not to smile.

'I know who you are, Miss Sarah-Jane Fletcher. There's no hiding from that rough haircut. I don't know if I should admit it or not, but I am responsible for the mess your hair is in. I'm assured it will eventually grow and you'll have your lovely locks back again soon.'

She paused with the knife hovering over her scone. The smell of hot scones cooled by thick, jammy cream.

'What do you mean, Mr O'Reilly?' she asked.

'It was me who dived into the water to save you. It was me who pushed you up for air. It was me who watched as you called your friends from the pier. It was me who covered your shoulders with a blanket and it was me who has continued to search for you since that day. And here you are.'

'Oh, my goodness. Did you also cut my hair away from the rope it was tangled in?' He nodded.

'I hope you don't mind. It was a matter of impossibility. The currents were not kind to your hair, twisting it about the rope as you were turned about.'

'Mind? No, indeed. Not at all. It appears you saved my life, Mr O'Reilly,' she said, her face relaxed into a huge smile. 'I can wear bonnets until my long hair returns. I am glad I was given an opportunity to thank you in person, sir. I'm sorry I didn't recognise you straight away, but I must've been in quite a state. Please don't take offence.'

'Of course. Please, call me Matthew. May I ask if the other young ladies were spared?'

'Yes, they were rescued by some fishermen,' she said.

'I'm so pleased. I heard that most were saved and returned to Yarmouth by train.'

'Yes. That's also what I did after the initial shock had worn off. My friends and I stayed at the Hotel de Paris overnight.'

'That was a good plan, Miss Fletcher. That day was exhausting for everyone, I think.' She nodded, sipped the last of her tea and prepared to leave.

'May we meet again, Matthew? I would enjoy a walk on the promenade with you to discuss this further. My mind would appreciate some clarity.'

He thought how forward this young lady was, but he didn't mind her forthrightness. After all, it was also his desire to see her again.

'Yes, I'd like that too. Can I escort you to your carriage in the meantime? Where are you staying?'

She told him about the guesthouse with the blue windows and blue door in Sheringham on The Boulevarde.

'Perhaps we should meet tomorrow morning if the weather is suitable. I could be ready by ten o'clock, if that is convenient.'

'Yes, that would be excellent, Sarah-Jane. I'll look forward to it,' he said. 'May I collect you at your guesthouse?'

'Why don't we meet here at the inn?' she suggested. As he had made an appointment with his solicitor at nine in the morning to sign his Will, this would be most suitable for him.

'I'll meet you here at ten tomorrow morning then.'

She stood, collected her purse. He stood, nodded.

'Yes, until ten tomorrow. Goodbye, Matthew and thank you very much for everything.'

Matthew watched her leave the room, descend three steps and glance back at him through a lace-defined bay window. He gave a little nod. She was beautiful, even without all her hair. He wondered what his prospects for the future might be with such an adorable wife.

Chapter 14 – 14C

Two years later, Cartia woke up, frightened. It was all happening at once. She sat bolt upright, frozen. It was so dark, she wasn't sure she had her eyes open. The terrible storm crashed around the cottage, a loud knock on their door, a man's urgent voice outside. She wondered if it might be Daniaen returning but realized he would never interrupt their night in such a way. It took a while to realize it was Henry. Mother responded first.

'Coming, son. Don't wake the whole village.'

Eyes adjusting, she could just make out her parent's shapes as they moved around the room. Father felt his way to the door and lifted the latch. Her eyes adjusted gradually to the dark to note that Father still wore his nightcap and had his shirt on, his long bare legs visible in the moonlight. Beyond the woven willow-wall, mother was pulling her day tunic over her chemise. Cartia pulled off her nightcap as she fell from her straw cot. She reached for a blanket and wrapped it around her shoulders.

'Henry, my boy. Come in, come in. Why are you here on such a stormy night?' he asked, pulling him into the dry room. His eyes bulged, and he turned his head frantically from one person to the next. She couldn't make out if he was frightened or excited. Mother came into the main room, fully clothed. She watched the door swivel on the stone at its base. As it was tied to the top of the house frame near the horseshoe, its swing was not easy to manoeuvre so father held the door with two hands and pushed his shoulder against it to avoid icy gusts of wind from wafting into the cottage.

'It's Emma. She's in tormenting pain tonight. Can you come, Mother?'

'Of course, Henry,' she said. 'That's happy news but we must not tarry. Cartia, fetch Mrs Finch. No need to be concerned. Do you have hot water at the ready?' Mother took control of the situation, picked up a bag of clean rags, a knife forged from carbon steel in its hand-stitched leather sheath, a cake of pure white soap and a basin to wash the baby when it arrived.

'Cartia, we need a bundle of rush lights from the shed. Henry, you have tallow lights at your cottage, but the rush lights don't have that fatty smell that can turn a stomach when your wife is in labour.'

'Yes, we have buckets of water in the room. She's been poorly since dusk. Our tallow lighting is a bit dull, and it does have a strong smell,' said Henry. He was pacing about the room, frenzied and yet smiling. 'Cartia, if you get the rush lighting, I'll fetch Mrs Finch and I'll meet you back at my cottage.'

'Yes, Henry. That's good. I'm going to dress first. It's wet and freezing cold,' she said. It was the first time she had been involved in the birth of a baby and was quite thrilled that Emma had asked her to attend. She tossed the blanket on the straw and reached for her warm clothes.

'I am shaking with cold and worry and excitement,' said Henry, dripping into a pool of muddy water near the threshold where, over time, a rut had formed. The storm continued to throw buckets of drenching rain, lightning flashed across the sky, which lit up enough for Cartia to run to the garden shed to find the reed piths which she'd soaked in rendered animal fat just a week ago. They hung from the back shelf of the woodshed to set.

Another two years passed. There was still no sign of Daniaen, but she had been given a message by a traveller, so she knew he was well and working hard.

At Henry's cottage, all was ready for Emma to give birth a second time. The bedroom was like a womb: warm, dark and quiet. The midwife, old Mrs Finch, was hanging religious effigies and covering the windows with tapestries to fill time. She'd brought them all into the world, so the village had a deep respect for the old lady. Cartia and her mother set about helping Emma from her bed and into the birthing chair where Georgie had been born two years ago. The pains were washing over Emma, faster and faster. She puffed and rested, clutching an effigy of St Margaret between contractions. She kept telling Mother that she was so tired and could not do this anymore. Mother whispered soft encouragement to her.

In the living room of the cottage, James and their father supported a worried Henry, while little Georgie was curled up asleep on a straw mattress with a woven blanket wrapped around him. None of the men could enter the birthing room, for the midwife forbade it. She needed peace and prayers. The priest had stayed with the men for a while; prayed and chanted gently to protect both Emma and the new babe. He said he would return at a later hour when the baby was delivered to bless the child and give it a name in baptism. Early in the life of the little one was the best time for baptism in case they did not survive. Cartia knew only two thirds of women and half the babies lived through the birth and the priest was often called in to comfort a family in their darkest hour.

Her legs splayed, and bending forward, she screamed, grit her teeth and held her breath. They all held their breath. The head was now visible, tufts of silver-brown fluff. Emma relaxed a while. Mrs Finch took care to keep the area clean as bright red blood ran down both legs. Cartia noticed how Emma had closed her eyes as she was resting before the final push. Her frown was gone. A minute later, Cartia felt dazed as the baby was delivered and Emma still had her eyes closed, her head bent to one side, unmoving. Quiet. Mrs Finch cut the cord as the baby cried, and she asked for Emma to be moved onto the bed. Emma must have fainted from exhaustion, as her body was loose and floppy when they lifted her from the birthing chair and onto the bed.

Mother was overjoyed as she washed the little girl with the precious soap from Flanders. Mrs Finch seemed agitated, pushing whole towels between Emma's legs and applying pressure. She rested Emma's legs up onto a pillow and wrapped her in a warm blanket.

'Ask your brother to fetch the doctor, Cartia. As quickly as possible.'

'Emma, wake up, you have a little girl,' said Cartia. 'How did you not feel her coming?' Her lips were a pale blue colour, her face was pale.

Mrs Finch looked up. 'Hurry, fetch the doctor,' she said, louder than before, the urgency in her voice sending a chill into the room.

Emma lay still. Her bright red blood was filling the bowl at the end of the bed. The baby cried. She could hear the happy sounds of relief in the adjoining room. She knew Reverend Broun would be coming in to bless the baby after mother cleaned her. So much was happening, yet Emma lay still. She noticed a metallic, fishy smell. She took the new mother by the hand and kissed it. After that, the night was a blur of sadness. She had lost her friend, and her children had lost their mother.

The baby was baptised Emily Jane. Henry was inconsolable. Her brother was twenty-one and a widower with two babies.

Chapter 15 – 2013

Ginny strained to see through torrential rain as the windscreen wipers tried their best to clear her view ahead. Josh's car was parked in the lane at the back of her old property with the engine purring, as they witnessed the demise of her home. It was see-sawing back and forth on the edge of the collapsing precipice, ready to tip into the sea, eighty feet below. She was grateful for the company of this young reporter in his hire car.

'How long have you lived in that cottage, Virginia?' he asked.

It seemed like an eternity, but it was only since she'd moved back to England. She liked his manner and was enjoying listening to the drawl of his words when he spoke. She thought of her husband and her family, whenever she heard an Australian accent. That's the reason she'd given permission for this interview. He was taking notes on his iPad, and she believed he sympathized with her situation. He said he was from a Brisbane newspaper when he arrived at her room, but she'd forgotten its name. She'd look at his business card when she got back to the care home.

'Oh, a long while now, son. My parents owned a stone cottage north of here, but I couldn't live in that. Too many sad memories,' she said. 'My brother's family lives there now. He's a thatcher, like our father, and works with his own son now.'

The gusty wind rocked the car from side to side with a ferocity she understood. The sort of wind that lifts roofs off houses and sinks boats flipped over at sea. It was a different wind here, one that bites your skin with sand, tastes of salt, and caused villages to perish under tons of sea water. She watched him scribbling away at a pretend keyboard and wondered how it all worked. The technology these days left her cold. There was no privacy; strangers wanted all your details, databases ruled that world. Nevertheless, she was still curious. Her world was far less complex now, but it hadn't always been so.

'How does it feel to see your home about to collapse over a cliff? Do you feel sad or angry?' he asked, not looking up from his iPad.

'Not much I can do about it, is there? No point in being angry at the sea or Mother Nature. I feel it's the end of an era for me, I guess,' she said. 'When I bought this house, there were two other streets between the sea and me. Bit by bit, erosion by seawater surges has taken the lot, washed it all away.'

'Were you frightened when you saw the other houses go?'

'Yes, a bit worried. But it gave me time to find something else to move into, and to get the furniture out. The council gave me some money for the block. I got the charity shop to clear the house out in the end. They were very kindly.'

'I'm sure they would've appreciated the gesture, ma'am.'

'Yes.' She went quiet. Outside the car, the noise was loud. Rain pelted against the side of the car and streamed across the window. She remembered that day clearly. Most other things were in and out of her memory within moments, but that stayed solid. She couldn't explain it really, how some things slipped away and some memories refused to go. She remembered the truck backing up, two men filling it with her mother's worn tapestry lounge suite, the oak dining table and chairs, then the two beds. How they stuffed her freshly ironed linen into a few plastic bags and tossed them in the back of the truck as though they shouldn't matter. The old telly went, even though she told them it no longer worked very well. She had stood by and watched her life move on. After they left, the place was empty. She found a broom in the back shed, so she swept it out, left it all nice and tidy.

'Did you keep anything at all? Some photos, maybe?' he asked.

'I hoped to move into a care home when a room became vacant. I'd only had a small room there so I couldn't take much with me at all.'

'Do you have any family nearby? Sons, daughters?'

'My, you ask a lot of questions, young man. Are you sure your Brisbane readers would be interested to know if I have family living nearby?' she laughed. 'They only want to know what interests them and how this news affects them. Twelve thousand miles away, I doubt they'd want to know what happened to me.'

'Perhaps you're right. Australia is a long way from here. I was just curious.'

They sat and watched the teetering building for an hour or so. She wondered if he'd like to join her for a sandwich for lunch. He was a nice young man a long way from Brisbane. She knew what that felt like, being such a long way from home herself in the past.

'Would you like to come back to the care home for a cuppa and a sandwich? It'd be warmer than this and you could ask me more questions for your report, if you want.' She smiled, and he nodded.

'That would be very nice. Thank you.'

The windows fogged up a bit despite the fan pumping warm air through. He took out a cloth from the glovebox and wiped it over the windscreen, put the car into gear and slowly moved forward. She took a last glance at the back of her home as he drove off down the end of the street.

‘How did your Christmas steam train ride go yesterday, Carly? Was it fun?’ asked Josh. Their friendship was growing, she felt, even if it might be a little slow.

The storms had given them some reprieve, though a light shower pitter-pattered on their umbrellas. There was even a break in the clouds so that the light was filtering through enough for her to record the event with some confidence. Josh seemed quite chatty in the car.

‘Oh yeah. I spent the day organising the twins. I took some fun photos to share with you – I’ll show you later. Don’t laugh, but we dressed in fancy dress. I had to remember to peel off my reindeer ears before leaving the station, along with the red nose and eye lashes. It was such a relief to remove those false eye lashes, although the twins laughed as they watched me flapping my long lashes at them. When I first put them on, it was like I was being attacked by a large, black insect!’

‘I wish I’d seen that! You’re a good sport, Carly. I bet the kids thought it was hilarious,’ said Josh. ‘What else is Christmas for, if it’s not for making children laugh?’

They’d been so well behaved and full to the brim with excitement when she’d told them of her plans to go on the Christmas steam train ride. Their grandparents had waited in the car at the other end of the journey to collect them, so it all worked out well.

‘Kids are a great excuse to do the silly things we enjoy, don’t you think?’ said Carly.

'Yes. You're probably right.'

'I need to get a feel for the right angle. What did you say your story here was about?' asked Carly, as they walked down the lane the following weekend with two cameras and a tripod slung around her shoulder.

'It's about how the environment has changed and whether that change is due to natural geology or human intervention or something else. The reason I'm doing it this way, is that local evidence shows there's a long history of these changes. It's not all happening just now and only now. I think it's on a continuum, way longer than we think. Projections into the future don't look good either. I read reports that say up to one hundred buildings could be lost around here by 2105.'

'It's such a huge thing, looking at the whole crumbling coastline. There's been defences put in place, I know, but not everywhere and they don't always last very long,' she said. 'Remember our visit to the museum? I was fascinated to learn about Shipden being under the sea since the fourteenth century. Imagine living back then. It must've been a scary time.'

'Yeah. Things change. But who's to blame? Anyone? Or is it simply that nature is never complacent. Never-ending changes which we just must live with? That's why I've interviewed some of the oldies in the area. Their long memories are priceless.'

'Yeah, they're pretty special in that they've seen things we haven't. I think social history is far more interesting than actual history we learnt at school. You know, dates and kings and stuff.'

'Yes, I agree, I think. Though I did enjoy history lessons too. It taught me how to research properly,' he said. 'It's about listening to scientists who look at long-term history, so we can predict a future. But my story will include real people and how it affected their lives.'

Carly realized she was more a hands-on learner, which was just as well because she did not have the opportunity to go to university. Caring for the family had become her first priority. He probably had a cushy upbringing with university thrown in. She'd had a different type of education, which she felt had made her resilient and taught her she could cope. She didn't regret any of it, although she would've loved to have felt the support of both her parents in her teenage years.

'The weather is clearing a little bit, so let's see if we can get a few photos, Carly. Do you want me to hold an umbrella over the camera?'

'No thanks, Josh. All good. Seems to have cleared up for the moment.'

Josh and Carly folded their umbrellas as they stood together, looking out at the blue horizon, mist hovering between the sky and the sea. There were two distant wind-farms visible, together with several gas platforms just on the edge of their vision. Seagulls glided across the scene, buoyed by an invisible, dynamic lift in the wind.

'I couldn't see any of this earlier,' he observed. 'It's clearly an amazing place to have lived, but the old girl must've been scared to death watching the land give way in front of her.'

'Yeah. Shocking. What made you interview that old lady, Josh?'

'Oh, nothing in particular, really. There've been many lives affected. I've interviewed quite a few people impacted by these surges. If you mean, how did I choose her? Well, in the local news,

I saw a photo of her watching the corner of her beloved bungalow teetering over a cliff and her bathroom on the sand below. That did it for me. I had to find her, so I rang the local paper and spoke to the editor. He was helpful. I suppose I don't represent competition working for a paper so far away,' he said.

'What was it like, bringing her back here?' she asked.

'I thought she might freak out, but she didn't. She was a bit of a character. She'd been through quite a lot in her lifetime. Probably enjoyed getting out of the care home in a car,' he said, his rare smile lighting up his eyes.

He should do that smile more often, Carly thought. He did not relax and enjoy the moment for long. His eyes were on her, probably wondered why she was staring at him. It felt awkward, so she looked away as he spoke.

'To be honest, she seemed settled in her mind about it all. She told me over a cup of coffee that she used to live in Western Australia. Can you imagine? What a different life that would've been.'

She nodded as she put the tripod together for a few more photos. She wondered if this lady might have been someone she knew from back home. Or if this lady knew anyone from Broome. Probably not. Western Australia is a huge place, what were the odds? She was probably from Perth. She recalled how, when people here realized she was Australian, they often asked her if she knew a friend of theirs who lived in Sydney or Melbourne. They had no idea of the immensity of the country. And they often thought kangaroos hopped down every street.

She adjusted the lens of her camera and started recording the remains of the small bungalow. The whole side of the building was gone this morning. She took in the angle of the chalk-lined cliff-face with bathroom essentials spread erratically down to the stony beach. A wet towel caught on a small bush, fluttered about in the wind. Someone's life, their private belongings scattered about for all the world to see.

More than sixty years had passed since the horrific storm of 1953, but Ginny Williams bore the thought with a deep sigh. It all became too much to bear for her so, after twelve long years since the drowning of her baby brothers, she had set sail for new horizons. There had been deep gloomy threads throughout the years since their death. She had decided to cut those threads by migrating to Australia as soon as she could. Cath and Fred, her whole family and her village were sorry to see her leave but understood her pain and the possibility of a brighter future in a country inviting them to emigrate in the early sixties.

In the new country, she'd met and married her Michael, an Australian with a scrappy bush hat made of rabbit fur felt, a wide brim to protect him from the scorching sun. He was known as Mikey to his mates. His teachers at St Mary's College, a Catholic high school in Broome, called him Michael, of course, for that was his Christian name. By the time he was in his twenties, the name Mikey seemed to stick to him like the sticky heat of northern Australian summers.

Mikey was often involved in free-for-alls at the local pub when he'd had a few too many. His mates would sling him out of the pub door to find his way back to his parent's little bush cottage on the edge of Broome. In the mornings, he would sometimes find himself curled into the dusty old sofa on the timber verandah, his Dad giving him a bit of a kick on the way past while he adjusted his own Akubra hat, ready to start his day before the sun came up.

Farming was relentless, but it was a steady living. His father and his grandfather had been farmers since the beginning of white settlement in this area.

At church, inspiration and guidance was in Latin. The kids he went to school with had grown used to the Mass and to one another. They had understood the rituals of the Catholic church, even if they had not understood all the Latin. They knew what was expected of them and attended the youth group on Friday nights. It was the right thing to do, no doubt about that at all. Every single Sunday, without missing a beat, Mikey came to the church to be absolved of his sins and to start anew on Monday.

Ginny first noticed him after Mass, soon after she and Val settled in Broome. He stood under the Golden Wattle near the side of the hall. In her twenties, she had long, dark plaits, which she knotted at the top of her head so the breeze might cool her neck.

She and her friend, Val, had met Peter and Mikey at the local Greek café, a short distance from the church.

'G'day. I saw you at church on Sunday. I'm Pete,' he had said, in a flat tone. 'This is my mate, Mikey Williams."

Ginny had intertwined her fingers. She tightened her grip until the knuckles showed white. Truth be known, although she enjoyed meeting new people, there was something in Mikey's demeanour she felt wary of. She wanted to see a spontaneous smile or a gesture from him. But nothing came. It was as though he seemed trapped, standing behind Pete and glancing over toward her now and again, those dark eyes watching her every move too. These local overtones were lost on her.

'Hi. Nice to meet you. I'm Virginia, but they've always called me Ginny,' she turned to her friend, who had a wide grin from ear to ear. 'This is Val. She's not a Catholic so you haven't seen her at Mass.'

Val shook her head, her blond bob shining like long streaks of sunlight. 'Hi. Groovy shirt you're wearing, Pete.'

Ginny grinned at her friend, now wide-eyed with anticipation of a bit of fun. Flirting was such spontaneous and outrageous fun. Why not? she thought. Even though Ginny felt her impetuous response was a little disconcerting, it accentuated her false courage. Val seemed to be more uninhibited than she was. Different backgrounds, she guessed, for her mother, Cath, had taught her that self-control was always important.

Pete looked at his mate and moved in closer to Val. 'Thanks. Got to keep up the image, you know,' he laughed, moving into a model pose in his psychedelic paisley shirt in maroon and gold. 'So, you're a couple of poms. I'd recognize that accent anywhere. Gotta watch that pale skin up here. You could frizzle up and burn. Which part of England are you from?'

His red hair and blue eyes flitted from Val to Ginny, who were both giggling. Val spoke.

'Ginny's from North Norfolk and I'm from London. We should sound completely different, but I know what you mean. Been here a little while.'

The boys nodded in reply.

'My mother's from Scotland. Edinburgh, I think,' said Pete. 'Would you like to join us for a milkshake or something?'

That explained the red hair and freckles and the advice on sunburn. The other guy, Mikey, was the quiet, silent type when it came to girls. Not much chatter from him. Ginny thought he was handsome and had observed him from afar for some time at Mass on Sundays. She figured she was in safe hands, so to speak. His eyes never left the red dirt under his thongs while Pete took control of the arrangements.

Ginny and Val both agreed to join them and, for the next hour or so, they had all slurped chocolate milkshakes, cold and refreshing from tall, anodized stainless steel cups. Icy beads evaporated and rolled down the outsides of the cup. It was like yesterday. Ginny recalled it all, smiling from her room at the nursing home. She remembered how they had arranged to meet at the picture theatre to watch 'A Hard Day's Night' because that was exactly what the girls wanted to see. Everyone loved the Beatles and their music. She remembered how the boys turned up with a box of Jaffas to eat at half time, while the ad's were on. In those days, everyone who went to the pictures had to stand for the National Anthem and then watch the newsreel. Sometimes they showed another film before half-time. After intermission, they often had a cartoon and then the main movie was shown.

There had been so much anticipation around that movie, and they had enjoyed it. Well, Pete didn't see too much of it, she didn't think. When she glanced over, the wash of lights from the screen fell upon his back. Val didn't seem to mind his attention, so she hadn't said anything at the time. Mikey had not made a move on her this way, although he held her hand after a while. Three weeks later, he had asked her to dance at the local Catholic ball and that was that. They were married the following year and, like all their Catholic friends, began to settle down and start their large families.

A few weeks after Ginny arrived in the town, she learnt the meaning of Pinctada. She had never heard this word, so she was curious as to its meaning. She'd carried a notepad around in her purse to jot down the new words in her new country. She discovered the meaning of 'Pinctada' from the unassuming Mikey. His mother had a special brooch made of mother-of-pearl which had evolved from the inner shell layer of saltwater oysters found in those parts. On their wedding day, he presented Ginny with a velvet box. Inside was a mother-of-pearl necklace with matching earrings to remind her of the first thing they had talked about in Broome and a ring with colourful, local gems and tiny diamonds.

First came baby Carly, in the second year of their marriage, with her thick, dark curls and the rest of the brood followed in quick succession. With years of interrupted sleep, Ginny must have been sleep deprived. Cooking for the family plus all the seasonal farm workers meant every moment of her life was busy. But there were also the good times. Christmas and toothless smiles and fun times. Then, one day, one ordinary, unassuming day when the last child was still a baby, Ginny had to get out of there. Broome, the heat, the storms, the red cliffs and pink sands. The flies, the sandflies, the bugs, the crocs. She had felt like a caged hen. The struggle had been too much for her.

She knew that Mikey would be heartbroken. She knew the older kids were of a decent age to manage themselves and him. She grabbed the youngest and ran. She left a brief note to say that she loved them but had to leave. He would know where to find her, so she didn't leave an address. From her coat pocket, she pulled out a velvet box, opened it one last time to glance at the lovely mother-of-pearl necklace and earrings, slipped off her wedding ring and left it near her note.

Dressed in her finest Sunday-best outfit, she closed the screen door for the final time, stepped off the verandah and hurried down the garden path. The hot sun at noon hid behind a thin wispy cloud. Diffused, muted light burst through a Golden Wattle planted in their front garden. She waited for a taxi at the front gate, moved her fingertip gently over the worn handle of her old leather suitcase which had once again joined her to fly back to the other side of the world. A tear escaped and her hand quickly whisked it away. She re-positioned Kellie on her hip.

She knew that it was what she did not say that would fill their minds with dread for many years after she'd gone. But she could not stay in that place any longer. She could not explain, or she'd cave in and change her mind, as she had done before. She was suffocating. She felt the world was like a continuous hot, sandy desert, and that she had fallen into a hole, grasping a lonely tree root by one hand, dangling into a dark abyss.

All these years later, curled up in a lounge chair in the care home, she could still recall the crunch of crushed Pinctada shells under her sandals and could conjure up the sound of the old church bell, which had been moved into the bell tower of the new church in Broome. It never sounded right anymore. Like her, it did not belong.

Chapter 16 - 1888

It was nine o'clock on the dot. Mr Blake's secretary watered plants in the window-box as Matthew sat in the solicitor's waiting room. The town of Cromer was already awake and ready to begin another day. Matthew had noticed the inn nearby served a few guests for breakfast, but he'd already cooked porridge and tea much earlier, on his portable gas cooker. He was focused on being on time with Mr Blake, and he felt excited to know he would meet Sarah-Jane at ten o'clock at that establishment.

He jumped several stairs at a time bursting with enthusiasm for such a promising day ahead and shocked Mr Blake's secretary when he rushed into the office ten minutes early. While he sat waiting, he thought of Sarah-Jane and the day ahead. After their walk along the new promenade, he might show her his converted bathing machine. He might even open the old box he'd found buried in the shingled sand at the Shipden ruins. That might amuse her. At nine o'clock, he was informed that Mr Blake would see him now.

When the appointment was finished, he shook hands with Mr Blake and thanked him for his efficient work. All done and dusted in such a short time. Mr Blake kept his Will and other documents in his office safe, so Matthew didn't need to carry any paperwork with him on his walk with Sarah-Jane. That pleased him.

Outside, several carriages drove by, pulled by majestic horses. One of them pulled up in front of the inn and he watched as Sarah-Jane was assisted from the carriage by a driver. She was standing opposite him in a crimson and white dress, swathed to her ankles and a blue bonnet covering her cropped hair. She carried a parasol on her gloved wrist, together with a blue purse. He could see everything so clearly from here. She was looking to her left and to her right. Then she saw him on the opposite side of the busy street and gave a little wave.

Suddenly there was a loud noise which sounded like an explosion, but he soon realized it was fireworks, as they lit up the grey sky behind the inn. He wondered why someone had set them off in broad daylight. Maybe it was a test run or someone had set them off by mistake. That was how he felt right now. Fireworks. He returned the wave. He wanted to be with her so they could enjoy the sparkling lights together, so he stepped onto the road, and hoped to cross in the gaps between horses pulling carriages. He saw his opportunity to cross over to her when a fruit and vegetable cart was slowing the traffic.

Another burst of fireworks lit up the sky. He saw her look behind in the direction of the noise and he watched her smile at the display. They would have such an enjoyable day ahead of them.

The two horses, who had plodded along pulling a heavy load, had now sped up. He realized they had been spooked by the fireworks, so he also increased his walking pace. There were several loose cobble stones on the road. He tripped, tried to balance himself and fell. There were abrupt sounds of frightened horses, a driver's loud voice yelling at him to get out of the way, dust, the horses panicked and out-of-control. The painful realization that he could not escape. He curled into a ball and held on.

Sarah-Jane hurried to his aid, rested his bloodied head on her lap. Tears flowed. The horses galloped down the high street and disappeared near St Peter and St Paul's church, fruit and vegetables tossed from the cart in their wake. Men surrounded the poor wounded gentleman, who had been crushed by both the terrified horses and a heavy cart. An off-duty doctor attended soon after and pronounced him dead. She held him close for a few moments before he was taken away by a St John Ambulance Association cart. She knew that her life was about to shatter like a mirror dropped on a tiled floor. Life was now in slow motion.

She glanced up at the embossed window of Messrs Blake and Keith. The solicitor was observing a disturbance in the street below. She could see his horrified expression.

Chapter 17 – 2013

For the past two years, Carly had celebrated Christmas at the guesthouse in Sheringham. She imagined that might be the case again this year, so she pulled out the pen in her backpack and added her name to the list near the front door. She could remove it if something else came up. But she knew she could never be alone on Christmas day. She knew most of the residents so they would enjoy themselves; have a few laughs.

She had become one of the mainstay guests since her arrival in England about three years ago, when she'd turned twenty. The hustle and bustle of London was the destination for most Australian travellers abroad, but she hated city crowds, particularly in summer. It messed with her mind that people from all over the world were zigzagging along the same footpath. All higgledy-piggledy. She'd felt quite overwhelmed. They all had different non-verbal rules for walking in crowds and each person did their own thing. They didn't know whether to walk on the left or the right.

It was the same in London's Underground. She recalled standing on the left travelling down the escalator to the Jubilee Line or the Victoria Line. Deep into the bowels of the earth, people were calm and orderly, which suited her. She had always liked sensible, orderly and organised things. The frustrated man behind her was visibly upset that day because she had stopped him from his frantic rush down the escalator. She had suddenly realized that she was the only one not neatly standing on the right side of the step. Back home, they would've stood on the left. She couldn't get out of London fast enough. Within a week she'd organised her train ticket to Sheringham, and her room at this guesthouse not far from the coast and hadn't returned to London since. She chose Norfolk because her grandparents were from a village along the north-east coast somewhere. Her father used to keep their address but had lost it long ago.

Carly had always wanted to be the heroine and bring her mother home again, but her mother was not easy to find. In fact, she had almost given up looking for her. The only evidence she had to go on was an obscure note she'd left on the kitchen table, together with some jewellery her father had given her mother on their wedding day. Carly wore the ring on her right hand to remind her to always be on the lookout for her mother as she travelled around England.

Recently, she had found a new word. A little hobby of hers; collecting odd words. Her mother had taught her to do that. This word seemed to explain why a person might up-stakes and leave their home and return to where they came from originally. Denizen. Google described a denizen as a person who lived or is found in a particular place. She wondered if Broome had inscribed itself on her mind but maybe not her mother's. She wondered if her mother's reality had been set in a different place and time, before she had landed in Australia back in the sixties. The fifteen years in Broome might have been a struggle her mother had not anticipated when she had married her father. She had been angry with her mother for a long time, but now she believed that everyone had a right to feel content in life, and she longed to speak with her to understand her perspective.

She had thought about this for a long time. Maybe her mother had yearned to return to these green hills and valleys and cobblestone villages for years, but Carly could not recall her ever saying that she had wanted to return. Landscape defined us. It truly never left us. Her mother had exchanged one landscape for a completely unfamiliar one. Even years later, her inner self may have found her new environment so alienated from where she'd come from, she might've longed for the familiarity of home. In her darkest hours, she might've noticed the strangeness of the quality of light as it fell on a building, or the sound of summer insects in the evening. Perhaps she struggled with her sense of self on those occasions and longed to return to her home in England. Had fragments of her memories built up over time, indelibly impressed on her mind?

Carly recalled when her mother displayed some old black and white photographs of her grandparents and their stone cottage with the most beautiful, thatched roof. Back then, Carly had never seen thatching before, and thought all roofs were made of aluminium or tiles. She also mentioned her grandmother's name was Cath and that her grandfather was a thatcher. She recalled a deep sadness washing over her mother's face when she spoke about her childhood.

In Australia, life must've been so different for her. The weather was completely upside-down and even the time of day and the expensive phone toll meant she could rarely phone England. Just once a year, at Christmas. It must've been impossibly hard for her mother, who wouldn't have said anything to upset any of them. She remembered her as a kind woman who was always busy. Hands in sinks, changing nappies, quietly getting on with the job of mothering all those babies. Christmas, in the middle of summer when mother was at home, meant a full English hot roast after church. She always seemed to be in the background, quiet and fulfilling her role with grace and ease. Nobody asked her if she was happy, so we all assumed she was. Even her father was in shock at her sudden disappearance.

Carly sat on the front step of the guest house and watched threatening clouds sail by. She liked the fresh air and hated being cooped up inside. It gave her some time to herself. She thought again about her new word. When she returned to 'her' place, where she grew up, she imagined her own self blurring into other selves. Like when she went to a school reunion once. Most of their discussions were of the many shared, early life experiences. These were not only about classrooms, but the deeper memories of shared space, light, buildings, struggles, sounds, smells, the tuckshop, friends. Temporal connections, also spatial. She considered the boy on her school bus and smiled. He was one of those memories, faint now, warm youthful experiences. Particularly in summer, smells of sweaty teenage bodies crammed into the school bus. All a part of creating a picture of who she was going to grow into.

She rubbed her arms, as the gusty wind picked up litter and tossed it along the footpath. Again, her mind kept pushing to sort out possibilities. Like the wind, it blew in cold gusts and then settled a while. She had learnt much since she moved over here. It gave her time to ponder, to question, to step back and look at situations with more forgiveness. She generally tried to fit the mould carved by expectations of others and she wondered if that was what her mother had done for fifteen years; tried to please everyone else to keep the peace.

The Catholic social structure, which her parents were part of in Broome, meant that the church her parents belonged to had encouraged large families by banning the new contraceptive pill in the sixties. Maybe her mother decided she had too many demands placed on her. Almost in revenge, Carly escaped that structure, those same demands, and thought of herself as carefree, although what does that really mean? She still must pay the rent.

Carly had moved to the other side of the world to get away from the pressures linked to her large family. Every moment she remained within their loving grip, life became more complicated for her. Yes, she admitted missing the laughs and camaraderie, but her mind was relaxed and peaceful here. The quiet was almost tangible. At first, it took a while to adjust to it. Life had been one turbulent drama after another with eight siblings. And it was never neat. One problem dealt with, next one emerging – no, they were overlapping like a map of London's underground. They had shared the experience of life together, but they bore it in isolation.

Warm thoughts of Christmas spent at home in their community were always special to her. She recalled the unity of coming together, shaped by the larger family of the local church. Other families with many children all in happy moods, together at the same time. There was never much money to go around so none of the children had expected expensive gifts. Many were homemade or second-hand, but nobody cared. There were tubs of plasticene, footballs, a baby budgie for the old birdcage, new undies, bright ribbons for long hair, maybe a homemade dress, colouring books, cut-out dolls, jigsaw puzzles, marbles and lollies.

Mothers all over town somehow produced a rare meal of a roast dinner with delicious stuffing and veg in the middle of the long, hot days of summer. Sweat poured from happy brows under paper party hats, recycled each Christmas. A fan clicked above the table, and a sweet caramelising aroma permeated into every corner of the house causing tummies to rumble in anticipation. It did not seem to worry Dad that, just hours earlier, he had wrung the chook's neck, sat under the tree near our front gate and plucked out the feathers.

It was one of those rare moments of peace, when father had us all holding hands around the dinner table before the meal and

Grace was said with a deep sense of compassion. It wasn't so much that he was a deeply religious man but at Christmas, all the joys and realities of a large and healthy family became overwhelming, and he was grateful. Christmas was about spontaneity, sharing, fun but the dominant emotion had been love. Simply, love.

Carly missed her mother's guidance, but she'd been taught well to cook and care for others, like all the girls. Home was always to be a place of sanctuary for this cast of characters with different personalities. There was an exhaustion in learning to negotiate, to share space, to carry each other's burdens. She found it relentless, but this pressure bonded her family together like glue. No bully was brave enough to confront any of them in the schoolyard, for their loyalty to one another was their strength.

That was one of the reasons she had travelled to the other side of the world for a while. Yes, to search for her mother. The other reason was to find herself and to become more aware of her individuality. She considered this self-centred factor a weakness in some people, who only had themselves to consider.

In England's coastal villages, she had found a stillness in the chaos of her busy mind. In photography, she had discovered a stillness of focus and time to reflect on the minutiae of life and nature. No arguments with siblings were a bonus. No close hugs from her younger brothers and sisters, who tussled for best positions whenever she read them a bedtime story. No more baby powder, fresh-out-of-the-bath kids to chase about. The balance was getting better. No more queues for the bathroom. She'd bought a ticket to England and also bought time for herself.

She closed her arms in a hug and remembered, with a jolt, that day when she had returned home from school to an empty house for the first time. No smell of damper cooking in the oven, the stuffiness of a house closed all day in summer, a note on the chrome and Formica kitchen table. The house had felt empty and stretched somehow as she stood alone in the empty kitchen staring across the lino floor.

She wondered how their story could possibly continue without her mother in it. She'd hoped that Mother might somehow come home soon. That she would still bring her joy and pain and laughter and do all the shopping, the cooking, and sorting them all out. Things would keep happening to them because there would be no story resolved without her. Carly felt awash with fear. It was impossible to believe the truth; to truly believe that there would be a final moment to remember her by. It'd felt worse than if she'd died. Her young mind hoped she would return soon, of course, and she hadn't given up that hope until Christmas, exactly ten years ago.

She stood up, brushed away her insecurities, which she'd discovered, don't really go away, and went inside to join the others by the warmth of a crackling fire. There was another view of how life might be lived, and it was right here, right now. Not better or worse than home in Australia; just different.

She blocked the icy wind outside, leaning on the heavy front door. Petunia was sorting out some letters into mailboxes in the foyer. Slotted, timber shelving with room numbers painted in black above the old buffet cabinet. A noticeboard near the mailboxes shared information, like the times to eat meals and a little mud-map to find the old guesthouse so newcomers wouldn't get lost. Carly liked the order of it, even if each mailbox was not much in the way of security. Mostly they remained empty these days but with Christmas approaching, occasionally there were cards and parcels. People tended to write emails these days.

She glanced at her room number. Curious, she retrieved a letter with international stamps lined up neatly in the top right-hand corner. Petunia smiled, 'A nice, fat letter from home then, Miss Carly? How lovely for you.'

'Yes,' she turned to the back of the envelope. 'It's from one of my sisters who hates using a computer. Thanks.'

Carly went to the window seat of the lounge room to read her letter. She didn't feel like sharing her mail with the other two girls in the room. Why would Sally write to her rather than send an email? So silly, really. She shook the envelope and realized there was more than a piece of stationery inside. She slipped her finger into the gap and slid it across the side of the envelope. A letter. And several blue aerograms from England. How strange. The aerograms were all addressed to her Aunty Val in Broome and were wrapped in blue ribbon. Why would Sally be sending Aunty Val's mail to her? She unfolded the letter her sister had written. She wrote that poor Aunty Val had died from breast cancer a few days before. Carly's heart sunk, her focus heightened. Sally wrote that Val had not wanted any of the family to mention her illness to Carly so she wouldn't have to make the decision as to whether or not to travel back to Australia.

Another empty feeling. She didn't know how to respond to this news. Aunty Val had been like a mother to her. The shock of her death numbed her emotions. Her immediate thoughts were that the family needed her, and she was awash with guilt at being so far away. It felt like their world had turned upside-down again. She folded the letter in half, refusing to believe it to be true. The rain had whipped up again, bashing against the tall bay windows. She reached for the folded red blanket and wrapped herself in it.

A while later, she opened the letter from her sister to continue reading through misty eyes. She blew her nose on a tissue she always carried with her and wiped a tear away. Sally wrote that Uncle Fred looked lost and alone, so her father helped with the arrangements. Uncle Fred had given these aerograms to their father. He had told Sally that he didn't know what to do with them. He'd asked her to post them to Carly, as she would know what to do.

In her hands were the flimsy old aerograms, sent at a time when posting mail overseas was very expensive and these had been a cheaper method of communicating. The writing was familiar. She turned to look at the return address. It was from Ginny Williams, her mother. She frantically flipped through the other aerograms. They were all addressed to Aunty Val and written by her mother. The postal imprints were from dates throughout the years between when her mother had left Broome to a Christmas card posted last month. She sat bolt upright in her seat, her hand resting over her thudding heart.

'Carly, are you okay? What's up?' Petunia placed her hand on Carly's shoulder and gave her a gentle hug. 'Is it bad news from home?'

Just breathe.

Chapter 18 – 14C

Every evening, Mother smelt the pork to see if it was rancid, checked the flour had not been visited by rats, and the garden peas were not damp and rotten. Cartia learnt what to look for. Fish was also on the menu most days in their village. Her father, Wills Leman, owned one of the trawlers so there was always fresh fish on the table. They were not permitted to sell fish from their home, but fishermen were able to bring home fish for their families to eat. Most of the fish went to the market after the King's men took their share. Most people she knew ate two meals a day. The first meal was dinner in the mid-morning and supper in the late afternoon.

Cartia worked in the cornfields until mid-morning from the early hours before sunrise, six days a week. Daniaen had not returned nor sent a message to her. She worried that he might never return but did not give up hope entirely. She worked hard to take her mind off him, but the corn was now as high as her head, and she remembered their first moments of love in this very field. Thoughts of beautiful Emma were not very far from her mind as well, but she was expected to carry on. So was Henry. He joined his father's fishing boat crew, and she continued to work on the land.

In a good year, the heads of wheat glowed in a golden haze, moving in rhythmic waves in straight rows all along several long fields. One year they would grow wheat in one field, rye in another and leave the third to lie fallow. After a few hours work from sunrise, most of the villagers walked home in groups to consume the meal prepared in a cauldron for them at home. She was hungry by mid-morning and didn't even mind boiled cabbage with her pork.

'I'm home, Ma,' she called, pushing up the latch. There were no keys in these cottage doors. 'What can I smell? I'm starving.' She smelt before she saw that the cabbage had been boiled for hours. Her mother taught her that green vegetables, when eaten raw, were potentially harmful to eat, so they were all cooked for a long time. Her mother was ladling a soupy mixture of fresh vegetables from their own garden into wooden bowls.

Emma's funeral was held at St Peter's last Friday and she was laid to rest in a grave overlooking the German ocean. Their sadness weighed heavily but they pushed on. Death was commonplace. The child would never know her mother and that troubled the family. Henry would need their support until he found himself a second wife.

It was Wednesday. Villagers are required by the church not to eat animals on Wednesdays, Fridays and Saturdays during Lent and Advent. That would be a sin. Most of the animals were slaughtered in November, before the cold set in, as it was too expensive to feed stock during winter when wheat and vegetables were few. They enjoyed communal feasts at this time when meat was plentiful. If they had an abundance of meat at that time, the leftovers would be salted and stored for winter.

Mother made a maslin of rye and wheat bread for dinner. Nothing is wasted in their home. Any bread left over would be soaked and given to the pigs. In the morning, she milked the goats and churned the milk into cheese. The chickens pecked at the ground, had long lives and provided them with many eggs. When the hens finally stopped laying eggs, they would provide the family with delicious Sunday dinners, but this was a special treat and didn't happen often. They preferred the many eggs which they laid over time.

Late afternoon, supper was served. Cartia was drained after a strenuous day in the fields, and her father and brother were exhausted, fishing out at sea in all conditions. They looked forward to their runny green pottage made from peas and leeks, herbs and salt.

Henry caught a hare in his trap, and it was hanging in the woodshed. After supper, Cartia fetched the hare and brought it to her mother. She will help to flay it, pick the bones clean and put them into a pot with the blood, seethe the pieces and soak them in cold water. Mother could make a broth in the morning from garden vegetables, almond milk from the market, and minced onions. While it's gently boiling over the fire all morning, she will add powder of cloves, cinnamon, mace and a little vinegar. Just before the family comes home for dinner tomorrow, mother will have added the soaked meat and bones to the broth.

There was not much variety in their food, but they were hearty meals.

One Sunday dinner in the summer of 1317, the family enjoyed a roasted pig leg, cooked outside in the warmth of mid-season. Henry added some peat to the fire, while he balanced little Emily on his hip. Georgie was floating his small wooden boat in a water tub and Cartia watched him, her chores finished for the morning. She would always feel an immense hole in their family without Emma. She tried to encourage the children to be happy. She thought they had an amazing way of acceptance and living in the moment. They were so young when Emma died that it was the adults who would miss her the most. Henry was now twenty-four, the two babies were born when he was twenty and twenty-one.

She and her mother cared for both children when Henry could not. Mother said it would get easier as time moved on, and they hoped she was right. The village community helped to supply food or encouragement and much more. Many of their own family had seen the same tragic end to child birthing. There were times he was lost in grief, and they were the worst days. Most days he went to work, sometimes on the family fishing boat and sometimes volunteering as a carpenter at St Peter's church. It was not his trade, but he enjoyed the healing point of focus in carving. Pews now had armrests with intricate designs of corn, wheat, a dog or angels. The angels resembled their beautiful Emma, who was buried in the churchyard.

She watched her brother wipe some mess from three-year old Emily's face. That little face was like a miniature version of Emma. It was unusual for a man to be so tender with children. Their father stood nearby adding lard to the carcass of the pig on the spit. She thought he looked disturbed and a bit embarrassed.

'Have you thought about taking another wife, son?'

'Father, forgive me. I can't do that. I still have a constant ache in my heart. Maybe one day when the children are older.'

'The children deserve to have a mother while they are young and you need a woman to help you raise them,' he said. 'You will miss Emma forever, son. That does not mean her children should go without.'

Henry stoked the fire once more. 'Maybe. I will think on it. Her sister has offered to take the children into her family in Crowmere. That might be best for now,' he said. 'Love is supposed to set you free, but the longer I stay in our cottage, the more I feel trapped. I have much to consider.'

'In the meantime, our family home will be their home when you're at sea. But we are getting old and will not always be able to cope,' he said. 'Emma would want you to be happy.'

'Yes, I know. Thanks, Pa.'

Cartia turned around to see Matilda and James, chasing the twins into the farmyard. Laughter broke the grey mood which had set in. The twins were a little older than Georgie and full of confidence. They raced over to where he was playing and asked to join in. They had brought their own boats which their uncle had carved for them.

'I don't know how you find the time to make their toys, Henry, but they love them,' said his father. Cartia was glad to hear a change of subject before her sister came closer. Matilda was with child again and it upset her to listen to talk about Emma dying in childbirth.

'And I enjoy making them,' said Henry. 'They seem to bring a smile to their little faces, so that's a blessing.'

'Good morning, everyone,' said James, moving over towards the firepit. 'That smells better than anything.'

'James, nice to have your family visit us this fine Sunday,' said her father. 'How is my daughter keeping? How are the prices of corn now? I believe you had a bumper crop this season.'

'Matilda is fine, sir,' he answered. 'You heard right. We had such a good harvest that the price went down a bit from last year. Too much corn flooded the market. It fell to six shillings and eight pence this week.'

'That's still a valuable harvest, James. Well done. The church will be pleased with that tithe.'

'Reverend Broun discussed it with me after today's service, Wills. We must be thankful for the harvest and for plentiful food. There's talk of a drought ahead so I'm considering storing some away; take it to one of the mills to have it ground and stored in sacks. It's the subsidy taxes that are bothersome. I paid two shillings this year.'

'Yes, I heard that too,' said Henry. 'Good work, James. The well near St Peter's will need to be maintained better if there's to be a drought. We need that fresh water when our run-off barrels go dry.'

'Son, that's a good thought and I'll see to it that Reverend Broun is aware of this. It's he who arranges to keep it maintained. We can't leave it to the regulators to do anything. The village is too small, and we are too far away from them, even though James is paying his two shillings tax.'

Cartia slipped her hand through her sister's arm. Matilda looked exhausted but she was still laughing with the children. The girls sat on the bench until their mother called Cartia into the cottage. While her sister rested on the bench with her knitting resting on her bulging stomach, she carried the wooden bowls outside, together with a sharp knife for father to carve the roast. They all washed their hands in the bowl provided near the open fire. Shadows were short. It was about eleven o'clock.

'Henry Leman, you'll have to move yourself and the children from this cottage,' said Cartia, in the firmest voice she could muster. Her brother's stubborn reluctance to any changes in his life upset her. She understood his need to keep his memories of Emma alive but, the truth was clear as the ocean lapped at his gate. Houses in the street in front of him were already under water, having succumbed to advancing tidal surges. It seemed to her the only choice was where to re-build his life.

Henry had been out fishing on father's boat all morning and had spent time transferring their catch to the merchants who came to negotiate a fair price. Cartia watched Georgie and Emily after she finished in the fields. Most of the time, his sister-in-law was able to care for them, but her child was unwell today, so their mother had cared for them. It was a team effort, organised each day. Work had put some routine into Henry's life, something he craved right now. He seemed to be constantly distracted otherwise. A compass without an arrow to point north. His wife had gone, and he was unable to accept her death well, even though many other women in the village suffered the same fate.

'I know, Cartia, I know. It's hard for me. Sometimes the weight of it all is suffocating,' he said, cuddling his daughter to suppress his tears. 'She was my future. Our future. This cottage was a big part of our story.'

She wasn't without sympathy, but he needed to see the truth. His neighbourhood was sinking underneath the grimy ocean. One big storm would be all it would take to wash right over the top of their cottage. She lay her hand on his and placed her cheek on his shoulder.

'Come on, then,' she said. 'Let's start packing up. I've brought some sheets with me today and we can start to move things a little each day until everything is safe. Father has made room in the garden shed as a temporary place to store your belongings. The children will be safer there, Henry. We live closer to Crowmere and beyond the creep of the tides.' She saw him nod his head. 'Our cottage is small, but we'll manage somehow. If you like, I'll fill these sheets, and we'll take them there now. You can stay with us tonight and we'll find alternative accommodation in the days to come. We don't have to do everything straightaway, but you must start now.'

He nodded, wiped his eyes with the back of his hand. He smelt like fish and salt. Most of the fishermen smelt this way, so it was a familiar smell.

'While I collect your bedding, why don't you take the children over to the churchyard to visit Emma's grave? It might ease the pain of moving, not having to watch me pack up.'

'Thank you, Cartia. You're the best sister. I think I will do that,' he said. He held Emily and called Georgie, who was building a sandy heap near the fence, watching seawater run into the rut he had made with his tiny hands.

Cartia could see him in the churchyard, both children sat at his feet near Emma's grave. He had insisted on a plot overlooking the ocean, as Emma had loved to keep watch for his fishing boat every afternoon. His figure was bowed, hat in hand, when a black raven swooped down from the church tower, hovered over him, both silhouetted against the grey sunset. A few drops of rain. She watched as he lifted the children and took shelter in the church. From the porch, he was still staring at her gravestone at the far end of the churchyard.

Chapter 19 – 2013

Carly ordered a takeaway from the coffee shop in Morrison's, near the Cromer railway station. She had been looking for a post office and smelt freshly ground coffee in a café with little red teapot shapes on every surface. She stood waiting for her drink and a baked pastry, admiring their display of unique teapots on several shelves. These days she found that her English friends preferred coffee to tea, and that surprised her. One of the things she recalled were the pots and pots of tea her mother consumed in Broome.

'Here you go, Miss,' he said. 'Nice and hot for a chilly morning.'

She wrapped two hands around the cup.

'Lovely and warm. Thanks. Could you please tell me where the main post office is?' The guest house usually looked after any mail to be posted. She hadn't needed to go to a post office the whole time she'd been in Sheringham.

'Not around here, love. It'll take you ten minutes or so to walk to High Street. It's opposite the church there, next door to the co-op. You could catch a bus, but it's only half a mile,' he pointed left, down Holt Road.

'Oh, near the church. Yeah, I know where that is, thanks,' she said, sipping her coffee.

The parcel of aerograms received from her sister was the real reason to wander around the post office, watching people come and go. There was a possibility her mother might be there to collect her mail from her post office box. She had already called around to the address on the back of most of the aerograms and found new owners living there who hadn't known where the previous owner had moved to. All they could tell her was that her mother had lived in that house for less than a year before she had to sell it. She wondered why she had to sell up so quickly and move somewhere else. Unfortunately, they did not have a forwarding address.

The Christmas card had a post office box number address on the back of the envelope, so she had written a letter to that address last week and hoped her mother would contact her. Every day since she had posted it, she had dropped into the post office and sat on a bench nearby and watched the owners of each post box come to collect their mail. For some reason, her mother was not one of them. Yet.

She stood, sipped her tea from a disposable cup and wondered if she should bother walking to the post office today. Half a mile. She looked at her phone. She still had time to get a bit of exercise and walk into the centre of the town.

Ginny fumbled for her keys in her handbag. Her post box key was detached from her car keys on a separate ring. It'd been quite some time since she'd decided on a post box, and, really, she ought to clip them all together on one ring. It's finding the time, she had told herself. Not that she was really short of the illusion of time now she was in a care home. The car was gone now so why she kept the spare keys in her handbag, she'd never know.

She only kept the post box so her friend in Australia could keep in contact with her. She had written so many letters to her over the years. Such a good friend one would find very difficult to find again in this lifetime. How she missed news of her own children. She must make some arrangements to have the post delivered to her new accommodation at the care home. The admin lady said she wouldn't mind checking her box next time she's in Cromer. I'll take this key to her, so she'll have it on her next time she is at the post office. Now, what was her name again? Funny how her memory could recall things from way back, as clear as if it were yesterday.

Chapter 20 - 1963

It was day three of her journey to the other side of the world. Eighteen-year-old Ginny felt her legs weren't quite so wobbly today, so she ventured out of her cabin, shared with her new friend, Valarie. They'd only known each other for three days but were already the best of friends. She still had to pinch herself to believe she was standing on the ship's deck and watching an endless blue ocean. Here she was, leaning on the outer handrail for support, watching seagulls diving for scraps thrown by the kitchenhand. For more than ten years, she had envied her siblings as they left home. Now it was her turn, and she would go as far away from the sadness of that night as she could possibly go. Australia.

Her older brother took over the family thatching business after his apprenticeship, so he'd stayed in the village.

Father had been very busy in the wake of the tidal surge back in the early fifties. The flood damage along the north-eastern coast had taken its toll, although some things could not be mended at all. Many neighbours had lost their homes to the sea, some of the bungalows needed re-building, most required maintenance. Their old, stone cottage had stood its ground through one of the worst storms in British history. They hadn't realized that the storm was smashing homes, lives, futures, until they emerged from the cottage the following day. For their own family, the loss had been heart-breaking.

They had buried her tiny twin brothers next to their aunt and two cousins in the local churchyard. The villagers never really recovered from their grief. So many were dragged out as their homes collapsed. Others were drowned in their own beds.

Father, Ma and her Uncle Bob were brittle for a very long time. She remembered trying to push her parents to shop for essentials or to cook a meal for the children. If it hadn't been for the caring of the village church, they may not have survived.

In the aftermath, the solid little church was still standing on the hillside, with a few older cottages, including their own. The flood hadn't gone down for weeks, topped up by constant rain. When she was a child, it seemed to her that the rain was never going to stop. She could still recall the putrid smells as the sea backed away, when bodies floated in along the broken shoreline, and so much sadness stuck in her mind.

They had lived upstairs for a year afterward. It was simply uninhabitable downstairs, and the sticky stains and stench were unbearable in winter when all the windows had to be closed. Mould and rising damp became the new challenge until the following summer. How they kept going through that storm and picked themselves up again after, she still wondered. With all that, the family considered themselves fortunate in comparison with others.

She looked beyond the horizon, where the colours intermingled with intense sun diamonds, so brilliant she could not find the edges of the ocean and the sky. A new wave of hope caught her breath. She delighted in the freedom she now had and hoped that the town of Broome would bring her a future where she could be happy again.

In England she had been to college, learnt secretarial work so she would be able to earn her own money and support herself in Australia. Her typewriting skills had already helped her to save enough money for her ten pound fare. Father had written to the priest at the Catholic Church in Broome to say she was coming. Ma had packed a blanket, some linen, and a cookbook. There had been tears at the port but also an abundance of love and good wishes. She would be missed, and she would, in this foreign land, long for their company too, no doubt, but what an adventure she had in front of her. In six weeks, things would be very different; just the way she wanted them to be. Maybe she might meet someone special to settle down in this new country. Maybe.

The girls read that Broome, now, in the sixties, was a bustling and wealthy pearling port, which exported pearl shell around the world. She'd only ever seen her mother's string of pearls which she wore on Sundays to church.

There were talks on board where the speaker showed slides of Western Australia. She and Val found these speakers very exciting and helped prepare them for what she thought Australia would look like. Perth is over a thousand miles from the dusty northern town of Broome. Many of the inhabitants of Broome were from the recent mining boom, some of whom landed from foreign shores just like Val and herself. She felt they wouldn't be lonely when so many others were also new arrivals.

'Val, look over there,' said Ginny, pointing towards the wide bay with a long wharf stretching out to sea.

She and Val had clung to one another since they shared a cabin on the ship. Now they were planning to begin the rest of their lives in Australia and swore to stay together. Maybe get a flat in town.

'That must be the Deepwater Wharf at Entrance Point they spoke about,' said Val. 'Lots of construction still happening there but looks like we'll be landing at it soon.'

The two girls observed the busy port as their cruise liner eased its way in. Tiny waves lapped onto the foreshore and ran along pink coloured sand, rippling in gentle motion towards enormous rocky ledges beyond. There was so much to take in; it was quite overwhelming.

Burnt orange sea cliffs lined the shore, unlike the chalky white bluffs with which she was familiar. These were intense and met the blue sky with rocky strength. Nothing frail about this land, she thought.

'They've nearly finished the wharf,' she said. 'Still lots of workmen and equipment about.'

'It must be the longest timber wharf in the world,' said Val.

'Maybe.'

'These big ships can't pull in too close to the shore, so we'll be landing nearer to this end, won't we?' said Val.

'I think so. I guess we should head back to our cabin and get ourselves sorted out,' said Ginny.

'Welcome to Australia, my friend,' said Val, laughing, giving Ginny's cardigan a tug as she turned to go.

After six weeks on board the ship, Ginny felt a little overwhelmed at the vast scale in front of her. She was acquainted with small villages, moody grey clouds and inhospitable weather. Here, squawking flashes of white seagulls welcomed them with spontaneity, the sunshine dazzled with promise, there was solidity in the soaring cliffs. No doubts at all. This is where she was meant to be. She couldn't wait to buy a postcard to send home to Lizzy and Tom, who had promised to visit her one day. She twisted around and hurried along the deck to reach her cabin. Let the adventure begin.

Chapter 21 – 2013

Josh had set himself up quite nicely in his holiday unit. He had connected to the internet, though it was more expensive than he had imagined. Work would pay for it. His expenses were covered. The one thing he could not control was the constant rain, so the internet was useful for research on those wet days when he was stuck inside. He smelt the chops sizzling in the grill. The loin chops were joined, not separated in the centre as they would've been at home and had cost him thirteen pounds a kilo, so they had better taste as good as they smelt. He'd also bought some Eccles cakes from the pier shop. The buttery, flaky pastry with a sumptuous fruit filling was a local treat, sugar coated.

Yesterday he and Carly had visited the Henry Blogg Museum, where he found information on the history of Cromer's lifeboats and the volunteers, who he had seen practising their skills. He decided to include their heroic efforts in his report as these volunteers had been in battle with the sea for centuries in some form or other. He made a note in his phone to contact the Coxswain for an interview as soon as possible.

Cromer's lifeboats and Coastguard volunteers were all out on Cromer beach when Dave's phone rang. He did not recognise the mobile number, but took the call, a bit annoyed that he hadn't switched off his phone earlier.

'Hello. Coxswain speaking.' The chap said he was a journalist from Australia.

'Okay, yes. I'm quite busy this morning, Josh. We're about to start training sessions. Can I phone you back later this evening? Yes, I have your number on my phone, unless you have a landline you'd prefer me to use. Okay? Thanks for ringing, bye for now.' He switched off his mobile and slipped it into his pocket.

To prevent accidents when the lifeboats were needed the most, part of the routine maintenance and safety practice included a free-fall abandon ship launch. It only happened every three months or so, but it was essential all the equipment required was in good order and that the men were dressed and ready to go, as if it were an actual emergency.

All morning Dave and the crew had been racing to the lifeboats, securing themselves in their seats and commencing the launch procedure up to but not including the actual release of the lifeboat. Too many accidents had already been recorded around the globe where the crew had climbed aboard the lifeboat, discharged the release-hook and the lifeboat fell into the sea too quickly, the unprepared crew hospitalised with back injuries.

'We take this sort of training very seriously,' said Dave, who had been with Cromer Lifeboats in the volunteer crew for ten years. He was facing several novices who looked the part in their new protective gear. 'What do you think, will we have another go?'

Murmurs of polite agreement came from nodding crew members, so they repeated the routine again.

'Let's see if we can all be sitting in the boat with kit on in record time. If someone is drowning out there, they don't want to know you were held up because you had to comb your hair.'

Dave tried to make the simulated conditions as real as possible. It was essential these men came back for more and so he made it enjoyable for them as well. He had been on enough operating crews to know how frightening it was out there in a storm.

'You local lads will recall the tolling of the underwater bells of St Peter's.'

'I used to hear those bells regularly,' said one of the new chaps. 'It was eerie how we knew it couldn't be happening, but nevertheless, there it was. My brother and I used to hide under the bed and listen intently on a stormy night. Sometimes it was there, sometimes it was not but I have heard the bells in the middle of a storm.'

'Why is that so strange? Does someone ring the church bell?' Another newbie.

'Not St Peter and St Paul's church, mind you,' said Tom. 'As the story goes, it's the bells from Shipden. St Peter's collapsed over the cliff, hundreds of years ago. The whole village too. The church with its belltower went last and it's still there.' He pointed out to sea, his eyes glassing over. 'About two miles west of the pier.'

'And you say you can hear the bells ringing?' asked Henry.

'I can only speak for myself and my brother. We were born here.'

'I was born in Yarmouth. I haven't heard any bells since I've moved to this area.'

'They tell me that children hear the bells more than adults. Maybe that's true.'

'Anyway, I'm about to blow my whistle not a bell. Are you ready?' asked Dave. True or not, this was a conversation which might take up the afternoon, and he wanted to get home for lunch.

He lifted the whistle to his lips and blew. As they ran about, he timed them.

'Great work, chaps. Our timing is getting much faster each time we do it. Next month a lifeboat will be launched by free-fall from the lifeboat station with only the operating crew on board. Some of you might like to join that crew if you feel confident enough.'

'If we come back again next week to do it all again for a couple of hours, I should be right by then,' said Sean. 'I wouldn't like it to be the real thing and not have had any experience in launching the boat.'

'Right. Fair enough,' said Dave. He also introduced them to Cromer's set-up. 'The station operates two lifeboats - one for inshore work and the other for offshore work mainly. Just a bit of history for you to think about, and then I'll let you wander through the Henry Blogg Museum over there. Welcome aboard.'

'Thanks, Dave. I enjoyed that.'

'Me too. I'll be here next week.'

'Okay, guys. Henry, if you're from Great Yarmouth, you should look up what happened to a boat called The Victoria in the eighteen hundreds. It came from there, like you. It met with the church tower we spoke about earlier,' said Dave.

Cromer lifeboat station stood proudly against the North Sea, its deep waters lapping at hardwood boulders of the pier. When the call to duty came about, the all-weather Tamer boat would be released from quite a height, straight into the sea, down a slipway. Once in the water, an inflatable boat sits on the transom ready to be deployed for an emergency rescue.

Dave glanced over toward the onshore building, now with deep blue doors, looking cheerful. He thought its age was showing proudly and it was right on the shoreline, very handy to everything. For the past couple of years, it had stored the current inflatable lifeboat with no rigid hull plus all the safety helmets and wet-weather gear. He had seen this one operating quite a few times and had a deep respect for the little craft.

Dave looked around the men as they wandered off. Some were too old for this type of physical activity, some too young and a few scattered in the middle age group which he would probably choose as crew in an emergency. But the others had their place too. Including them all in training kept them fit and healthy, gave them something to be proud of and they did enjoy the camaraderie that went along with voluntary work.

This day was like any other Saturday, when the public used the beach for walking their dogs. He had seen plenty of weekends go by without the need to launch a rescue, but it only took one tragedy on one day. Any death was one too many.

'So, thanks for coming along today, chaps.'

The following weekend, he was pleased to note that the novices had returned.

'Before we go out in the inflatable, I'd like to go through what we did last weekend, if you don't mind. Repeating myself a million times helps you when the odds are against you out in a dangerous sea. You might even thank me one day.'

The men appreciated the lightness of his classes. Most had been working all week, had families of their own to support.

‘Okay. If you were living along this coastline in December of fifty-three, you would remember the storm of that year. The sea surge was one of the biggest in living memory, when flood water swept down the coast killing over three hundred people,’ he said, pausing for a moment to allow this to sink in. ‘That’s why we’re going to get this right.’

He read aloud the words written on the handout each volunteer held tightly,

‘One. Check equipment and documentation to ensure that all components of the lifeboat and launching appliance are in good operational condition.

Two...’

‘So, any questions before we get into our wet gear?’ He paused. There were no questions. ‘Okay. Today we have a slight wind; thirty knots and a bit of light rain. You know the wind can turn to a gale at any time, especially in winter. Good time to practise what you’ve learnt. What do you say?’

William, Henry and Sam were the first to volunteer to go out with him. The others watched on the bench. All the men were chatting about local events while they shared the change room to be fitted out.

‘Right. You have two minutes to don your kit. Go!’

When they pulled on their yellow wellies over waterproof pants, none of them knew what was about to happen in the very near future.

Chapter 22 – 14C

By the time Henry's cottage was empty, tides had crept further inland, covered his fence and lapped at the walls of all the cottages along his street. Neighbours had filled their carts with furnishings and family and set off for nearby Crowmere, Blakeney or as far away inland as Alysham. Every evening, he became more restless, and Cartia felt it was unlike him to be this way. She would keep a keen eye on him as his grief had not left him. Shipden was being swallowed by each wave trickling along its beach and in winter, by waves of tremendous size and strength as they came crashing further and further inland.

'The stone foundations will be all that's left soon,' he said one night after supper. 'All that work for nothing. No home, no wife.'

Mother put an arm around his shoulders. 'Life has dealt you quite a blow, Henry. We all feel for your losses. It's a dark time for us all.'

'The fishing has been good of late,' her father said. 'Yes, that's about all. No, there's the health of Matilda's young ones and Georgie and little Emily. We can stand up and be thankful for that. So many other folk have been struck down with sickness.'

'Yes, we should remember to be thankful. Praise be to God,' said her mother.

It was early evening, when Matilda and James arrived at the farmyard with her new son, their twins gripping her skirt. James was smiling.

'We have news. I have had permission to build a cottage at the other end of my land. The ocean will never encroach upon Crowmere property. We're too far from the water, so we would like to offer it to you, Henry, if you'll allow us, to build another home for you and the children. We will all help you, my friend.'

Cartia knew she had tears welling in her eyes, watching the family hugging each other. Matilda noticed her wiping her cheek and held her for a few moments.

'It's alright. It's a wonderful gift. These are happy tears,' she said.

Henry had stood up, eyes wide, staring at James and Matilda. He struggled to find the words he needed, but he would do so in time. Mother asked for calm so the smaller children would not wake. Henry lifted the latch and went outside, moonlight falling on his path to guide his way to Emma's gravestone. Cartia followed in silence, knowing his intention. A storm was brewing; the northerly wind gathered dry leaves and whirled them along the road. He sat on the precipice of the graveyard overlooking the sea below. Waves grew in intensity. The sea had imposed itself onto his life. The sea, persistent in its rage, crashed against cliffs which had once been a gentle incline full of wildflowers in summer months. Now it was all gone, a chalky cliff faced the might of the ocean.

'Take me too!' he called, standing now with his arms outstretched. A gust of icy wind whirled around him, showering sea spray until he was soaked. Horrified, she watched him collapse, crying loudly. The raven squawked from his nest in the tower of St Peter's.

She ran through the rain, gathered him up and pulled him away from the edge.

'No, Henry. This is not the right way. Come. Let's go home.' He might've been surprised to see her nearby, but he didn't say. He pushed dripping hair from his eyes and let her lead him through the churchyard, past the well, up the cobbled street and back to the cottage on the far edge of Shipden.

Chapter 23 – 2013

'Maybe she's passed away. Sorry to be so blunt,' said Josh, trying to be helpful. His voice was kind, conciliatory. They had returned from a busy day capturing the collapsed cliff from all angles. The house teetering on the top, the bathroom scattered below. She explained about the aerograms from her sister, and the recent enquiries she had made with the post office. For privacy reasons, they would not give her any details of the person who rented the post box.

'I'm sorry, Carly, but that has to be a possibility, considering you actually wrote her a letter and she hasn't responded.'

She stared into his eyes, then glanced away to gather her scattered thoughts like they were wisps of butterfly wings caught on a breeze. Truth is, she had already thought of that too but did not want to give up hope just yet. It was not that her mother was very old. She would probably be in her mid-forties, early fifties. It is a thought she had when she was informed of Aunty Val's death from cancer. The aerograms showed that she was very much alive when she had written them. She'd appeared to be in excellent health and her mother seemed very pleased to read the family news which they'd shared with each another over the years. Of course, she only had half the conversation – her mother's. She liked to imagine that there was another pile of aerograms written by Aunty Val with a pretty pink ribbon around them, somewhere in a drawer in England.

Through the written tone and voice of her mother, she listened to her innermost feelings expressed to her best friend. It was through these words that Carly was able to piece together what had happened all those years ago. How unhappy she had been in Australia, so far from her home in England. It seems she'd returned to care for her parents in their old age, for both died soon after she had arrived in England, so she assumed the guilt of living so far from them in their hour of need was simply the last straw. She had taken her baby and returned to England. She wrote that she had to go, the pull was far too great. In one of the more recent aerograms, Ginny mentioned a heart condition she had been diagnosed with. It was then impossible to fly back to Australia, so she had decided to stay. But Carly wondered what had happened to her baby sister. Why hadn't she let father know of her whereabouts? There were questions still unanswered. She wondered if these questions would ever be answered.

Josh finished checking his phone, stood and pulled his backpack onto broad shoulders.

'Those photos should be sorted through tonight, Carly, if you have time,' he said. 'I'll be sending part of the article in about lunchtime tomorrow.'

'Yeah, okay. No problem. I'll put the better ones on a cloud by morning. I'll send you a link.'

'Thanks. You should also put together an invoice and I'll send it at the same time.'

'Yep, gotcha,' she said. The smile stretched across her face before she could think about it. She would love him to smile back but he was a person who just wanted to get on with the job. He always seemed to have a wall up between himself and others. Like some sort of protective barrier. She wished he'd drop the drama and just relax a bit. What did he need protection from? Chill out. Still, this was good money, and she always enjoyed capturing the scene for his articles. Truth is, she'd love to be the scene he wanted to capture.

This latest story was interesting, and they'd be following it up with an interview down the track a bit. The lady who lost her home to the sea now lived in some sort of care home.

It was like watching a younger version of herself walking towards her while she waited for Josh outside the foyer of the care home. Carly glanced away before the girl might take offence at her staring.

He wasn't late, she was early. She managed to get a lift from one of the Americans staying at the guesthouse, so she would catch the bus over to Holt when they finished the interview. She hoped it wouldn't take too long. She planned to take the twins to the beach this afternoon, even though it was a dull day with storms predicted. As she waited, spits of rain gathered in the gusty wind. The world was supposed to be warming up but definitely not today. No point in planning an outing around the weather over here. You'd never do anything as it's always miserable in December.

The teenage girl was quite close now, about to walk past where she sat on the bench. The girl's dark plaits were just as her own thick hair looked whenever she used to plait her hair, dark curls escaping along the strands to her waist. She had been dropped off at the entrance driveway, from a car with a cute, thatched cottage logo emblazoned along the side panel.

The young girl glanced her way as she walked past, looked back at her and broke out in a smile. She had a confidence in her step which Carly hadn't had. She was tall for her age and must've been no more than ten or eleven on closer evaluation. The electronic doors parted. She entered the foyer and closed her umbrella.

Down the road a bit, the car had pulled into a curb. One of the odd things about living in England was car parking rules. She couldn't get used to cars parked against the direction of the traffic. She had watched as it squeezed itself into a space, both cars facing each other on the same side of the road. If headlights were eyes, it would look like the cars were having a chat. A tall man opened the car door near the footpath, aligned it with the gutter, switched off the engine and retrieved a bag from the back seat. He tucked his scarf into his coat, opened his umbrella and quickly crossed the street to follow the young girl into the care home.

He walked straight past Carly, head held low, frown deepening as he paced closer to the doors. Then he vanished inside. She rubbed her arms and hoped Josh wouldn't be much longer. Several other visitors rushed by her. One of them sat on the other end of her bench. He was a bit dishevelled. Without looking up in an obvious way, she hoped the wind would change direction. She pulled out her mobile phone and sent Josh a message, to remind him it was chilly waiting for him. He was five minutes late. As she closed her phone, she glanced over to the roadside and saw Josh, who was standing outside a taxi, and about to respond to her message.

'Over here, Josh,' she called, waving from the shelter of the drive-through. He waved and hurried along the path. She took a few steps away from the bench and nodded to the chap near her. He wore dirty, red sneakers and a thick overcoat with the collar turned upward to cover his ears. She noticed the lip piercings as the wind gusted and flipped his greasy hair up. He looked familiar. No, just a layabout avoiding the rain.

He was soon forgotten when she set to work. As Josh was about to interview the lady from the care home, she adjusted her equipment onto a tripod in the visitor's lounge on the first floor. The usual musty, sour smell of a closed building and sounds from a family of visitors across the other side of the vast room. A heater with wood burning fiercely behind a small glass window, reflected a warm glow onto Josh's face when she checked the focus on her camera. He checked his notes, pulled out a pen from his shirt pocket. She was used to his no-nonsense style now, though she often wondered why he appeared to her as cold at times. When they were alone, they enjoyed each other's company. If only she could penetrate that invisible wall he put up whenever they got closer. Two Aussies, stranded on an island together. They should snap together like pieces of jigsaw. It was a puzzle, that's for sure.

Josh stood up, his whole face smiled in recognition of this lady coming towards him. She dressed in warm trousers and a handknit, mohair jumper and looked pleased to see him again. The nurse assistant helped her to sit in the lounge next to the tall man she had seen entering the building earlier and the young girl with the plaits. The lady's hair had greyed, she seemed short of breath, even in the wheelchair. Josh positioned himself in front of her, Carly behind him with her camera already taking photos of the occasion. She assumed they were this woman's family, and she was right. Josh introduced himself to them and also introduced her as his photojournalist. They gave their names as Tom and Kellie.

'I'm really just a photographer for the newspaper articles Josh writes here. But thanks for the compliment, Josh,' she said, shaking the hand of the man on the lounge. 'Is it okay if I take a few photos while the interview takes place?'

'No problem at all, lass,' he said, pausing for a moment. 'Have we met before somewhere?'

'No, I don't think so,' she said, adjusting her tripod for a wider shot.

'Could've sworn I'd seen you before. I don't usually forget a face.'

She looked up and grinned. No, she was pretty sure the first time they had met was when he rushed past her downstairs earlier. He was probably just trying to make polite conversation.

'Okay. Can we begin?' asked Josh, as he switched on his recording app and placed his phone on the coffee table in front of them.

'Yes, then we can all enjoy a cup of tea,' said the older lady. 'But, before we do, I'd like to ask Carly about her ring.'

Josh turned to face her, and they both looked down at her ring.

'Of course,' she said, holding out her hand to display the ring. It was an unusual ring with colourful stones haphazardly scattered along the gold base with small diamonds between each coloured stone. Her father had given it to her before she left Australia, as a gift for her upcoming twenty-first birthday.

The girl was called Kellie. She stood up and took a closer look. 'It's really pretty.'

'Thanks, it belonged to my mother,' she told her. 'It's part of a mother-of-pearl jewellery set. My sisters will get the other pieces when they turn twenty-one.'

They were all interested in it for a few moments, but she noticed Josh from the corner of her eye, shifting in his seat. She retracted her hand and returned to the camera, at the same time as the lady started breathing heavily and when she looked in her direction, she saw her eyes fixed on her hand, her ring. She glanced at Josh to see what he'd do. He called the nurse over, as the lady held her hand to her heart. She heard her cough a few times, gasping for breath.

Kellie jumped up, rushed over to the woman, who was now in obvious distress. Her breathing was too fast and audible. She was puffing like she had been in a marathon. The nurse got the wheelchair and assisted her into it.

'I'm sorry, young man,' said the nurse. 'Maybe another day?' The last they saw of her, she was wheeled down the corridor to her room. Soon after, another more senior nurse scurried through the lounge, and down the corridor.

'What happened?' asked Josh. 'Is she alright?'

Kellie gripped her uncle's arm, her face pale. 'Can we go down to her room, Uncle Tom?'

'Not yet, Kel. Let's wait until the nurses have gone.'

He turned to Josh. 'Sorry about your interview, Josh. Perhaps we'd better call it a day. If you like, I could contact you when my sister's more up to it. It's her heart, you know. That's why she's in here really. She's quite young to be in a care home but she needs twenty-four-hour care now.'

'Absolutely, mate. I'm in no hurry. We could come back whenever it's convenient for her,' said Josh. He switched off the recording app and returned the phone to his coat pocket. Carly had just noticed he'd worn a suit for this occasion and thought that was perhaps a little formal. Maybe it was his formality which caused the episode for the poor woman with heart problems. It had all happened so quickly. She hadn't really seen the woman's face, as the lady had sat in front of Josh, who obscured her view. Other than his formality, she had no idea what had happened to cause such an emergency. Well, at least she'd be on time to catch the bus to Holt and take the twins to the beach for an hour or so.

'You want a lift home, Carly? Share my taxi?' Josh asked, as she carefully packed away her equipment.

'No thanks, Josh,' she said. 'I'm going to catch the bus to pick up the twins from Holt. Believe it or not, we planned a trip to the beach today. Not exactly the weather for it, eh?'

'No, not really. You're not planning for a swim are you?'

'Of course not. Just a muck about in the sand and a bit of a walk along the promenade to the pier for a treat.'

'I bet they love to see you coming up the road. One outdoor adventure after another!'

'I suppose so. Better than being stuck indoors, which is what most sensible people do on days like today.'

'Then let me at least carry your tripod and camera bag. You can collect it later.'

'Actually, that would be very helpful. Thanks, Josh,' she said. 'Let me know when you want to do this interview. Might be a couple of days, I guess.'

'Yeah. I'll text you. She didn't look well, did she? Still, they didn't call an ambulance, so I assume that sort of thing has happened to her before. Glad she was okay when I drove her out to see her house recently.'

'Oh, don't even think about it. Scary. I'm sure they'll contact you soon. What else did you have planned for today, Josh?'

'Think I'll try to do that interview with the lifeguard chap.'

'Right. I'll be somewhere on the beach with the twins, so not far from there.'

Chapter 24 – 2013

Carly didn't know where to look now, though she was on a constant vigil for sounds, running from the pier toward the beach huts as the storm returned with a vengeance. If only the twins would call out. Silence was the enemy, not that it was quiet with the gale-force winds howling, the angry sea throwing seawater at the tidal wave defences in front of her. She monitored the beach huts remaining. She was almost sure she saw Tariq go into the blue one but couldn't be sure. She watched the sea consume the remains of summer 2013. Waves funnelled along seaward walls north of the promenade, huge waves flew into the air, unable to escape in retreat and filled every space between there and the cliff edge fronting the town.

Tears mingled with sea-spray, her hair matted, and her body was beyond cold; her fingers numb. She tried to slip into drifting waters which swirled around a wooden door but pulled back as one end of the door sank into a whirlpool. She wrung her hands together, called out, but the wind swallowed the sound of her voice. She turned to face the cliff, the cold wind blew against her back. She bent forward on her knees, dry-retching, and spat out the salty taste from her mouth. In the distance, a muffled noise.

Above the sounds of squawking birds, howling wind, crashing waves, she thought she heard a faint, frightened scream.

She leant toward the beach huts, ears pricked, waiting for more. But nothing. Maybe it was not a scream. How could she be sure? She lay flat on a rock and listened intently, watching seawater steal the door from one of the remaining beach huts.

The noise was deafening.

'Tasneem? Tariq? Where are you?' Carly screamed, her call swallowed by an angry North Sea in December.

Strong currents pulled on the brightly coloured doors of beach huts and threw timber planks high above crashing waves, plummeting into the turbulent sea. Through rolling sea-mist and driving winds, Carly lay flat on the rocky edifice, her eyes darting among the debris of beach towels being sucked under a wave. Plastic beach toys and timber floated on the ebb and crashed down on the rocks. She covered her ears with her frozen hands, the wind raced along her spine, and her clothes were soaked through. Yet another wave pushed itself from blackened depths and burst into the retreating power of the ocean, this time throwing collapsible chairs against the next wave and smashing them to pieces above her head. Tinsel from an ornamental Christmas tree and seaweed twisted. Red baubles floated in gathering jetsam, jammed between crevices of rocks nearby.

Furious and wiping away welling tears, she screamed again and again into the place where the twins had been heard just minutes before. Her heart racing, she glanced either side of where she was crouched on her knees. The scattering of families walking along the promenade had left the area. The man with his dog, gone to find shelter. She had never felt so alone. So cold, numb.

'Help! We need help!'

Sharp gusts whipped her hair from its ponytail and plastered it to her head. She struggled to stand but was knocked over twice, the second time she lost her grip on the surface of the rock which caused her legs to slip off the rocky surface. Her ankle smarted. She pulled herself back up, her eyes never leaving the surface of the water below, her voice now scratchy, her throat feeling taut, sore.

She needed to get help fast. Chances of saving the twins were dwindling with every wave, every moment. She put her hand on her chest to relax her racing heart.

Her other hand reached into the back pocket of her jeans and retrieved her mobile phone. She squinted through the sea spray, salt settling on the screen as soon as she flipped open the lid. Again, her eyes studied the water for any sign of the children, her ears listening for any feeble sound that might be one of them calling her. She couldn't feel her fingers but managed to key in the emergency number 999. Or was it 112 or 000? A flash of doubt. One of them was the European emergency number. Whatever. Why didn't they all have the same emergency number? 999 was ringing. A sense of temporary relief washed over her. A steady voice answered quickly. Her eyes re-focused on the sea crashing along the coastline. A beach ball, a few towels. More summer remnants from inside the beach huts tipping the waves or being dragging under.

'Emergency. How may I help you?'

How can she be so calm? Doesn't she know of the calamity happening down here? Breathe, just breathe.

'Coastguard, I think.'

'Calling the Coastguard emergency now. Where are you madam?'

'At the beach huts in Cromer, just south of the pier.'

'What is your emergency please?'

'Two children were in a beach hut and now the sea is destroying the huts. I can't find them!'

'I have contacted the lifeguards, madam. They will be on their way. Estimated time of arrival between five and eight minutes.'

A strange sense of relief washed over her. She felt trapped between calm and fear. She closed the phone and returned it to her pocket, looked up at the tall figure of a man silhouetted against the eerie skyline and running towards her. It was Josh.

Dave watched the BBC weather report with intent. He wasn't someone who watched much telly but tonight was different. He couldn't get enough of it. The news was dominated by deteriorating weather conditions along the coast. His wife joined him on the lounge. He could smell brewed tea, her floral perfume, the sweet roasting vegetables in the adjoining room and he was reminded of the aromas and warm comforts of home. A fire crackled and spat in the grate, dispersing a reddish glow on their upturned faces, focused on the latest storm reports.

He felt impatient and uneasy. Couldn't sit still. He jumped up again to put more wood on the fire. In all his years as a lifeguard, he always felt edgy when storms turned ugly like this one. Outside, the teeming rain slashed across the windows of their cottage, the door rattled, the wind howled.

'Sit down, love. You won't solve anything by pacing about.'

He sat down again. 'Sorry love, but I just have this feeling I can't shake off.'

'That's okay. Nothing has happened or you'd have had a call.'

'Yeah, I know.'

He took out his mobile phone and scrolled through posts. His brother was holidaying in Thailand so a few photos of sunny days, warm white beaches, and paper umbrella villages. Good for him, but that distraction didn't help. He read a few other posts but found his mind simply had too many tabs open and he couldn't concentrate to read the messages, so he slammed it shut. A small tree branch whipped at the front window, causing him to turn toward the sound, startled.

'Oh, Dave. Now look what you've done. My tea is spilt all over the carpet.'

'So sorry, Merl. Here, let me help you wipe it up.'

He reached for one of the towels drying on the clothes airer nearby and dabbed the carpet. He felt quite pleased to have something to do but didn't tell Merl that. She was now in a fluster because he used her best white towel to mop up the spillage.

The call finally rattled him into action. Adrenalin was already pumping through his veins in overdrive. Dave flew out the front door, mobile phone at his ear, keys rattling in his hand.

'Yes, got that. Thanks. On my way. Get onto the Launching Authority immediately. We need their permission. In the meantime, have you contacted the rest of the crew?'

'Be careful, Dave,' Merl called after him, closing the door to the easterly gale. He switched on the engine and waved to his wife, who stood at the window like she always had.

A tree had fallen on a distribution box in Thetford and caused it to explode. Several power lines were brought down. Thousands of residents in Norfolk lost power. With only candlelight in the shed, the men who had already arrived before Dave, had changed into their all-weather gear. The generator would be required today, so Dave moved to arrange this immediately.

'Hi, Dave,' a chorus of mumbles as he raced passed. He was not surprised to see that these particular men had arrived earlier as they lived nearby.

'Cars skidding across the road to avoid power poles. What a rough storm!'

'Glad you made it, Dave.'

He had listened to reports on the car radio to keep pace with the storm's damage. The RNLI has warned that people may die if they ignore the Met Office weather warnings. Although this was not unusual for the Norfolk coast area, it always put him on high alert for dangers at sea.

'Yeah, I'm glad you made it, too. Explosive wind pushed my car like a Tonka toy. Do we have a mechanic on board yet?'

'Yes, Dave. Kit on and ready to go,' replied Matt.

Dave, a coxswain who had steered his way through many storms, knew of the danger should the engine in the lifeboat play up during a rescue at sea. The Met Office announced a wind warning was in force so he'd been anxious all day, waiting for these moments, knowing someone would need to be rescued.

'Check each other's safety equipment,' he said. 'Especially the life jackets.'

Within two minutes, Dave had arranged for the generator to be switched on, was zipping up his wet weather coat and clipping his helmet in place. He looked around the room, saw the last man slipping on his wellies. They had practised this manoeuvre many times, so everyone raced ahead feeling confident and pumped.

Heavy rain lashed the Coastguard station where the boat was stored and ready to launch. He waited for the operations people to open the gates and release the switch to lower their boat. Several of the men were new to this experience so they were sitting near the mid-section and checking their equipment.

'Geez. Glad we had all that rehearsal time, Dave.'

'It always pays off.'

'Practice makes perfect. At least we hope it does.'

'Yeah.' The rest of the Rescue Team arrived, already soaking wet and on high alert but only seven crew members were required in the lifeboat. Excitement and anticipation were running high.

A loud noise as the bright orange lifeboat launched down the ramp, slipping effortlessly into a high and furious sea. The men held tight, bending low in the boat and glowing bright blue on and off against a pitch-black sky. He felt the front of the lifeboat slip into a wild sea, got it balanced and steered it north. He noted that five minutes had passed. All good so far. Enough men had arrived in time to launch the rescue, the others remained behind, ready to join them if necessary, in the four-wheel drive or the inflatable. An ambulance had already been activated and should arrive on or near the beach soon.

The operations team spoke clearly through the Automated Information System.

'Dave, you'll notice a young woman by the name of Carly Williams on the northern end of Cromer beach, right next to the beach huts at this side of the path, which is covered in deep seawater and she's near the rocks. She reported two small children missing. They were last heard calling from the blue beach hut approximately five minutes ago. She advised that there were two beach huts remaining upright with sea water lapping halfway up the door, stopping access to the hut. There are no windows. Over.' He found it difficult to hear through the noisy storm and the riotous sea lapping at the lifeboat. He directed the boat north-east to have the wind behind them as he fronted the rocks.

'Operations. Thank you. I'm listening. So, is there anyone else with Carly?'

'No. I don't think so. I have no further information.'

'Let me know when the ambulance arrives. Too dangerous at the moment inshore for the helicopter.'

'Yes. Understood.'

'We're navigating on a reach across breaking waves; they can roll a boat over if we're not careful. Then we'd all be in trouble,' he called. He kept a close watch on the crew, who were faced with six to eight metre sea swells and wind coming from an adjacent direction. Winds were consistently blowing thirty-five to forty-five knots, and they were being hit with gusts in the high fifties. Basically, Dave knew they were stuck in one big ocean-sized washing machine.

'Pete, check that the ropes are ready for a rope rescue.' He was a volunteer like the others, and an excellent rope rescue technician with years of practice. Dave knew this man could be relied on to assess casualties, and provide first aid treatment, if necessary, before transferring them to an ambulance or helicopter. He was a steady, reliable officer who had accompanied him on other operations. Solid. He also had a couple of little kids at home so this assignment would have personal meaning for him.

'I checked all the ropes, Dave,' he said, opening the storage box. 'All okay and ready to go.'

Dave focused on the sea ahead, gradually turning the lifeboat in towards the cliff, aiming at an area between the groynes nearest the beach huts. He hoped this person was not injured and the two missing children would be rescued but there was always that underlying fear that they would be too late.

Then, just when they thought it could not get any worse, it did. Another low-pressure system started barrelling in, sandwiching the boat between two storms. As the cross-waves pulled them in two directions, the crew were tossed like a proverbial cork in the ocean.

'Hold on,' said Dave. The lifeboat came to an abrupt halt. He jolted forward, gripping the wheel.

'I think that last wave has damaged us. Matt?' He checked the SIMS for more information. Looks like there's trouble with the propellor. He would wait for Matt to physically check the situation. Matt moved to the back of the lifeboat and checked over port-side.

'Dave, we've just lost the propeller. Looks like the strut has gone through the hull,' Matt yelled over the sound of the crashing waves. '.. and I think there's a small split under the bridge deck.'

Dave already knew that the propeller wasn't working as his speed thrust was all over the place.

'Hello. Operations?' The safety of his crew was the only reason he might have to cancel this rescue and suggest to the Operations Team that the smaller inflatable D734 be launched instead. The three crew members were already on stand-by and would be deployed immediately by tractor from the boat shed on shore.

'We need to return for repairs, Dave. The split is small but it's allowing water to seep into the starboard hull.'

'Okay. Abandon rescue,' called Dave, as he reached for the AIS microphone.

'Dave, the leak is causing seawater to contaminate the fuel tank. If we don't return quickly, we'll be in more strife,' said Matt.

'What are the possibilities of fixing it out here, Matt?'

Matt shook his head. 'No chance.'

Then they lost their second engine.

This rescue was not going to plan but, in his experience, in these conditions, it rarely did. His men on board were quiet, on alert and ready for any eventuality. He switched down from twenty knots to ten and returned toward the pier on the power of one engine.

We can try our best. That's all we can promise. Sometimes we can't save everyone but, like he told his wife, storms at sea are a bit like storms in life. And he knew that didn't always end happily and it made him feel on edge a bit. You can prepare for the journey all you like, but sometimes the unexpected happens and you find yourself being pushed around by the waves. As much as you want to turn back, often you have no choice but to keep pressing through. In those times it's so easy to slip up, feel frightened and overwhelmed. Right now he observed the wave breaks and the pull of the tidal rips as they entered the station to be hoisted up.

Chapter 25 – 14C

'The sea is too wild to take the boats out today,' said Father. 'Let Henry sleep. I have nets to repair, and the merchants will want to have access to their orders from the trading ships.'

'I watched one of those trading ships tie up to the new pier on Monday. They pulled in on high tide,' she said.

'They brought cheap goods from Asia. Did you see the rats scurry down the gangplank?' he asked.

'No, I did not. We have enough of our own without foreign vermin arriving by ship.'

'That's for sure! I must leave now. Send Henry down later, my dear. He can help me to be ready to set sail tomorrow.' He slipped on his wellington boots over warm socks, collected his pipe and covered his head with a beret.

Reverend Phillip Broun called it an act of God. Cartia listened as he related it to the story of Noah in the Bible. Outside the church, the sea encroached on their churchyard from two streams beneath the earth, one on either side of Shipden. Most of the village had disappeared already and he feared the worst for St Peter's. He said another stream behind and under the churchyard undermined the stability of the remains of the hill, which could be seen as a cliff from the beach. He had written to ask for some new land on which to build another church in Crowmere and this had been approved by the King himself.

People asked questions. 'But what of the well?' 'What of our new pier?' 'What of our livelihood in the marketplace?' 'Has God forgotten us?'

She watched her brother rush from the church meeting, in distress. The tide was out, and he walked down the side of the new embankment near the cliff edge. She glanced at her mother, who nodded approval. Cartia followed him down the side of the cliff to the honey-coloured sand below the churchyard. There was a carpet of broken stones, and flotsam from destroyed cottages. Stone pathways led nowhere. She saw him stand at the bottom of the worn cliff, looking up. Her shoe gripped each rounded beach flint, to find her balance with each step. Tribes of small crabs raced away from her body, across the sand.

'Won't be long before those graves tumble over the cliff and into the sea,' he said.

She joined him, looked up and saw he was right. The tip of each frontline gravestone protruded over the edge.

'That's terrible. People will be so upset.'

'Cartia. Emma is lying in the front row. I can't let her be taken by the sea. I swore to protect her forever.'

She understood his fear, but this problem could not be solved by them. It didn't seem fair at all, but they knew better than to question God. If it was an act of God, he must be very angry with the people of Shipden, and this confused her. They were good people most of the time. Many of them were poor, but they paid their tithes and obeyed the moralities set by the church.

'Do you think we should talk to the priest about this? Could he resolve this?' she asked.

'Yes, perhaps. He seemed to be only interested in the new church. Maybe he's forgotten that people who were buried here are a part of us.'

With new resolve, Henry moved quickly toward the side slope of the cliff and headed towards the church entrance to speak with Reverend Broun, and she followed. The community stood outside the church when they reached the top of the goat track. Instead of going home straight after the meeting, families gathered on the lawn discussing the collapse of their village and especially the church. Most of them had moved to Crowmere, to the south of Shipden, in the previous month but returned each Sunday for Mass. Horses and carts were tied up in an orderly manner along the side of the church, under the trees.

Henry searched for Reverend Broun, but he couldn't find him among the crowd in the churchyard. He entered the building and saw him sitting in the consistory court area, writing notes in Latin. Every Sunday afternoon he would listen to pleas from several local people on moral misdemeanours. Henry and Cartia sat on the edge of a bench seat nearby, and hoped he would look in their direction, so they didn't need to disturb him at his work. He noticed them, and asked,

'Hello Henry and Cartia. Did you wish to speak with me?'

'If you please, sir,' said Henry. 'I wish to ask about the churchyard. What will happen to the graves?'

'Alas, we can do nothing, my friend. Nature will do what nature does best. We have no control over it.'

'But couldn't we move the graves to the new church site?' Her eyes darted at him, shocked at her brother's impertinent question. She didn't like his tone.

'That would amount to heresy, son. Nobody moves the dead once they are buried.'

'I don't understand what 'heresy' is, sir.'

'It is when people go against what the church and God command. This court hears pleas for the detection and admonition of heresy.'

'How do we know what God would want?'

'It is written in the Bible, lad. There are rules and structures for life which we must follow. You know about the ten commandments? Yes, of course you do,' he said. 'If priests in the church, who have studied God's words, say it is a sin, then it must be so, and the people would be wise to listen to them. The Bible is written in Latin and must be studied carefully for many years to gain an understanding of these things.'

'Why would God want Emma to be taken by the sea? I don't understand.' He seemed more conciliatory now. Quieter. She'd noticed his moods go up and down in an instant, like he had no control over his behaviour.

'So many things are complicated for us mere mortals, Henry. We must have faith in the knowledge that God will care for us in the afterlife,' said Reverend Broun. 'Emma's soul is not in her coffin now. She is with God in Heaven.'

'So, you are saying that we would have to leave the cliff to collapse, if it will, and take her body out to sea?' he asked.

'Yes, I'm afraid so, my son. Moving it would be a terrible sin. We do not want to let evil win. God would be angry with us. Let her rest in peace, Henry.'

Her brother stood slowly and moved down the short aisle to his waiting parents, who were holding his two young children. Cartia turned and thanked the priest as they left.

Sunday morning, she woke with a feeling of dread. She was unable to place it at first, but then she remembered. This day was Emily Jane's fifth birthday. The date of Emma's passing. How would Henry cope? The routine of work would not happen today. Nobody worked on a Sunday.

Then she remembered that there would to be a special market held at the church to close the congregation. They had hired some minstrels and dancers to come to the marketplace in an effort to curb some of the apprehension they had felt in having to transfer to the new church in Crowmere. There would be music and fun for Emily's special day. That would lift their spirits. She tossed off her blanket and rose with more optimism than dread.

The children were asleep, curled up next to their father at the far end of the room. She tried to be quiet, removing her nightcap and wrapping her blanket around her shoulders. It was the latch on the door which woke Georgie, who sat bolt upright in fright.

'Go back to sleep, Georgie. It's just me going to the latrine with the bucket to empty.'

She was surprised to find her father was already awake. He was used to early mornings, so he found it difficult to sleep after sunrise.

'God be with you, Cartia,' he said. He was shovelling dirt at the far end of the cess pit.

'What challenge awaits us today, Pa?'

'God is always with us, every minute of the day and night, Cartia. He knows exactly what our challenges will be but how we handle them sometimes shocks Him too.'

She entered the wooden latrine at the end of the cess pit and poured the night's fluids into the hole as she did most mornings. She used an ewer and basin to wash her hands and face then stood nearby and watched her father.

'It's filling up faster than normal, isn't it Father?'

'Yes, it is. The men who drain it will be here tomorrow. I'm building up the edge near the road in case of overflow. Poor Mr Willers up the track a bit had to call in help to move carts, branches and rubbish when his cess pit overflowed onto the street. I had to drive our own cart on a diversionary route around the mess while they cleared the debris.'

'I heard about that. Overcrowding is the trouble. People are taking in family from flooded homes. Too many using the latrines.'

'It's only temporary, but we're a community who cares for one another as the Lord wants us to,' he said. 'We'll manage, Cartia.'

'Yes, Father,' she said. 'We will.'

She watched as a smile broke out on Emily's face and wondered at how contagious her joy was. In her lap was a tiny puppy. She said it was the best birthday ever and Georgie named him Scruffy. She lifted the fluffy pup and looked deeply into his eyes. Scruffy's tongue, pink and moist, licked her nose and she giggled. Even Henry smiled.

'You both need to take good care of him,' Ma said. 'Your father will show you how to do that. He might even build him a kennel. He must not go near the chickens or ducks, and you will have to train him, so he learns how to behave.'

Most of the day was spent at the church. Nobody she knew celebrated birthdays, in fact, many of her friends did not know the date of their birth. If they needed to have clarity for legal purposes, and this was rare, the church held records of their Christening and that was close enough.

The puppy had been part of a litter her father had seen struggling down at the pier. One day the mother dog was gone, perhaps died. Two pups remained, so he and one of the other fishermen each took one home. Father called it a blessing as it happened the day before Emily Jane's birthday and would serve to add some cheer to the dark day.

Market day was not Sunday, but they were given special dispensation. After the final church service, acrobats and dancers filled the air with their music and colourful entertainment. They came with their own minstrels, who played pipes and fifes and drums. She felt her heart race as she watched their energy and listened to the beat of the drums. Everyone looked happy, felt the same energy and some began dancing or clapping. She knew all the people who worshipped in Shipden; she worked with them, they were neighbours, she shared their sorrows, their pain, their happiness.

It was not unusual then that several of the men came to Henry as he leaned on the fencepost near the well. Every person in the village tried to help him in their own way and she felt grateful that their community understood his agony and the decision he had to make. But he would not be comforted. As time went on, she observed his behaviour as dour and unpredictable. Maybe the music would cheer him, but she doubted it. He arranged for his sister-in-law to take the children and Scruffy to live with them in Crowmere.

He went to bed early, without supper.

Cartia woke around midnight from a light sleep. It felt strange not having Georgie and Emily Jane as well as Scruffy in the cottage. An emptiness an adult could not fill. She heard light snoring, which was familiar, comforting. As her eyes adjusted to the darkness, she blinked to focus. Henry was gone. She curled back under the blanket in case he had gone to the latrine, and she let some time pass in a dreamy haze. He might be back in a short time.

The first sign of daylight filled the cottage with floating dust motes. She must've drifted off to sleep again. She glanced over to her brother's mattress. Empty. He would normally sleep in his braes and wear them the next day, but she noticed his tunic was not on the stool beside his bedding. The air was crisp, cold. It had been raining heavily but seemed to have steadied now. She reached for her blanket and clambered from her sleep. It had been a long time since she woke to find Henry missing. Perhaps he had wandered off and, being so sad, anything could have happened to him. In her hurry, her thoughts tumbled in horror. Her long hair fell from her bed cap in her haste. She slipped an undyed wool tunic over her long-sleeved undertunic and chamois undergarment which she'd worn for sleeping, tiptoed to the door and lifted the latch. Her parents were not awake. She didn't want to worry them as Henry might be in the garden shed working on his woodwork, so she lifted the latch and left the cottage without making a sound.

There was no light coming from the garden shed, so he wasn't at the property. Supposing he walked down to the churchyard? She'd found him sitting in his empty cottage before the sea washed away the thatch last week. Maybe he'd returned to his cottage. All these thoughts were fighting for her attention as she scurried north along the cobbled road to the other side of Shipden. She was deafened by the rush of blood beating in her ears and the howling ferocity of the windstorm.

Clouds filled the sky again. It was almost first light, but clouds blocked the sun. It reminded her of how Henry's own clouds blocked out the joy in his life and how much energy was being drained from him every day he was not at peace. There were shapes of abandoned cottages in the long grass on the sides of the cliff, as the wind blew through it and pushed the timber structures over into the sea, one by one. As they floated away with the outgoing current, only the remains of stone foundations were left behind. Anything loose was moving with the rhythm of sea and wind.

She checked to see if Henry was inside the remains of his cottage but sea water had submerged it to the top of the windows. She turned towards St Peter's church and thought she saw movement at the top of the cliff. Someone had piled dirt near the grave sites, so she was unable to see clearly. Something was bobbing up and down beyond the pile of dirt. She started running towards the churchyard. Several people had seen her and came out of their cottages with a sense of urgency, but they didn't go after her.

The pile of dirt was mounted at the side of Emma's gravestone and the hole near it was empty. She felt she would vomit and held onto the gravestone nearby to regain her stability. Where was her brother? What had happened to Emma's coffin?

Hysterical shouts, confusion.

'Henry! Where are you?' She stepped over the muddy pile of dirt and ran to the church for shelter as rain fell heavily. It was always left open, even now it was deserted and empty. Inside, she found her brother.

Henry was huddled in the corner of the room, frozen with fear and unable to move through the shattered glass. Beside him was a mud-caked spade.

'Come home, Henry.'

'I can't...move.'

'Yes, you can. I'll help you.'

'Cartia,' he said, tears streamed down through the dirt on his face leaving rivulets of pain. 'What have I done? God will be angry.'

She wanted to understand his gasping words, but he was not making any sense.

'Let's go and see our father. He'd be able to help, Henry.'

'No, not this time. I cannot go home, or he would be punished too.'

'Now you're worrying me, brother. Can you tell me where Emma is?'

'She is dead. In heaven.'

'Yes, but what has happened to her body, Henry? Where is she?'

Nothing. No reply.

'Henry!'

'If I told you, it would be bad for you,' he said. 'It has to be my secret.'

She could see there was no point in trying to change his mind. They left the empty building when the storm subsided. Henry walked alongside her, carrying the spade. Neighbours were curious but went inside as they passed by. She turned to look at the churchyard and noticed fresh diggings right beside the wall of the church building.

Chapter 26 – 14C

The whole churchyard was saturated when Father accompanied her to the church that evening. Everybody else was busy moving their remaining meagre belongings into carts and did not take much notice of two people going for a walk. She pointed to the area where she thought Emma now lay and they sloshed through the mud to that site.

Henry had not spoken a word and slept often. Most of St Peter's congregation now met at St Paul's in Crowmere. The congregation was planning on building St Peter and St Paul's church in the centre of that town. St Peter's church in Shipden had lost nearly all its churchyard over the eroded cliff, into the sea. Coffins were found floating; most had broken on impact when falling over the cliff and shattered into small pieces on the rocks at high tide. The rest of the village was preparing to see the last of their church and cottages.

'We should leave, it doesn't seem stable now, Cartia,' he said. 'Do you think anyone saw what had happened here?'

'I'm not sure, Father. Perhaps. The lady over the road watched me run in this direction when I was searching for Henry.'

Father was deep in thought as they walked up the cobbled street, through the deserted marketplace, past the well and abandoned village.

'Father, are you alright?'

'This is a sin. God will punish those who have taken the body.'

'We must pray for forgiveness then, Father.'

'Yes, Cartia. Henry cannot pray. He cannot speak for himself.'

Reverend Broun came to talk with the family, including Henry, who could listen but did not say a word. He said the locals were worried that evil had been invited into their village. They saw it as a disaster in the making.

'Maybe he has been struck dumb as a punishment for removing her body from the churchyard,' he said to Father. 'The idea of burial outside consecrated ground is beyond forgiveness.'

'God save us all.'

'The idea that such a well-bred Christian lad could do such a thing is almost beyond belief,' said the Reverend Broun, shaking his head.

'Henry is twenty-six. If we can encourage propositions from local village girls who know him well, we'd like to see him re-married,' said Reverend Broun. 'This would be best for you all.'

'Do you think it would heal his mind?' asked her mother.

'It's a possibility. Having a new wife to distract thoughts of his first wife often heals and revives young men,' he said. 'She would need to be patient and kind. There are several young women who work in the cornfields with Cartia who would be looking for a husband. Let me know if you'd like me to approach them on his behalf.'

'Thank you, sir. His brother-in-law is building a cottage in Crowmere for him. We had hoped the children might join him there, but it doesn't seem likely now. If he had a wife, it might give him some hope,' said Father.

'Yes,' agreed Mother. 'Hope is what we all need to keep going in these bleak times.'

Henry sat starring at the floor with his head in his hands.

'I am not going to ask Henry for the whereabouts of Emma's body. If he moved her within the churchyard, then it would be pointless. The cliff is within a couple of feet from the edge of the church now. Soon it will have disappeared under the ocean,' said Reverend Broun.

'God save their souls,' said Father.

'When will it rain again, Mother?' asked Cartia. 'The crops of corn surrounding the village are wilting from lack of water.'

'I wish I knew,' she answered. 'It is the longest time I can recall that we have not had rain. Our tubs and barrels are almost dry and the well in the marketplace has been inundated by sea water. They are digging two new wells in Crowmere. We will need to carry water two hundred yards if we do not have access to a horse and cart in a week.'

'Thirteen thirty is so incredibly dry. I'll never complain about muddy conditions again. Well, perhaps not for a while,' said Cartia. 'Rain is sent by God. Do you think the lack of rain, the ruination of our crops is because Henry shamed us all? Could it be seen as heresy? Are we paying for his crime?'

She surprised herself. Questions seemed to pour from her mouth. People were struggling and she did not like what they were saying about Henry behind their backs.

She didn't notice that her brother had entered through the open door and sat on a stool near the firepit. She turned to find him staring at her.

He opened his mouth to say something. 'No,' he whispered. 'No.'

Both she and Mother didn't know how to react to hearing him speak again. Henry was now thirty-nine. Many years had passed. He lived in his tiny cottage in Crowmere alone with his two children visiting him from time to time. Both children were of marriageable age themselves now.

St Peter's was still visible with only a few graves in the collapsed churchyard, but nobody used this building as it was deemed unsafe.

'This drought has left so many people hungry and weak,' Mother said. 'Will we ever recover, do you think?'

'God will bring us through if we have faith,' said Father.

A rat scurried through the straw in front of them and raced out the open door.

In the evening, Henry was busy in his Crowmere cottage. Cartia was visiting him and making supper, observing with fascination as he worked in silence to preserve his most treasured object. He had saved the box he had made for Emma and was adding to it. Her name was still engraved on the lid.

Inside the box he had placed the lace which she had worn on their wedding day and her red dress. Wrapped inside the lace was her marriage brooch, shiny gold with colourful gems. Cartia recalled how excited both girls had been the day after the wedding when she displayed her gift.

The circle shape of it was to represent his never-ending love for her. No beginning and no end. He wrapped the lacework around it and nestled it within the red fabric. On top of this he placed the iron horseshoe which he'd retrieved from their cottage now deep under the sea.

'One more thing to add and then it's finished,' he said, not particularly to her but she heard him muttering. Cartia's tapestry, sewn in blue and green colours had been hanging on the wall. With care, he pulled it from the timber frame and added it to the box.

'It doesn't belong here now,' he said. Their eyes met. She nodded.

He reached for the zinc solution and began to paint over the iron box to prevent it from rusting, even in salt water. Last week he had used a blue paint to prevent moisture from reaching the metal.

'I know what you mean,' she said, with her hand on his shoulder. 'You don't want to see this tapestry every time you come inside your new cottage. It's part of your old life now.'

'Yes, something like that,' he said. He placed the box, freshly painted, in his woodshed so the smell would not overwhelm.

She couldn't decide if she was pleased or not. If he was packing his memories away so he could begin his life without Emma, then that would be good. It was his intensity that worried her the most. His focus on the past had grown stronger over time. So much so that he couldn't see his way forward. It was like he was a fish caught in netting and could not escape.

Cartia returned to her home at daybreak, after Henry had left to work on their father's fishing boat. With Shipden's harbour silting up, a failing market, and the town partly destroyed, the trading and fishing boats now berthed in Crowmere. She liked to check on him regularly as he was still not well. Moving to a new town had appealed to him - a blank slate perhaps, a place so paradoxically placeless as to enable a kind of rebirth. Everything new to him. A place where he might start again. She breathed a long sigh. If only Daniaen had returned to her. Something must've happened to him, it made her sad to think such a thing. A traveller said there had been much work in the marshes around Norfolk, but she wondered if it was still so.

As it was a mild day, she covered her head with a shawl as the sea breeze continued to bite. There would be no fieldwork today. She was working every second day now. She noticed the corn dryers in the grain storage barns were only drying half the amount of corn. One of the two Shipden mills had closed and the queue at the other mill was short. She would miss seeing her friends and hoped they were able to find some work.

The village, slumbering in the mid-summer sun, looked bedraggled and smelt like mould, faeces and fish. Many of the residents had already left, leaving thatched cottages empty. Sewerage was no longer collected by the sewer men. The village had given up. She passed by several people who were known to her and spoke to them for a while. They all had the same worries; she didn't feel alone.

The inundation of Shipden was the talk of most residents, comparing themselves to others in similar positions up and down the Norfolk and Suffolk coast. It was only a few years ago that Dunwich had lost its harbour to the sea, and news of those residents came to them via travellers like her brother, Tom. It had come as a shock at first as Dunwich had once been the capital of that area and a major trading port. How could they fight the ocean? It obviously couldn't be done. She thought of the pier the townsfolk had paid for and erected recently. It had been a last-minute reprieve for their boats and as a defence in stormy weather. Word has it that the pier was breaking up and would collapse in the next storm.

Bells from St Peter's echoed over the remains of the village every evening for vespers at the twelfth hour after sunrise. There were no curfew hours in this town where one hundred and twenty residents once lived, unlike in London, where people must listen for the sound of St Martin's le Grand because the gates of the city close at that time. She had visited London once in her life with Henry. She had seen watchmen carrying lanterns to patrol city streets, making sure people were safe in their homes or staying at an inn, like they were. All the taverns closed, all boats were moored. Nobody wanted to be arrested as a nightwalker in the city. She shivered at the thought of being thrown into those filthy prisons she'd heard about. It was different living in a village by the sea. There was a certain sense of safety not found in the cities. But Father still insisted they return home by the time the bells rang out.

Mr Westcott, the local butcher, moved his cart of meat to the market in Crowmere and greeted her with a loud voice as he passed. He stopped his horse and asked if she would like to ride on the back of the cart, as it was empty after a day's trading.

She almost said no, for the walk was doing her good. But she decided to return home to help mother with the chores. She slipped up onto the tray, her legs dangling off the back.

'How have you been, Mr Westcott? How is that new baby of yours?'

'He's going to be a fine butcher in the marketplace once he's grown, Miss Cartia.'

'Oh, so he has a loud cry?'

'Yes, at all hours of the day and night.'

'It won't last forever, sir. You will be blessed with a fine son to help you in your future business, I'm sure,' she said.

'Yes, I hope so. His mother is exhausted, but we will be fine.'

He was usually a kind person with a grand sense of humour and came across as a happy soul. 'Have you heard about the sickness in London, Cartia?'

'No, sir. What's news there?'

'Many people are hit by a plague of some sort, brought in by rats from the sea.'

'What? No, I hadn't heard such news. That's terrible.'

'People are covered in black bruises, I heard, and many have died.'

'I hope it doesn't come here. We have enough things happening in Shipden.'

'So do I, lass. So do I.'

'People have called it the Black Death,' he said. 'Here's your cottage, Cartia. My regards to your parents. God be with you all.'

It was the summer of 1348 when a visitor from London appeared in the marketplace looking for a safe place to live. He was a short, stout man of middle years with a greying beard. His wife sat in a heavily laden cart pulled by two Clydesdale horses.

Cartia went over to the cart and asked the woman if they needed directions.

'Good morning to you, madam, you're looking lost. Strangers in town stand out.'

'Hello. That's very kind of you,' she said. 'My husband and I would like to settle somewhere in Crowmere. They say it is easy to find a cottage in the northern parts, near the woodlands.'

'Those properties are being eroded by the sea, madam. I don't think they would be suitable for you for very long,' she said. She was surprised to see the woman's eyes flood with tears.

'Are you alright, madam?' She reached out and patted the horse near her while the woman found her handkerchief. 'Beautiful horses. What would we do without them?'

'Indeed. They are gentle creatures for such strength,' she said, wiping her face, blowing her nose. 'I'm sure we'll be alright soon, but I'm tired.'

'Travelling any distance can be exhausting,' she said.

'There's more to my sadness. All my children have died in London, so my husband and I are hoping to find a safer place to live. Now you tell me the land is falling into the sea,' she said, wiping away a tear from her cheek. 'It's too much to bear. The journey has been overwhelming.'

'I'm so sorry to hear of your troubles, madam,' she said. 'There are properties further inland which might suit you better. Have you considered Alysham? Or Holt?'

Her husband returned to the cart and swung himself up to join his wife on the bench seat.

'Good day to you, young lady. Thank you for keeping my wife company, while I conducted some business. I've bought a small cottage nearby. We will be living in Holt and must go before the bells toll for vespers.'

'My pleasure, sir.' His wife was still weeping and dabbed her eyes with a cloth.

'My wife is upset. We have had to leave our home in London. When the bubonic plague first struck us in recent days, so many of our friends and neighbours died. First the bruises, then within five days they were gone. Dead. We drove our cart past men burying the dead in makeshift graves at the Charterhouse Square pit. It was not the stench so much, but the ground was not part of a religious property' he said, shaking his head. 'Not on consecrated grounds, you see.'

'That's dreadful news, sir. I wish you both well in Holt. Maybe I will see you again another day.'

'It could've been worse, Miss. Six hundred years ago the whole country was in darkness for nearly two years. Crops failed with no sun. People starved and got sick. At least we can see where we're going,' he said. 'We'll be right. We're a country with a history of survival.' He winked and picked up the reins. With a snap of his wrists, they began to move.

She bid them farewell and watched those magnificent horses moving gracefully down the road.

'It's those rats from the orient!'

Mother was shouting as she paced in the cottage that evening. Maybe her instincts were correct, but Cartia had never heard her mother raise her voice before and was shocked. She reached for the jug and poured her some water.

'Calm yourself, Mother,' she said. 'I've never seen you so upset.'

'What else could it be? The pestilence is out-of-control and will spread to all our families. Living in the countryside, even in Shipden, will not protect us from this evil. You mark my words.'

'They have called it a bubonic plague,' she said. 'It is indeed very frightening, Mother, but nobody knows what has caused it to start.'

'We know the trading vessels from China have been to places like Spain and other European countries before coming here. Each of those countries is reporting hundreds of deaths from the plague,' said her father. 'It is possible that the vermin on board those ships have deposited the sickness and spread it along each port of call.'

'I heard also that a horseman came off one of those trading ships in London and he was already infected with it,' she added. 'I spoke with a couple today from London who had lost all their children to this plague. The woman's face was drenched with tears, Mother. They've left London to go to Holt, but I spoke with them in the marketplace in Crowmere.'

'I heard the news from a passing traveller too,' said her father. 'People are leaving the city in droves to be safe.'

'We must pray for God's protection and mercy,' said Mother. 'I will go to St Peter's after supper.'

'I'll help you do the animals and cut up some vegetables for supper, Ma,' said Cartia. 'Then I'll go with you to church. St Peter's is almost empty now. Would you prefer to pray at the Crowmere church this evening at vespers?'

'No, God knows me better at St Peter's.'

'You know God is with you everywhere you go,' said Father. 'No need to go anywhere special to pray but I think it helps us focus on our words better on consecrated ground. Do you need me to go with you, my dear?'

'Cartia will accompany me, and we will be home soon after vespers.'

‘Then I will keep fixing my nets and talk to God while I do it,’ he said, smiling.

Chapter 27 – 2013

Josh had been a Nipper on Stradbroke Island's Point Lookout when he was young but never advanced to being a Lifesaver. Now he wished he had those advanced skills, but he was a confident beach swimmer, and he occasionally went surfing. He realized he had never been in the surf when it was as wild and as cold as this. He squatted beside Carly on a rock near the wrecks of those beach huts he had admired a month ago. The turbulent North Sea swirled into a dangerous spiral in front of him, pulling debris into charcoal depths across the submerged footpath. Carly had to scream at him to be heard over the noise of the storm and the sea, even though they were less than a step away from each other.

'I think the twins are in one of those beach huts still standing, but I can't be sure which one,' she coughed, choking on sea-spray. 'I heard voices calling for help about ten minutes ago. I've yelled for them, but it's so noisy, I can't make out their little voices! I'm so frightened for them, Josh!'

'It's the one closest to you. It belongs to their grandmother,' said a dark voice. They turned to see Kyle, the guy at the Holt train station, windswept and wet. Unfazed. His red sneakers gripped a rocky edge.

"You have no choice. I can't swim," he said with chilling calmness. 'The beach hut will collapse soon and wash the children into the sea.'

'Okay. Thanks, mate,' said Josh. He hadn't noticed that Kyle had joined them on the beach and wondered how he knew they were there. Right now, he didn't really care to ask. He surveyed the remaining beach huts and didn't like the chances of anyone getting near them. The whole path was covered in gullies of water, swishing back and forth with each crashing wave. He called as loudly as possible with his hands cupped but still did not hear any voices in return. He noticed Carly was trembling, her eyes misty and wide.

'Carly, settle down and phone the emergency number for the lifeguards,' he said.

'I already did that. Any other ideas, Josh?' She looked back at Kyle. Alarmed, she recalled what it was about him that had frightened her. He seemed to have no fear at all. What was wrong with him? He was always appearing in odd places. What did he mean about the twin's grandmother owning one of those beach huts?

'Goodo,' said Josh. 'There's a rope over there. I'll tie it around my waist and swim across.'

'Are you serious? No. That's dangerous.'

'Carly, I have to try. The lifeguards will be here soon but maybe not soon enough,' he said. 'Kyle is right. I wish we knew how those kids are coping right now.'

He retrieved a long branch, stretched his arm out over the rock and pulled a thick, water-logged rope towards him. They both knelt on the rockface above the path, the north-easterly wind gathering speed, and tied the rope around his waist, testing its strength with a big pull. Kyle took the other end of the rope and wound it around a rock, holding the remainder around his waist.

The tide pulled and pushed him as he lowered himself into the foamy waters below.

'It's freezing in here!' His mind was focused on where he was going to swim, but he had no idea what he would do once he got to the hut. He'd work all that out as he went along. Carly looked terrified. He had no time at all to do anything but swim.

'Move quickly, Josh,' yelled Carly, shaking in her boots. 'Or you'll freeze.'

He looked back at Kyle, reassuring himself that the rope was secure. Kyle nodded. The sea rose and fell in a rhythmic pattern pushing Josh on the crest of the wave, swimming toward the remaining two beach huts. The rope became taut as he was swept beneath the water in a rip, holding tight as it dragged him out towards the sea. His legs kicked to push him up to the top of a wave, going with the rip. His arms scooped through the water with as much pressure as he could muster. All he could hear was Carly screaming as he fought to stay upright. Soon the sea was so cold he no longer felt his feet kicking. His ears were ringing and his head ached.

He glanced over towards where she was kneeling, near the rope knotted around the rock. Kyle was pointing behind him. He watched as she suddenly moved to stand, jumping up and down, waving her hands in the air at someone or something in the direction of the Cromer pier. Behind her, blue lights flashed, silhouetted against dark, sombre clouds.

'Carly. The rope,' he called, choking through a mouth-full of putrid, salty water. Fear clouded his senses as he struggled to reach the twins. Then the rope, which he held in his hand, went limp.

Tasneem says nothing but I know what she's thinking. She does that well – which is what I can't do. My sister has a long think before doing things and I am the opposite. I get things done fast. When I try to think first, I get distracted and must build up courage all over again or thoughts get so tangled and muddled in my head that I find it hard to solve problems sometimes. Out of the two of us, she's the thinker and I'm not.

'You can't be serious, Tariq!'

'I am serious. Come on.'

'We'll be in trouble.'

'No, we won't. Come on. Quick, before Carly notices.'

I slipped from the bench on the wharf and looked back at my sister, knowing that she wouldn't be able to resist the pull of adventure. After a few steps, she followed with an umbrella in her hand, but not before checking where Carly was.

'She's still talking with that fellow with the long hair,' I said, not giving her too long to think or we'd miss the opportunity to escape. We really wanted our buckets and spades, and I knew exactly where my Gran kept them in the blue beach hut. 'Come on. We'll be back before she turns around.'

Rain had soaked the beach and now it'd stopped, so that's awesome for sandcastles. I just don't know why Tasneem thought she might need the umbrella. I didn't comment on it. Whatever makes her okay to come with me. There's a lot of give and take when you're a twin. We've been together before we were born seven years ago. She came first and then I arrived five minutes later. That's the way it's always been, even at school and at church and in the car. I admire how she can sit still and wait for things.

'Tariq, why do you need to go and see inside a beach hut in this awful weather?' she asked me.

'The rain has stopped and because nobody is around now.'

'They aren't here isn't a reason to look inside their beach hut.'

'It's not like it's breaking in, stupid. It's our Gran's. She won't mind. Besides, we both want to get our buckets and spades out, don't we?'

'Yes, but don't you think Carly should be with us?'

'She's taking too long. We'll save her time and she'll be pleased we got them ourselves, won't she?'

'I suppose so,' said Tasneem.

She slipped her hand under the beam at the base of the colourful beach hut and retrieved the key to the padlocked door.

'Hurry up, Tasneem. Quick.'

'I've got it now,' she said as she handed it to me. I stretched up and held the padlock steady with one hand and slowly inserted the key with my other hand. The padlock sprung open, the key chain dangling from the lock. The door creaked open. Tasneem looked over her shoulder at the waves making loud crashing noises and foaming into shore.

'Tariq, look at the sea. It's really wild. I'm scared.'

He thought how beautiful it was, the foaming line dissipating at the sandy flintstones.

'Don't be a scaredy cat, sis. Let's do this quickly then and get back up to Carly.'

'Yes, hurry, hurry.'

We bundled ourselves into the wooden beach hut, looking around at the empty beach. I felt a tinge of guilt for leaving Carly and looked up toward where she had been standing on the pier. Her red jumper was just a blob from where I was standing. The blob of red was jumping up and down, waving in my direction. My sister was already in the hut reaching for the plastic buckets, so I followed her thinking that the sooner we get these buckets and run back to Carly, the better, now she's noticed us gone.

I heard a loud crack of thunder and spits of rain fell onto my head. A gust of wind whipped a curtain of light rain at my face. I stepped up inside and slammed the door behind me. Now I was dripping wet and catching my breath.

'What did you close the door for, Tariq? We can go now.'

'The storm blew in my face.'

She sat on the wooden bench with the green bucket and spade in her hand. There seemed to be a reluctance for her to move and I figured she probably needed to think again. Meanwhile, I dragged a stool over and reached up to the shelf for my own bucket and spade, even though I knew we wouldn't be able to use them now the storm's returned. Obviously, I can't go back empty-handed. The wind outside was shaking the boards underneath us and, with every crashing sound, a trickle of sea water crept in under the door. There aren't any windows so I can't see what's happening outside, and my tummy has big butterflies in it, and I realized I don't know what to do next.

'We need to get out of here,' said Tasneem. 'Carly will be wondering where we are.'

'I saw her waving to me from the pier. She knows we're in here.'

'Oh no. Now we're in trouble again.'

'Let's just sit here and wait for this rain to stop. She won't want us to get wet, will she.'

'I have my umbrella. Let's go.'

'Can we give it five minutes? It went away before...'

'Okay. But no longer than five minutes,' she started counting to sixty, five times, while the hut began to sway a little with some sort of rhythm, back and forth.

I looked around for something to distract my sister. The counting was worrisome. Another gust of wind and strange sounds like things breaking, dislodging one of Gran's boxes from the shelf above her head. It fell to the ground at our feet, smashing the lid off at an angle. Tasneem screamed and stopped counting.

Rain was pelting against the beach hut. I could taste the salty air being pushed between the wooden slats in the walls. Everything was wet and I started to shiver uncontrollably. Tasneem told me my lips were going blue. Inside the box on the floor was a picnic blanket, still dry, so I pulled it out carefully and wrapped myself inside.

'It must be five minutes now. Let's go,' she said, speaking far too loudly so I could hear her above the noise outside. 'Come on, let's go.'

I was squatted beside the dislodged plastic box, curling up a bit to keep warm inside the blanket. She pushed past me and pressed down on the door handle. She seemed to be having a hard time opening it. This was annoying, for I would have to remove myself from this warm spot and open it for her before she became upset. That's another thing about my sister; she cries when she gets worried and that just worries me more. So, I stood up and tried to push the door at the same time as turning the doorknob. The door stretched out a tiny bit when I leant on it, enough to wash heaps of water in, swirling under and around the lower edges of the door and into the hut. We were now standing in water up to our knees and the door was stuck. We both screamed.

Fear is like shocks rushing through my body. It leaves me exhausted but alert, my hands flew everywhere trying to escape. I had not locked the door so why did it not open? My sister stood up on the bench, screaming for help and holding on to the old box. The blanket floated below. More crashing noises outside, then I heard something like tin banging on the wall behind us.

I picked up the floating lid to the box and climbed up next to my sister, who was crying and now as shivery cold as I was.

'What do we do now?' I asked her.

'Did you say before that Carly saw us?'

'Yes, she was waving. I know she did.'

'She'll come soon, I'm sure,' she said. 'You'll have to sit still and wait.'

I watched her slide down the wall to squat, her thumb slipping into the space where her missing front teeth had been. The noisy wind rattled the hut and whistled down between the wall of the hut nearby.

Even though it was all my fault, and I'd put us in danger, I relaxed a bit knowing that help was on the way, but I could not keep still for long. Carly would be here soon. Between us on the bench was the old plastic box where the blanket had been. I was about to place the lid onto the box, when my hand reached out for the smaller box inside. I'm going to keep that box safe. Gran will be pleased that I saved it for her.

Then I heard it. Someone was calling our names. It sounded far, far away. Probably Carly using her panic voice. We'd be out of here soon. Then I didn't hear her. We were both too cold to speak after a while. The sea water was slowly creeping higher, so both of us bent our knees to our chins shivering on the bench. I started to feel really sick, like I wanted to vomit.

A muffled sound of voices, thunder, lightning. The sea water covered the bench so we both stood up on it, taking turns to sit on the plastic box between us. Someone banged loudly on the door. I think it was a man's voice.

'Are you in there? Tariq, Tasneem. It's Josh, Carly's friend.'

'Yes we are,' said Tasneem's tiny voice.

'Yes!' I called, much louder than I meant it to be. 'Please open the door so we can come out! The key's in the lock.'

'Too much water weight against the door, Tariq. Are you okay?'

'We're stuck inside and very cold.'

'We've called the Lifeguards, and they'll be here shortly to get you out of there. I can't stay here, guys. It's freezing in the water. Hang in there, you two.'

'I want to go home,' called Tasneem through her tears.

The plastic box floated. We both stood up on the bench. The sea was curling around our legs and we were so cold. Darkness descended. I was afraid of the dark at night, but this was not night-time. The storm took away the sun. I held onto my sister, who was wet and cold. Blue lights suddenly flashed across our bodies, thin streaks splitting through boards in the wall. Then a man in a helmet ripped through the roof above us, making a hole and dropping a rope to us. When we looked up, rain fell onto our faces and into our eyes.

I tied the looped rope around my sister, and they pulled her up. Her feet dangled in mid-air as I let her leg go. Soon, the rope came down again, so I got into its loop, holding on tightly to the smaller box. It was quite heavy, but I didn't want to leave it in the hut. There was an ambulance waiting. They wrapped us in some foil blankets, but I can't remember anything else after that. I think I might've fallen asleep, but I remember Josh talking to the Coastguard and Carly having her foot bandaged. The guy with the long hair was gone.

Tasneem and I both woke up in the hospital in Norwich. Gran and Pa were sitting beside our beds, and we were happy to see them.

Chapter 28 – 14C

In the soft Shipden twilight, she sat quietly on the floor of the abandoned church. Mother was holding her hand, her head bowed, eyes closed in prayer. They sat on those empty boards and listened to the sound of waves breaking rhythmically over the pebble shore and against the northern wall of the church. A calm washed over them. After a while, they stood and looked out of a glazed window to the north. Other windows were shattered but the northern windows were intact.

'Mother, I think we should go home.'

'My prayers are done. Let's go,' she asked. 'What was that?'.

'The church is rocking. Come on, Ma, it's dangerous to be here now,' she said. 'Oh, there's another shudder, stronger than the last.'

They rushed from the church and watched from the cobbled street as the church wavered, the strong wind both terrifying and exhilarating at the same time. It was beginning to rain again and everything was bleak. An icy blast sent them racing for shelter. It bit hard, penetrating coats and scarves and gloves.

Cartia blinked through the rain at a lone figure silhouetted against an angry, moonlit ocean, kneeling near the edge of the churchyard. It wasn't unusual to find sadness in such a place, but it was always harrowing to observe. She didn't know what to do. Should she leave mother and see if the man was alright? It was getting dark, and they hadn't brought a lantern with them. What did this person want in the churchyard, well after the bell for vespers had tolled? Who was this person? Was he friend or foe?

As they hurried down the road, she glanced over her shoulder again but couldn't see anybody. The whole side of the church was invisible to her, swallowed by shadows. Her quick glance didn't detect any movement. She convinced herself it might've been a statue of the Virgin Mary or an Archangel resting on the last row of graves and not a man at all.

They slowed their walk, puffing and gasping for air. Rain on her face felt like needles on her skin. They tucked their heads further into their capes and observed the puddles expand across their path.

'You alright, love?' asked her mother.

'Yes, we could seek shelter in one of the empty houses, if you like,' said Cartia. She was keen to get back home but would be relieved to find any shelter at all. They both looked up at the line of thatched, timber cottages as they kept walking. Several of them had lights in shuttered windows. They hadn't all left the village yet. There was a sense of something new and frightening happening since they had walked through the village earlier.

Some of these homes had a cross painted on their cottage door. They had lived in Shipden their whole lives and knew every resident. Most were fishermen, some were farmers or clothiers or weavers. Most of them labourers, illiterate, struggling with little or no formal schooling but they were hard workers from strong, reliable families. They looked at the painted cross on the door of Mr Bacon's cottage and turned to one another with grim expressions.

'Does that cross mean the Bacon family has the plague?' said Cartia. 'There are six children living in that cottage.'

'God be with us, Cartia. Best we continue straight home,' said Mother. 'The plague has hit Shipden.'

'Yes, Ma. What's a bit of rain after a drought?' said Cartia, trying to lift her mood. Nobody laughed.

A mud-caked spade lent against the outside of their shed. She didn't recall it being there before they left. She supposed her father had used it before the storm came. It was strange for him to leave tools lying around. Muddy shoes were removed and placed on short sticks, upside-down under the thatch overhang.

Father had spread some dry straw over the dirt floor, an aromatic, sweet smell. Earlier today, she had noticed a sharp, musty, almost metallic, odour. She knew this was a sure sign the old straw was mould-affected and musty. It would've harboured fleas, which were biting her legs last night. Fleas were particularly bad now.

'Thank you for replacing the straw, Father. It smells sweet,' she said. 'Good thing you finished it before the storm.'

'You can both sit and dry your feet by the firepit. We need to talk,' he said.

'We have some news for you too, Father,' said Cartia.

Mother placed the kettle on the fire and sat on the stool. Cartia sat on the floor mat.

'It's Henry,' he said. 'I caught him sneaking about the tool-shed. He wouldn't speak about why he needed the spade, but I gave it to him to borrow.'

'I saw it leaning on the shed in the yard, Father,' she said. 'It wasn't clean. Maybe he needed it to do some job at his cottage.'

‘Then why be secretive about it?’ he said.

‘His behaviour is erratic to say the least,’ she said. Mother nodded. ‘He is still not quite well.’

Father wondered if we knew of any reason Henry might have needed to borrow the spade. It seemed odd that he couldn’t say what he was doing with it. They discussed this while tea was poured. He was not worried about him borrowing the spade, he was worried about his son’s behaviour.

‘Will,’ said her mother. ‘We noticed something very worrying walking back from St Peter’s. There’s a black cross painted on the home of the Bacon family.’

‘No. That’s shocking news. These are dark times coming. If such a good, righteous family could be affected, we will all suffer,’ he said. ‘We’ll pray for them.’

Wet clothes were removed behind the wattle screen. Her warm cape was woven from their own sheep wool last summer, so was almost waterproof from the lanolin. They wiped themselves down and dressed in their nightwear, spreading wet clothing on every surface to dry. A pervasive sense of foreboding crept into her dreamy state.

There would be no work for her tomorrow. In the morning, she would walk to Crowmere to visit Henry, take him some of the pottage left over from supper tonight. First the drought, now last night’s heavy rain. The fields would be saturated. And now the plague had arrived in Shipden. The cottage was cold and damp, but she felt exhausted, drained from events over which she had no control. She soon settled onto her covered straw mattress and slept a restless sleep.

Father and Henry were unable to take the fishing boat out today as the water was too churned up, so Cartia packed a basket of vegetable pottage and a fresh loaf of bread and began her walk to Crowmere. More crosses were painted roughly on cottage doors while tidal surges trespassed on coastal properties. An eerie, sick feeling washed over her. The shock of it all was overwhelming. She sat for a moment by the side of the road near the old Oak tree that Henry used to chase her around in much happier times. Although the path was wet, she was thankful it was not raining.

People walked past, sometimes nodding to her or quietly bidding her a good morning. Dark eyes set back from bony cheeks, matted hair, patched tunics. Even the children looked scrawny, gaunt and without hope in their manner. They were not running, laughing, smiling. Instead, they clung to their family group or a mother's apron, some crying, some beyond that and listless as they wandered past her. Everyone covered their nose and mouth in some way. It felt frightening to be among people. They say there is no cure for this disease, and no stopping the sea from flooding the whole village. How does one keep on going like this? One foot in front of the other, she thought, as she picked herself up and continued her journey towards Crowmere. Surely it must end soon.

She noticed several more cottages bearing the black cross scattered along the route to Crowmere. If people remained in their homes, all would be well for the rest of them. Father said people had been appointed to sit and watch outside these doors. She saw them, with masked faces, pass food and drink to the people inside, and then sit back and guard the entrance.

It felt surreal to Cartia, who was almost at Henry's cottage, to witness all this melancholy. She sensed that his use of their father's spade was such a silly thing to discuss with any urgency. She suspected there was more to this and wondered if it was anything to do with his fanatical focus on poor Emma. Every time she saw him lately, he seemed to ramble in a distressed manner. As she turned the final corner, she prayed that he would be able to focus on reality and explain to her what was happening.

Thirteen forty-seven had been such a difficult year for everyone and, from her observation, it was starting to look like it was going to get a whole lot worse.

The cottage door was open when Cartia arrived.

'Hello, are you in there, Henry?'

'Behind the house, in the garden plot,' called Henry.

She put her basket in the cottage, removed her cape and walked around the side of the cottage. She was surprised to see James and Matilda were visiting him too. She tried to be cheerful, restrain the panic in her voice.

'James, Matilda, good morning. So good to see you. Are you well?' she asked, trying to be cheery but it didn't work. She leant against the fence post and sighed. Her sister came over to her, placed a hand on her shoulder.

'Hello, Cartia. Yes, we're alright. It's really frightening, isn't it? We'll need to be very careful,' said Matilda.

'So many people are sick. I walked past homes of people we all know, who have a cross painted across their doors.'

'Yes, we've seen them too. It's disturbing. I watched them carry bodies out to the cart yesterday evening,' Matilda said. The two girls sat together in silence while the men bent over a worktable, in discussion. 'Come and see what Henry has made. Have you seen this beautiful memory box?'

'Yes, I hope it helps him. To be honest, I came to check on Henry. Brought him something nourishing to eat. We can talk on this more later.'

They both wandered over to the workbench, happy to find something else to talk about.

'God be with you, Henry,' she said, giving him a gentle hug. 'Yes, the box is wonderful. I watched him paint it a few days ago, so it wouldn't corrode quite so fast.' She thought they all looked a bit on edge, though Henry seemed comfortable in their company. He had been putting another coat on the iron box which held the carved, wooden box containing his fond memories of Emma.

'Final coat done. I'll take it to her later,' he said.

'What do you mean, Henry?' asked Cartia. Here he goes again, off on some nonsense talk. She wondered if the other two had noticed. Their expressions gave nothing away.

'She'll be happy when she has her important things,' he said.

'She would've been proud of the effort you've made to keep her things safe and sound, my friend,' said James. 'Let's have some dinner. My timepiece says it's eleven o'clock. Cartia has made a pot of pottage for us.'

'Yes, I have. And I carried it all the way to your cottage, Henry. Come along.'

Matilda walked with Henry back toward the cottage entrance with James and Cartia ahead of them, discussing the bleak conditions she'd noticed on her walk to Crowmere.

'But you must move on now, Henry. Emma is gone, my dear,' said Matilda. She placed her hand on his shoulder in a loving gesture. He looked at her, blinked a few times and walked on, carrying the heavy box into the cottage.

Once inside, the box was placed on the windowsill and forgotten. Henry had removed the food from her basket and started to build up his firepit. It wouldn't take long to raise a flame as the coals were still hot. Cartia placed her pot on the grate and stirred so the vegetables did not stick. She found some wooden bowls, and set them out on the shelf, along with a sculptured ladle Henry had made from a dried Holly branch. She thought about talking of lighter subjects. Reality was just so hard. So worrying.

'How are your children, Matilda? And young Jack – has he found work yet?' she asked.

'I think they're all well. As you know, the twins have both wed but not blessed with children yet. Better left for a while, I think. Especially now. And then there's the pandemic, of course, to add to their worries,' she said. 'Jack is trying his luck in London. He knows of a baker there who is hiring an apprentice.'

She paused for a moment. Matilda looked flustered. 'I'm frightened for our Jack in London. I'm very concerned about the sickness, Cartia.'

Meanwhile, Henry and James pulled up stools just outside the cottage. She couldn't make out what they were discussing but it was good to see Henry in conversation and quite animated as well.

'Yes, I've heard that it's horrible and many people in London have died. But Jack is tough and healthy, Mati. He will return home if he needs to. Some people have called it the Black Death because of the black bruises which appear on their skin,' she said. Her sister was looking intense, and her frown grew deep.

'Yes, Black Death seems to be its name,' Matilda said. 'I think we'll notice great changes coming soon, Cartia. I don't know how Henry will cope with it all. He doesn't seem to connect well with restrictions and boundaries anymore.'

'I'm glad we were able to meet today, Mati. We may not have the chance again for a while.'

'Yes, I think we will need to stay at home,' said Matilda. 'I hope it's not for too long.'

'I'll look after Mother and Father. You keep watch, if you can, on our brother,' she said.

'Yes. Try to stay happy, little sister. You might be able to finish some knitting. We have quite a bit of wool in the basket now, after that long summer.'

Henry and James had left their stools and walked to the top of the field. Henry was caring for some animals which belonged to James and was being paid a wage of four pence a day, the same as field workers. It was enough to get him by, as father's fishing business was no longer viable. Maybe it would improve again in time.

'I went to the market last week,' she heard James tell Henry. 'They're talking about closing them for a while because of the plague running rampant through the country.'

'Yes, I heard that too,' Henry said. 'It is not all bad though. Prices dropped so I was able to buy myself a horse for the sum of six shillings and eight pence. I also bought a couple of cows for a shilling each, a pig to fatten up for five pence and two lambs for winter wool at two pence each.'

'Good buying, Henry. Times are poor for trade when families cannot find enough food to eat. We have plenty of land for those animals, but they'll need to live off grass and scraps. We might not be able to afford to feed them all over the winter months. The empty, old barn will be useful though,' said James.

'The cornfields were too dry before the downpour the other day, so Cartia has very little work. I think she goes into the cornfield every second day or so now. Not much of a harvest this year but plenty of straw, so I'll make sure the animals get some of that,' said Henry.

Cartia heard her name. Funny how that happens. The rest of the sentence was a mumbled blur, but she always picked up on her name.

'Are you calling me, Henry?'

He turned in her direction, waved and shook his head.

Matilda set out their hot pottage and bread. 'Dinner's ready,' she called.

Hands were washed in the tub near the door. James proceeded to pray the blessing on their food. With so many people hungry in the village, they were especially grateful for the hearty pottage to fill their bellies.

'Did you bake this bread yourself, Henry?' said James.

'Funny, James. No, Cartia brought it to me this morning.' They broke the bread and dipped it into the steaming pottage. 'Mother has taught her well. James, can I ask you to help me with lifting something later today?'

'Yes, that is fine, Henry. I'll come by your cottage just before the bells ring for vespers. Is that a good time for you?'

'Yes, thank you. I won't keep you too long.'

Chapter 29 – 2013

Anna frowned and looked up at the clock on the wallpapered wall of her kitchen. She's only half concerned that Carly is an hour late and the twins are not racing about the house, ravenous after a visit to the beach. Despite the cold weather, there had been a pause in the rain showers this morning and Jack, although he hadn't said anything, really needed to have a break from their constant chatter.

If she was honest, the peace and quiet was a treat. They had been so lucky to have met Carly, who had endless energy with the little ones. Her hands-on experience at home had taught her how to manage the twins and keep them occupied, even in these rainy conditions. It had not stopped raining all week. Unless you had the webbed feet of a duck, it was necessary to keep everyone, including her grandchildren, indoors all week. It always seemed to happen in the holidays. Tons of rain. Big tidal surges all along the coast. Heavy rain and storms.

She carefully stirred coffee into her own cup and poured tea into a mug for Jack. She hadn't minded when her son had asked if the twins could stay with them for a while. He and his wife were renting a small holiday van in Hemsby, about an hour from Holt on the A149.

Although the sun was not warming the sunroom at all, the light was much brighter as they sat for morning tea. Jack walked from where he had been painting scaled figurines for his miniature ship, to the plush cane armchairs and coffee table.

'About time Carly brought the children home, isn't it, love?' he asked. 'Those storm clouds look rather threatening.'

She placed the drinks on the table with a plate of homemade biscuits and nodded.

'I wonder if she missed the bus?'

'She'd have rung on her mobile phone, don't you think?'

'Yes, I imagine so.'

'Oh, nothing to worry about, I'm sure. Probably engrossed in building a sandcastle.'

'Yes, maybe that's it. The twins said they were going to get their buckets and spades from our beach hut, but I forgot to tell Carly. I'm sure Tasneem will let her know. I told her where the key is hidden. Do you think I should phone them?'

'No. Like you said, the twins will tell Carly about their beach toys in the beach hut. They must be the only ones anywhere near the beachfront today. It's much too cold for summer activities like that,' he said. 'Good thing you put their wellies and coats on this morning, Anna.'

'They probably won't even go on the beach if this weather keeps up. Just wander around the shops checking out the Christmas window displays,' said Anna. 'Though it's nice and peaceful, isn't it, Jack? I love those kids to bits, but their chatter and their energy can be hard to deal with at times. We're just not used to it after all these years. Biscuit?'

He reached for a shortbread and started nibbling at the end of it. 'I suppose,' he said. 'It was interesting the other day when we drove over to Hemsby, wasn't it? It looked quite nice, where they're staying.'

'Hemsby is lovely in summer. I'm not too sure how they will go if we have a major storm surge though, Jack. The locals are getting quite nervous about it.'

'Aziza has a bit of a project to do down there. They won't put themselves in danger, I'm sure.'

'Of course, silly me. I know they'll be fine. Now, where are those youngsters? Time is moving on a bit. Maybe I should phone Carly,' said Anna. She reached for her phone. By the time she opened it, she heard someone knocking on their side entrance door.

Jack was already concentrating on his model's paintwork, so she got up to answer the door.

'It's probably them now,' she said, collecting the afternoon tea tray and taking it with her to the kitchen before opening the door. A gust of cold wind burst into their warm home. To her surprise, two police officers stood stoically on her welcome mat. She knew this could not be good news.

Her heart sank.

Chapter 30 – 14C

'Where are you wanting to carry this to, Henry?' asked James, who had arrived at his cottage as the bells stopped tolling.

'St Peter's. I want to give it to Emma,' he said.

'Emma? Are you sure, my friend? The whole cliff will crumble soon and take everything with it,' he realized that this was not news to him. That he must've taken this into account.

'If it pleases you, Henry, we will do it. Matilda is cleaning up after supper. Is Cartia still here?' James asked.

'Yes, she is. She thought it best to wait until we all could go together,' said Henry. 'Cartia, are you coming now?'

'Yes, I am. I'll just fetch my cape,' she said.

'We don't want to hold James up too long,' he said. 'I appreciate his help with this box. It's too heavy for one person and I don't have a cart.'

'Off we go then,' said James. 'You take one side, and I'll take the other. You did well to connect those handles to each side.'

'I appreciate your help, James. It's a long walk. Heavier than you think it should be,' said Henry. Cartia came to the door as they started down the road towards Shipden. 'Come on, Cartia. Hurry up.'

She closed the cottage door; the shutters were already closed. She skipped down to where the men balanced the box between them.

'Where are you going with that box, Henry?' she asked. 'Everyone else is carrying things away from the village, not into the village.'

'I'll explain more when we arrive at the church,' he said. Each cobble stone was uneven and slippery, so progress was slow.

Cartia felt out of her depth and longed for the familiarity and raw hope of happier times together. It was as though a giant stood over the place, casting a deep shadow over them. Her brother was no longer the same. He should not feel so alone. He ached for the company of his friends and family who would always be there for him, but he had trouble reaching out to them. A silent tear rolled down her cheek as she listened for sounds in the piercing silence of the empty marketplace near the church. All she could hear were the waves and the trees whispering in the wind. The only birds were a couple of ravens perched high on the tower. She longed for everything to fall back into place again. She wanted to hear the villagers sing in the church, the market buzz with activity and women's voices as they discussed the affairs of their day while drawing up the bucket from the village well. Again, she thought of Daniaen, of his safety, and if he would ever be able to come for her. Was this the end of the world? The final judgement? Everything was so dark, and sadness weighed like a heavy blanket on the shoulders of the deserted village.

Henry and James carried the heavy box to the northern part of the stone church wall and dropped it near a heap of freshly turned dirt. There wasn't much distance between the church and the precipice, so she stayed near the gate. The tide was out, a full moon glared through a split in the dark clouds.

Cartia stood at the gate, watching the men from a distance. When she searched the familiar beach at low tide, she was horrified at what remained of Shipden's thatched cottages. All that lingered were lovingly laid stone paths, collapsed limestone walls and slab foundations. Seaweed hung from rafters, meticulously split from local woodland. Like her brother, many had put countless hours into building their cottages and she could only imagine how painful it was for them all to witness this destruction. A few feet away, the two men were facing one another, her brother holding a spade.

'So, what's happening, Henry? Why are we here?'

'I'm going to bury this box with my wife,' he told James. 'Then I can move on.'

'But these are all your memories of her, my friend,' said James.

'Memories can haunt you, James. It's too painful to remember her in this way. She will always be in my heart,' he said.

'What can I do to help you?' he asked Henry.

'You and Cartia should go home now, so you will be safe from harm.'

'Harm? Nobody's going to harm you. How might you do this? What's your plan?'

'I've already loosened the soil with the spade some time ago. I'll bury my box with her. She's already lying here,' he said, pointing nearby. At this revelation, James moved back a step. He seemed shocked. Cartia had already guessed that he had moved Emma's coffin to a safer place but hadn't mentioned it to anybody.

'I moved her coffin, James, and I understand this would not please God. I moved her here so she wouldn't go over the cliff into the sea. I believe God wouldn't allow the church to be destroyed.

This is still consecrated ground, near the church so I felt she's safer here. That's the harm I speak of – a vengeful act of God. Now, please, go. Let me get on with this,' he said.

'God be with you, my friend,' said James. 'If you must do this to move on in life, go ahead.' He moved his hand to rest on Henry's shoulder for a few moments and turned to go out of the churchyard.

There was nobody else around this part of town now. No-one would notice a man digging in the ruined churchyard. Most of it was gone. Tumbled over the cliff and into the ocean.

'He doesn't want us to wait for him,' said James at the lych-gate. 'Let's go.'

'If you don't mind, James, I'll wait nearby. You go on ahead home and tell the others what's happening. I'll be here for him when he's finished. I think he's going to need support,' she said.

'Do you think I should wait too?' he asked. 'I will wait if you need me, Cartia.'

'No, he's my brother. You go back home to Matilda. You have further to walk, and night is setting in.' She sat on the road verge where she had a clear view of her brother.

'Alright,' he said, convinced she was safe waiting for Henry. 'I'll let your parents know where you are. I don't think he'll be long.'

She watched James hurry away, thankful for his support.

'Cartia Laman?'

There stood a tall man with a facemask wrapped over half his face. At first glimpse, she didn't recognise him and startled at the sound of his voice in the dark. She pushed herself off the stone wall to face him, to squint through filtered moonlight, closer to his features. He probably could not see her very well either, as the sun's light had almost set over a cloudy evening.

'Good evening, sir,' she said.

She couldn't explain the reason, but she felt she knew him. She adjusted her own facemask. Everyone was wearing them to avoid the dreaded illness.

'Yes, I'm Cartia.'

'Cartia, I've been trying to come for you for so long,' he said, removing his facemask. 'Did you not marry after all this time? Did you wait for me?'

She couldn't believe her eyes. There he stood, an impossible figment of her imagination, perhaps? A ghost? He stepped closer to her, through the soft sea mist.

'Daniaen de Rek? Is that truly you?'

She turned toward her brother, who was kneeling beside Emma's grave, the mud-caked spade on the ground beside him. Then, she turned back to face him.

'All this time I've waited for you. Are you real?' she touched the side of his face with a trembling hand. He laughed.

'Yes, I am very real, Cartia. I've returned from the marshes. The plague has stopped all dam construction, and the marshes are flooded. I will return there again soon, but I wanted to see you and to ask if you wanted to come with me,' he said. 'I've built a small cottage on a dry hill, closer to the dam.'

'My parents are old now. I can't leave them in a plague.'

'Yes, I thought as much. You're a very loyal daughter. Your duty to your family is almost over, Cartia. Perhaps we must stay until after the sickness has passed and work is abundant in the marshes again.'

She thought about the years which had passed, about the pain she felt when he had left the village to take work out west. How she had longed for him to return, day after day, for so long. She had refused to marry anyone else and only wanted to be with Daniaen.

'Can I think about this for a while, Daniaen? It's come as a great surprise to me that I would ever see you again. Yes, my family has needed me over these years and I'm glad I stayed to share their burdens. Maybe the time will be right soon to make the decision to leave them and go with you.'

'Would you still consider marrying me, Cartia?'

They stood under the lychgate of St Peter's church, maybe the last couple to do so. They held hands and smiled. She was amazed that he had come back for her, and felt her heart might explode. This was hope for the future, something she felt was gone forever. She had rehearsed this moment for a very long time. She drew a deep breath, stared into his eyes and whispered,

'I take you as my husband, Daniaen de Rek.'

'I take you as my wife, Cartia Laman,' he said. 'My father once said to me, 'You can't build a dyke on your own. We all flourish, or we all perish.' We will build a life together and flourish, my Cartia.'

Smells of rotting seaweed and dung blew in on the coastal breeze. Nobody was carting away the sewerage, the horse dung was not being cleared, the community had almost all left town. The only cart in the village was the body collector. Every evening, she heard the slow clip-clop of a horse and cart. The driver called for the dead in his monotone voice, asking for bodies to be wrapped and left outside cottages. In some places, so many had died that clergy were unable to perform individual burials anymore and instead had to bury bodies in a plague pit on the edge of town.

The clergy were particularly hit hard by the plague, the local church had recently lost so many. She knew of Robert de Wingerworth, a new priest sent to Shipden as a gift from the King when the Abbot of St Benet became ill. They had given up the most important thing that kept each one of them going through all the challenges of life and nature – hope.

She thought St Peter's church had also given up hope. It collapsed and shattered over those sandy cliffs one dark night when a tidal surge pushed its way deep under each side of the chalky edifice. The remaining walls gradually sank below the waves, taking the remaining graves, including Emma's grave with the memory box, to a final burial. The tower, resting on its side, lingered on the beach for many years at low tide. Flints covered the sand, together with fragments of bar-tracery from the windows.

On that dark, stormy night, the villagers who remained until the final day, swore they heard its bells tolling under the ocean at high tide.

Chapter 31 – 2013

Hospital smells not only brought back sharp memories, but they also gave Josh a conflicting sense of life and death, pain and pleasure, happiness and sadness. Hospitals are where he smelt all these contradictions together at a point of crescendo. He felt his heart race every time he entered a hospital foyer. He wasn't looking forward to visiting her today but felt it was the right thing to do. Slung on his shoulder were some magazines, her iPad, clothes, toiletries, and her mail retrieved quickly from her room at the boarding house. He wouldn't take a taxi. The hospital was in the middle of Cromer and easy to find so he had walked between showers. Besides, he wanted to walk off a few thoughts which had played on his mind.

Since yesterday, when he put his life on the line for her and the twins, he was feeling a bit on edge. Adrenaline raced through his veins, courage he wasn't aware he had, fear of the unknown. After years of heartache and disappointment, to feel himself come alive again was emotional and confusing, to say the least. He'd been scared. Scared to lose her, scared to step out of his comfort zone. He couldn't rationalize his behaviour this morning, gathering her stuff together and taking it all to the hospital. The games people play that he'd hated to be a part of but found himself swept up in, to protect her, to reassure her.

This would be a trying time for Carly too, so he must pull himself together and get on with it. As a fellow Aussie. He'd arrived at the entrance to the small hospital and entered a busy foyer.

'Carly Williams, please. She was brought in yesterday,' he said to an orderly, who rushed by with a trolley. He pointed at a large reception counter. There was a volunteer, who smiled at a young woman and pointed to the corridor on her left. He waited his turn in the queue. He must've been bored. He noticed the colours of the walls; bile yellow, the floor a pale chocolate brown with black edging. Ghastly colour choices but this part of the hospital felt quite new. A television monitor distracted visitors but nobody could possibly hear the audio. There was a sweet soft smell near the desk, several bunches of flowers in buckets. They masked the arid smell of antiseptic and cleaning polish. He'd buy a bunch for Carly when he could.

A couple of vending machines leant against the far wall. He wandered in that direction while the lady helped another lost soul find direction. He was next in line. He slipped some coins into the slot and retrieved a packet of chips from the window at its base. The packet reminded him that they are crisps over here, differentiating them from hot chips at the Fisho. He sat on one of the plastic chairs in front of the reception area and opened the packet, relishing the taste of a salty, vinegar-soaked morsel. He didn't eat many. They were too salty and made his eyes sting. Besides, the receptionist smiled in his direction.

He stood, threw the crisps into the bin and approached the information counter. 'I'm looking for my friend, Carly Williams, who was brought in here after a beach accident. She hurt her ankle during the storm.'

The woman checked her database. Some double glass doors nearby burst open. Several medical officers pulled a trolley toward the lift on the far wall, the patient moaned and bent sideways. Josh felt disrespectful, so he glanced away. Behind him he could hear people murmuring in low tones. The intercom announced the arrival of an ambulance. Several nurses with facemasks on sprinted past in crisp white shirts and black pants.

'Can get a bit loud here sometimes, sir. Sorry about the noise.'

'Can't be helped. I'm sure it's unavoidable. The storm must have everyone feeling on edge,' he said.

The woman looked up from her screen.

'Yes, it's been very busy, particularly the past few hours,' she said, returning to her screen. 'Carly Williams can be visited. She's on level one, the stairs are over there. Reception on level one will show you to her room.'

'Thank you. Could you tell me where the twins were taken?' Josh had seen the sign out the front which indicated they may have been taken to Norwich Hospital rather than here.

'Their names, please, sir?'

'Tariq and Tasneem Timms. They're about six or seven years old, I think,' he said. 'Friends of friends.'

He waited while she checked her computer again, bright pink nails clicking on the keyboard.

'They're not listed at this hospital, sir. For privacy reasons, I can't tell you about their condition. But I can say they've probably been transferred to Norfolk and Norwich University Hospital, Accident and Emergency department. Here's their phone number, sir.' She handed him a sticky note.

'Okay. Thanks again. Level one for Carly?' he confirmed. 'And these flowers, please.'

'Yes, sir. That's correct,' she said, accepting his Visa card and swiping it. 'Thank you.'

He chose some red roses with delicate little white flowers softening the edges with tiny red berries of some sort and he genuinely hoped she would like them, a momentary distraction. She'll want to know if the twins are okay. He had the phone number of the hospital and would check later if they had been taken to Norwich but, not being a close family member, the hospital would not divulge any information on their condition.

Early next morning, the sky was a soft velvet scattered with stars when Josh drove Carly home from the hospital. She had not needed to stay any longer, the x-ray indicated a badly twisted ankle, so she sat beside him, the flowers he'd bought for her still wrapped and placed across her lap. For now, the rain had moved on, but more storms were predicted tomorrow.

'Josh, thanks for delivering me back to my own bed,' she said. 'Nothing like one's own pillow.'

'Yeah, of course. We ex-pats must look after our own,' he said, smiled and glanced sideways at her. She looked a bit of a wreck, poor girl. What a traumatic experience for her and the twins. And him too. Being tossed around in a freezing, mad sea wasn't his idea of fun either. He was lucky the lifeguards turned up when they did. They all just needed to chill out for a bit.

'I'll give you a hand getting up the stairs if you like,' he said. 'But you will have to get used to using those crutches for a while.'

He watched the road ahead, weaved around deeper puddles and blocked drains. There weren't many cars on the road at that time of morning and he was grateful for that. In the back of his mind were the pressures of finishing his article and organising his return trip home in time for Christmas. But, right now, he was focused on Carly. He liked her independent soul, but sometimes it felt good to have someone else rely on him, to lean on his masculinity a bit. Not that he would want her to be too reliant on him. Nor too permanent. He thought about that as streetlight reflections caused unexpected movements in puddles on the road.

'Tomorrow I'll phone Anna,' she said, looking out the window. 'It's no good phoning the hospital again. They can't tell me anything. I have her mobile number, so I'll phone again. I've left a couple of messages already. Maybe she won't pick up…'

'Carly, I'm sure they don't blame you for what happened at the beach.'

'How can you be so sure, Josh? I was there, I was responsible for their well-being,' she said, blowing her nose.

'I know you were. But those kids were very naughty sneaking away like that. There's no way you would've allowed them to go to the beach huts at that time, if you'd had a choice,' he said. No matter what he said to reassure her, he knew she needed to hear Anna's voice.

'The weather turned so suddenly. We were on our way home,' she said. 'That stupid bloke stopped me. Apparently, he'd been one of my online students. It was a weird conversation really. Anyway, before I knew it, the children had gone and, when I looked for them just minutes later, I saw them go inside one of the huts and shut the door.'

'Kids are quick.'

'I know. Right? By the time I ran along the prom to reach them, the sea had swallowed up most of the other beach huts and the water was too deep to reach them.'

'Yes, I know. The water was high. It put too much pressure on the door, and they couldn't open it.'

'Josh, I haven't asked you this, but I've been wondering,' she said, watching his steady hands on the steering wheel. 'How did you know I needed help? I remember looking along the beach and watching this lone man running in my direction. Then I realized it was you.'

He flashed one of his smiles in her direction as he recalled the moment.

'Well, I was about to have that interview with the coxswain, Dave, and all the alarms went off as I entered the building. I didn't even get to meet him. Of course, I had to get out of their way, but I overheard someone say there were children stuck in one of the beach huts. You told me that you were taking the twins to the beach, so I put two and two together and decided to take a look myself.'

He watched her forehead fill with a deep frown. This was so unlike the vivacious person he knew before this accident happened. Carly's foot would heal way before her mental anguish.

'Thank you so much, Josh. I'm really sorry you had to go through all that.'

'Don't worry about me. I'm just fine,' he said.

Chapter 32 – 2013

After another brief stint in hospital, Ginny was relieved to return to her own bed in the care home. When she checked with the receptionist, who had very kindly emptied her post office box in Cromer, there had been several letters. She hoped that they wouldn't all be bills this time, as she thought she'd caught up with them by now. She really hoped for a letter from her friend, Val. She missed her so much and all the news of the children and Mike.

She had wondered for quite a while now why Val hadn't written to her. This was quite unusual for her friend not to write, especially around Christmas. Not even a Christmas card. She remembered posting Val a card just before she came into the care home. She was starting to wonder if all was well with her as she had been under treatment for breast cancer for some time. She had written her new post office box number on the back of the Christmas card to Val so, if she was able to, she would expect her to write eventually. She had used the last aerogram remaining in her stationery kit as the Royal Mail stopped making them last year and her own supply had run out. She missed the lightness of them, the brevity, the simplicity, the smell.

The receptionist brought the mail to her room in the afternoon after her lunch tray had been cleared away. It was so restful here. People were kind and generous, if not rushed off their feet. She flipped through the letters, discarded the advertising material. There was one letter from the local council inviting her to attend a course to keep her occupied. She didn't think so. Not now.

One thing for sure, there were no blue aerograms, no cards, no overseas stamps. It was back to square one, waiting for Val to write. Maybe she should write out of turn, which would not be the way of things for them, but she felt an urgency about it. She would write soon. As she pondered this, a small envelope dropped from her pile of advertising brochures. She picked it up, inspected it front and back. She didn't recognize the handwriting. She saw the Sheringham address on the back and didn't recall anyone from that address, other than her recollection of an older home currently used as a guesthouse. She knew the house well enough with its pale blue door and bay windows. The garden was just trees now and the once-proud building stood out in the street as the bus drove past.

She tore open the flap and pulled out a handwritten letter, only one page with a photo on it. The wonders of technology. She put on her reading glasses after giving them a wipe with her hanky. She sighed and began to focus on the photo first. It was taken in the late sixties, she remembered. Her eyes went to the tall man in the centre of this smiling family. Mikey, his hand resting on her shoulder, all smartly dressed for church and standing near the golden wattle at the front gate. She was nursing baby Kellie, twelve-year-old Carly was seated at her feet with the other children. My goodness, how she looked like Kellie. She had no photos of the family, so it was like stepping back in time observing all those happy, smiling faces. Now, what's this letter about and who wrote it? Who had access to this photo?

What? She could hardly believe her eyes. It was a letter from her oldest daughter, Carly. She felt her pulse race, concentrated on each word in front of her but her mind felt clouded, confused. She drifted to the address again. Is she here? She took a deep breath several times and started to read that Carly was searching for her in England. In the letter, she asked Ginny to contact her. She checked the date of the letter. She worried that a long time had passed since the letter had been written. Maybe she had already given up hope and returned to Australia by now. She would have a job to go home to, must be in her mid-twenties by now. She had left a mobile phone number and an email address in the letter. When Kellie comes in to visit next, she would ask her to contact her older sister. A sister she has not known since she was a tiny baby.

Her eyes welled up and she couldn't see the writing clearly. What would she say to her daughter after all this time? Would Carly be angry with her? Would she ever be able to forgive her for leaving? If she'd thought about her once in all this time, she would've been overwhelmed with a deep ache, so she survived by cutting off those links. Val had kept her informed. It was their special secret. When the doctor told her she could no longer travel long distances or by plane anywhere, she knew her life was anchored in England. How she missed those days in Broome, those long hot summer days sitting under the frangipani tree near the verandah with her children playing at her feet. Tears flowed freely now. Her chest felt tight, she rubbed her arm, which was aching a bit.

Strange things had been happening to her lately. Firstly, the young man who drove her to see her collapsing home. Then his interview which still hadn't happened. She felt quite guilty about that and must get back to him to re-schedule. Secondly, the girl with the ring. She would know that ring anywhere. She was sure it once belonged to her. Made especially for her by her husband and presented to her on their wedding day. How did this photographer get hold of her old ring, which she'd left on a kitchen table in Broome many years ago? Maybe it had been stolen or maybe he had to sell it to make ends meet.

It was too much for her to take in. Outside her window, a storm was brewing again, the charcoal sky darkening her room. Her body felt heavy, weary. She would rest on the bed for a while and let things fall into place later.

A week had flown past since the incident at the beach hut. Carly had rung earlier to say that her foot had almost recovered, though she still needed it bandaged and she still required crutches to get around. This morning, Josh had received a message from the care home that Ginny had requested he return to complete his interview, so he came as quickly as he could. His boss in Brisbane had been on the phone last night asking when it might be finished, so he felt an urgent pull to get things moving along.

This was his final interview before he submitted his story to the newspaper. His plan was to finish it this morning and work on the report the rest of the day. He called Carly to meet him there, but she had already left for the day so was unable to reach her. She had mentioned that she had an online class and would take an Uber when she'd finished. Photos, he decided, would have to wait until she was available. By then, he would have checked his report or be pretty close to it. He'd slip the photos in later. Tom and his niece were waiting for him when he arrived in the foyer of the care home.

'Good morning, Tom, Kellie,' said Josh, shaking hands with Tom. 'Is everything okay? I had a message from Ginny to come over this morning.' Neither of them looked comfortable with him being cheerful. Kellie had tears in her eyes.

'Josh, I'm very sorry,' said Tom. 'Sadly, my sister passed away a couple of hours ago. I would've called you to cancel, but I didn't have your contact details.'

'I'm very sorry to hear that. My condolences,' said Josh. 'It's never easy, is it?'

They sat and talked for a while. Kellie busied herself by making hot chocolate for them.

'Thanks, Kellie.'

'We waited here to meet with you. Is Carly unable to come today?' said Kellie. 'My mother died holding tight to a letter I'd like to speak to her about. If you could give me her email address...'

'Poor Carly twisted her ankle at the beach. I'm sure she wouldn't mind me sharing that with you, Kellie.' He tore some paper from his notes and on it wrote her email contact.

The girl pulled a piece of paper from her jeans pocket, smoothed it out on the coffee table between them and compared the email address Josh had given her with the one written in the letter. 'Uncle, these are the same email addresses. Carly is my sister.'

'So, Ginny was her mother?' asked Josh. 'But they didn't recognise one another the other day when we were all in this room. She's been searching for her mother for a couple of years. What are the odds...?'

'Ginny had a difficult life, but she struggled through with great resilience. She changed. Got old too early. That might be why Carly didn't recognise her. I don't know the whole story, obviously, as I only ever visited her once when she lived in Australia. I know she came home to our place about fifteen years after she left. She was exhausted when I think about it. Her heart was weak, but we weren't to know about that back then.'

'She had a large family,' said Josh. 'It would've been tough living in Broome back then.'

'Yes, she did. I met the first four when I was over there on holiday years ago, and she brought the youngest one back with her to England,' said Tom. 'This is her. Kellie.' She looked up and smiled at him.

'I can only remember living with Uncle Tom and his family. As Mum's heart grew weaker, she couldn't cope with my energy. Then, of course, her house was completely unsafe for a child to live in as time went on,' said Kellie. 'She used to live with Uncle Tom too when we first arrived, but she found it disturbing. When Grandma and Gramps died, she moved into their holiday house. That's tipped over the cliff now, I think. She told me Uncle Tom's house reminded her of their twin brothers who drowned in the floods.'

'I remember that morning in the fifties,' said Tom. 'Coming down the stairs, finding the twins in the pram, our parents holding each other, crying. Ginny was already downstairs. She was as quiet as a statue. Probably in shock. The rain and noise outside the cottage didn't stop. All that day, we were told to stay upstairs where it was dry but everything we touched was damp. The air, the curtains, even the walls.'

'I heard about those flood surges in the early fifties. It must've been very frightening for the whole family,' said Josh.

'It was. There were lots of tears shed that day. My aunt and two cousins drowned several cottages along. Like many others, their home was totally washed off its stumps and collapsed into the sea. We were lucky our old family cottage was strong enough to withstand the flood, but sea water came in under the door and filled it up like a swimming pool. My uncle, who had lost everything and everyone in his family, came to live with us until he was able to settle in London,' said Tom. He took out a hanky and blew his nose. 'Later we learnt that most families knew of someone who had drowned. Hundreds died, right along the east coast. Other low-lying countries also had similar problems. We helped people rebuild, of course, but my sister, Ginny, never really recovered from the shock. She left our village as soon as she turned eighteen.'

'Australia was advertising for people to emigrate for the cost of ten pounds, so she took them up on it,' said Tom. 'Married a local bloke, had babies. But I don't know if anyone can get over the shock of seeing your brothers drowned in their own pram. Ginny had lots of babies herself. I thought that would cure her, watching them survive and thrive, but I don't know.'

'She had intended to return to Australia,' said Kellie. 'but her doctor put an end to that idea, so she just stayed in England. Said she didn't want to cause a drama back home, so kept herself to herself pretty much, and I stayed on with my Uncle Tom and his family.'

'When I saw the photo in Carly's letter,' Tom said. 'I remembered it. When I got home last night, I dug out the album and there was my copy, which my sister had sent to our parents for Christmas one year. That's why I thought I'd seen Carly before, Josh. I recalled her from the photos. She's my niece.'

This was a lot to take in and Josh wished Carly had been able to be here with him today. Instead, she finished off her online course, with her twisted ankle up on a cushion. The minute he leaves the care home, he'd send her a message to contact Kellie. He imagined she'd be over-the-moon happy to hear from Kellie, but devasted to have missed the opportunity to spend time with her mother before she passed away.

Josh was able to speak for some time with Tom about the floods in the early fifties. He would use this information in his report, with Tom's permission, of course.

'And your parents? Ginny's parents?' he asked. 'Are they still alive?'

'No, they passed away soon after Ginny arrived back. The grief never left them, Mum especially. Dad had his work as a thatcher to take his mind off things a bit. He trained us boys to continue with his business. But Mum .. family was everything to her and she was crushed with guilt for falling asleep as the flood water crept into the house. I was very young then. It was a shocking time. She died first, and Dad died soon after – he couldn't live without Ma. They had been kids in school together. He didn't seem to know who he was without her.'

Chapter 33 - 2013

Carly finished her final class, picked up her crutches and hobbled down the hallway. Earlier, she had received an email from the girl at the care home, a relative of the poor lady who had lost her house to the sea. She was curious as to why Kellie wanted to speak with her and guessed she might've wanted to get a photo from her collection from that brief meeting. She would ask Josh when he was going up to the care home again and show her some photos then.

Petunia stood nearby and placed today's mail into the slots on the buffet. She wore flashing Christmas tree earrings and a wide smile.

'Good morning, Carly. How's your foot today?'

'Hi Petunia. Much better thanks, but I've been ordered to use crutches for another week, unfortunately,' she said. 'I might have to use my bottom to slip from step to step for a while longer.'

They kept their banter light-hearted. Petunia was always busy. 'Someone's at the front door,' she said, and placed the rest of the mail, mostly Christmas cards, on the buffet and hurried to the door.

'Hello. Merry Christmas,' she heard her say.

'Hi – yes, merry Christmas to you too. I'm wondering if I could see Carly for a while?'

Petunia opened the door wider. 'Yes, you may. Come on in.'

'Kellie,' she said. 'Please, come on into the warm fire in the lounge room. Thanks, Petunia.'

Kellie nodded as she walked past and followed her into the comfortable lounge room. It was empty, as most of the other residents had gone Christmas shopping. Carly had asked for them to buy a couple of gifts for her to save her from squeezing into the crowded shops. At the moment, she lived in fear of someone treading on her toes.

'So nice to see you, Kellie. Can I make you a hot drink or something?' Kellie removed her coat, scarf, beanie and gloves, flopped them over the back of a chair.

'Thanks, a hot chocolate sounds lovely,' she said. 'Josh told us about your trouble at the beach huts. How's your ankle now? I see you're still hobbling about.' They both moved over to the buffet near the wall, where a hot drink dispenser was available for guests and residents. There was also a covered plate with fresh scones and jam.

'Oh, I'll survive, swelling's gone now. It was the scariest time of my whole life! I slipped on the rocks. The crutches are more of a weapon in case someone gets too close to my foot,' she said. 'Good timing, Kellie, fresh scones.'

'And strawberry jam,' she said. 'I hope you don't mind me dropping by. I'm glad you're okay. I have some sad news to share with you and I think you'll be surprised at what I'm about to tell you, Carly.'

'Okay. Well, that sounds ominous. Let's get this drink organised and we'll sit over there, on the window seat,' she said, now more curious than when she had received the earlier email message. Kellie was very young to be out on her own in this terrible weather. Maybe her Uncle Tom had dropped her off in his car.

They settled on the cushioned seat, a worn-thin, blue velvet fabric, and sipped their drinks.

'Okay. Now what's all this about? I'm intrigued,' she asked Kellie.

'Did you know that my mother passed away?' she asked.

'Oh, no. I'm so sorry,' said Carly, placing her hand on Kellie's shoulder. 'I had no idea. Are you okay?'

Silly question. She didn't know what else to say or do. This poor girl had lost her mother unexpectantly. She appeared to be about the same age as she had been when her own mother went missing. It would be a terrible loss for her. But she hardly knew this young girl. Why would she feel the need to tell Carly in person? She could've sent a text message. But why would she bother to do that in her time of grief to someone she barely knew?

Kellie put down her mug, opened her backpack and retrieved an envelope. She recognised it at once. It was the letter she'd written to her mother some time ago. Kellie pulled out the letter and unfolded it. She looked up at her. She had tears in her eyes but seemed to be okay.

'That's the letter I sent to my mother, Kellie. How did you come across it?' she asked. The girl looked uneasy, but she put it down to the uncertainly Kellie must be feeling right now.

'My mother had it in her hand when they found her.'

It took a while to work this out. She was still in need of clarity. Why would Kellie's mother have had this letter?

Her mobile beeped.

'Would you mind if I checked this message, Kellie? I don't want to appear rude, but I'm expecting an important message from my work,' she said. How inconvenient for Josh to send for her now. Wait. As Kellie's mother had died, there would be no need for them to go to the care home to complete the interview. She glanced at

Kellie, who nodded slowly, and settled back into a cushion to wait for her.

It was from Josh. He had something to tell her and would like to drop by in the next few minutes. Was she available?

She opened the phone and wrote that Kellie is visiting atm.

He answered as she walked back to Kellie. Too late, I'm here. Open the door please.

This was awkward. 'Kellie, Josh has arrived. Would you mind if I let him join us? I could ask him to come back later, if you'd prefer,' she said.

'That's okay. I don't mind,' she said, folding the letter and putting it back into her backpack.

'Why don't I make him a hot chocolate?' She smiled, stood and began walking to the buffet.

'I'm sure he'd appreciate that, Kellie. We've both been through such a lot this week. I'll let him in.'

She held the lounge room door open for a moment and looked back at Kellie. She seemed composed, clicking the hot drink machine into action again. So many questions still hung in the air. Now Josh had arrived with news. She opened the front door and saw him sheltered under his umbrella, the rain gushing from its edges.

'Not much notice, I'm afraid, Carly,' he said, shaking the umbrella. 'I'll leave this in the stand.'

'Always nice to see you, Josh,' said Carly, gently closing the door behind him. 'Did I thank you for bringing me home from the hospital?'

He nodded. 'Profusely.'

He slipped his wet shoes off and lined them up along the shoe rack with others. She liked the way he had control of the little things. Everything had a place. Umbrella in the stand, shoes on the rack. Was he always this tidy at home? Controlling the things he can control, she thought, might be a way of life for him. It would take courage to risk his heart being broken again. But he doesn't lack courage. She'd watched him jump into the sea to save Tasneem and Tariq.

'As I said, Kellie has called in. I assumed her Uncle Tom dropped her off.'

He looked apologetic, pulled her close. 'I'm sorry it's come to this, Carly. It's not what you wanted, I know.' She felt startled. What was he talking about? She pulled away from his soft embrace.

'What on earth are you talking about, Josh?' He took a step back; his hands slipped into the pockets of his jeans.

'Oh, so you don't know yet?' he said. 'Let's go into the room with Kellie. I'm sure she has the same news as I do.'

'Okay. I do know Kellie's mother died suddenly. Is that what this mystery is about?' she said. 'You know what's really odd? That girl has the letter I wrote to my mother in her backpack.'

'Yes, I think I know why she has it, but I'll let her fill you in.'

The doorbell rang.

'You go inside and warm up, Josh. I'll answer the door. Petunia must be elsewhere in the building,' she said, using her crutches to lean on.

A gust of wind blew the door open when she turned the doorknob. All she could see for a moment, were two umbrellas. Under them were Anna and Jack. She hadn't seen nor heard from them since she came out of the hospital. A wash of guilt came over her. How would these two people ever forgive her? Maybe they wanted to chastise her for allowing the twins to go anywhere near the beach huts during the storm. Nothing she hadn't already said to herself, but it would seem worse coming from them.

'Carly, just the young lady we needed to see. I hope you don't mind us dropping by this afternoon. Anna said it was best we called in to speak to you face-to-face rather than talk on the phone. Is it convenient for you?' Jack hesitated, glanced at his wife.

'Of course. We're about to have afternoon tea. Come on inside, please.'

They placed their umbrellas in the stand near the door and followed her down the hallway and into the warm lounge room. She did not know what to say so remained silent.

'I see you've hurt your foot,' said Anna. 'I hope it's not too bad. Is it broken?'

'No, not broken. Just a bit swollen. Silly, really. The rock was slippery,' she said. 'I'm so sorry for the anguish I've caused you both.'

'Nonsense, Carly,' said Anna. 'That's why we've come to see you this morning; to tell you we're all okay. The twins are out of hospital and with their parents at our place.'

'It wasn't your fault,' said Jack. 'We had a few hours of worry once the Police came around, but they took us to the hospital in Norwich. Once we saw the children were improving with every hour, we relaxed. Of course, we contacted Carter and Aziza, and they drove home immediately.'

'We also spoke with Tasneem, who explained what happened at the beach that day. It seems they had disobeyed you and sneaked off without your knowledge. Little monkeys. I hope they've learnt their lesson and also very grateful they survived, thanks to your prompt action,' said Anna. 'The lifeguards said you and your friend, Josh, did all the right things to save them. It was a harrowing experience for you, and we must also ask you to pass on our thanks to Josh.'

They opened the lounge room door and a whoosh of warm air held them still. She gestured for them to come through, 'Now you can thank Josh yourself, Anna,' said Carly.

Josh was sipping his drink, talking with Kellie, nodding at her conversation. He turned, put his drink on the side table and walked towards them.

'Anna and Jack. So nice to see you. After all the recent drama, are you all okay? How are Tasneem and Tariq? We tried to see them in the hospital, but we weren't allowed in,' he explained.

Carly moved over to Kellie. 'I'm terribly sorry for all these interruptions, Kellie. Do you have time to stay a bit longer? I'd really like to hear what you have to tell me, but I know you're sad today and may not want to be here socializing with people. If you want, I can phone you later?'

'That's alright, Carly. My Uncle Tom will be here to collect me in an hour. I have time,' she said. 'That is, if it's still okay for me to stay now you have other guests.'

'I'd love you to stay. These are wonderful people who are the grandparents of the twins I babysit. Let me introduce you to them and I'll get them a warm drink too.'

She introduced everyone and made a coffee for Anna and a white tea for Jack. She'd remembered. She was so pleased with their visit. They hadn't blamed her for not watching the twins closely enough. In fact, they seemed grateful. They were very understanding people who knew what it was like to have young children and the antics they get up to. A weight had been lifted from her shoulders.

She listened to the sound of the storm outside. It was still December; the storm of all storms was the first thing people discussed. It went on for two days on the fifth and sixth of December and was sure to go down in history as one of the major events of this century. She listened to everyone trying to out-do each other with news of terrible events right along the coast. Anna reminded them of similar storm surges in the fifties when she was young, when thousands of people all along the Norfolk coast died.

Kellie had been sitting, observing the others. 'My family lost two babies in those floods,' she told Anna. 'My Uncle Tom and my mother were only young themselves when it happened. I've watched how it's affected them, and they never really got over it,' she said. Her hands twisted together, her eyes sad.

Anna came to sit with her, placing her arm around her shoulder. 'It's such a terrible time for everyone. These storms have been eating away at our coastline forever and so many people have suffered loss over the years.' Anna's phone rang. 'Oh, silly thing. I'm sorry. Would you please excuse me? I'll switch it off.'

She glanced at the caller ID and decided to take the call.

Josh was telling them about the sea being so cold when he jumped in to save the twins, when she heard the doorbell ring again. She'd leave it for someone else this time. After a few minutes, it rang again, twice this time. She excused herself from the room to answer the door to the impatient soul waiting to get in. It must be chilly outside.

It was the Police. Two of them, dripping under black umbrellas. Lightning lit up the sky behind them. She stepped aside immediately, and they entered, adding their umbrellas to the hallstand.

'Thank you, Miss.'

'Hello. Sorry to have kept you waiting – crutches are a bit slow. Who were you after?' she said.

They showed her their identification wallets. 'We're looking for Carly Williams. Is she here?'

Her stomach dropped. Someone has died, something terrible must have happened to one of her loved ones back home…

'That's me.'

'Don't worry, nothing too dreadful has happened, Miss Williams,' the younger one said. He must've sensed her inner panic. 'Can we have a moment of your time, please?'

They didn't mind that the lounge room was crowded as it wasn't a personal matter. They needed to inform her of an arrest. So, they joined the others, although they refused to have a hot drink as they were very busy and needed to get away soon. Chairs were placed almost in a circle around the bay window where Kellie was talking to Anna. At least, she had been talking, before the two policemen approached the group. How awkward they must feel when all conversation stopped as they approached, people always feared the worst news.

'Hello everyone. With Carly's permission, we won't be long. Let you get on with your day.'

The older police officer took a seat near Carly, the younger one stood behind him. Her heart raced. She concentrated on the older man's face, his eyes stern and his body set solid.

'Well, officer, what is it that you need to say?'

'Carly, I don't know if you remember a fellow from your class - a Mr Paterson?' he paused. 'Kyle Paterson.'

'I teach online, so I don't always get to know the students very well. Do you have a photo of him? Is he missing? Has he done something wrong?'

'Yes, his photo is online. Can you pull it up, George? We're building a case against him. He's been arrested and we've had him in for questioning regarding a complaint from the public.'

His colleague opened his phone and searched, found the photo and showed it to Carly. She looked over at Josh, who also looked at the officer's phone.

'Oh, Kyle. Yes, he seemed to pop up in all sorts of places,' said Carly. 'We had quite a strange conversation a few days ago, which I rushed away from. I was babysitting and he distracted me. Asked me a question about my accent and where I came from. When I realized the twins had disappeared, I turned around in time to see them go inside the beach hut, so I ran after them.'

'He turned up later near the beach hut during the storm,' said Josh. 'I met him earlier too. When I first arrived in England. I'd gone to the railway station in Holt. He followed a couple of young women onto the steam train.'

'One of those young women reported she'd been followed from the train at Sheringham,' said the policeman. 'Actually, Carly, it was your friend, Rose. She said you were also followed by him too. That's why we're here today. Is this so?'

'That seems like a long time ago now, but, yes, I was. I didn't realize it was Kyle though. I certainly hadn't realized he'd been a student of mine either,' she said. 'Is Rose alright?'

'Yes, apparently her stalker didn't harm her physically. Just frightened her and walked off,' said the officer. 'I believe this is a pattern for him. We've pulled together quite a few reports of a man with red shoes, who followed young women, particularly in the evenings. But whether he hurts someone or not, they do get a scare, and the experience is threatening. Makes women think they can't walk alone when they're followed like that. Anyway, we may need you to give evidence at the station, if you don't mind, Carly. It can wait until Monday.'

'No problem, officer. I remember those red sneakers. He was also at the care home I visited. I'll give it some more thought. He might've been stalking me in other places.'

'Yes, please do. Here's my card. Josh, if you could also give us a review of what you saw at the Holt railway station before Monday's deadline, that would be helpful. Perhaps you could both attend the police station at Cromer before next Monday?' he said, nodding agreement with Josh. 'We'll see ourselves out. Thank you for your time and have a merry Christmas, folks.'

The police officers left the room. The conversation noise moved up a notch.

'My mobile rang before, Carly,' said Anna, above the chatter. 'I'm afraid I told my son and his family to call in here on their way home. The twins wanted to say goodbye to you, and this seemed like a good opportunity.'

The room was abuzz, as though a party was brewing. She thought of Kellie, probably overcome with grief at the death of her mother and needing some peace. But Kelly was in deep conversation with Jack, so she was okay for the moment.

'Anna, that's lovely. I'd really enjoy seeing the kids before they return to London. I think we all need a cuddle after our ordeals.'

The front doorbell rang, and in rushed Tariq and Tasneem with Aziza and Carter, who she had not met before now. The children flung their arms around her, she crouched down to see them property. 'Are you alright? Not broken anywhere?'

They laughed. Then they went all serious when Aziza introduced herself and her husband and suggested the children might have something they needed to say.

'Yes, Mother. Carly,' began Tasneem. 'We are very sorry.' She was interrupted by her brother.

'It's all my fault, Tasneem. I'm very, very sorry. I promise to think more before I do things in the future. My Dad says I have to slow down a bit,' said Tariq, smiling. 'I'm going to be a lifeguard when I grow up.'

'That's good. They need people who can think quickly. They do need people who think things through properly first though,' said Carly. 'I'm sure you could use your superpowers as a lifeguard, Tariq.'

'I want to be a doctor,' said Tasneem. 'They fix people.'

'They fixed us well, didn't they?' she said. 'The lifeguards and the doctors and nurses.'

'Yeah. Would you like a hot chocolate? A scone with jam?' she asked. The children nodded, adults laughed and followed her down the hallway, the children amused by the crutches and wanting a turn.

Before she sat down, the doorbell rang again. 'Here we go again.'

Kellie jumped up, gathered her coat and checked her watch. She looked at Carly, a frown forming on her smooth, youthful forehead.

'I have to go now, Carly. That'll be my Uncle Tom.'

'Kellie, ask him to come in and have some morning tea with us, if he can spare the time,' said Josh. 'I'd like to chew his ear a bit more about the fifties floods.'

'And I really need to hear what you came to tell me,' she said to Kellie, as she closed the door behind her.

'Alright. I'll ask him. He might like to be with me when I tell you the news, Carly,' she said.

Petunia came in as Kellie left the room. She added more fuel to the fire, gave it a poke, and shut the window of the stove. The old fireplace was still in situ and the mantlepiece was adorned with Christmas candles and green tinsel. In the corner of the room stood a Christmas tree. Soon the door opened, and Kellie brought her Uncle Tom into the room. Everyone was introduced and Kellie made him a coffee. She hoped he wasn't put out by the noise and crowded room. He looked a bit out of place today, rings under red eyes, quiet.

'Now, Kellie, please tell me your news before someone or something else happens to interrupt us,' she said.

'Yes, okay,' Kellie said. 'As you already know, my mother passed away yesterday – her heart stopped. She'd been unwell for some years and there wasn't any more they could do for her.'

The mood turned sombre as they listened to her continue.

'When the nurse found her, she thought she was asleep in her bed, but she wasn't asleep,' she paused. 'Mum held this envelope in her hand. The nurse gave it to my uncle later and we could see it was from you, Carly.'

'I went home the previous day and dug out some photos my sister had sent to me over the years,' said Uncle Tom. 'Some lovely photos of young Carly with the rest of that family. I recognised her that day when she was taking photos for your article, Josh.'

'Apparently I look like you did when you were my age,' said Kellie.

She agreed. It was a remarkable likeness. But that would mean, her Uncle Tom was that lady's brother, her uncle. Was Kellie her cousin?

'You know, when I first saw you, I thought I was seeing my younger self coming towards me. Are you somehow related to me?' she asked.

'Yes, she is. I'm your Uncle Tom, Kellie is your sister, Carly. I think you would've last seen her when she was just a baby. The lady at the nursing home was your mother, Ginny.'

'That's what I was going to tell you,' said Josh. 'That's why I came around this morning.'

For a moment, it all seemed surreal to her. Like a dream, an out-of-body experience. Tariq and Tasneem sat on the carpet, watching it all unfold. Anna and Jack nodded to their family that it was time to go home and leave them to sort themselves out.

'What, I can't believe this,' said Carly after a long pause. 'That's really sad. I had hoped to bring my mother back to Australia with me one day. I had so many questions to ask her. Kellie, you're the baby we all missed so long ago. I'm glad you're okay.'

She knew she was babbling. They had much to talk about but now was not the time. She held out her arms and Kellie came over to be held. She was grieving her mother's death and excited about having a sister here.

'We needed to tell you as soon as possible,' said her uncle. 'Before the funeral.'

Anna came over to her, whispered that she would leave them to it. She asked if Carly and Josh might like to come over for lunch tomorrow.

'Yes, of course. That would be lovely. I'm sorry about the debacle. I'll show you out.'

'No, no,' said Jack. 'You stay here. We'll catch up with you tomorrow around midday, if that's okay.'

'Okay. Twelve o'clock. Got it. Bye kids,' she watched them all don their coats and leave.

Carly quietly moved about the room, deep in thought. She collected the empty mugs and placed them on the buffet tray. Kellie pulled back towards her uncle and slipped her arm through his. It was so sad for Kellie to lose her mother. But she felt different. Not so much sad, but more disappointed, a goal unable to be reached. She realized she'd grieved the loss of her mother since she had left the family ten years ago. It was almost a relief to allow her to stop the search. Emotions were mixed as she could not pinpoint exactly how she felt. She was pleased to know what had happened to Kellie and to be reunited with family. That tempered any anger she might have felt under the surface.

'I'm living with Uncle Tom's family at the stone cottage where our mother grew up, Carly. Could you come to visit one day, do you think?' said Kellie. 'We'd love to show you everything. One day I might visit you in Australia and meet the rest of my family. I don't remember anyone, not even my dad.'

Chapter 34 – 2013

Everyone left in the next hour, except Josh. The two of them sat around the crackling wood fire on cushions, staring into the flames. Several of the residents had joined them in the lounge room, but sat at the other end, leaving them to ponder over the events of the day.

'You must be exhausted,' he said. 'What a day!'

'Thanks for staying back. I need some company right now.'

'What do you mean? There's plenty of other people living here to give you company,' he teased.

'But none of them understand this weird situation as you do, Josh. Thanks for being here.'

'Now, that I have no choice about,' he said. He was filling in the space with light conversation, hoping she would find him easy to get on with. Was it her rosy cheeks tonight, warm from the glow of the fire? Was it that she needed him? Whatever it was, there was no denying an awakening under his skin which he hadn't felt for a long time.

'My article is almost finished,' he said. 'I really appreciate the trouble you went to with all the photos. You've quite a talent for photographic journalism.'

'I guess you were just lucky then,' she said.

'You want to go to the pub for a bite to eat?' he asked.

'No, thanks. I don't feel very sociable.' She looked away, tears welling in those deep, brown eyes. She really was beautiful, even in sorrow, her dark hair fell along her shoulders, glinting when she moved. 'I should send an email back home to Sally and Dad and the rest of them.'

'I could order a pizza,' he said. 'Or you could help me finish off what I made for tea last night. The trouble with cooking a casserole is that it lasts for days when I live alone.'

'If you don't mind me sending the email first, I could do that,' she said.

He assured her that he would wait for her. He retrieved his coat and scarf and waited, reading the newspaper while she went upstairs. The newspaper was full of photos of the last week. The whole eastern coast had suffered damage. Someone had taken a photo of the destroyed beach huts being washed out to sea with the tide. That brought back memories of their own encounter. He became aware that he'd taken a deep breath as he recalled sinking with the rips pulling him under the surface of the waves. He was lucky he'd been washed up to the chest-high water near the door to the beach hut. He remembered calling out to the kids and how Tariq responded. Soon after that, with Kyle's help, he was able to scramble out of the water over some large rocks. They had both been shocked when the rope had snapped.

The paper reported on the many heroic actions by the lifeguards with some photos. He recognized a chap called Dave being interviewed near the rubble of the pier. He wondered what made a man like that volunteer for such work and admired his bravery, his community spirit. On the next page was a story about Kyle, together with his photo. Not a big story. He hoped they could turn him around with treatment of some sort eventually.

Next morning, Carly was tingling from head to toe, staring out the window at the lighthouse from Josh's holiday unit and, beyond that, at the sunrise melting over the North Sea. She couldn't stop smiling. The world and its confusion had stopped last night for her.

She turned her cheek to his hand resting on her shoulder and sighed.

'Are you okay?' he whispered, kissing her neck. 'That was a bit unexpected.' They both laughed.

She felt his arms around her as he spoke. She had never known what she had been missing until now. She turned to face him, 'It wasn't exactly a planned moment, but wow….'

'Yes, wow is the right word. Have you ever had a boyfriend before, Carly?'

'No. I never had the time really, looking after the family after Ma left. You seem to know what you're doing though,' she said, smiling. His eyes sparkled, a mischievous look. He held her hands.

'I'm nearly thirty, so I hope so. You seem happy enough this morning. Must've been my casserole that inspired you.'

'Oh, that. Yes, it was delicious. Fancy a bloke knowing how to cook a decent casserole.'

'It's all about the timing,' said Josh. 'In fact, most things are all about the timing.'

They both sat on the edge of his bed; she slipped a blanket around herself while he put some clothes on. She watched his body move; graceful, slow movements. Purposeful. Gentle. Her head was spinning a bit, and she had no energy. Utterly happy. She curled into the blanket and rolled back onto the bed.

'I'll make you a cuppa. You just relax,' said Josh, kissing her forehead as he left the room.

It was unexpected last night because Josh had not wanted to get involved with anyone, here or anywhere else. The prospect of another long-distance relationship left him nervous. Last time it was okay for a while but soon, the distance had become too cumbersome. They had to re-adjust their lives after every visit and couldn't move forward. Last night his rigid walls had crumbled. Now this amazing young woman had come into his life. What should he do with this? He felt elated, there was no denying that. It was not a one-night stand, he felt sure of that too. But how would this work for them? Maybe he should get on with putting on the jug and stop trying to look too far into a future which was so slippery right now, it was like nailing jelly to a wall.

When he returned to his bedroom, Carly was asleep, curled up in a blanket. She looked both dishevelled and peaceful, unbelievably beautiful. He didn't like to disturb her but knew she'd promised Anna and Jack that they'd go to their home for lunch today.

'Wake up, sleepy head. We've slept in a bit, I'm afraid,' he said. 'Here's your tea.'

She stirred, opened one eye. 'Okay. Thanks for the tea.' She pulled herself up and took the hot mug. 'Are you having one too?'

'Yep. I made myself a coffee. Not a tea person, really,' he said, walking over to where he'd placed his mug. 'There's just so much I must learn about you. It might take a while to get to know one another, but I've got the time.'

'That's the truth of it,' she said, sipping her tea. 'We've had a working relationship up 'til now. I've been independent, not attached to anyone. You have too, I thought.'

'Not exactly,' he said. 'I have been married before, but only for a few short years. She passed away quite young from cancer.'

'I had no idea, Josh. That's terrible, I'm so sorry. Does anyone ever get over that?' she asked.

He wanted to tell her the truth of how empty the space she had occupied in his heart was. It probably always would be, but it was getting better with time. So, he explained how he felt now.

'And a few years later, I met someone I went to school with through Facebook. After all my hurting, here was another woman I could love. It was frightening at first and it took both of us quite a while to settle. But the problem was, she lived in another state.'

'Oh no. So, what happened? Why didn't one of you move?' she asked.

He felt irritated with those questions. The answer wasn't as simple as a sentence. Today wasn't the day to go into all this. 'I dunno. Just too hard, I guess.'

'Anyone else broken your heart?'

'No, not really. That's enough, don't you reckon?'

'Well, my story is very dull by comparison,' she said. She placed her empty mug on the bedside table and twisted around to face him.

'I don't know how we can make this happen, Josh, but I believe you might be my story.'

He felt the words sting a little. Yes, it was pleasurable to hear. Everything about her was pleasurable, everything he wanted. He wanted more. She reached for his coffee mug and sat it next to hers.

'I don't imagine I can go out today,' she said. 'I feel that everyone will look at my extra-large smile which, you must admit, is a bit odd in the middle of winter storms.'

'That's okay. It's up to you entirely, Carly,' he said. 'But you'd better ring Anna and let her know you'd rather stay here and cuddle up with me today.'

She sat bolt upright in the bed, legs over the edge and kept the blanket wrapped around her on the way to the shower. She only needed one crutch this morning to hop to the bathroom.

'Of course, I'd completely forgotten. My mind is like fairy floss this morning!'

He took his clean shirt and jeans from the cupboard and placed them on the bed, placed another towel on the rack and stepped into the shower with her.

'I thought you'd like me to scrub your back. Okay? We have a bit of time.'

'Oh, okay, Josh. I feel like I'm floating on air.' She turned her back to him. He lathered his hands with sweet-smelling soap, the rain shower falling over them, between them, rolling down their backs as they embraced. He smothered her with soap, memorizing the curve of her back, the soft shape of her. He closed his eyes, smelt lavender, listened to her quick breathing as he slowly rubbed her thigh. He felt her turn to him and opened his eyes. She was filling her hands with lotion, and began to rub his chest, kissing him. Her soapy hands slipped lower and lower. He drew a slow, deep breath.

'Carly, careful. We won't get to our lunch appointment,' he said, turning around and leaving the cubicle. He heard her tense laugh.

'Are you okay? I'm sorry, Josh. I really don't know what I'm doing.'

'Of course, I'm okay. Too okay,' he said, and felt himself smile. He reached for his towel and wrapped it around his waist, cleaned his teeth and left the bathroom. Too much too soon, he thought. He needed time to compose himself and land safely back to earth. But he felt so warm inside and thrilled to see Carly accept him as a lover, as 'her story'.

Chapter 35 – 2013

It was Jack who answered the front door to let them in. They folded their umbrellas and placed them into the umbrella stand. Carly felt like a glow-worm and hoped it wasn't too conspicuous. Josh seemed to bounce back to his normal self so much easier than she did. Good thing that was the case as she felt quite scatty, and she hoped nobody would notice if she slid into the house behind him.

'Come on in, you two,' said Jack. 'You'll be glad to get back to Queensland, Josh. All this rain and the flooding and all.'

'I am sure you guys must have webbed feet,' said Josh. 'I simply cannot get used to all the bad weather, day after day. Doesn't it get you down a bit?'

'You get rain in Queensland,' Carly said. 'But it's mostly in spring and summer, isn't it?'

'It is. Much the same in Broome, I suppose,' said Josh. 'Although I haven't been there yet.'

'Yet? You're welcome to come and visit me when I get back. No, it's not the same as Queensland,' said Carly. 'Dry, dry and drier for most of the year, until October. Then in come the cyclones to wake us all up.'

She longed for him to visit Broome one day, to know he was hopeful for them to have a future together. He placed his hand around her shoulders, pulled her close. An impression of a smile. Not a real smile, not the sort which melts, but pushing himself to smile. Why is he doing this? Maybe it was her. Although she felt pleased in the moment he held her, she also felt an alarm, a throb.

A deep yearning. Evidence of the night before, she supposed. Their relationship was changed now, awkward and with a commitment he may not be willing to pursue. She would pull back a bit, let him catch up, if he really wanted to.

Jack led them out to the sunroom at the back of the cottage, where they sat around a table. It was like a conservatory, glazing on every wall panel, a place to sit and enjoy the garden or work on his hobbies. She noticed he had been making some more miniature sailors for one of his sailing ships. It seemed like a long time ago since she had seen him at the Sheringham pond.

Anna and Aziza came into the room with trays of food and drinks. Tasneem carried some serviettes, and cutlery.

'Tariq will be here in a minute,' said his twin. 'He's having a huff about something.'

'Don't mind him. He's upset because he's lost something that was special to him, Tasneem,' said Aziza. 'We'll resume the search after lunch. We have guests right now.'

'It's so good to see you again, Tasneem. You look fit and healthy. Are you okay?' asked Josh from where he stood looking out the window at a crisp, winter garden.

Tasneem set down the cutlery and placed a serviette on each setting. 'Yes, thank you. I'm okay. Tariq usually does the bread plates but he's not going to help until he finds his box.'

'Well, he might have to go home without it,' said Anna. 'We've looked just about everywhere. Boys and their special boxes. I remember my boys having a special shoe box under their beds when they were little. Some things never change.'

'I haven't actually seen this box before,' said Aziza. 'He found it. He says he saved it from the sea.'

'I wonder if the ambulance officers might know where it ended up. It might be at the ambulance station waiting for someone to collect it,' said Jack. 'Do you remember seeing it, Carly?'

'A box? You know, I can remember his box. He was lifted from the beach hut by the lifeguards. He carried a box with him. The ambulance officers were wrapping my foot, and I looked away when they drove me into the local x-ray rooms. Tasneem, do you remember it?'

'Yes, I do. We sat on it to keep our feet dry,' she said. 'Is that the box he's looking for?'

'I believe so,' said Anna. 'Go and ask him'. Tasneem skipped from the sunroom, into the lounge room where her brother sat, arms crossed, lips pouted, legs crossed and scowling.

'Tariq. The box. Is it the one we found in the beach hut?'

He relaxed a little, uncrossed his legs, leant forward. 'Yes, do you remember what happened to it?'

'No. Not really. I remember what it looked like.'

'They took it from my hands and then pulled me up through the roof on a rope. They wrapped us up in silver foil like a barbequed potato and drove us to the hospital. But where is my box now?'

Carter came in from the kitchen, clapped his hands and asked the children to wash their hands, ready for their lunch. The sweet, caramelising smell of roast beef and vegetables wafted into every room. They both jumped and raced each other into the bathroom. The box was forgotten for a few moments.

The meal was shared around the dining table on a pretty, blue tablecloth.

'May I leave the table please?' asked the twins, together.

'Yes, as long as you're quiet,' said Carter. 'Go and watch some television before we have to go.'

'I can't go. I don't have my box,' said Tariq.

Josh had been busy reading the news headlines when all the fuss was happening with the box mystery. 'What's in the missing box, Tariq?'

'I don't know. It was in the beach hut.'

'What makes it so important to you then?'

'I found it. It's mine.'

'I have a box of yours in the boot of my car. Is that it? Don't you remember? I told you I would bring it to you when you got out of hospital,' said Josh. The boy's eyes lit up.

'Yes, I forgot! Thank you. May I have it? Now?'

'Can it wait until I finish my lunch first?'

He agreed to wait and sat on the floor next to Josh's chair, playing quietly with a toy car. The adults all looked at Josh and wondered why he hadn't said anything before now.

'I'm sorry,' he said to them. 'I'm tired. I worked late last night. I didn't think about it until now.'

She couldn't help a big smile appearing, listening to his excuse.

The outer box was quite heavy when Josh lifted it out of his car. It was probably still full of sea water. He carried it inside to the waiting children and placed it on the tiled floor.

'It might be full of water, so go carefully,' he said. 'This is a very old box, I think.'

'I think you're right, Josh, it's quite old,' said Aziza, who loved all things old, preferably historically ancient. 'Tariq, I'll sit here with you and watch. It might hold some very old treasure.'

'Pirate treasure, Mum?' asked Tasneem.

'Who knows? Let's watch as Tariq opens the box.'

The rusty padlock was snapped with a bolt cutter. They all gathered around as he tried to open the lid. It was stuck. Carter returned from Jack's toolbox and jimmied it open with a chisel.

'Thanks, Dad. Now let's open it,' said Tariq. He slowly lifted the leather-hinged lid. 'It smells like the sea but it's not wet.'

Inside the box was another box. A smaller, wooden box with one word carved on the lid. His tiny fingers felt each letter etched into the lid. E...M...M...A.

The British Museum's local Finds Liaison Officer contacted Aziza by phone a couple of days after she had taken the box in for assessment. It was indeed ancient, handmade and included antique items dating around the middle of the fourteenth century. The outer box was very heavy, and she wondered how her seven-year-old had managed to lift it.

How did it find its way into a beach hut? Who was Emma?

She might never know the answers to these questions, but she did know it must be given to the British Museum. There were not many artifacts left from that period, so it was amazing that her son had discovered it in Cromer. The North Sea has many hidden treasures, and this one had been under the ocean for hundreds of years.

'Tariq, there's something we need to discuss,' she said. 'It's about the box you found.'

'Yeah. I know. It's old,' he said. 'It's mine.'

'Of course. Tariq, we're not allowed to keep things from history for ourselves. That would be selfish. We need to share them with everyone else in the country because they are very important. They represent where we all came from.'

He looked a bit shocked that the box could no longer be considered his own. She expected the reaction. Eyes downcast, shoulders slouched, he seemed quite sad.

'Carter, do you think we could help the twins make special boxes of their own?' she asked her husband. 'They might like to help us make them or paint pictures of the beach on the side. What do you think?'

Carter nodded and she watched as his mind got to work designing a solution. 'Come on, Tariq. Will you help me? Tasneem? Your very own box can contain your dreams or special things you'll collect, and you'll be able to keep them under your beds.'

The children were delighted, Tariq a bit slower than Tasneem to catch on, but the excitement of the new boxes soon became infectious.

'That's great,' Aziza said. 'We can start to plan today and buy the timber tomorrow. Okay? In a little while, the old heavy box will be on display for the public to view at the museum and we'll all go along to see it.'

'Yeah,' said Tariq. 'My own box. The old one belonged to a girl anyway.'

'Carly, could you please come and take some photos of this ancient box and its contents?' asked Josh into her mobile message bank. 'I need these to add to my article before I send it in.'

He wondered if she planned to speak with him again after he hadn't contacted her since that night in his unit. He didn't mean to be dismissive, but it might've looked that way to her. She meant far too much to him, he realized now. He felt he may have burnt his bridges with her on a personal level but hoped she would give him another chance.

She phoned him an hour later, saying she could help him the following afternoon. The call was quick. It was a work assignment, after all. Neither of them mentioned anything personal. She promised to meet him at Anna and Jack's home where the box was being stored until it was collected by the department.

Maybe she'd had second thoughts about him, or was she just annoyed at his reticence? Maybe it was a one-off night of heated passion. It hadn't felt that way, but it never did. He had longed for her presence so many times since that night, but he became overwhelmed with all the potential problems. He understood the pain of loving someone who lived in another place, and the impossibility of that.

How could they go forward when she lived in another country? Or, indeed, even when she returned to Broome, they would still be too far apart. No, he couldn't see any way out of this. Better if it was left alone. Besides, his ticket to return to Queensland was being prepared for him and he had to collect it in the morning. As much as he yearned to be with her, she may not feel the same now. Wouldn't she have contacted him otherwise? He couldn't imagine her sitting at home watching her phone, hoping he might ring her. Not Carly. Not outspoken, confident Carly.

Chapter 36 – 2013

Carly and Rose sat waiting for the train, their scarves wrapped snuggly around cold ears. They were on their way home from Norwich castle museum, a day out together before Carly returned to Australia for Christmas. They had already talked about that chap who had followed them home from a previous train journey and were relieved that he was being investigated by the police. She rubbed her hands together to keep warm through woollen gloves. Her mind was elsewhere, in a state of limbo.

'I have one last job to do. Josh rang. He wants me to meet him at Jack and Anna's place tomorrow,' said Carly, her hands pushed into the pockets of her blue woollen coat.

'What are you going to tell him?'

'Nothing, really. Only that I'll be travelling back home soon.'

'He'll have to find another photographer, I guess. None quite as good as you, Carly.'

She didn't want him to find another person to work with him, but she felt it was time to go. She knew that, if she stayed, her heart would be broken by this man. He acted like he didn't care about her. The weather is cold enough, without him freezing over too.

'Thanks, Rose. I wonder about him sometimes. I'm certainly not going to chase him.'

'Sometimes we must be a bit brave, though. Don't you think? Otherwise, we miss the opportunity altogether,' said Rose.

She thought Rose had hit the nail on the head. She turned her face away and brushed a tear from her cheek. How would she face him now? She remembered how he had pulled away from her advances in the shower. How embarrassing was that? Two weeks later, and she was still blushing.

'He's had a couple of very upsetting experiences in the past, and I think he's struggling to get past them. I've never had a boyfriend before, Rosie, so I'm confused,' she said. 'I can't read his thoughts, and he hasn't phoned or texted me. I think he just wants me as a colleague or a friend. Maybe that's enough. Maybe he can't handle anything else.'

'I'm sure he'll talk to you about it soon. You two got on like a house on fire before,' Rose said. 'He probably needs some time to think about it. You must decide if you can wait, I suppose.'

In the distance through a long tunnel and pea soup air, they heard a train roaring towards them. Other people stood and walked to the line, ready to board. The station master made the announcement. Carly took Rosie's arm and together they joined the queue.

'Did I tell you that I said my farewells to Kellie and Uncle Tom's family after Mum's funeral? I had dinner with them in the cottage my mother had grown up in, where that horrible flood in the early fifties rocked her world,' she said. 'I have some photos to show you. Wait until you see the thatching on their cute cottage.'

'Lovely. We could look through them on the train,' said Rose. 'I bet they'll miss you. Do you think your sister will visit you in Broome some day?'

'She's already saving up her pocket money, so I hope she does. I also met my Aunt Lizzy, who is a few years younger than my Mum. She might fly out with Kellie. She sounded keen. My family was certainly excited when I wrote to Sally with all the news. Dad said he wanted to hear all about it when I return home. Of course, he was sad to hear that Mum had died.'

'Will you be home for Christmas, do you think, Carly?'

'Wouldn't that be special? I haven't had Christmas at home for a couple of years now. I do think I'm ready to go, Rosie. I've got what I came here for, though it's disappointing that I couldn't spend time with my mother. I really wanted to know what happened to her, and now we know.'

'I'll miss you too, my friend,' said Rose.

'We'll definitely keep in touch, Rosie. I have your email, and you have mine. One day I'd like to show you around my part of the world,' said Carly. 'It's a different sort of beautiful than here. It's where we store the sun.'

'Oh, funny. Okay. We haven't had too much sun here, have we?!'

She looked out the window of the train as it rushed past several clusters of old terrace houses, not a tree in sight. Winter light was fading, deepening shadows to the west. Ten minutes down the track and farmland came into view. Green fields, at last.

'One of the most amazing things you have over here is history, Rosie,' she said. 'Aziza sent me a text this morning. You know that box I'm to take photos of tomorrow? Well, apparently it dates way back to the fourteenth century.'

'That's incredible. Ancient. When you told me about the marriage brooch inside, I looked it up on the 'net and it was a gift to brides from their husbands after their wedding night,' said Rose.

'Yeah. The word on the box was Emma, so maybe she was the bride, way back in that time. Maybe she died in the plague around that time, like so many others. Who knows?'

'One thing for sure, she was much loved by her husband. His testament to her memory appeared in this century because he created that sealed box to protect Emma's special box, all safe and snug inside.'

'Yeah. How romantic is that?'

'There are also bits of hand-made lace and bits of red fabric. Aziza told us the fabric was called Lincoln Scarlett and would've come from one woollen mill in Lincoln. The colour and weave were rare for that period.'

'Pity more of it didn't survive. Given the theme of the box, it might've been Emma's wedding dress. What else did they find in the box?'

'A few things. A horseshoe, the frail remains of a tapestry, almost in fragments, so fragile. Wedding dresses were not like tulle and white back then. More likely that she wore her Sunday best dress. Didn't matter what colour it was.'

'Any precious jewellery apart from the brooch?'

'Yes, I think there was a gold wedding ring.'

Rose was right. It was romantic. Whoever buried that box, which was found after many years under the sea, must have loved Emma heaps. Why couldn't she find that kind of dedication? A young man in Shipden, his dreams in tatters, had put together a box of memories to be buried with his wife.

'I don't want to keep bringing this up but I'm glad they found that guy who followed us. What's his name?' said Rose, bringing her thoughts of romance to a sudden halt.

'Oh, Kyle. Yeah. He was some creep. Scared the living daylights out of me at the time,' she said. 'I'm not going to let it affect me though or he'll have won. Are you okay now?'

'Yeah. Sort of worries me a bit still, Carly. I'm not scared all the time, but I still get that sudden prickle. Especially at night. I'll be going about my business and wonder if that man trying to make awkward conversation might follow me off the train or wherever I am,' she said. Carly nodded, reached out to touch her hand.

'The court case comes up soon. Will you need to testify before going back home?' asked Rose.

'No, apparently the court will accept my affidavit, and I've already written that at the police station. Did you do that too?'

'Yes, I did, but, apparently, I might be called as a witness. I guess they don't need us both to testify. Josh will need to go to the police too, I think. He saw Kyle get onto our carriage before following us that night. He must've followed one of us, was turned off and then later followed the other.'

'Yeah, I suppose so. I did confront him, and he took off. He must've left me and traced your steps instead. I don't want to think what might've happened if he'd gotten away with it,' she said. 'For many people, fear is a fact of life. I have a friend who carries around a pepper spray in her handbag. Blimey, I'd never find it in time in my handbag! Be quicker to run.'

She tried to make light of the situation, but it really did frighten her too. He'd been arrested now, so it was a bit irrational to be worried about him. Better to move on.

'Wow, it's much warmer inside the carriage!' said Carly. 'Now, would you like to check out my photos?'

They snuggled into a double seat and flipped through the photos on Carly's phone as the train ventured at a slow pace for the next hour or so, into the starry evening.

Chapter 37 – 2013

Josh set up the lights for Carly, displaying the box and its contents on a blanket. Her arrival would make him feel more grounded but, for now, he felt like something was missing. The outside box itself was quite ordinary to look at but the beauty lay within. It protected Emma's memory, whoever she had been, her story written in artifacts.

'Aziza, can we talk about these things? The box, the wedding brooch, and the other things?' he asked.

'Sure, Josh. What do you want to know? I'll try to answer your questions. I have had the officers from the British Museum here and they're really excited by the find.'

'What could they tell you? What might happen to the box and its contents now?' he asked. 'Do they have any idea who Emma was? Has the age of the box been confirmed?'

'They were extremely interested. We don't know who Emma was, but we do know she was a young bride in the fourteenth century, about the time of the mid-century Black Plague. She could've met her end in that plague or in childbirth or TB or any number of illnesses, or simply starvation as they also experienced a drought mid-century. Everywhere was unclean, rats, no proper sanitation,' said Aziza. 'Where will they eventually put these objects? Firstly, they'll arrange for expert staff to collect this box. It'll be all catalogued and eventually put on display in a museum. They don't have too many objects like these from so far back in history. They are irreplaceable and priceless.'

He could hear movement at the front entrance. Jack was asking Carly to step inside. He put aside his notebook and pen and waited for her to arrive in the lounge room. Anna appeared first, carrying a tray of sponge cake and tea, Carly and Jack followed behind soon after.

'Can I take your coat, Carly? Your backpack?' asked Jack.

'Hi everyone. Sorry if I'm late. The bus is a bit unpredictable this weather. Thanks, Jack. I'll just hold onto my backpack. My camera equipment is inside,' she said, removing her blue coat. 'Where are the twins?'

'They've gone with Carter to see the Christmas pageant,' said Anna.

'Oh, how lovely. I guess it can't be held in the Pavilion now. The storm saw to that.'

'That's right. The Pavilion will be mended in time for next year's pageant, I'm sure,' said Anna. 'We were just discussing the contents of the box you're about to photograph for us, Carly.'

'Fascinating. I'm going to miss all this ancient history,' she said.

She smiled, her eyes glanced over to him. 'I see you've set it all up for me, Josh. Thanks.'

'Over to you now,' he said, tightening a knob on the spotlight stand. 'Anything else you want me to do?'

'No, thanks. That's fine.'

She opened her backpack, started clicking together her camera and lens. She behaved like nothing had happened between them. Like it didn't mean a thing to her. He guessed that this was the end of his journey with Carly Williams. Might be just as well.

They can both relax and get on with the job now. He reached into his coat and pulled out his flight ticket, waved it in the air.

'What's in there?' asked Anna.

'My flight home to Brisbane in time for Christmas,' said Josh.

'I knew that was your timeline, so well done, Josh,' said Jack. 'It's always good to be home for the festivities, if that's possible.'

Anna and Aziza were pleased for him too.

'So, you're going home,' said Carly. 'I hope you've done whatever it was you wanted to achieve.'

'Yep. The bloke who had the broken legs is mending and should be back over here after New Year some time, so it's time for me to return.'

'Your family will be pleased to see you,' said Anna.

'Yes, I didn't think I'd make it for Christmas this year.'

'We were just getting to know you. One day you must come back and visit us,' said Aziza. The twins will be older, but they will always be grateful for your help at the beach hut. And you too, of course, Carly.'

'I hope I can visit as a tourist one day, Anna. After all, I haven't had a crab salad at Cromer yet. Seriously though, you live in a fascinating and beautiful country.' said Josh. 'If you're ever down my way, please drop in,'

'We're not likely to travel that far,' said Jack. 'Are we, dear?'

Anna smiled. 'Never say never, Jack.'

Carly finished her work in silence. It was strange not hearing her chirpy voice and laughter. He decided to let it go. Why make things more difficult than they needed to be? He walked closer to where she was working, feeling edgy and hesitant. He took a deep breath not knowing how she would react. He cupped the side of her face with his hand. She leaned into his touch, her eyes locked with his.

'Carly, thanks so much for all your hard work. Your creative photos made all the difference to the success of my trip,' he said, as he stepped towards the door. 'Maybe I'll bang into you in Australia somewhere one day.'

She let her camera dangle on its neck strap and smiled the softest smile he had seen. Their eyes only met for a moment before she returned to her job.

'My pleasure, Josh. Thanks for the job. And everything. Bye.'

He wanted to rush over to her and hold her, apologising for his lack of empathy, for being a coward. But the truth was it was too hard. He both wanted to never leave her side and, at the same time, to run. He was surprised at his lack of confidence. He couldn't find the words to tell her without getting tangled. So, he said nothing at all. He simply said his farewells to everyone and left. It was easier for them both.

Love affairs, in their beginnings, were all about the present. But there's a point in each – an event, an exchange, some other unseen trigger – which forces the past and the future back into focus. For him, it was the lessons from his past. He'd been too full of the wonderful surprise of her to look beyond immediate happiness. The more he thought about this aspect of his past experiences, the more frustrated he'd become. His mind was aflutter with 'what ifs' and he realized how much he would regret hurting Carly but could see no other way out.

He clicked his methodical mind into gear. His thoughts drifted to facts. The return of his rental car this afternoon and then to finish packing. His flight would leave early tomorrow morning from Heathrow airport to Singapore, so he had a train trip from Norwich to London this evening. After a couple of days in Singapore, he would arrive in Brisbane.

Carly did not believe for one minute that it was meant to end like that. Rose was right, she should have said something, made a phone call, sent a text message, something. But no. She didn't want to make more of a fool of herself. How stupid is pride? Now he had gone forever. She touched on the emptiness of that thought and felt nauseous.

'Carly, are you alright? I guess you're going to miss his company,' said Anna. 'Come here.'

She felt Anna's arms pull her near and she patted her on the back. She bit her lip to stop an overwhelming urge to cry.

'I suppose I will miss him a bit. I did enjoy working with him,' she said.

Aziza poured her another cup of tea and handed it to her. 'Thanks. It was so sudden,' she said and sat on the lounge near Jack.

'I thought you two might hit it off,' said Jack. 'Looks like I was wrong.'

'So did I,' she said. 'Never mind, more fish in the sea and all that.'

'So, when are you planning on leaving us, Carly?' asked Anna. 'You mentioned you hoped to be home soon.'

'I bought my ticket too. I'll be leaving in a couple of days. Long enough to say goodbye to all the friends I've made while I've been living here. I do appreciate your friendship and the opportunity to play with your gorgeous twins.'

'Carly, how can we thank you? Just know you're always welcome back here with us. I know you've found some relatives in England now, so you'll probably want to return one day,' said Aziza.

'Thanks, Aziza. If you come to the land down under, please email me and I'll meet you at the Perth airport or in Broome.'

She finished her tea and helped clean the dishes. Jack drove her home to the guesthouse in Sheringham, near the pond, where it all began.

'I wish you a hearty breeze in the pond for your boats next summer, Jack.'

'Thanks for inviting me to have coffee with you that day, Carly.' said Jack, smiling. 'All the very best to you for your flight back home.'

Chapter 38 – 2014

It had taken him a year to get to this point. Josh glanced at the Brisbane airport clock. Through thick glazed walls, an inky sky dotted with stars. A few tired travellers lingered in the Qantas lounge, draped over seating or each other, listening for passenger calls to board. He poured himself another coffee to stay awake. Plenty of time to sleep on the plane. Nearly eight hours from Brisbane to Broome, but it would seem much longer.

He couldn't wait to see Carly again. His stomach churned with nerves, hands sweated. He would like to meet her family, see where she came from. Apologize for being a jerk. It was two in the morning, a long stretch ahead. Her excitement was palpable when he received a reply to his message, even though it was midnight in Broome.

When he returned from England, he had thrown himself into his work. His editor seemed to enjoy the angle he had taken with the series of articles. The public loved Carly's photos which accompanied the online version. The printed version highlighted her photo of Ginny's house tipping over the edge of the cliff, and a handtowel caught on a twig. He had a copy of it framed. For the past year, he'd walked past the chalky cliffs in this photo and remembered that day. The public had identified with these real people and with the impact climate change continued to have on their lives. It could've been any one of us. He hoped these stories would open hearts to an awareness of the natural environment to make choices that benefit the earth.

In the serenity of his farm, he'd created some fictional characters, blended them with facts, and called his work The

Missing Village. He mixed his research with interviews to gain a clear picture of what life must have been like for a family living in a fourteenth century fishing village and another family who had lived in the fifties in the same area, who had suffered immeasurable pain and loss. In the clarity of his mind, another chap kept appearing, so he included Matthew O'Reilly's voice from the nineteenth century too.

People were numbed by science and its warnings. He wanted to bring those facts alive for his newspaper readers, to show them some of the consequences of those tidal surges and dangerous weather patterns. Let the public see for themselves that nature is fearsome and climate change warnings should be respected. He thought of those stories, of the people he had encountered along the way. Of coincidences like the photo, which he had discovered in a Norfolk newspaper from 1889. Someone back then had taken a picture of a lady holding a man, who had been run over by a rampaging cart and a couple of Clydesdales. There had been a sad story about this young man, who had been known locally as one of the heroic swimmers who had saved people from drowning after their ship had collided with the remains of St Peter's in Shipden. He was able to bring it all to life again in his stories and responses from readers, and his boss, were encouraging. A sweet-sounding voice echoed through the terminal,

'Good evening, ladies and gentlemen. Calling passengers for Broome, Qantas flight number ...'

He collected his small backpack and travel documents. Others stretched, yawned and joined the queue. He had never felt so sure of himself. He'd had plenty of time to mull things over in his mind. He knew his life would be messy with Carly living so far away but the risk was worth it. If she still wanted him around, perhaps they could work it out.

Carly felt anxious waiting at the Broome airport terminal. Earlier, she had managed to force her breakfast down. She'd cooked a pavlova last night after his text message, but it failed in all ways a pavlova could fail. It made no sense to her – why was she so unnerved by his visit? At least she hadn't been squashed up in a plane all night, like the bedraggled lot who had just arrived at the airport. She scanned the weary faces for Josh. She still couldn't believe he had contacted her. The text came unexpectantly, and she nearly fell off her chair. Her sister, Jenny, thought she had won Lotto. Maybe she had, but she would reserve that conclusion for a later date.

It felt like waiting for a cruise ship at an airport. Like it was never going to happen. She had loved him like this since their eyes met at the pub in Cromer. It's amazing how much one person can affect another and in such a short space of time. She hadn't really felt he was comfortable around her. Knowing she wasn't loved in return was hard but made even worse after they'd spent that night together. She'd felt so special then but totally discarded the day after. A castoff, like a piece of second-hand clothing. Was she in for more of that treatment? This time she was determined to stand up to him if it didn't feel right. Why would he fly all the way over here? Maybe it was for work? She had almost given up hope of a reconciliation with Josh. Although she wouldn't want him to be still tethered to his past, she understood that his pain would never totally go away, that he had been changed by those experiences. She knew he had courage, and she felt sure he could move forward, but did he know this?

She'd changed too but in a more positive way. She had succeeded in finding her mother. She'd even met her English relatives and gained a little sister, who would be visiting her before she goes to uni. She had grown in other ways too. She had been able to survive by herself, earn her own living, find her own way around the world with confidence. Over the past year, she had gained control of her life back home. There were so many things life might throw at us that we cannot control, and she felt her resilience had been stretched on several occasions. The mental angst of the Jubilee line. The crowds in London's summer. Cliffs falling into the sea. When children sneak away from you and get into strife. When a parent went missing and how she'd managed with the aftermath.

With new certainty, she now had less conflict in her life. Her photography work was growing. Last year, in England, she was not as well prepared to deal with Josh. Now she would be ready for whatever he had in mind.

Honestly, she didn't know how she would react after all this time. She was awash with questions and no answers. She'd stay flexible.

As soon as he stepped off the plane, the oppressive heat was suffocating. Descending the rickety passenger stairs, Josh put on his sunglasses and cap, saw a sign Gateway to the Kimberley in the distance and another sign closer with a line of camels wandering across a sunset, saying Welcome to Broome. He collected his bag and wheeled it toward the exit gate. He was sure of one thing: she would not be wearing her blue coat in Broome today.

He was excited at the prospect of seeing Carly again, and to hear her laughter. He wasn't without nerves though. She may not be feeling the same way as he was, after all, it had been a year since he'd left England, and he had taken so long to realize that she was his future. He was sure now. It felt right, as though something they had was ripped apart into little pieces, but it might yet be mended. He may still have a chance to change direction. He felt positive about his own feelings for Carly, but he had no idea how she perceived him now. He looked around as he entered the terminal building. Not many people scattered about, so it should not be hard to find her.

Then their eyes met. She was standing near a palm tree, outside the front of the terminal, waving at him through a window. He headed outside, felt the difference as the door opened. The air was like a wet blanket thrown over him, the soil so red beyond a few patches of tended garden. Asphalt tarmac, red dirt, car park, tropical palms. He hadn't really known what to expect, but it was certainly not like any airport he'd seen. It was too sticky-hot, but he only had eyes for her. Nothing else mattered right now.

'Hey, you!'

'Hi, Josh. So nice to see you again.'

She wore denim shorts with a red blouse. He was glad she had kept things casual between them. A quick kiss and a long hug.

'Man, I've missed you,' he said, pulling back but not letting go of her hands. 'Let me look at you. You're a feast for my eyes, Carly. Did I tell you I've missed you?'

Laughter came easily to them, but he felt a tension between them that hadn't been there before. So much time had passed, it had to be expected. Was he too late?

Carly had to catch her breath. It wasn't simply allowing time to melt away and letting trust in again. She may also have to be brave again, forgive and move on. If she didn't put herself out there, she'd be missing out on the life she wanted. Would it be hard to be emotionally vulnerable with Josh again? Yes, it would be a risk. All year, she had been grieving the life she had discovered with him. Without him, life lost much of its vibrancy and sparkle – and they could be such an awesome team.

She was glad he hadn't given her much notice. She might not have chosen to be waiting for his plane to land, waiting for him to collect his luggage and then waiting for him to find her outside the terminal. Waiting a whole year. Now he was standing here, looking into her eyes, full of anticipation, holding her hands. It seemed surreal, it left her nervous, on edge. He might pop like a bubble and disappear again.

'Are you okay?' he asked. 'I'm sorry I didn't give you much notice. I'm sorry about a lot of things.'

'Yes, I'm very okay. I'm thinking of pinching you to make sure you're here.'

'Oh, please don't do that. I don't want to look back, Carly. Let's not pretend I haven't been absent for the past year in more ways than one, but I've come to ask for your forgiveness. I hope, in time, you can have confidence in me again so we can get to know one another a bit better. We'll take it slowly. What do you think?' There was a pause, which felt uneasy, so she told him the truth.

'You really want to know what I think, Josh? It's been tough. Honestly, you left so suddenly, I assumed I'd probably never see you again. It's exactly what my mother did to me all those years ago. Fair dinkum, I've been confused and hurt.'

'I know. I'm so sorry. I didn't handle things well. It was the whole distance thing. I was freaking out about repeating my history. I think I've got myself sorted now and I hope it's not too late.'

'Yes, I knew that was the problem, but you didn't talk to me about it. I'm glad you came. That took courage. Anyway, let's have a coffee. One thing I learnt in England was that everyone must have a coffee or tea to let things settle a bit,' she said. 'You can tell me all about what you've been up to. I did see the online version of your articles, Josh. The Missing Village was an awesome series. I have so many questions and the first one is - how long will you be staying?'

'I hope I can look around Broome for a few days with one of the locals. Got to get back to the farm after that. I'm so pleased you enjoyed the articles, Carly. I'd love your help on my new assignment. I've called it The Vanishing Islands in the hope of drawing attention to the plight of communities losing their whole island to the sea around Australia,' he said.

'Sounds like an interesting project, Josh. Let's talk more on it later. In the meantime, you're welcome to stay with us.'

'Are you sure? I don't mind staying in the hotel.'

'No trouble at all, we have heaps of room.'

'Honestly, Carly, my initial thought was to see if I still had a chance with you. See if we can work something out that suits both of us. Now I'm standing here with you, I want more already.'

'Let's just wait and see,' said Carly, who couldn't stop smiling, no matter how much she tried not to. 'You'll need to work a lot harder than that.'

They laughed, walked toward Carly's car, his arm draped around her shoulders, the other pulling his bag along. For a while, all she could hear was the sound of small wheels rolling over loose tarmac and feel the heat rising through her sandals.

He pulled her close and kissed her forehead as they walked. She liked the feeling of him next to her, and the solid tread of his footsteps beside her. She tucked herself against his underarm. She liked the quick glances he threw her, his softness. In fact, she liked him very much.

A large flock of white cockatoos lifted from the grass, squawking into an endless indigo sky. A few cars pulled out from the almost empty carpark at the exit gate. Tiny flies rested on his face, so he removed his hand from her shoulder and flicked them off. She noticed he was quick to replace his hand on her shoulder again as she led him towards her car. She glanced up at him, held his attention and said,

'Take my hand, Josh, and don't let go. It might be a rough ride,' she smiled. 'The man I want is one who would love me as much as whoever made that ancient box for Emma.'

His eyes squinted against the bright sky as he observed a flock of Silver Gulls settle on a nearby gum tree. She waited and watched him move his thoughts back to her.

'And you deserve nothing less.'

The Raggedy Men of Cromer Pier

A foggy night
on slippery slats
with rusty nails,

droplets on
the white safety rails,
salty on the watchman's fingers,

shaken over slithers of squids'
rotting flesh. There's a sound
of slop, slop, as if death

were walking. From the mouths
of men, the men in rags
float and hover beyond the pier,

above the church bell that rings
under drowning waves which play
the samphire strings orchestra.

Towns can die, and here
the legend of a famous pier began
where the townsfolk

left as a gift, a ley line
between land and sea
and I wonder

about the moment when sea
gushed between flint and mortar
and the town moved inland,

began crossings
on the night boat
to Shipden-under-sea.

During the Middle Ages, Shipden village was washed away by the sea. Desperate men slept on the beach and swam out to pillage anything of value. From time-to-time, ghostly apparitions are seen in the sea, others report of a bell ringing.

Publishing permission (2025) by English poet, **Lynn Woollacott**. First published: Reach Poetry Magazine (UK) and online at *placesofpoetry.org.uk* .

Acknowledgements for The Missing Village

A book such as this, with multiple levels of history intertwined, doesn't just roll off the printer. It took years of writing and research. I have so many people to acknowledge and thank sincerely. My appreciation not only extends to each of these people for their area of expertise but for their generous and helpful attitude to my writing endeavours.

I aligned Josh's story and character with a dear friend of mine, and I thank him for allowing me to do this. However, Josh is pure fiction, so most of his character and his challenges were developed in my imagination. I'm not sure if he'd want his name in print, so I will err on the side of caution and keep him a mystery.

Angie and Sid Timms, my wonderful friends who live in North Norfolk. With their assistance, I was able to fill my senses to write scenes dripping with the atmosphere of being present. I wonder if they'll recognise themselves in a couple of the characters!

Beta readers: **Brigitte Prince**, a retired English teacher, who facilitated the first edit with valuable comments and slipped my work into a consistent tense. **Leah Tedman**, my beautiful daughter, who encouraged me to modify Cartia's secret tryst with Daniaen. So, I did. **Diane Carroll**, a lifelong friend and confidant, who can pick up an error at forty paces. Di's feedback about writing more on Daniaen and Cartia's story is valid, and I'll consider this more as a sequel. **Gill Tilney**, who is always willing to read my stories and provide encouraging feedback. Brigitte, Leah, Di and Gill – thanks for helping me to polish the work and for your uplifting words.

Zena and Steve Pye from The Albion Hotel in Cromer for permission to use their Victorian era hotel and their names in a scene where Carly meets Josh for the first time in chapter one.

Richard Harbord, author of *Shipden alias Cromer, Norfolk's Most Cosmopolitan Sea-Resort, its Origins and Early Development.* A Town Planner and architect, he's now retired and writes succinct and thorough prose, along with maps, images, history and research, giving a real sense of the scale of the early development of Shipden. I was able to imagine the topography of

Shipden in the 14th century and compare it to changes in the landscape today.

Mark Warner, Branch Manager of Jarrold's bookshop in Cromer, Norfolk. He went out of his way to post Richard Harbord's research book to me in Australia moments before they all went into lockdown for Covid-19.

The Cromer Museum was where I first came across information on Shipden village, its demise and what it looked like today, under the sea. The museum is set in a row of late 19th Century Victorian fisherman's cottages with 19th Century furnished rooms, and the clothing people wore. My 19th century story was easy to visualise after seeing how people of that time lived in North Norfolk. Also, the stories of Henry Blogg and the history of Cromer lifeboatmen were well displayed in the **Henry Blogg Museum** nearby.

I'm grateful to **Paul Watling**, who is the current Coxswain/mechanic at RNLI in Cromer. Thanks for your professional advice on the RNLI equipment and training in Cromer.

Andrea Beckham, Historic Environment Assistant (Records) Norfolk Historic Environment Service, Norfolk County Council Union House in Norfolk for the copies of early maps of Norfolk and for scanning reports on deep sea diving off Cromer in more recent times.

Helen Leighton, Practice Manager, Department of Planning and Conservation, for her helpful links to historic records.

Hannah Jarratt, Technical support assistant, Coastal Management, North Norfolk District Council who sent me numerous background links to explain the coastal erosion plans and emergency communication plans for coastal towns.

Scientists, **Naomi Oreskes** and **Erik M Conway**, for their insight into the future, in their book, *The Collapse of Western Civilization, A View from the Future* (Columbia University Press 2014).

Nick Stone, photographer and blogger (invisibleworks.co.uk) who introduced me to the Paston family, who had lived in Caistor Castle in 1440 for 100 years. Their documents have been digitized at the British Library, and they offered me access to that family's personal papers…a rare view of real people from that era.

Google Books has digitalized books on Norfolk's cathedrals and market towns to the east of Norfolk. It's so easy to get online to read old and ancient manuscripts. *google.books.com*

Peter Stibbons, who allowed me to use a slide from his great-grandfather's slide collection (1880's) for The Missing Village. Courtesy: Randall/Salter Magic Lantern Slide Collection.

Lincoln Tedman, my wonderful son-in-law and a manager of Pilotage Services Gladstone, who used his vast knowledge with marine terminology to edit my draft in the Cromer storm chapter of 2013.

Redland City librarians. The impact of running a novel writing competition with a prize of being mentored was life-changing for me. Author, Louise Cusack, was generous with sharing her wisdom. Since then, I have written three novels. Redland librarians sniffed every corner of the earth for answers to my enquiries. They also introduced me to the vast resources at Trove and the British Library.

Queensland Writers Centre and **Australian Society of Authors**: for helpful counselling and linking writers across this vast land.

Society of Authors, London, for longlisting The Missing Village in their unpublished manuscript (international) competition, The McKitterick Prize. I cannot tell you how thrilling this was!

I've written this novel in the spaces between many important family events, which included caring for my parents, who are no longer with us and the birth of two precious grandsons. I'd also like to thank my sister, Judy, and my adult children, who are always on the sidelines, cheering me on in loving ways over a lifetime: Anthony, Leah, Tim and David, and their families.

…and thanks to you! I hope you enjoyed *The Missing Village*. If you belong to a Book Club, the next two pages will be of interest to you.

With gratitude *Jill Marley*

Book club – discussion points

Questions:

1. In the 14th century, what was Cromer called?
2. So, how did Henry fight the 'unnatural storms eating away at hillsides' (prologue)? Was he successful?
3. What is the German Ocean called these days?
4. Are there lingering questions from the book you're still thinking about?
5. What was your favourite part of the book?
6. If you could give the book a new title, what would it be?
7. How did your opinion of the book change as you read it?
8. If you could ask the author anything, what would it be?
9. What did you think of the writing? Are there any standout sentences?
10. What was your first impression of the book?
11. Was The Missing Village plot-driven or character-driven? Or a mixture of both?
12. Read your favourite passage.
13. How did the settings affect the story?
14. If Josh hadn't taken up the opportunity to fly to England, do you think the story for Carly might have been different? How?
15. Cartia made a nosegay. What was this, and how was it used?
16. How did Kyle know that the blue beach-hut belonged to Anna
17. What was the marriage brooch a symbol of? Do we still have jewellery we consider as symbolic?
18. Which characters from The Missing Village grew and changed throughout the book?
19. Which era were you most drawn into? Why?
20. Which character did you relate to the most, and what was it about them that you connected with?
21. How do you feel about the ending of this book and how the author wrapped it all up?
22. Do you think Carly should take Josh back?

The Missing Village - possible answers:

1. In the 14th century, what was Cromer called? (Crowmere)
2. So, how did Henry fight the 'unnatural storms eating away at hillsides' (prologue)? Was he successful?

Henry felt he was successful in justifying his actions to God and hoped, in return, for peace and prosperity in the land. However, he failed to change the environment in any way whatsoever. The Black Plague still happened. Cliffs still fall into the sea.

3. What is the German Ocean called these days? (*The North Sea*)
4. Are there lingering questions from the book you're still thinking about?
5. What was your favourite part of the book?
6. If you could give the book a new title, what would it be?
7. How did your opinion of the book change as you read it?
8. If you could ask the author anything, what would it be?
9. What did you think of the writing? Are there any standout sentences?
10. What was your first impression of the book?
11. Was The Missing Village plot-driven or character-driven? Or a mixture of both?
12. Read your favourite passage.
13. How did the descriptive settings affect the story?
14. If Josh hadn't taken up the opportunity to fly to England, do you think the story for Carly might have been different? How?
15. Cartia made a nosegay. What was this, and how was it used? (*Women carried these fragrant bouquets to help mask the stench of the streets and unclean bodies.*)
16. How did Kyle know that the blue beach-hut was Anna's? (*He helped to re-paint it.*)
17. What was the marriage brooch a symbol of? (*A gift to his wife from a husband, after their wedding night.*)
18. Do you still have jewellery you consider as symbolic?
19. Which characters grew and changed throughout the book?
20. Which era were you most drawn into? Why?
21. Which character did you relate to the most, and why?
22. How do you feel about how the author wrapped it all up?
23. Do you think Carly should take Josh back?

www.ingramcontent.com/pod-product-compliance
Lightning Source LLC
Chambersburg PA
CBHW030626310726
48979CB00003B/905